SOUTHERN LITERARY CLASSICS SERIES
C. Hugh Holman and Louis D. Rubin, Jr.
General Editors

PREVIOUSLY PUBLISHED

Chita, by Lafcadio Hearn, introduction by Arlin Turner, Duke University

In Ole Virginia, by Thomas Nelson Page, introduction by Kimball King, The University of North Carolina at Chapel Hill

Tiger-Lilies, by Sidney Lanier, introduction by Richard Harwell, Smith College

Adventures of Captain Simon Suggs, by Johnston Jones Hooper, introduction by Manly Wade Wellman

The Letters of the British Spy, by William Wirt, introduction by Richard Beale Davis, University of Tennessee

The Planter's Northern Bride, by Caroline Lee Hentz, introduction by Rhoda Coleman Ellison

The Knights of the Golden Horse-Shoe, by William Alexander Caruthers, introduction by Curtis Carroll Davis

IN PREPARATION

The Partisan Leader, by Nathaniel Beverly Tucker, introduction by C. Hugh Holman, The University of North Carolina at Chapel Hill

THE
VALLEY
OF
SHENANDOAH

THE
VALLEY
OF
SHENANDOAH

OR
MEMOIRS OF THE GRAYSONS

by

George Tucker

With an Introduction by
DONALD R. NOBLE, Jr.

The University of North Carolina Press
Chapel Hill

Southern Literary Classics Series
Copyright © 1970
The University of North Carolina Press
All rights reserved
Manufactured in the United States of America
Cloth edition, Standard Book Number 8078-1143-2
Paper edition, Standard Book Number 8078-4055-6
Library of Congress Catalog Card Number 70-123106

The 1824 edition used in duplicating this work is in the Rutgers University Library, New Brunswick, New Jersey.

INTRODUCTION

In his preface "To the Reader," George Tucker, speaking as the "editor" of *The Valley of Shenandoah*, puts forward two reasons for having written the novel: to present a "faithful picture of the manners and habits which lately prevailed in one of the most distinguished states of our confederacy," and to offer an "instructive moral to the youth of both sexes" (vii). To these aims might be added a third: to show that loose and careless living and a foolishly excessive generosity, combined with repugnance toward financial matters, can not only bring ruin to a family's fortune but ultimately, if circuitously, lead to moral collapse as well. George Tucker was uniquely suited to write *The Valley of Shenandoah* and to make these points, for while the plot of the novel is fictitious, the depiction of early nineteenth-century Virginia life and the dearly purchased realization of the need for economic care came directly out of Tucker's varied and sometimes dissolute life.

Since George Tucker is unknown to most twentieth-century readers, and since his life bears directly on his work, a biographical sketch seems in order. Tucker was born into a merchant family on St. George's Island, Bermuda, on August 20, 1775.[1] He received a good education there, reading and studying in a "Latin school" under a tutor and later reading law. Feeling that his opportunities in Bermuda were too restricted, Tucker sailed for America in August of 1795, following the death of his mother. By no means was he a typical immigrant. His kinsman, St. George Tucker, was established in Williamsburg and, after an expensive visit to Philadelphia, Tucker went to him there for money and advice. St. George helped him and advised him to enroll at the College of William and Mary.

Williamsburg was an old and declining town, but Tucker found congenial company and led a life that should still produce envy in a healthy undergraduate. Post-revolutionary Williamsburg may not have been the gay capital it had once been, but there was sufficient diversion to

1. The information that follows is drawn largely from Robert Colin McLean's *George Tucker: Moral Philosopher and Man of Letters* (Chapel Hill, N.C., 1961), the best study of Tucker to date.

keep Tucker from studying very seriously, although his admission of studying *only* in bed before breakfast must surely be at least part boast or *sprezzatura*. Upon graduation in 1797 *ex speciali gratia*, Tucker made a journey to New York City, where he met John Jay and George Clinton, and then to Philadelphia, where he was introduced to George Washington.

Returning to Williamsburg, he courted and married Mary Byrd Farley, an heiress and the great-granddaughter of William Byrd II. In his "Autobiography" Tucker says that the girl's charm and fortune had attracted a great many suitors. Unfortunately Miss Farley was seriously ill, probably with consumption. Tucker's proposal was accepted, however, and after their marriage in October, 1797, the couple went to Bermuda, largely in an attempt to improve the bride's health. By May, 1798, they were back in Williamsburg enjoying an active social life. Two years were all they were to have, however, for Mrs. Tucker died on May 25, 1799. Her wealth had given Tucker an unfortunate opportunity to develop his worst traits, so that after her death he found himself still incompetent to practice law and, due to irregularities in his wife's will, not the wealthy man he had assumed he would be. Only after twenty years of litigation was Tucker able to gain possession of even a portion of his wife's estate.

Had Tucker known himself better, he would not have expected to become a successful lawyer in Richmond, for upon moving there in the summer of 1800 he at once joined the swirling social life and became a well-known and well-liked man about town. In 1802 he married George Washington's great-niece, Maria Ball Carter. After proving a failure as a courtroom lawyer (as a result both of incompetence at law and of poor speaking ability), he served successfully for one year as commissioner of bankruptcy.

Tucker's politics had undergone a significant change since his departure from Bermuda. Whereas he had been a pro-French "republican," almost a Jacobite, when he came to America, now, perhaps because of his station, wealth, and acquaintances, Tucker had grown more conservative. Although a pro-Jefferson Republican, he manifested ambivalence at one point, in a speech in favor of certain Federalists. This resulted in a quarrel and subsequently in a "challenge" to one Lewis Harvey, although the duel never took place.

Tucker seems to have had unerringly poor financial judgment. While spending freely and losing regularly at cards, he speculated unwisely and lost money in real estate transactions. In 1806 he was accused, perhaps unjustly, of mishandling funds of the Richmond

Academy, of which he was a trustee. At this point, the fall of 1806, needing to retrench financially and to take stock of his life generally, Tucker moved himself and his family to his in-laws' estate in Frederick County in the Shenandoah Valley. This retrenchment took time, and there were setbacks. In 1807, on a visit to Richmond, Tucker was actually arrested for an old debt—an event that greatly embarrassed him but strengthened his resolve to straighten out his financial life.

No doubt he missed Richmond and his previous style of life, but he found compensation in his growing financial stability and some amusement in local goings-on. In May, 1808, he moved south to Pittsylvania County, where he built a house and purchased slaves. Had he moved to the west sooner, he said, he "should have been so much more advanced in . . . profession, so many thousands richer in purse, and so many years younger in health and ambition"[2] than he was. As it was, Tucker was hardly lacking in ambition; he practised law, wrote essays on topics of local concern such as the clearing of the Dan River for navigation, and was elected to the State Legislature in 1816. After moving

2. Tucker to St. George Tucker, Oct. 9, 1808, Tucker-Coleman Collection, Colonial Williamsburg, quoted in McLean, *George Tucker*, p. 20.

to Lynchburg in 1818 he was elected to Congress the following year.

At this point, just as matters looked most promising, his luck changed again. Tucker met new misfortunes in real estate, and financial problems that had been increasing for a decade finally forced his father-in-law, Charles Carter, to sell his own estate at public auction. Tucker and Carter's brother-in-law, Lawrence Lewis, managed to buy twelve of Carter's slaves, presumably family favorites. On the small estates in western Virginia, slaves were probably much more personally regarded than they were in the deep South. Certainly, in *The Valley* the Graysons' bankruptcy and sale of their slaves is morally painful as well as socially disgraceful. The Graysons feel that they have failed in their responsibilities toward their slaves when they must allow them to be sold, some to the feared deep South.

Although re-elected to Congress for a total of three terms, Tucker served without distinction. His gambling and spending in Washington brought on financial worries that must have seemed repetitious even to him, and more serious problems arose at home. Of his six children, Harriet died in 1816 and Rosalie in 1818, and his only son was exhibiting the emotional instability that would finally lead to his hospitalization in Philadelphia in 1829. His wife Maria died during pregnancy in 1823. These misfortunes may have deterred him from achieving a more striking record as congressman.

During all these years, Tucker had been pursuing, if desultorily, something of a literary career, probably as much for social as for literary reasons. He had contributed numerous pieces in various genres to several Virginia newspapers. He had been writing verse, much of it satirical, since boyhood, and continued that practice in Virginia with the encouragement of St. George Tucker, who was also an amateur poet. Tucker also gained some reputation as an essayist and commentator on local and contemporary issues. His pamphlet, *Letter . . . on . . . the Late Conspiracy of the Slaves* (1801), contains several ideas that attract the attention of today's reader. Tucker was aware of both the practical and moral problems that slavery presented. He foresaw more and larger revolts as slaves increased in number and inevitably became more educated and organized. He saw the financial unprofitability of the slaveholding system and recognized it as a counterproductive force that encouraged white slaveowners to sloth and all that went with it, a force that drove white workers to emigrate to the West, where they would not have to compete with slaves for work. Tucker's proposed solution to the problem was the colonization of American slaves on a piece of land west of the Mississippi, to be bought from Spain by the U.S. government.

In these early years, and indeed through *Voyage to the Moon* (1827), Tucker wrote many satirical pieces and "letters" and seems to have thought of himself as a kind of Swiftean satirist, mocking the foibles of contemporary Virginians. *Letters from Virginia, Translated from the French* (1816) is probably Tucker's work. In it, slavery is attacked on both moral and economic grounds, and there is satire of rural lawyers and avaricious Yankees, topics that Tucker could not resist. The French "Traveller" who is the *persona* of this volume shares Tucker's enthusiasm for genteel society. Tucker's reputation as a writer had earlier, in 1803, led many in Richmond to attribute to him William Wirt's anonymously published *Letters of the British Spy*, which was written in the form later used by Tucker in *Letters from Virginia*. *Letters from Virginia* was well received, as was Tucker's *Essays on Various Subjects of Taste, Morals, and National Policy* (1822), which both Thomas Jefferson and James Madison read and approved.

Jefferson's approval, along with Tucker's reputation as a writer, his prestige as congressman, his acceptable political views, and his personal connections (his kinsman Thomas Tudor Tucker was Treasurer of the United States), probably were responsible for Tucker's being offered the professorship of moral philosophy at the newly formed University of Virginia. In addition to $1,500 per year and life-time tenure, the position would afford Tucker the chance to be with his family and among the cultivated society that he so admired. Surprisingly, however, Tucker hesitated, for in the summer of 1824 he had written *The Valley of Shenandoah* and had high hopes for it. He stated his position candidly in a letter to Joseph C. Cabell, who had approached him about the professorship.

I have for more than a year conceived the project & indulge in the hope that I might pursue the business of authorship as a profitable calling—I have (but this is a secret) actually essayed the public favor in a novel just published in New York and should I meet with any thing like the success which has attended Cooper, I should think my prospects of profit much greater than any professorship could hold out—He has made about $5000 by each of his novels—and the Valley of Shenandoah, my new work was written in two months —The situation to which you invite me would almost put a stop to my efforts as an author.[3]

If his novel were successful, Tucker did not intend to tie himself down to a life of teaching.

3. Tucker to Joseph C. Cabell, Jan. 1, 1824 [misdated, actually 1825], Cabell Deposit, University of Virginia Library, quoted in Richard Beale Davis, *Intellectual Life in Jefferson's Virginia, 1790-1830* (Chapel Hill, N.C., 1964), p. 305.

Unfortunately for his hopes at rivalling the author of the Leatherstocking Tales, however, *The Valley* was almost totally ignored at publication, and on February 21, 1825, Tucker wrote to Cabell accepting the post.

From this point until his retirement in 1845, Tucker taught with moderate success and wrote a great deal, mainly in the areas of political economy and history. These writings have been treated in considerable detail by Tipton R. Snavely in his *George Tucker as Political Economist* (Charlottesville, Va., 1964) and are of little interest to the student of literature. Tucker did, however, write two more novels. *A Voyage to the Moon*, published pseudonymously in 1827, is a rather entertaining satire of contemporary manners in which the "author," Joseph Atterly, accompanies a Brahmin to the moon and there observes the follies of people who do such ridiculous things as decorate their bodies with the plumage of birds. In *A Voyage to the Moon*, Tucker also castigates quack doctors, some of whom he may have known in the course of his family's illnesses, and "blowhard" lawyers, with whom Tucker must have been involved personally as well as professionally. Tucker's third novel, *A Century Hence*, completed in 1841, was never published. It takes place in 1941 and is essentially a futuristic romance in which a young couple from feuding families suffer misunderstandings and difficulties. Neither of these later books has the strength of *The Valley*, probably because *The Valley* gains its power and convincing qualities from Tucker's first-hand knowledge of his material, while the two later works are the creative productions of a man not notably gifted with imagination.

In 1845 Tucker retired from the university, freed his slaves, and moved to Philadelphia with his third wife, Louisa A. Thompson, whom he had married in 1828. He remained active after retirement, publishing his *History of the United States* in 1859. This, along with his *Life of Thomas Jefferson* (1837), gave him considerable renown, although not the fame as a novelist which he had coveted.

On a trip to the South, where he spent his winters after the death of Louisa in 1858, Tucker suffered an accident. In January of 1861, while disembarking from a steamboat in Mobile, he was struck on the head by a falling bale of cotton. Brought to his son-in-law's home in Virginia, he lingered for three months and died on April 10, 1861.

George Tucker was clearly an amateur novelist, but perhaps because he was dealing with a locale and material he knew well, *The Valley* is remarkably free from imitation. There are, however, some influences that should be noted.

Tucker had read many of the eighteenth-century novels, and *The Valley* does display some of the conventions of the sentimental novel. The women are highly emotional and blush, faint, or develop illnesses when under stress. The lovers seem especially transparent, and it is a wonder they can keep any secret, let alone that of a seduction and pregnancy. Tucker also makes extensive, and I think successful, use of letters, especially between lovers, in a manner reminiscent of Richardson's *Clarissa*, to which *The Valley* bears other obvious similarities. *The Valley* is loosely constructed and filled with digressions, and in the manner of Sterne, Tucker apologizes for this practice even while indulging in it.

Even though Tucker utilizes many of the techniques of the sentimental novels, however, he makes clear his disapproval of that kind of fiction. He feels that novels can fill an impressionable reader's head with "false and exaggerated conceptions of human life—of the elevated and transcendant virtue of lovers—the raptures of sentimental love, and the necessity of loving to fulfil the destiny of every human being, at least of every young person" (I, 91). Louisa's seduction can be attributed partly to the false notion of love she had learned from novels. *The Valley* was designed to serve as a warning against just such romantic excess, and Tucker advocates a much more practical kind of marital union—one based on affection, surely, but also on the joining of families and property.

In *The Valley*, as in so much of his writing, Tucker indulges in satire in the style of Dryden and Swift. He names quarrelsome country lawyers "Worricourt" and "Barbawl"; he portrays the rising middle class as foolishly ostentatious; he ridicules the fop "Belmain" for his mannerisms. This is simple and transparent satire, but Tucker seems to enjoy it greatly.

In 1824 there had not been much fiction produced in the United States which one could propose as influences on Tucker. His spurious preface seems similar to Washington Irving's hoax in his Diedrich Knickerbocker's *History of New York from the Beginning of the World to the End of the Dutch Dynasty*, but this device goes back at least to Cervantes, and Scott makes use of it. Tucker's wish for anonymity, however, is a typically Southern attitude. Many Southern writers felt, as Scott did, that the public did not hold the writing of novels to be entirely respectable. Tucker mentions in a letter that there are "hundreds of very prudent & knowing people who are very well convinced that a man who writes for the public cannot be a lawyer or a man of business."[4] Philip Pendleton Cooke later remarked on another aspect of this same matter: "As a lawyer reputation and fortune await me . . . . As an author . . . a painful fear of the world's censure."[5] In the antebellum South, letters were generally regarded as properly the avocation of a gentleman who made his living and his real contribution to the commonweal through law or public service.

Francis Pendleton Gaines, in his groundbreaking study, *The Southern Plantation* (1924), insists that the tradition of the plantation novel begins with John Pendleton Kennedy's *Swallow Barn, or A Sojourn in the Old Dominion* (1832) and is then continued through the works of William A. Caruthers, William Gilmore Simms, and on into the twentieth century. While Tucker's novel did not have enough readers to be the origin of a tradition, and indeed has a somber theme that is seldom to be found in the literature of the plantation tradition, *The Valley of Shenandoah* does contain a number of the elements found in the typical plantation novel and does provide, as

[4]. Tucker to St. George Tucker, Feb. 3, 1814, Tucker-Coleman Collection, Colonial Williamsburg, quoted in McLean, *George Tucker*, p. 72.

[5]. Philip Pendleton Cooke to Beverly Tucker, Dec., 1835, quoted in Jay B. Hubbell, ed., *The South in American Literature, 1607-1900* (Durham, N.C., 1954), p. 506.

Tucker intended, "a faithful picture" of Virginia life. The Grayson estate, with its commodious house, outbuildings, fertile fields, and happy slaves under the protection of their benevolent mistress, could serve as the setting for any plantation novel.

The activities with which Tucker's characters divert themselves are much like those practiced by rural aristocrats anywhere in the Old South. The families visit and entertain one another; there are barbecues and other social functions to which all the gentle folk go to eat, drink, and dance; and the men have those pastimes exclusive to them—hunting, gaming, and heated political discussion. No one is concerned much with the management of his estate, and there is a general mood of festivity, hospitality, and prodigality. The lower classes of whites enjoy their "Fish Frys" and the slaves have their all-night "shocking" parties, at which their labor is eased by singing and by liquor provided by their generous owners.

It is not in these plantation trappings, however, that the strength of *The Valley of Shenandoah* lies. It is rather in the realistic treatment of those aspects of plantation life which brought the Graysons to ruin and which have caused the break-up of many old estates, thus allowing some of the less cultured but thrifty middle class to achieve economically what they never could have achieved socially.

Colonel Grayson, deceased before the novel opens, is responsible for most of the misfortune that attends his family, slaves, and property. A sympathetic appraisal might describe him as having been overly generous and rather thoughtless. It is implied, however, that his inattention to affairs approached irresponsibility, his hospitality approached prodigality, and his signing of notes for others demonstrated a naïve evaluation of human nature. It must be remembered that others must pay for his mistakes. Loss of fortune through prodigality or disdain for business matters has, then, moral and psychological implications as well as practical ones.

Those of the rising middle class, represented in this novel by the Fawkners, make no such mistakes. They pay strict attention to business, sign no notes for others, and, although they cannot resist some ostentation to declare their prosperity to the world, generally live modestly and avoid gambling and other vices. Tucker recognizes their virtues, although he indicates that they might be a bit more generous where circumstances warrant it. What Tucker laments is the break-up of the old social order. The middle class will occupy the estates of the upper class but cannot provide the cultural and polit-

INTRODUCTION xxiii

ical leadership the leisured aristocracy had provided. In this respect bankruptcy becomes more than personal or familial in scope. For a gentleman to go bankrupt is injurious to the state, depriving it of a leader who could direct its cultural and political destinies. A cultured aristocrat without money is an aristocrat still, Tucker tells us, but he is rendered impotent. The newly rich are merely rich; it will be generations before they can assume cultural or political leadership.

In his examination of Virginia society, Tucker was not concerned with the upper class alone, and the threat posed to them by the rising middle class. He intended to portray characters from all levels of Shenandoah society. In a chapter devoted to this subject, he describes at length the Germans and the Scotch-Irish who recently migrated to western Virginia. Tucker is obviously not fond of the Germans. They have drifted down the mountains from Maryland in search of good farm land, which they work industriously and successfully. They are thrifty businessmen, faithful husbands, and good fathers, but they are dull and clannish. They are "without ambition, and without literature" (I, 52) and they make no contribution to public affairs. The chief entertainment of the Germans seems to be getting involved in complicated, spurious lawsuits. They are essentially "the dray-horses of society—not fitted for the turf" (I, 53). One can sense the prejudice or provincialism in Tucker's attitude towards the Germans, who are decidedly "foreign" in appearance, customs, preference in foods, and, especially, language.

The Scotch-Irish, Tucker tells us, present a strong contrast in almost every way. They can be passionate, public-spirited, imaginative, and generous but are often lazy, drunken, and improvident. They more or less inadvertently provide America with many of her pioneers, since many Irishmen, like the Graysons' friend McCulloch, lose their farms through carelessness and are forced to move west. Because they are gregarious and English-speaking, Tucker believes the Scotch-Irish will be quickly assimilated into the general population and that many will surely rise to high places.

It is Tucker's examination of the lowest class in Shenandoah society, the slaves, which perhaps holds the greatest interest to a twentieth-century reader. *The Valley of Shenandoah* provides an unusually full account of the "peculiar institution," by a writer in an excellent position to render this account.

The bulk of the commentary on the Negro and slavery comes in Chapter IV. Gildon, an inquisitive Yankee, wants to learn all he can about plantation management and Negro slavery. To begin with, Edward explains to him that "they are perhaps better supplied with the necessaries of life than the labouring class of any country out of America" (I, 63). At "Beachwood" this was probably true. At "Easton," the Graysons' other plantation, run by an overseer, conditions are not as good. The overseer stints on medicine and food, overworking the slaves as a part of his efforts to cheat the Graysons as much as possible. Where the master is not present, that familiarity that humanizes the institution cannot spring up. Most feared by the slaves, of course, is the deep South and the indigo plantations, where the climate is unhealthy and the plantations do not raise their own food supply.

There is a good deal of familiarity between the Graysons and many of their slaves, and the affection runs both ways. "Granny Moll," a standard fixture in the literature of the plantation tradition, has served and loved four generations of Graysons in her eighty-four years. She identifies with the family and feels their fall deeply. Old Jeffrey, a retainer of the Fawkners, is "a shrewd, artful, ready-witted knave, who, having long assumed the privilege of great familiarity with his superiors, was at length suffered quietly to enjoy it" (I, 32). Characters like Jeffrey have survived in the tradition, through fiction, plays, and motion pictures, until very recently. They no doubt existed, but they have achieved a mythological strength far out of proportion to their actual numbers.

Edward Grayson, presumably speaking for Tucker, voices sentiments concerning slavery which are only slightly more conservative than those Tucker himself had shown in his *Letter . . . on . . . the Late Conspiracy of the Slaves* or *Letters from Virginia, Translated from the French.* "We, of the present generation find domestic slavery . . . [an] evil . . . [that] admits of no remedy that is not worse than the disease. No thinking man supposes that we could emancipate them, and safely let them live in the country. . . ." (I, 61), and it is impractical and perhaps cruel to send them abroad. The slaveowner must seek "to *mitigate* a disease which admits of *no cure*" (I, 62). He is "fully aware of its disadvantages—that it checks the growth of our wealth—is repugnant to its justice—inconsistent with its principles—injurious to its morals—and dangerous to its peace" (I, 63). Edward rationalizes by claiming that one born to slavery does not intensely suffer the deprivations of freedom, just as one born blind does not suffer as much as one who loses his sight. Slavery is not excessively inefficient, either, for some slaves work hard from personal or "family" pride, while if some are "disposed to work less, they are sometimes compelled to work more; and fear, and habit, and the little emulations I have mentioned, make the result not materially variant from that of freemen'' (I, 69). All in all, since the practical problems of emancipation seem, to Edward, too great to be overcome, an admittedly immoral and inefficient system must be continued in as humane and productive a way as possible.

On the psychological effect of being a master, an owner of human beings, Edward and Gildon have a serious and interesting disagreement. Gildon, who is after all the villain of the piece, is a Yankee who has not owned slaves and does not "know" Negroes. It is he who comes out with the "master-race" rhetoric. "There must be something very pleasant, after all, in having so many persons over whom you are supreme and sovereign lord. Don't you feel, Edward, when riding over these vast domains of yours, something like a feudal Baron?" (I, 60). (Gildon had tried acting like a feudal baron in Dutchess County, New York, but the un-cooperative tenant farmers had insisted on acting like his equals.) "There is something very fascinating now confess it, Edward, in this unlimited control, let us fiery republicans say what we will. Indeed what is the love of liberty but the love of doing what we please? and, consequently, he who is proud of his own freedom, is equally gratified at controlling the freedom of others" (I, 60). Edward refutes Gildon point for point. He insists that love of freedom and love of tyranny are not the same thing and that "he who has a proper sense of his own rights, has a due respect for the rights of others" (I, 61).

Despite Edward's obvious humanity as a slave-owner, there is one aspect of slavery, the act which is the very heart of slavery, the slave auction, which cannot be defended. Tucker's description of the sale of the Graysons' slaves takes up most of Chapter IX of the second volume and is in many ways the most moving incident in the novel. Edward realizes and acknowledges the horrors of the slave auction: "The weight of his fetters, the negro, who has been born and bred on a well regulated estate, hardly feels" (II, 206). Such a slave is relatively comfortable and sometimes even feels a part of the "patriarchal family" (II, 206). "But when hoisted up to public sale, where every man has a right to purchase him, and he may be the property of one whom he never saw before, or of the worst man in the community, then the delusion vanishes, and he feels the bitterness of his lot, and his utter insignificance as a member of civilized society" (II, 207).

In admitting the immorality of slavery and in insisting that slaves are well cared for, Tucker occupies a position shared by other enlightened border-state Southerners of his day. John Pendleton Kennedy, speaking through Frank Meriwether in *Swallow Barn*, says,

slavery, as an original question, is wholly without justification or defence. It is theoretically and morally wrong—and fanatical and one-sided thinkers will call its continuance, even for a day, a wrong, under any modification of it. But, surely, if these people are consigned to our care by the accident, or, what is worse, the premeditated policy which has put them upon our commonwealth, the great duty that is left to us is, to shape our conduct in reference to them, by a wise and beneficent consideration of the case as it exists, and to administer wholesome laws for their government, making their servitude as tolerable to them as we can consistently with our own safety and their ultimate good. We should not be justified in taking the hazard of internal convulsions to get rid of them; nor have we a right, in the desire to free ourselves, to whelm them in greater evils than their present bondage. A violent removal of them, or a general emancipation, would assuredly produce one or the other of these calamities.[6]

Tucker differs from Kennedy in his greater realization of the humanity of the Negro and the Negro's capacity to feel the ignominy of

6. John Pendleton Kennedy, *Swallow Barn, or A Sojourn in the Old Dominion* (New York, 1832), ed. William S. Osborne (New York, 1962), pp. 455-56.

his position. Not until George Washington Cable would another Southern novelist write so bluntly of the inhumanity of the caste system and its effect on the Negro, and Cable was attacked violently for his opinions. The fact that Tucker was not so vilified shows that in 1824 the debate over slavery was still open. Tucker could criticize the institution because defense of that institution had not yet become the touchstone of Southern patriotism. Tucker's description of Virginia plantation life, and of slavery in particular, could be critical, and therefore realistic, in a way that later novels might not.

As the reader will notice at once, *The Valley* shows many signs of amateurishness and plain carelessness. Major events are insufficiently foreshadowed; minor characters appear and disappear without explanation; the characters remaining at the end are disposed of with unmannerly abruptness. Presumably because of the great haste with which he wrote, Tucker makes a number of grammatical errors, and even allows Colonel Grayson and Major Fawkner to exchange ranks from time to time. In the 1824 edition, which is reproduced here, there is no Chapter V indicated, although it seems clear the break should come after the discourse on slavery in Chapter IV, or at about page 70.

In *Letters from Virginia* Tucker had advocated a simple style, and mainly he follows his own advice. Avoiding flowery language for the most part, Tucker is conservative in his attempts at dialect and at using speech mannerisms to delineate character. Characterization is not a strength of Tucker's, either. Most of the characters are stock romantic figures, made of pasteboard. James Gildon, the villain, seems an exception. He is not a straight melodramatic seducer-villain; in some ways he is the victim of forces within him and without, which cause him to be the destroyer of the Grayson family and of himself.

In providing his "instructive moral to the youth of both sexes" and presenting a "faithful picture" of Virginia life in the last decade of the eighteenth century, Tucker accomplished more than he intended and more than other and better Southern novelists, writing later, were able to accomplish. As Richard Beale Davis puts it:

> One must grant that George Tucker's *The Valley of Shenandoah* is not quite a full-fledged Virginia novel, for the nostalgic atmosphere which usually accompanied glorious deeds or plantation life is not its main tone. Only in the twentieth century, when the critical spirit had again meshed with the creative, could novelists like Ellen Glasgow in *Barren Ground* or Willa Cather in *Sapphira and the Slave Girl* see

Virginia life in its full irony and paradox as Tucker had, and one may argue that even they never quite overcame a certain sentimental myopia. Like them, Tucker probed and analyzed *con amore*.[7]

Tucker was fortunate. In the twenty-five years between the setting and the publication of the novel, slavery had not yet become the obsessive issue it later became. The Missouri Compromise of 1820 pacified and reassured Southerners for almost a generation, and it was during this breathing spell that Tucker wrote. He had the freedom to examine and criticize Southern society—its stratification; its feudal characteristics; the conflict between the rising middle class and the old, declining, planter class; and, especially, the institution of slavery. He could maintain his neutrality, pointing out both the evils of slavery and the hopelessness of emancipation. He could discuss the failings of the upper class, as they were not yet under attack.

Events during the years following the publication of *The Valley* combined to deny this opportunity to other writers. In 1831 Nat Turner's insurrection served to polarize opinion; the Virginia legislature voted only seventy-three to fifty-eight against a motion to emancipate. Almost all the "ayes" were from the western counties or the old planter class, both

7. Davis, *Intellectual Life in Jefferson's Virginia*, p. 312.

of which groups could claim Tucker as a member. Having voted to retain slavery in the face of insurrection at home and increased criticism from the North, Virginians and other Southerners then took steps to protect themselves from their slaves and to eliminate incendiary criticism. On the practical level, this assumed the form of stricter enforcement of slave codes and systems of control and patrol. On the intellectual level, it took the form of censorship by public opinion. Criticism of slavery or of the class system by a Southerner became impossible. It became the duty of Southern writers to defend slavery and to glorify the Southern way of life. Simms and other writers were encouraged to turn from the novel and from their natural subject, the society around them, toward the romance, the way of Scott, and the past. They were hindered from examining an area that Tucker, an inferior craftsman, gave promise of dealing with. If we accept Hawthorne's brief definition of the novel, as set forth in the "Preface" to *The House of the Seven Gables*, as a form of composition "presumed to aim at a very minute fidelity, not merely to the possible, but to the probable and ordinary course of man's experience," it may be that George Tucker's *The Valley of Shenandoah* is one of the very few *novels* to be written in the South in the nineteenth century. It is an awkward book, yet it points the way that Southern fiction might have taken had Southern writers been able to keep their intellectual freedom.

A Note on the Text

The text here reproduced is that of the first edition, published in 1824.

This edition contains numerous errors, which are the result of Tucker's haste in composition, the roughness of his manuscript, and Charles Wiley's carelessness in printing.

Tucker wrote the 636-page novel in only two months, in the summer of 1824. It does not seem likely that he had much time to revise or polish his work. The manuscript was in such poor shape, in fact, that Harper's, to whom he first submitted it, offered him five hundred dollars for it on the condition that he remain in New York City to supervise the printing. Otherwise, they would have to hire someone to decipher Tucker's handwriting. Instead, Tucker gave his manuscript to Charles Wiley, agreeing to divide profits and expenses. Wiley soon afterwards went out of business, and all Tucker received from the arrangement was several hundred copies of his novel, with no cash.

Some errors can with reasonable certainty be attributed to Tucker himself. For example, Colonel Grayson is called Major Grayson on page one, and Major Fawkner is called Colonel Fawkner on page twenty-two.

Other errors, such as the omission of any designation for Chapter V in Volume I and the duplication of the Chapter III title in Volume II, seem obviously the printer's. Tucker was probably justified in complaining that the novel was "ill-printed."[8] In a critical edition of *The Valley of Shenandoah*, responsibility for the many irregularities in the text would have to be established.

There was at least one subsequent edition of *The Valley*. In 1828 Orville A. Roorbach published an edition, a copy of which is in the Library of Congress, but this edition seems to have followed that of 1824 and reproduced its errors. The 1828 edition apparently fared no better with the public than had the first edition.

Tucker, in his "Autobiography," mentions that *The Valley* was "reprinted in London and was translated into German."[9]

8. Tucker to St. George Tucker, April 25, 1825, Tucker-Coleman Collection, Colonial Williamsburg, quoted in McLean, *George Tucker*, p. 28.

9. George Tucker, "Autobiography," quoted in *ibid.*, p. 88.

The Valley of Shenandoah

Volume I

THE

VALLEY OF SHENANDOAH.

CHAPTER I.

On the banks of the beautiful river Shenandoah, in the county of Frederick and state of Virginia, lived Mrs. Mary Grayson, the widow of Colonel Grayson, a meritorious officer of the "continental line," in the war of the revolution.

She had married at an early period of life the man of her choice, and as her husband had been tender, generous, in easy circumstances, and very generally respected, her life had passed away in unclouded serenity, until about eighteen months before the beginning of these memoirs, when a bilious fever, in depriving her of her husband, had first taught her the knowledge of real misfortune. Her grief having gone through the usual gradations, had now subsided into a soft and not unpleasing melancholy.

She was the mother of a son and a daughter, to whose education and welfare she was determined to devote the residue of her days, and her thoughts were at this time principally occupied with the future destination and pursuits of Edward Grayson, who expected to complete his course of studies at the college of William and Mary the ensuing winter.

It was about the middle of July, after early candle-light, that a little mulatto girl, in blue striped homespun, came running into the parlour and exclaimed to Miss Grayson, " Oh Miss Louisa, Master Edward is come, and the young gentleman is with him."

A mighty bustle ensued, as is usual when the tranquillity of a life in the country is interrupted by the return of one of the family; a consequence however, on the present occasion, which was produced far less by the weariness of monotony, or the hope of hearing news, than by the affectionate regard which was entertained for Edward by every member of the household. His sister ran to the door to meet him: the servants, one after another, greeted him; and his mother rose from the little table, where she had been reading some work of rational piety, to embrace the future prop of her house.

Some time was spent in the exchanges of affectionate greetings before any notice was bestowed on Edward's companion: but he was soon welcomed with the cordiality due to a particular acquaintance—for though he had seen the family only for a short time, in a visit they had made to the lower country about two years before, yet he had particularly recommended himself to their favour by his agency in a dispute between Edward and a fellow student, which had threatened a serious issue; and this affair had laid the foundation for an intimate friendship between these young men, though they were widely dissimilar in character, disposition, and principles.

James Gildon was the only son of a wealthy merchant in New-York, and had been sent to Williamsburg for the purpose of breaking off an attachment which did not comport with the sordid and ambitious views of his father. He possessed respectable talents, a pleasing person, a lively, cheerful temper, and genteel and insinuating manners; he was studious to please, and often successful in pleasing, and yet all these social and agreeable qualities were not sufficient to prevent, though they were but too successful in disguising, an utter selfishness of disposition.

In his temper Edward was reserved, somewhat haughty in his manners to those who were not acknowledged inferiors, (to whom he was all mildness and condescension,) and possessed of the most scrupulous and fastidious honour. In person, he was tall, thin, with gray eyes, light hair, and a long, thin, but very pleasing visage.

Gildon, without being positively short, was lower and stouter than Edward, had a full, round face, florid complexion, black eyes, and hair of the same colour. His talent for satire, seasoned as it was with a sprightly vein of wit and pleasantry, was much relished by the saturnine and somewhat misanthropical humour of Edward. The latter believed his friend to possess a good heart and honourable principles, although he occasionally supported, by way of argument, theories in love and politics which did not accord with his own refined and high-minded standard of right: and their discussions on these topics, while they served to give greater zest and animation to their intercourse, commonly terminated in some witty sally or humorous anecdote of Gildon, by which he tacitly seemed to surrender the triumph of the argument to his adversary; and thus prevented that coldness and alienation which difference of opinion and frequent altercations are apt to produce among young men of the same age and standing.

Louisa Grayson was now in her eighteenth year. Her form had acquired a roundness and symmetry which it had wanted when Gildon had first seen her. Her manners, too, were improved in ease, and her face in spirit and intelligence. His fancy had often pictured to him the little pretty blue-eyed sister of his friend, but he found (what does not often happen on such occasions) that these ideal representations had fallen short of the reality. He was delighted at the discovery, and with difficulty could repress that gayety of heart and exuberance of spirits with which beauty naturally inspires a young man of three-and-twenty, whose heart is not already engrossed, and who is conscious of his own powers of pleasing. But this being the first time he had seen the family since the death of Colonel Grayson, a sense of decorum made him sober, and as far as practicable with one so excitable and so excited, serious and grave.

"Have you not grown very much, Miss Grayson, since I had the pleasure of seeing you in Richmond? I think you about two inches taller."

"Perhaps so, sir; I had an attack of the ague and fever last autumn, and it is said sometimes to increase the stature of those who but for that had attained their growth," replied Louisa, not availing herself of the implied compliment he intended to her age.

"Your looks give indications of any thing but ill health, Miss Grayson."

"'Tis true, sir, ever since my recovery, my health has been unusually good," said Louisa, either not perceiving the intended flattery, or not finding it unpalatable.

"But you surprise me," said Gildon, "in talking of agues in this part of Virginia. I thought they were confined to the lower country; that the goddess of health had fixed her favourite residence in the mountains, and that there her votaries sought her in the sickly season."

"I caught my ague, indeed, in the lower country soon after we met you in Richmond—but the climate in this part of Virginia is supposed to have undergone a change for the worse of late years, and agues in some situations are now very common."

"Pray, Miss Grayson, what has become of that handsome, agreeable young gentleman I saw in your party."

"Without being sure, I should have known him by that description—I presume you mean Mr. Belton; he is now at his residence in Baltimore."

The ice being thus broken between those young people, they were instinctively led to make themselves agreeable to each other; and the conversation thus naturally sliding into a subject more congenial to their tastes than that of climate or disease, and more favourable to their wishes, soon became more lively and interesting. They thus gradually fell upon the easy footing of old acquaintances; and partly from the pleasure received, and still more, perhaps, from the consciousness of the pleasure communicated, each began to think the other one of the most agreeable persons in the world. Such are the sweet illusions of beauty and youth!

During this time, Mrs. Grayson and her son were carrying on in the opposite corner of the room, a dialogue of a different description. She made the most anxious inquiries about her son's studies and adventures, and future plans—asked him to explain what he had occasionally hinted at in his letters; and dilate more at large on what he had previously explained. Nor was she so engrossed with Edward's concerns as to be unmindful of those of her friends and acquaintances in Williamsburg and its vicinity.

"How are the C——'s my son? You wrote me they were now living in Williamsburg."

"Yes, madam, the Colonel has purchased a pretty good house there; the one formerly occupied by Mr. S——, for the purpose of educating his children, and he means to pass his winters there, and his summers on this side of the Blue Ridge."

"I presume Ripley will now go to decay."

"I was there once this spring with my friend William, and it is very much out of repair. The portico is rotting down, and the whole building begins to look like a ruin."

"Poor Ripley," said Mrs. Grayson, with a sigh. "Some of the happiest moments of my life have been past there. But my aunt B——, had she returned to Flowerdale before you left Williamsburg?"

"She stayed until the 4th of July, and set off

with her grand-daughters two days afterwards. The old lady said that the sight of so many of her old friends in Williamsburg made her young again. But she took care to tell us, that the old city is not the place it was. She would insist on carrying me one morning to see Lord Botetourt's statue, and was quite shocked to find it exposed to the weather, for not long ago the corporation pulled down that part of the Capitol which covered it to repair the other part."

"The city must, indeed," said Mrs. Grayson, "be greatly changed. What sort of girls are Mary and Eliza?"

"Mary is very handsome, and I am told very like what her mother was. Eliza is a pretty figure, and has much sprightliness, and such pleasing manners that she is much more of a belle than her sister. Young Etheridge, of New-Kent, is addressing her."

"What, the son of old Etheridge, who kept the tavern at the Court-House?"

"The same, madam, but he is a very clever, genteel young man, and his father has left him a good estate on Pamunkey. I told you he had bought Pelham on York river."

Mrs. Grayson looked thoughtful for a moment, and then calmly said, "it seems to me that estates change hands much oftener than they used to do—but I suppose it is right it should be so."

A new train of thought being apparently now excited in her mind, the conversation took another turn, and she communicated very freely with Edward on the state of his father's affairs, and on the plans she had formed, with the aid of Mr. Trueheart, her executor, for their settlement. After a free interchange of opinions between the mother and son on this interesting subject, the conversation becoming general, Mrs. Grayson addressed some inquiries to Gildon, and Edward glided round to the chair of his sister and in a low voice said,—when did you hear from the Elms, Louisa?

"But yesterday," said she, "I received a letter from Matilda, and she promises to spend a week with me as soon as her father returns from Hampshire, provided I will agree to accompany her to the Fredericksburg races in the fall. I cannot consent to leave mama, but I shall not tell her so till we meet, lest I should deprive myself of the pleasure of seeing her."

"I admire your policy," said Edward, in a tone of good natured raillery, though he was evidently much pleased with the intelligence.

Louisa, then turning to Gildon, who had carried on a conversation with Mrs. Grayson without quitting his seat, broke out in a strain of enthusiastic panegyric on her young friend Matilda Fawkner, which at once displayed the powers of her native eloquence, the ardour of her friendship, and those captivating graces which animation and generous feeling lend almost to any countenance.

Edward, looking at his sister with more than usual affection, remarked, "I fancy, my sister, you are endeavouring to repay the encomiums which Matilda so often bestows on you;" thus seeking to recompense his sister for the gratification she imparted to himself.

Mrs. Grayson looked first at one child and then at the other; her inward delight suddenly beaming through the habitual pensiveness of her countenance, like the moon showing its face from behind the cloud that had obscured it, and she would have been completely happy but for the recollection that her parental pride and joy were no longer participated.

Louisa, in a little while, for the well-timed compliment of her brother, soon took occasion to whisper something in his ear, which evidently gave him great pleasure.

Supper was now announced, consisting of a broiled chicken and sliced ham for the travellers, and of fruits, milk, and sweetmeats, the ordinary evening's repast for the family at this season of the year. They sat at table till eleven, though the young gentlemen had made rather a long journey, and they retired to their respective rooms to enjoy that repose which naturally follows bodily fatigue and the calm pleasures of rational society.

In the morning, after breakfast, Edward, according to his practice, ordered horses for himself and his friend to take an hour's ride, giving his favourite riding horse to Gildon—and aware that he would have much assistance to give to his mother towards settling his father's intricate and perplexed affairs, as well as in superintending the business of the farm, in which his companion could bear no share, he thought that politeness dictated that he should at once begin the course which prudence prescribed.

As soon as the family had withdrawn from the breakfast-table to the drawing-room, or parlour as it was commonly termed there, he went up to him with that air of mingled frankness and courtesy which it is so difficult for any one to catch who has not been bred a gentleman, and said, "My dear Gildon, I beg that you will now consider yourself at home. My mother will often require such little services as I can render her, while I am here, and I must leave you to amuse yourself in the library, or with my sister's piano. I have directed my man Phil to saddle Saracen and bring him to the door for you every morning, and you may exercise your discretion, and ride or not as you like best. If you please, you may try his gaits this morning. I am sure you will excuse these separations, as I can often have the pleasure of your company when I cannot assist my poor mother."

"Say no more, my dear fellow," said Gildon, "it would be a very mistaken politeness which would seek the accommodation of a guest at the expense of one's own; and I should feel ill at ease if I saw that I put you out of your way. I know you have much to do, and I insist that while I am here you will pursue the same course as if I was away; and I, on my part, promise you to act as if I was at home: and as an earnest of this treaty of accommodation and ease, I will decline the honour of backing the Saracen this morning, as I have not more inclination for riding at present, than I have for a second breakfast: besides, I am desirous of seeing your sister's improvement in music (if she will favour me so far) since the evening she was so much embarrassed at Mr. Randolph's, in Richmond."

"I fear, sir, you will find that my skill in music has not grown with my growth, and the instrument is sadly out of tune; but it may serve to afford a little variety, and relieve you from some of the weariness of a country life after the gayeties of Williamsburg."

As she rose to go to the piano, Gildon, with the familiarity of an old friend, but the gracefulness of a courtier, offered his hand and conducted her to the instrument.

"As you please then," said Edward: "I will even ride Saracen myself, and, until I see you again, good morning to you both."

Gildon was lavish of his compliments to Louisa after the first piece. He extolled her taste and execution, and mentioned several new songs, some of which she had not heard, and others she was then practising. From music they passed to poetry, and from poetry to novels; and while they were discussing the merits of Mrs. Radcliff's Mysteries of Udolpho, Mrs. Grayson made her appearance; on which, Louisa withdrew from the instrument, as her mother had never taken any pleasure in hearing her play since the death of her father, who had been devotedly attached to music, and was himself an excellent performer on the German flute.

This lady was then in her fortieth year, though, until the late ravages which grief and care had made in her face, she looked ten years younger. She was rather under the middle size; handsome from regularity of features, but still more so from the expression of mildness and benignity which her countenance conveyed.

She had been the mother of five children, but three had died in very early infancy. Her recent afflicting loss had thrown a degree of seriousness over a character naturally rather cheerful than gay; and given a pensive cast to her features that made them more interesting.

She had received as good an education as the country afforded; and while she had been familiar with books, she had been well instructed in those arts of house-keeping which have been too much neglected in modern days. In the mysteries of the dairy, the kitchen, in all its branches of roast, boiled, and stewed; of potting, pickling, and preserving; of making bread, beer, soap, candles, and curing bacon, which are so essential to a Virginia matron, and for which this description of her citizens was once so distinguished, Mrs. Grayson was a perfect adept. In the useful and domestic arts of spinning, weaving, dying, and bleaching, she had no ordinary skill.

Mrs. Grayson had been much taken with Gildon's manners and exterior, and his studied attentions to herself had not been without their natural effect. Not doubting that he, in common with all who approached Louisa, would feel the force of her charms; and attributing his present visit to the impression her daughter's beauty had already made, she had taken the subject into consideration, and finding on inquiry that Mr. Gildon the elder was a man of fortune, and that his son was about to be received as a partner in a large mercantile concern in the city of New-York, she felt no objection to the match except the distance that would separate them; but she made up her mind to give an assent to what she considered as so likely to take place; and the rather, as the penetration of a mother's eye had soon discovered that the pleasing manners and sprightly conversation of Gildon had not been seen with indifference by Louisa.

Colonel Grayson, assured of his wife's prudence and equal affection, had left his property to her for life, with the power of distributing it between his children according to circumstances; and she had already resolved in her mind the details of such a division as would at once be just and convenient to the different parties—though it pained and somewhat alarmed her to find that the more insight she obtained into her husband's affairs, the greater was the amount of his debts, and more impaired was his fortune found to be.

It was this unpleasant discovery which had induced her to remove from their mansion in Charles City to their estate in Frederick, which had been hitherto used as a summer retreat, and where she thought she could, by her presence, make a valuable estate more profitable, and pursue a more rigid economy than comported either with the generous, and rather thoughtless, hospitality of her husband, or with the idle, social habits of her neighbours.

She began a system of retrenchment in the whole of her expenditures; reduced the number of her domestics from eighteen to eight; her carriage horses from four to two, and a house with ten large rooms to six moderate ones. The furniture of the family mansion of Easton was partly transferred to Beachwood, and partly sold for the purpose of paying off some of the debts of the estate. Easton was put under the management of Mr. Barclay, a distant relative.

Beachwood, their retreat in the Shenandoah, had very great beauty in the eyes of one accustomed to the unvarying surface of the lower part of Virginia. The house was on the brow of a gently sloping hill on the north-east side of the Shenandoah, not far from Ashby's Gap. The low grounds of the estate which though somewhat wider than usual, were still narrow, stretched above and below the house more than a mile each way; and were alternately green, yellow, or black, as the rich soil happened to be bare, or its crops to be growing or ripe.

In front, the Blue Ridge rose in majestic height, stretching as far as the eye could reach to the south-west on one side, and the north-east on the other; though a bend in the river-hills stopt the view in the last direction after five or six miles. The mountains, thickly covered with wood, presented a high, dark, and somewhat gloomy barrier to the vision in summer; but in autumn, they exhibited in gay profusion the brightest colours of the painter's pallet. Here, every shade and variety of red, crimson, and yellow, may be seen intermingled and relieved with different coloured evergreens; but, as the bright tints predominated over the sombre, it was a very gay and pleasing object to the eye, and the effect of its lively and varied hues overcame the melancholy associations which the fall of the leaf is so apt to awaken.

The house itself was a modest mansion of rough blue limestone, in the form of the letter L, having three rooms on a floor. Below, were a passage, drawing-room, dining-room, chamber, and a large closet which had been used as a dressing room, and was now the lodging room of Louisa. The three rooms above were bed-chambers. A large kitchen garden was on the east of the house, containing a succession of falls as the ground sloped to a little rivulet, which was formed by a limestone spring, not half a mile from the house. But the most beautiful part of the view was the river, presenting always to the eye, except after a heavy rain, a smooth surface and a limpid stream when near, and a broad sheet of mirror when seen at a distance; in which the mountains with its woods all crimson and gold; its jutting cliffs and patches of cleared land, were doubled to the eye, and inverted in their position.

This beautiful stream was not then ruffled by those boats that are now wafted on it with their rich freights, to Georgetown and Alexandria. It furnished no other variety than a horseman fording, or a wagon occasionally rumbling over its rocks; or in floods, a ferry-boat passing to and fro, with the aid of a rope stretched across from bank to bank.

Two or three small clearings of land, with a small cottage, out-houses, and orchard to each, appearing here and there in occasional hollows of the mountain, pleasantly varied the woodland scenery, especially in early spring. The situation was equally recommended by the fertility of its soil, the beauty of its scenery, and (compared with the situation they had lately occupied) the salubrity of its air and climate. Its solitude, and picturesque scenes, were well fitted to nurture that tender and romantic cast of feeling for which Louisa had already been remarked by her young acquaintance at Easton. But it is now time to turn our attention to Edward Grayson.

CHAPTER II.

The same lively interest, the first in the bosom of a young man of twenty-two, which prompted Edward's inquiries of his sister, made him now turn his steps to the Elms.

Among the most intimate friends of the late Colonel Grayson was Major Fawkner, the proprietor of a good estate about four miles higher up the Shenandoah, which has been already mentioned, and was called the Elms. They had both been officers of the revolution, and although they had served in different parts of the country, one having been under General Washington to the north, and the other under General Greene in the south; yet, as they had at the close of the war been both members of the Cincinnati; both warm supporters of General Washington when the country began first to be divided into two angry hostile parties which threatened to destroy the happiness of the country, in disputing about the best means of promoting it; and had been both thrown into the same neighbourhood, they became extremely attached to each other. During the Colonel's summer excursion to Frederick, they saw each other almost every day, and the families interchanged dinners once a week. The Major was naturally generous and high minded, but being rather of an indolent, easy disposition, he had insensibly fallen into the views of his wife, and had become more bent on making money than had been natural to him. He was a man of mild, amiable manners, but with something of that precision and exactness which military men are apt to acquire.

He had married an heiress, from whom he derived the estate on which they then lived: A woman narrow-minded and ambitious, priding herself on her own wealth, and graduating her respect to others by theirs. A few years before, they had a son and two daughters; the youngest of whom had died of a prevailing epidemic when nearly grown. Her son had been, next to the sale of their crops, the chief object of her anxious thoughts; so that her excessive and mistaken fondness had made a constitution, originally a weak one, yet more feeble and delicate.

This youth had died of a pulmonary complaint about four years before, and Mrs. Fawkner's desire of amassing property, which had before seemed to exist only for the sake of her son Steener, as he was called, seemed, if possible, augmented and redoubled when this apparent motive was taken away. She was more pinching in her household; more pressing on her husband to collect the debts that were due to him; more disposed to chaffer with the merchants with whom she dealt in the neighbourhood than ever; and more on the lookout for good bargains in land, negroes, or bonds.

As her daughter Matilda, who was not thirteen at the death of her brother, and who had, with her sister, been always treated as an inferior, grew to womanhood, and improved in person and mind, she presented a new object on which her avarice and ambition, and restless, intriguing disposition could operate; and she began to look around for a suitable match for her. A match by which she might bring into the family an estate still larger than her own.

When her darling Steener was alive, she had considered Edward Grayson as a very desirable match for Matilda, and in the frequent intercourse of the families, she was ever extolling to the children the good qualities of one another; and her course of policy might, if their own recommendations had been far less than they were, have made them pleased with each other. But, in truth, her agency was entirely unnecessary.

Edward, as we have seen, possessed all those qualities of manners, mind, and person, that were calculated to recommend him to the heart of a woman of taste and discrimination, who is, perhaps, after all, the best judge of merit in the other sex. And Matilda Steener, besides being one of the loveliest in face and person, possessed a sweetness of disposition and kindness of manner, united with dignity, which had made her an universal favourite.

She was tall and slender, had dark brown hair and eyes, and a skin that rivalled the conch shell in the fineness of its texture, and in the brilliancy of its tint. She had long viewed Edward Grayson with the partiality which his own merits, as well as his pointed attentions, were calculated to inspire: and on his last visit he had come to an explanation, though they had indeed long understood each other before; and she, without any disguise or affectation, candidly confessed that his pure and virtuous attachment was cordially reciprocated.

When she communicated the fact of his declaration to her mother, she was surprised and distressed to find that it did not meet her approbation. Mrs. Fawkner remarked, "that Major Grayson's affairs were not settled—that his estate had not been profitable for some years, and it was well known that he had incurred considerable debts in Alexandria—that Mrs. Grayson had confessed to Colonel Fawkner, that the farther she looked into her husband's affairs, the more discouraging she found them, and that Barbawl, Colonel Fawkner's attorney, had told her in confidence the week before, that the estate was threatened with a security debt, which, if it was made to pay, would nearly swallow up the whole—that Edward Grayson was to be sure a very genteel and amiable young man, of good talents; but if he should lose all chance of being able to keep Easton or Beachwood, he would be no better match than Barbawl or young Dr. Cutaway, both of whom had ventured to declare themselves lovers of Matilda, and had been rejected by the general consent of the whole family." She insisted that Matilda should think no more of Edward, at least for the present; and finding that she persisted in acknowledging her decided and unchangeable preference, she made Matilda consent not to think of marriage until some further development of his affairs; which Matilda the more readily agreed to, as she was convinced that if her mother's ill-omened predictions should prove true, Edward's pride would not suffer him to insist on obtaining her hand until he had first obtained a respectable standing in his intended profession.

From this time, Mrs. Fawkner put every engine at work to change her daughter's affection, and to break off the match ; and her efforts, though meant to be conducted with art, both with a view to save appearances and to insure success, were so manifest, that they had greatly diminished the intercourse between the two families, and substituted form and ceremony between thé elder members in the place of the most friendly and unreserved intimacy.

With the young people there was no diminution of friendship or cordiality. Matilda and Louisa saw each other often, and the former endeavoured to disguise the motives of her mother's objection as much as she could ; and as she was known to be planning a match between Matilda and her cousin Frederick Steener, she ascribed this preference on the part of her mother to her well known partiality for her own family.

This young man was an orphan child of a deceased brother, possessed of a good estate in Berkley, and for whom her father was guardian; and no more eligible match, in point of fortune, presenting itself to Mrs. Fawkner's imagination, she was entirely bent on promoting it, though her kinsman was, in fact, an awkward, unpolished, yet good-natured clown ; and had a richer rival offered for the hand of her daughter, Frederick's pretensions, though of the noble house of Steener, had been as promptly rejected as were those of Edward.

Mrs. Fawkner had not manifested her opposition before Edward had left Frederick, in the preceding autumn, for Williamsburg ; and he had been ignorant of it, but for some slight intimations in the letters of his mother and sister, who, however, unwilling to pain him, and confiding in the undisguised affection of Matilda, had given a softened representation of the fact.

As the time approached for an interview, his fears gradually augmented, and he began at length to imagine to himself the vicious arts which so intriguing a woman may put in force to effect her object ; and in spite of himself, to fear that Matilda's constancy would not be proof against the busy, well-planned schemes of her mother.

The Elms are situated near the banks of the river, having a small rivulet meandering on one side of the house and discharging itself into the Shenandoah, in a gentle current, through a rich black loam. Two rows of elms, which old Cornelius Steener, the father of Mr. Fawkner, had planted in remembrance of his native country, Holland, form a long avenue from the gate on the public road to the house ; and the same association of ideas made him prefer this low situation, surrounded by water, to a beautiful eminence, about half a mile back of the house. which commanded an extensive view of the river and the adjacent country. Yet, as the irregular mansion he had built, was encircled by grass of the brightest verdure, and the grounds about it were decorated with clumps or rows of weeping willows, poplar, aspin, and such shrubs and vines as delight in moist situations, all flourishing in unusual luxuriance, it was not devoid of a certain species of beauty, and conveyed the agreeable ideas of fertility, abundance, and comfort.

Nor was it as unhealthy as might have been at first supposed; it being found by experience that the fogs and noxious exhalations from the river often pass over, (like the boasted policy of the Romans,) the lowly dwellings on the rivers' banks, to attack those who had sought to elevate themselves above their reach.

A large kitchen garden, and another of fruit-trees, in which old Steener had been very curious, occupied nearly three acres on the other side of the house; and in its walks and bowers, Edward and Matilda had passed many a delightful moment, and had tasted that purest and sweetest of human enjoyments, which love imparts to two young and innocent bosoms. Nor did they know the full extent of their happiness, until they were threatened with its loss.

In the corner of this garden, where a light railing separated the two parts, Matilda had obtained permission to exercise her fancy in the erection of a summer house—not being pleased with the heavy and tasteless structure which her mother had put up in the centre of her own garden, as she always called the first enclosure. This was Matilda's favourite retreat; and here, when Louisa Grayson visited her, they passed their summer mornings and evenings in reading, needle-work, or painting, in which art she gave indications of a great natural talent. Here it was, too, that Edward, a few evenings before he set out for Williamsburg the preceding autumn, first ventured to make a declaration which his words, and looks, and actions, had plainly indicated a year or two before. This circumstance had made the retreat doubly dear to Matilda, and it had been her favourite amusement in the following spring, to plant around it new shots of the coral honey suckle, to trail those vines of the multiflora so as to close every remaining aperture, by which the rays of the sun could enter; to add to the damask roses and jasmines on the outside, and to deck the little knots of flowers in front with the rarest and most beautiful exotics she could procure. It seemed, indeed, to engross her so entirely, that Major Fawkner, in his frequent journeys from home, whenever he procured any valuable flower-seed, would say to his daughter that he had brought her something for her hobby while Mrs. Fawkner would sometimes complain that Jerry, the gardener, was half his time in waiting on Matilda—that her own garden was overrun with weeds—and Mrs. Busker would, that year, have pease and cucumbers a month before her.

It was in this favourite spot, still dearer from the reflections it awakened and the visions it raised, than from its shade, and beauty, and fragrance, that Matilda was engaged in her usual morning pursuits, when a servant announced Mr. Edward Grayson to his master, then sitting in the dining room with a bundle of papers before him. Edward immediately entered. He was cordially welcomed by Major Fawkner, and with a show of politeness by Mrs. Fawkner. The Major said to the servant "where is Miss Matilda? run and tell her Mr. E. is here.—I suppose she is in her hobby, according to custom. Edward, secretly flattered by the intimation which this remark conveyed, quickly said, " nay, do not send for Miss Matilda—let me see what improvement she has made in her summer-house.

Stop, Mr. Grayson, said Mrs. Fawkner, I believe Matty is in her dishabilles this morning; she won't like to be taken by surprise.

" Why, wife," said the Major, " For the matter of that, Matilda is always neat and tidy."—

" She is neat enough in all conscience," said Mrs. Fawkner. But—

When the lovely object of dispute entered the room; having, as soon as her kindly officious maid Nelly had informed her of Edward's arrival, obeyed the impulse of her feelings and run into the dining-room. Her hair, indeed, in wild disorder, hung over her forehead and down her shoulders, in rich profusion, and so far justified the remark of her mother; but in every part of her dress besides, which was a light muslin frock, drawn at the bosom and wrists with pale blue ribbands, she was dressed with the neatness of a new doll, and the precision of a quaker.

She ran towards Edward, and held out her hand, but immediately reading the displeasure in her mother's countenance, and remembering that he was now her declared lover, she checked herself and made a formal courtesy, but still giving him her hand. Edward saw at once the change, and felt an undefinable sort of uneasiness ; for what sudden coolness in his mistress, ever escaped the lover's vigilance ?

After the compliments and inquiries, usual on such occasions, Mrs. Fawkner, whose mind had been brooding over the attachment which she had once so much encouraged, but which so little accorded with her present views and wishes, said " I hope you left all well this morning, Mr. Grayson, at Beechwood. I hardly ever see your mother now. I laugh, and tell her that pride keeps her so much at home now that she drives but two horses."

" That is the last motive in the world to operate on my poor dear mother," said Edward; "but, perhaps, she has some right to complain of you, on the score of visiting."

" Why, indeed, I have not been out as much of late as formerly. Major Fawkner has been obliged to go to Alexandria and Baltimore this spring, and I must attend to the business of the farm. Every thing is at six and sevens when we are both away. You know overseers require as much looking after as the negroes themselves. They tell me the fly has been very troublesome in your wheat, and that your harvest turned out badly.

I have been so little awhile at home, that I have not yet learnt the condition of the farm.

"Well, the Major thinks, now the old General has resigned, the price of wheat will fall ; and if it does, and the fly continues to destroy our crops, I know not what will become of us. The times are hard enough already. Barbawl tells me that people on the other side of the mountain are mightily in debt. Oh, has that suit of the sheriff, whom your father was security for, been decided yet?"

" It has not, madam," said Edward, with an impatience that he in vain strove to suppress.

Matilda endeavored to change the conversation, by asking if they had a splendid exhibition on the fourth of July, at Williamsburg ; and, on his proceeding to answer her—said Mrs. Fawkner, with a view of concealing her real sentiments, " Barbawl says he thinks they cannot recover, or at least that they ought not. And if they should, that all the other securities must contribute an equal part ; and that it will not be more than four or five thousand dollars apiece."

"The whole claim, madam, I thought, was but four thousand dollars, and that it was likely to be reduced considerably."

"I am very glad to hear it. Well, your father was so willing to be every body's security. There's Joe Cheekby, Frederick Steener's guardian, with his oily tongue would have persuaded the Major to have been one of his securities, if it had not been for me; and they tell me that he is in a fair way to be ruined."

"You were my guardian angel then, I admit," said Major Fawkner, "but I hope Cheekby will come out yet," he added, "for the sake of my neighbours."

To Edward, these last remarks gave more serious concern, as he knew that his father, with his accustomed good nature, had been one of this Cheekby's sureties to his guardian's bond; that he had vested the large funds of his ward in purchases of waste lands, which had at first yielded great profit; but which, by excessive competition, and the flagrant frauds which had been practised by the land speculators, had now proved very unsaleable, and that most of the co-securities had partaken of Cheekby's speculation, and were sharers in his loss; and he was alarmed on account of his mother and sisters. Suppressing, however, his feelings, he again attempted to have some conversation with Matilda, but finding he was liable to perpetual interruptions from Mrs. Fawkner, who would always contrive to say something that was calculated to mortify or alarm him, he now, indeed, felt the full force of his mother's remark, that she feared he would find things much changed at the Elms, and he rose to depart, when the Major, with his usual good nature and kindness of heart, urged him to stay to dinner, and on his refusal, expressed a wish that he would ride over often and take hunt with him, adding that though he was getting rather too unwieldly to *start*, his rifle would do as much execution as ever *at a stand;* and he was about naming a day, in the following week, when his considerate wife reminded him that he was to go over to Hardy, by appointment, to survey his new purchase.

"You are right, my dear. See what it is, Edward, to have a wife: 'twill be well to appoint a day as soon as I get back."

Edward took his leave, with feelings very different from those with which he entered the dwelling. His horse was bought out by old Jeffrey, formerly the valet of Major Fawkner, but now his hostler—a shrewd, artful, ready-witted knave, who having long assumed the privilege of great familiarity with his superiors, was at length suffered quietly to enjoy it; and who, looking on Edward as his future master, had been in the habit of addressing him in that style, which he supposed most likely to conciliate his favour, present as well as future.

"Ah, master Edward, I'm glad you've got back—

we have all been wishing for you—we hav'nt killed a buck since you left us. Master can't hunt without you—we have all been wishing for you. There have been a good many fine gentlemen here this spring; but I tell the black folks here, that there's nobody like master Edward."

" Poh, poh," said Edward, " you are at your old game, Jeffrey," throwing him a quarter of a dollar, and less displeased at his flattery than at the ideas of rivalry which his remarks, connected with Mrs. Fawkner's behaviour, had indicated.

" There's young Mr. Stevens, with his two fine nicked bays, with black manes and tails ; and Dr. Sticquein, from Loudoun, in a mighty fine sulkey ; but it all would not do." Looking to see how far he might venture in his career of impudent familiarity. Edward, making no reply, suddenly mounted and rode off.

As he slowly trotted along the avenue of venerable elms, he recollected the high and buoyant feelings which had filled his bosom when he last passed through them an hour before, and contrasting them with those he then felt, he could not but indulge in the most gloomy anticipations of the future. He even fancied that the behaviour of Matilda was constrained, and had something of coldness in it, and he asked himself if it were possible that his absence for six months, and the attentions of two or three coxcombs, could have wrought the change. When he passed through the gate which terminates the avenue, he instantly cast a last look at the house which contained what most interested him, and found all his hopes and confidence revive, as he saw Matilda standing at the window and following him with her eyes, as she was wont to do in her first days of unconscious love. He gave the reins to Saracen, and in less than half an hour was at home.

CHAPTER III.

EDWARD had not been long gone and Matilda retired to her own room, before Mrs. Fawkner, in that sharp tone of reprimand with which she often addressed her husband, exclaimed, " I wonder, Major Fawkner, you can give that young man such pointed encouragement, always inviting him to hunt, and to visit, and what not. You know he has addressed Matilda, and you must see that he is not disagreeable to her; but, for my part, I have no notion of allying myself with a falling house. If what Barbawl tells me is true, they will certainly have that debt to pay, and then, I suppose, we must maintain the whole family."

The major, who sat apparently in deep thought, said, " Why, really, that securityship of poor Grayson gives me a good deal of uneasiness, and if the whole should fall on his estate, it would leave little else but the land; but as to Edward, I think him a fine young man—one who will rise in his profession; and I fear that matters have gone too far between him and Matilda to be now broken off, so that, I think, wife, we had better make the best of it."

"That is always your way now, Major Fawkner, letting every thing take its own course, and sitting down contented. You would have given up that debt of Eaton & Shewaway, if I had not teazed and worried you, till you made them give you a mortgage on their property in Alexandria; and you would never have bought the Briarfield, if you had had your way, and deferred the purchase a week longer."

"Well, my dear wife," said the Major, partly convinced by those examples of her superior foresight and decision, and partly to put a stop to further reproaches,—"what would you have me do? I must treat the son of my old neighbour and friend with civility. I could do no less than ask him to visit us."

"But you are under no necessity of making him an inmate, and getting up visiting parties to keep him for ever dangling after your daughter Matilda shall never marry a beggar, with my consent; and, I think, if you were to speak your mind plainly to the girl, and tell her of the imprudence of the match, that she could be brought to turn him off, though she is very much disposed to be headstrong of late. Depend upon it, my dear husband, (for she had found by experience, it was best to infuse a little kindness in her peroration) if we do not put an end to this business in time, we shall live to repent it; and, for my part, I can't make up my mind to see a child about to sup sorrow and not try to dash the cup from her lips."

The easy temper of the Major was alarmed at this picture of distress; and without giving himself the trouble to examine into its probability, he said, "to be sure, my dear, it would be as well to see how Edward can maintain a family before he encumbers himself with one; and, at any rate, until he is settled in his profession, I will advise Matilda to keep matters in suspense; or perhaps, my dear, you had better tell her what we think on the subject, and she can tell Edward." Mrs. Fawkner, content with her present success, did not urge the matter further. She had not brought her husband to that point of opposition that she wished, and was determined on effecting.

Edward, on his return, found his sister and her lively friend yet engaged in an animated dialogue, in which the parties being secretly pleased with each other, and both too conscious of pleasing, the hours passed off unheeded in their flight. Gildon had detailed some of his college adventures with his happy vein of humour—described, with witty satire, some of the belles of his acquaintance—entertained his fair and delighted auditor with a description of the theatrical wonders of the New-York and Philadelphia theatres—Mrs. Merry and Mrs. Whitlock, Hopkinson and Fennell—with also the fashionable scandal which was then current in the better classes of society. "Bless me," said Gildon, with some surprise, purposely exaggerated, "have you returned already? You made but a short visit—it seems scarce half an hour since you left the room."

"Did you find the family at home, brother?" said Louisa.

"They were," said Edward, "and your friend sends you this geranium. I am glad to find that your time does not pass heavily."

Mrs. Grayson cast an anxious and inquiring glance towards her son, and read in his countenance a look of care and perplexity which were not usual with him on a return from the Elms, but she was afraid to discover the current of his thoughts.

"When do our neighbours talk of visiting us, my son?"

"Not soon, I apprehend, madam, as Major Fawkner's business calls him frequently from home this summer; and you know Mrs. Fawkner hates to leave the farm when he's away. Matilda hopes to be able to spend a day with you in the following week, and desired me to present you with this product of her little garden," handing a beautiful half blown moss-rose.

Mrs. Grayson, who had long been in the habit of regarding Matilda as her intended daughter-in-law, and felt for her the affection of a mother, received the gift as a sure omen that whatever may be the sentiments of the rest of the family, the most interesting member of it was unchanged; and yielding to the sanguine hopes of an easy temper, and of a mother's partiality, she thought that any obstruction which Mrs. Fawkner might raise, would finally yield to the constancy of Matilda's affection, and the rare merits of her son.

"She was always the sweetest girl in the world," she said, as she received the fragrant gift.

Louisa then launched out in a strain of the most rapturous praises on her young friend, whose superiority of understanding, accompanied by the greatest good-nature, without the least particle of pride, had obtained its natural ascendency over a mind ardent as was Louisa's, and much given to admiration.

Gildon then observed, " how easy it is to see, Miss Grayson, that you were brought up in the country. Now, you may meet with fifty young ladies in our large cities, before you would see one who could be thus lavish in her praises of another."

" Because," said Louisa, "we can seldom meet with one so deserving."

" Well," said Gildon, " I shall write to my friends that the rarest thing I have yet met in the mountains of Virginia, is one young lady, not yet twenty, and not without some small pretensions herself," in a tone of good-natured raillery, "who extols a neighbouring belle to the skies. From your description, and the ecstacies of Edward, in his occasional rhapsodies by moonlight, I should like to see this phenix—but, for my part, I think there is sometimes as much merit (giving a significant look towards Louisa) in bestowing praise as in being the object of it."

A trampling of horses was now heard in front of the house; and in a minute, a tall raw-boned man, with sandy hair, pale gray eyes, and rather rugged features, dressed in gray home-spun, entered the room.

"Oh, Mr. M'Culloch, Mr. M'Culloch!" they all exclaimed.

He ran up to Edward, "how goes it my young friend? you're welcome back to the mountains. I am rejoiced to see you in the back-woods again, safe and sound from the Tuckahoes. I have been afraid that you were engaged in some of the riots which have lately broke out in old Williamsburg; and I know you are as good pluck, my lad, as if you were a thorough bred Cohee, though you were born and raised in Oyster-land. In riding out this morning, I met with my old neighbour Hatchett, who told me he was coming here, and that you returned yesterday; so I thought I must give you a shake by the hand, and see whether the lowland air had worsted your complexion, or city airs had spoilt your manners."

"I flatter myself you will find me not much altered in so short an absence. But how are Mrs. M'Culloch and your little folks?"

"Why, the chicks, God bless them, are all well, and merry as a brood of young partridges, but the old squaw is a little complaining of late. I tell her she frets herself sick about debts, and short crops, and such scurvy plagues of life—begone dull care is my motto. If the fly destroys two or three more crops, we must push off to Kentucky, and feast on bear-hams and buffalo-hump; unless Citizen Hatchett here could lend me about seven or eight thousand. What say you old cent per cent?" with a loud good-natured laugh.

The personage whom he addressed, who had entered soon after him, and who had been received by the family in a style that betokened acquaintance merely but no intimacy, was a sharp-visaged, pock-marked, sallow-looking man, apparently about fifty, dressed in a coat and vest of a rhubarb colour, with his thin gray hair tied close to his head.

"Mr. M'Culloch is always running his rig on those who live on such poor lands as we," said Hatchett, with a self-complacent smile. "If I had had ever so much money by me, it would have been gone long ago. I never heard such complaints of the scarcity of money."

"What, old buck, you have been doing a brisk business this summer, have you? Did you ever see the time when it was not scarce with some people—with such runagates as myself, who see no use in the dross but in spending it; and who will neither pinch my belly or back so long as a dollar can be had in an honest way? And I doubt, friend Benjamin, whether I do not have more pleasure in spending an hundred dollars than you have in making a thousand—and I am sure mine is the easiest task of the two."

"Every man to his taste, Mr. M'Culloch," said the money-lender, who wincing under the unrestrained banter of his companion, and not knowing what would come next, told Edward he wished to say a word to him in private, and with great awkwardness of gait, but an air of no little self-importance, shuffled out of the room.

"Now, look at old Maw-worm," said the free spoken mountaineer, "with his face as yellow as the gold he worships, and his heart as hard as the iron chest which contains it. I suppose he has picked up some bond of the poor major's, or like enough, one for which he was some worthless fellow's security, and as soon as he hears of Edward's arrival, he loses no time in exacting promise of payment out of the present crop; or, perhaps, will offer forbearance for the trifling consideration of thirty-three and a third per cent. I shall tell Edward to have as little to do with the old Jew as possible."

"Why, Mr. M'Culloch, I thought that you and Mr. Hatchett were on very friendly terms," said Mrs. Grayson.

"He, an old blood-sucker! the Shylock of the valley. It is true I sometimes make a convenience of him, and get money from him when I can get it no where else. But I never spare the old curmudgeon the less on that account. I know that he bears me no good will; but so long as I have an acre of the Clover Flat left, or a woolly head to work it, he will always be ready to take my paper at a discount. I think that every bond he gets of me affords the old hunks double pleasure; for it at once gratifies his malice by helping me to my ruin, and his avarice by his unconscionable gains. I pray, dear madam, that you will tell Edward to beware of him."

"I hope," said Mrs. Grayson, "if your suspicions are just as to the subject of his application, that he will not be so unreasonable in his exactions as you suppose, nor Edward so imprudent as to submit to them."

Young Grayson now entered the room with a face in which chagrin might be easily seen through an assumed appearance of careless ease.

"Well, has old Screwtight been pestering you already with his d——d *claims,* as he calls them?" said M'Culloch.

"He merely spoke of a small matter of business," said Edward, with seeming indifference.

" Yes of *business* that is no business of mine.—Excuse my freedom, madam, but I always scent out mischief when such vermin are near. But tell me, Edward, how run politics in old Williamsburg? I fear you have come back an arrant jacobin. I was a bit of Frenchman myself at first; but ever since the bloody work of the guillotine, and the attempt of Citizen Genet to bully the old general, I have given them up, and I am now afraid they will lug us into this war before they are done."

Edward and Gildon now both took up the cudgels for the cause of liberty and France—regretted that the United States had not generously given their aid in the noble struggle in which that gallant people were engaged for their independence, instead of adopting the cold, timid, selfish course of neutrality; and they unhesitatingly expressed their conviction that our policy might be fairly ascribed to the unbounded influence of England and her numerous partizans and adherents, dispersed over every part of this country.

The dispute was waxing warm, and while one party forgot the respect due to age, the other made no allowance for the ardour and impetuosity of youth; when Mrs. Grayson, to whom such scenes were not less rare than unwelcome, considerately interfered, and with that characteristic mildness and sweetness which it was difficult to resist, said, " Fie, gentlemen, do you dispute on politics before ladies ? If so we will leave you. Mr. M'Culloch, I thought you had more gallantry."

"Nay, madam," said the veteran, "excuse me. I don't in general regard these political railers. Your thorough going democrat is so prejudiced it does no good to reason with him; but, I confess, it makes me sorry to see the son of my old friend, who you know, madam, was always ready to fight at the least disparaging word against the old general, taking sides with this faction; and I wish to put him in the right path if I can. But I fear," added he, with a good natured smile, "that he was so thoroughly inoculated with the disease, while in Williamsburg, that he is past all cure, except what time and experience may bring. I will then even leave him to their salutary operation."

Edward, brought to his recollection by the gentle admonition from his mother, observed, that as he despaired of making Mr. M'Culloch a convert in politics, he hoped he could now convince him of the efficacy of plaister of Paris, which was then getting into use in that part of the country; and proposed they should take a walk to a clover field on which it had been used by way of experiment. The ladies left the parlour, and the gentlemen repaired to the field of clover. Here narrow slips or belts, of a more luxuriant growth and a deeper green traversing the whole field, were as plainly marked to the eye as the different colours on a piece of striped cloth.

"In these," said Edward, "plaister has been scattered at the rate of a bushel to the acre; while on the intermediate spaces, where the clover is yellowish and thin, and of a stinted growth, there has been none."

"This, indeed, looks as if there was some virtue in this French plaister? but now, are you sure you have not, like other prophets, taken some pains to verify your own predictions, and ploughed these green slips deeper or better, or sown the seed a little thicker, or that your manager has not done it for you? for, as David Hume says, in his chapter on miracles, it seems much more probable that there has been some trick practised, or some mistake committed in one of these ways, than that such wonderful effects should be produced by peppering a little dry chalk over the ground. I could as easily believe that a man would fatten sooner by smelling a beef-steak than by eating it. No, no, my boy, you must try this again and again, before you will convince me."

Edward and Gildon were diverted at their friend's incredulity; Grayson observed, "It is no wonder we cannot convince him in matters of politics and speculation, when he won't yield to the evidences of his senses."

The sturdy enemy of prejudice and innovation remarking then that the old squaw, as he often termed his wife, would wait dinner for him, insisted they should dine with him the first time they went abroad, and spend as much of their leisure hours with him as they could; and mounting his large, raw-boned, iron-gray horse, he paced out of their sight in a twinkling.

Edward then observed, "there goes one of the honestest, best hearted men I ever knew: but as you perceive, one of the most opinionative and inflexible. Fortunately, his feelings are always amiable and good, or he would often be intolerable. He is of Scotch-Irish extraction, as we call those who emigrate to this country from the north of Ireland. They form a considerable portion of the population of that part of this state which lies west of the Blue Ridge; and those who are fond of such curious general speculations, often dispute which make the most valuable description of population, these, or the descendants of German emigrants, or Dutch, as they are commonly called, with whom they form a most striking contrast.

"I did not know," said Gildon, "that these two descriptions of settlers made any considerable part of your population in Virginia, as I knew it did in Pennsylvania. I thought your people were more homogeneous, and were principally of English descent."

"That is true with the eastern part of Virginia," said Edward.

"I should like to know," Gildon then remarked, "the great leading features of these classes, and in what particulars they most strikingly differ."

"Well," replied Edward, "let us sit down on the log at the foot of yon shady sycamore, and I will endeavour to exhibit to you the characteristic virtues and faults of each. My old friend M'Culloch is a favourable specimen of one class, and a lady in this neighbourhood is an unfavourable specimen of the other."

They walked on to the place proposed, where a sycamore, on the river bank, bending its large white trunk and massy branches over the stream, formed a shade impervious to the rays of a July sun. But as Edward's dissertation may seem very dull prosing to some of my readers, it is put in a separate chapter, that those who choose it, may pass it over without breaking the thread of the narrative: though we would modestly hint, that sometimes the mountain, whose waste and barren surface exhibits neither flower nor leaf, often contains valuable materials to those who will take the trouble of searching a little deeper for them.

CHAPTER IV.

"The German settlers with us have generally migrated from the western parts of Maryland and Pennsylvania, and are for the most part born in those states, and not in Germany. But they retain their original characteristics in the first generation without much change; and when they have lost the peculiarities of language and manners and customs, there are some traits of character less visible to ordinary eyes, which they will probably retain long afterwards, which will impress themselves on their posterity for many generations, and will, no doubt, have some effect in forming the compound that is hereafter to make our national character.

"They are, with few exceptions, a pains-taking, plodding, frugal people; and sober more in consequence of their industrious pursuits, their slight relish for social pleasures, and their habits of thrift, than indifference to liquor. On the contrary, they seem to have that love of strong drink, which, natural to man, in every climate, is strongest in wet and cold countries. They are, in short, mere Germans in this propensity; and many a one will get drunk at another's expense, who will scarcely drink at all at his own; and will lay aside his sobriety altogether, when he has fallen into habits of idleness. He is, in general, a good domestic character, a kind and faithful husband, and a provident master of his family. His contentious humour spends itself among his neighbours, and is shown, not in riots and brawls, but in lawsuits; not in the courtyard, but within the walls of the court-house. When once engaged in law, they never quit it until every expedient of new trials, rehearsings, chancery suits, and such like instruments of the "law's delay" are exhausted; and so long as the lawyer can keep up the jig, these his favourite clients are ready to pay the piper. There is nothing for which they will part with their money so freely. I remember to have heard a gentleman of the bar tell my father, that a Dutchman, (as they are inaccurately termed, the few Hollanders among us being distinguished as low Dutch,) called at his office one day and wished a suit brought against one of his neighbours, with whom he had had some petty dispute. As he gave a tedious unintelligible account of the quarrel, the attorney thought it best to question him:

"Did he strike you?"

"No, he did'nt shtrike, or I would have peaten his d——d prains out."

"Did he offer to strike?"

" No—dat's de same in law."

" Well, did he slander you?"

" I has no proof of dat."

" Has he got any of your land?"

" No, indeed! Do you think I would let him get any of my land?"

" Has he done any injury to your cattle, or any of your property?"

" I don't know that he has."

" Well, friend Stophal, I can't see that you have any ground of action. I don't know what sort of suit I can bring."

" Don't know!" he indignantly asked, "why bring a *spite suit!*"—And persisted in his wish, though he was assured he would eventually have the costs to pay.

" In selecting sites for their habitations, they always place them near the water, commonly on some little stream, on whose margin they can have a meadow—if large enough to turn a mill, so much the better. The grass and hay which these wet situations afford, enable them to keep their horses and cattle fat, and to supply, at moderate prices, their less provident neighbours with butter, cheese, small meats, and some excellent vegetables.

" Most of them mingle the pursuit of some handicraft trade with that of husbandry, and are blacksmiths, wheelwrights, hatters, and the like; in which occupations they sometimes attain a skill far above mediocrity, though they are commonly very deficient in taste. Their gardens furnish them abundantly with potatoes, beets, peas, beans, and other culinary vegetables; but the favourite product of their kitchen garden, is the cabbage; which, by pickling and subjecting to the acetous fermentation, they convert into sourkrout, an excellent antiscorbutic, and well adapted to counteract the effects of eating salt meat. They cultivate buckwheat very generally, partly on account of the cakes they make of its grain, and partly for the sake of their bees, of which they keep great numbers, since this plant continues to bloom long after all other flowers have disappeared. The honey thus extracted from the buckwheat, is again brought into contact with it at their tables, as it is commonly eaten with their nice buckwheat cakes.

"Their wardrobes are abundantly supplied with such clothing of linen, cotton, and wool, intermingled in different proportions, and variously striped with blue, red, and yellow, as their own looms can afford—and, except that they are not sufficiently attentive to cleanliness, every thing about them exhibits both comfort and abundance.

"Thus possessed of the means of gratifying his principal wants, which are chiefly sensual, without ambition, and without literature, the mind of the German settler is contracted, and his disposition selfish. He takes little concern in public affairs.

He votes indeed at the elections, but always for the candidate by whom he can make the most; or in the absence of the motive of interest, for him who can flatter the best. A stranger to all literary gratification, and knowing that he has succeeded very well without learning, he gives little or no schooling to his children. Having the wants, which are merely animal, gratified, and being of a phlegmatic temperament, he is comparatively without emulation, without generosity, without public spirit. He cares little what is passing beyond the walls of his little *pomœrium;* and all questions of politics, or religion, or learning, which stir up the busy passions of men, and have awakened the feelings of his ancetors, are less than shadows to him, for they are not even perceived."

"Your picture is a very unfavourable one," said Gildon. "Methinks they resemble these great worthless sycamores; they hold a place on the rich banks, which a more useful tree would occupy if they were away."

"Not so," said Edward; "for though they are in many respects not altogether to my taste, yet I hold them to be an useful class of citizens in their place, and to perform a good part in the great drama of life. They are the dray-horses of society—not fitted for the turf, as the high-mettled racer; nor for the chase, as the Chickasaw; or our own old field breed; nor for war, as the

Arabian; but well qualified to execute that coarse but useful labour, which society requires; and to keep up the comparison you have made, you see this tree is not without its use, as it affords to us, and occasionally to the cattle that pasture in these fields, the benefit of its shade. It makes the best coal for our smith's shops, and growing kindly to the water's edge, and very rapidly too, it keeps the river, in time of floods, from washing away its banks. They rapidly start up where nothing else would spontaneously grow; they enrich the ground by shading it, and by much that they return to it; and in good time, they will give place to trees of more value and usefulness, and be themselves consigned to the smiths' shops. Though I am not sure but other trees may be found that would afford these advantages, and yet be further useful for timber, firewood, or fruit; if so, the time will come when we shall have more leisure to cultivate them, and they will take the place of these barren sycamores."

"But go on," said Gildon, "with the other part of your picture."

"The Irish character presents in almost every thing, a strong contrast to that which I have just placed before you—as ardent and impassioned as the others are cold and phlegmatic—as imaginative as the others are dull, they run into the most violent extremes. Yet the Irish who have migrated to this country, being for the most part from the North of Ireland, which was settled by the Scotch, partake of the character of the latter. When bent on the pursuits of gain or ambition, they manifest great enterprise and perseverance; but are often idle, indolent, and improvident. Nothing is more common here than to see one of the Scotch-Irish, who has inherited a piece of good land, when it was to be had for the trouble of surveying it and paying two dollars an hundred acres into the public treasury, on which he might easily have got rich, by a course of extravagance and bad management, be obliged to sell it before he is thirty. And some of the best estates in this Valley, are constantly passing from the hands of the Irish, who were among the earliest settlers, into those of the more frugal Dutch.

"The Scotch-Irish have both the virtues and vices of bold, daring characters, and sanguine temperaments. Hardy, restless, brave, and enterprising, they have been the most successful warriors against the aboriginal proprietors of the country, and the advance guard of civilization; and when once society, in this our wilderness, was accommodated with the useful arts, and broken to the restraints of law and civil government, they have ever proved its most conspicuous ornaments. They exhibit nothing of that frigid sameness of character which distinguishes the Dutchman, whose phlegmatic temperament makes him indolent, and sometimes reckless of the future, and sometimes patient and persevering in amassing wealth. If our Irish are uniform in any thing it is that, whatever may be the course they take, they push it to extremes. Should you here see one wasting his substance in thoughtless extravagance and unwarranted luxury, you may there behold another engaged in a course of rapid and adventurous speculation. And even when aspiring to build up a fortune by the slow gains of some regular pursuit, there is an extraordinary boldness and decision in his career. As a grazier, or a miller, or distiller, his operations are carried on upon a large scale, and if he fails, (as it must be confessed he often does,) he can commonly say with Phæton, "*tamen magnis excidit ausis.*"

"In the affairs of the government, he feels the liveliest interest; and being commonly a presbyterian in religion, he has more than the usual pride and intolerance that that sect has been thought to inspire. They have been, for the most part, federalists, since our country has been divided into two parties, though I hear a large majority of them belong to the other party in Pennsylvania. It is somewhat curious, but it has justly been remarked of the Irish emigrants to America, that when settled together in great numbers, they are commonly good democrats; but when dispersed about singly, or in small parties, they are apt to be federalists."

"I suppose," says Gildon, "the federalists, who beat us in the art of making proselytes, are able to gain over small numbers, but they cannot convert large ones."

"I don't think that the reason," said Edward. "When they are collected in great numbers, they retain their original feelings of resentment to the British government, and zeal for the rights of the people, and they find the principles of the democratic party and its systematic opposition to the existing administration, accord better with the character of this party, than do those of the federalists; but when single, their original political feelings, having nothing to keep them up, die away after a while, and being often regarded as Englishmen, by our countrymen, who are not very nice in their distinctions, and consider every European speaking English, as an Englishman, and all others as Frenchmen, they gradually get the feelings and predilections of those with whom they are confounded. They thus more naturally associate with the federalists, who view the English with favour, and most of whose principles of government differ not widely from those of an Englishman, except in the article of hereditary right. You know an Englishman or a Frenchman always continues the same wherever he may live; but it is otherwise with an Irishman, who feels his country degraded by its dependence; he readily identifies himself with the country he adopts, and becomes a Frenchman in France, a Spaniard in Spain, and an American in the United States." "I believe," said

Gildon, we must be proud of our country, before we can love it."

But to return—The Irish every where show a ready disposition to encourage learning, and every other liberal institution. Where there is one German who is taught the dead languages, there are fifty Irishmen. These speaking the same language with us, and having no irreconcilable peculiarities in manners or modes of living, they are more assimilated to the natives, and occasionally hold places in the legislature, the militia, and the magistracy. If the German settler may be compared to the drayhorse, the Scotch-Irish resembles the light and spirited riding-horse, a nobler animal by nature; and, when free from defect, destined for worthier purposes, but more liable to accident; and if by some mischance, unfitted for the saddle, of less utility than one of a heavier and a coarser breed.

"My old friend, M'Culloch, who has left us, has most of the characteristic virtues and faults of his race. He has their intolerance in religion; their intemperance in politics; their prejudices, local, personal, religious, and political. He is an intolerant presbyterian—an intemperate federalist —has a general prejudice against all Tuckahoes— a particular one against old Hatchett, and was equally warm in his attachment to my father. This affection he has transferred to every member of the family, and it is this which makes me forgive him his politics, and bear with his narrow prejudices against republican France. Though he affects to speak rather carelessly of his wife, he is known to be a most tender husband, and she well deserves his utmost affection. Indeed, it has been his extreme indulgence to a numerous tribe of children, and a restless, scheming disposition, which has impaired a good estate, and will drive him, I fear, at last, into the wilds of Kentucky or Tennessee. But while he suffers himself to fall into the nets of old Hatchett, he is ever putting me on my guard; and a little before we parted, he urged me most pressingly to take no steps towards relieving my father's estate from a debt which it may have to pay, on accouut of a securityship, without first consulting him, who has experience in these matters, and like a guide-post, as he says himself, can show the way to others, though he cannot take it himself."

Perceiving now, some distance above them, a number of reapers, which by reason of a bend in the river and an intervening hill, had been previously intercepted, Gildon inquired if they had been mowing hay. "No," replied Edward, "we are now in the midst of our oat harvest; and, as I have not seen many of our field negroes or people, at the quarter, as we call it, if you have no objection we will return that way to the house."

"With all my heart; I want to see as much as I can of your system of farming, and of managing a plantation in Virginia. I have sometimes a thought of turning a southern planter or farmer myself. I hate our long winters and harsh springs; and there must be something very pleasant, after all, in having so many persons over whom you are supreme and sovereign lord. Don't you feel, Edward, when riding over these vast domains of yours, something like a feudal Baron? My father had a little farm, in Duchess County, on which he worked from four to five slaves; and although he had much more valuable lands rented out, (and a large territory gives a man no little consequence,) yet my view of these fertile lands never gave me half the gratification that was afforded by a sight of the blacks. I thought that the tenants were always jealous of the superiority which they believed I assumed; and, except now and then a mean fellow who wanted indulgence for his rent, or had not complied with the covenants in his lease, they were always taking pains to show me they regarded themselves my equals. There is something very fascinating now confess it, Edward, in this unlimited control, let us fiery republicans say what we will. Indeed what is the love of liberty, but the love of doing what we please? and, consequently, he who is proud of his own freedom, is equally gratified at controlling the freedom of others."

"A very ingenious piece of sophistry, upon my word," said Edward. "You think, then, that the same sentiment which makes a man wish to be master of his own actions, makes him wish to control the actions of others; or, in other words, that the love of freedom and the love of tyranny, are one and the same thing. No; be assured that he who has a proper sense of his own rights, has a due respect for the rights of others; and common sense must dictate to every rational mind that the wish which he recognizes of being his own master, is also felt by others; and that that is the most perfect system of civil liberty which can best gratify the desires of all: and it is imperfect in proportion as it falls short of this result, until it degenerates into downright despotism, where only a single person is free, if indeed the fears and dangers that environ him suffer him to be so."

"A very pretty dissertation this for a Virginia planter," said Gildon. "You must have intended it for part of an oration on the fourth of July. I dare venture to say there is an audience in sight which would readily subscribe to your doctrines."

"I was aware," said Edward, "that you consider these principles as inconsistent with our practice—but nothing can be more unfair than the charge of inconsistency. We, of the present generation, find domestic slavery established among us, and the evil, for I freely admit it to be an evil, both moral and political, admits of no remedy that is not worse than the disease. No thinking man supposes that we could emancipate them, and safely let them remain in the country; and no good or

prudent man would run the risk of renewing the
scenes which have made St. Domingo one general
scene of waste and butchery. Nor has any practical scheme as yet been devised for sending them
abroad—and we should pause a while in deliberat-
ing on its practicability, when we recollect that history tells us of no country which has ever been
able to rid itself of so large a part of its population
as the blacks now compose in the southern states.
The expulsion of the Moors from Spain comes
nearest to it—but, besides that their numbers
were much fewer; they had only a narrow sea to
cross, and they were in another continent. Their
banishment too, was complete and for ever. While
here, they must either be colonized on our borders, at all events on the same continent, or they
must be transported to the distance of three thousand miles. In this choice of difficulties what are
we to do? What can we do, but to select the least
formidable? and since we cannot confer on them,
or restore to them (if you will) some of those
rights which we ourselves so highly prize, without
endangering not only these, but every other we
possess, we must even set down contented, and
endeavour to *mitigate* a disease which admits of
no cure. Because we do not indulge in idle declamation about the injurious consequences of domestic slavery, yet do not infer that our politicians
are not insensible to them. The theme is an ungrateful one—like any other natural defect or mis-

fortune which is incurable. We are fully aware of its disadvantages—that it checks the growth of our wealth—is repugnant to its justice—inconsistent with its principles—injurious to its morals—and dangerous to its peace. Yet after giving the subject the most serious and attentive consideration, and finding it admitted of no other safe remedy but what time may bring some centuries hence, they are fain to acquiesce in their inevitable destiny, and now consider all speculations on rights which cannot be enforced, but at the expense of still higher and dearer rights, either as the ebullitions of well-meaning but short-sighted enthusiasm, as sheer folly, or the hypocritical pretences of the lovers of mischief. And while we set task-masters over our slaves—give them coarse food and clothing—and occasionally subject them to punishment—while those who are most successful in the management of them, spend the profits of their labour, sometimes foolishly enough, yet neither is their situation so bad, nor ours so enviable, as you might at first suppose. They are perhaps better supplied with the necessaries of life than the labouring class of any country out of America. They have their pleasures and enjoyments according to their station and capacity, and probably enjoy as much happiness, with as few drawbacks, as any other class of our population. The error on this subject proceeds from a white man's supposing himself in the situation of a slave, without recollecting that these people were born slaves, and that there is as much difference between their feelings respecting their condition, and those of a white man, as is the privation of sight to one who is born blind, and one who has become so.

"Nor is the pride of conscious power so strong a sentiment as you seem to apprehend. I believe that slaves are more often regarded as instruments of gratifying avarice, than the love of power. If I know myself, I am, as a slave-holder, a stranger to the latter sentiment. Those who are born masters, are no doubt very authoritative—very impatient of disobedience or contradiction—but they find little more to flatter their pride in their power over their slaves than in that they possess over their horses or dogs; (or if that sounds harshly, and conveys an idea of their degradation, which I certainly did not mean,) no more than the authority which a parent exerts over his children. It will be found that the average profits of their labour does not permit us to extend to them greater indulgences and more comforts; for, as things are, where there is one who derives a large profit from their labour, there are two or three who barely make both ends meet; and not a few who every year, without much extravagance, eat into their capital, and find, that after deducting the cost of their maintenance, the fruits of their labour yield little over a rent for the land."

"Your estate is a profitable one, is it not?" said Gildon.

"I know not what it might be under judicious management. But under the system pursued by my father, of extraordinary confidence in his agents, and extraordinary indulgence to his slaves, I imagine, from what I have been able to see of his affairs, that it did not yield him two per cent. on his capital."

By this time they had reached the harvest field, in which Gildon saw nine strong, athletic negro men, in the prime of life, cutting down a heavy crop of oats with their long scythes and cradles; while about twice the number of women and boys were following them, some of whom were binding up the sheaves, and others forming them in small stacks. They were plentifully supplied with whiskey, which no doubt contributed to their good humour, though every where the gathering in the fruits of agricultural labour is an occasion of feasting and hilarity. An overseer, a middle aged man, of a serious aspect and steady demeanour, was looking on the work, directing their operations, and occasionally assisting. He greeted Edward very cordially, though respectfully, and Gildon saw that the slaves all welcomed "Master Edward," and "my master," "and my young master," in a manner that convinced him, whatever might be the condition of other slaves, the bonds of those of Beachwood, sat lightly upon them.

Those who were near came up and shook hands with him, and to each of them he had something to say, by inquiries about their children, or their own little crops or gardens, or poultry. They all testified the most unaffected joy at seeing him, with the exception of a young man about his own age, who, hanging down his head under the pretext of picking up the oats, never ventured to approach, or even turn his eyes towards Edward. He had, it seems, won the affections of a favourite house maid of Mrs. Grayson's, when he had been the chief dining-room servant, which trespass, the same dame nature who had inspired it, had also brought to light; and for this act of gallantry, which had not been sanctioned by the consent of their elders, nor was warranted by the immature years of his sable Helen, (she not being fourteen,) though he was ready to make honourable amends, and did so in fact: he was sent to the crop, and put under the overseer, by way of punishment. As the negroes about the mansion-house are better fed, better clothed, and more intelligent, they look upon themselves as the superiors of the crop hands; and no degraded courtier feels deeper mortification than a slave who is thus taken from the house and put in the crop, or sent to the quarter.

Edward yet felt an attachment for this boy, who had been brought up with him, and had been the humble play-fellow of his early years until this act of profanation. When he saw his deep shame and humility, he felt his ancient good-will return, and approaching him, carelessly said, "well Peter, how do you like working in the crop? how are you?" holding out his hand. Peter, who had long since been reconciled to his new situation, and wanted only Edward's sanction to address him, seized his hand and with the graceful bow of a courtier, and a countenance lighted up with joy, strongly manifested by two rows of large white teeth, and a pair of prominent staring eyes, said, he hoped his young master had been well since he had been down the country. In answer to the question put to him by Edward, he replied: "I like it very well, sir, but I would rather wait upon you."

"I have often heard," said Gildon, "that the labour of a slave, was but half that of a freeman, yet I scarcely think that I ever saw our stoutest and most active labourers work more willingly, or with better effect, than these bondsmen of yours."

"Perhaps," said Edward, "this is not a fair specimen of their ordinary performance, both on account of our presence, and because harvest is a kind of holiday work. The occasion of securing the reward of the year's toil, is always a cheerful one; and they have, at this time, an extra allowance of food and a liberal supply of whiskey, of which they are all extravagantly fond. But on a well regulated estate, on which the slaves have been properly brought up and well managed, their labour, when they are actually engaged, differs little from that of freemen. They have, too, their feelings of pride and their emulation with the neighbouring farms, and with one another, which though not operating so generally, or so steadily as self-interest, operates at sometimes, and on some individuals, quite as efficiently. I am sure there are several men in that row who as completely identify themselves with our family as if the crop was their own. See that man who is third from the leader of the set: he was long the foreman, that is, deputy overseer, on the Easton estate, and it was his pride to lead the row in every rural employment, whether of topping or suckering tobacco, or planting, or pulling fodder, or cradling, but he is now getting in years, and nothing consoles him for being obliged to yield the post of honour, but that it is occupied by his sons; who for strength, activity, and faithful attachment, are treading in their father's steps. Their grandmother is yet alive, and though weak in sight and somewhat deaf, is otherwise healthy in body and mind. She has successively nursed my paternal grandmother, my father, and us, and seems to feel for us in regular succession, all the attachment that she could feel for her own children. She almost wept this morning when I called at her cabin to see her."

"You think, then, that considered merely with the eye of an economist, slavery is not a national evil," said Gildon.

"Far from it," replied Edward. "It does operate to lessen very greatly the productive labour of a country—but not, I think, in the way it is commonly supposed. It is obviously the interest of the slave to make as little and consume as much as he can, if you attribute to him the first feelings of our nature, the love of ease and enjoyment—and this seems a sufficient cause why their labour, and skill, and care, should be less than that of freemen. But if they are disposed to work less, they are sometimes compelled to work more; and fear, and habit, and the little emulations I have mentioned, make the result not materially variant from that of freemen. And in like manner, if they are inclined to consume more, they are often compelled to consume less than they would do if they could command the fruits of their own labour. There is many an industrious, ingenious slave, now clothed in oznaburg and napt coating, who, if the master of his earnings, would wear fine linen and broadcloth. No; it is in the effect which slavery has on the whites, that the chief mischief is produced. It consigns this half of the population to idleness, or tends to consign them, both by making their labour less necessary, and by making it degrading. You observe that twice the number of menials are necessary to a man of small fortune here that are so to a man of large fortune with you. For none of our citizens, male or female, will perform the smallest domestic duties for themselves. Believe me, it surprised and a little shocked me, when I first saw, in the houses of some substantial farmers in your state, sensible and well bred females get up from table to hand bread, or cider, and aid in setting dishes on the table—or the master of the house saddling and bridling his own horse, and bringing in logs of wood for his fire. As our whites who can command the labour of slaves, are not permitted to work by their prejudices and their pride, for want of other employment, they are very much exposed to the seductions of gaming and drinking. Its moral effects, however, present a wide field for speculation, and are not unmingled with good. But whither is this discussion leading me? Our dinner hour is now at hand, and my mother, who is a disciple of the old school, will expect us to make some alteration in our dress for dinner, if it be only to have our boots brushed, and our heads powdered—Good morning, I beg pardon; good evening Mr. Snead—and they crossed the fresh stubble till they reached the hill which runs parallel to the river, and following the path at the foot of it, they proceeded to the mansion house. When within an hundred yards of the house, the kitchen bell sounded, and Gildon expressed his fear they would not be in time, but was told that it was the practice to ring twice, with an interval of half an hour, both for breakfast and dinner, by which the members of the family had time to give a punctual attendance, and to make those preparations in dress that were then deemed indispensable in the best houses in Virginia, but which are now pretty generally dispensed with.

Gildon found Primus in his room with all the apparatus of water, towels, brushes, powder, and pomatum, by the aid of which he soon made himself more comfortable as to his feelings, and not the less so, I imagine, from the persuasion that he would appear to more advantage in the eyes of the fair Louisa. While under the operation of this youth, a slim, black, and rather ill-favoured chap, but shrewd, lively, and obsequious, he felt a disposition, which is rather more natural than strictly proper, to glean some information upon the subject that had most occupied his thoughts since he had reached Beachwood.

"Upon my word, my good fellow, you are a most accomplished friseur—old Lafont never made a better pigeonwing than you have given me."

"I served my time in Fredericksburg, sir."

"You must have kept your hand in since your young master was away. I suppose you have dressed many a fine gentleman within the last six months."

"I have sometimes tried my hand, sir."

"Well, and what spruce beaux have you dressed?" looking in the glass and pressing down one of the side curls then in fashion.

"Why, sir, there was lawyer Barbawl, and Mr.

Jim Dunder, and Mr. Ben Dunder, and Dr. Tiresang, and Mr. Belmain, from South-Carolina, sometimes."

"And why," said Gildon, "did you not always dress him?"

"Because he brought his own servant, sir."

"And which of all these fine gentlemen did you like best?" said Gildon, taking up a clothes-brush and looking in the glass while brushing his clothes.

"Why, sir, they be all very clever gentlemen to me—but I think Mr. Belmain was the spryest man among the ladies. He be so handsome—he dress so fine—he talk so sweet."

"I suppose, then, you would like him," hesitating and rather doubting whether he was not going too far, "for a young master?"

"I prefer master Edward to any other gentleman—he is so generous and so good—but Mr. Belmain have no chance to be my young master this time. My young mistress is so hard to please."

"How do you know that?"

"Oh, can't I see? You think nigger got no eyes? He is mighty rich they say, and his man tell me he was a going to call here again on his way from the springs this summer. He had such a pretty phæton, and two such elegant bays, and a led horse besides. But according to my notion Miss Louisa won't go to South-Carolina; it is too sickly."

Gildon having now nothing more to adjust or

to brush about his person, by way of pretext for continuing this dialogue, and satisfied for the present with the information he had obtained, descended to the parlour, where Primus soon appeared with a nimble step, but a face as demure as if he had never seen Gildon before, and presented to him a silver salver, on which was a black bottle and some glasses.

"Is that toddy cool?" said Edward.

"It is just taken from the spring, sir."

"I believe that is a drink which is not much known out of Virginia."

"Not much with us, except in some southern families, or when it is provided specially for them. But I have learnt to drink it, and it is now my favourite beverage."

Louisa was dressed in a loose muslin tunic trimmed with her favourite pink coloured ribband, and a straw gipsey, lined with the same colour. The heat of the curling irons had given an unusual glow to her complexion, naturally delicate, which the reflection from her gipsey heightened still more, and she stood in the full blaze of youthful innocence and beauty.

Gildon thought he had never seen a face half as lovely, and could scarcely forbear complimenting her on her good looks and taste, but the bright vision which so won his admiration, also chastened it, and produced an unusual degree of respect. He, however, paid what is a much truer homage to her charms, and the force of which all females know by instinct : he turned his eye towards her, and in a fixed gaze seemed for a moment unconscious of all besides. He soon recovered his presence of mind, and addressing himself to Mrs. Grayson, began to speak of the pleasures of farming and of rural life—varied in summer by a trip to Bath, or some other watering place ; and in the winter, by a visit to the metropolis, or some of the northern cities. Louisa, pleased and flattered that one who was familiar with scenes which her imagination had represented as so fascinating, should find any thing desirable in so secluded a situation, could not but take credit to herself for some part of his animated eulogium on the pleasures of retirement; and while she was conscious that more gay and social scenes were coveted by her youthful heart, excited as it was by an ardent fancy, she did not seek to weaken or controvert a taste that she could not but consider an indirect tribute to her charms.

They were summoned to dinner in very different frames of mind—Mrs. Grayson and her son, thinking, in spite of themselves, on the difficulties in which the debts and pecuniary engagements of Colonel Grayson were about to involve them—while they each had their separate causes of anxiety which sadly harmonized with the gloomy and unpleasant picture that was common to both. Every thing that looked like difficulty, or threatened disaster, reminded her of the loss of that friend who bore the chief brunt of such evils, and when misfortune, by the balm of conjugal sympathy, was deprived of more than half its force. The very virtues and attractions too of her children, gave a keener edge to her sufferings when she recollected with how much pride he would have beheld the fondest anticipations of his early life completely realized. There mingled too with Edward's anxieties, fears for the loss of Matilda, whom her friends might prevent from accepting his hand, and whom, if that obstacle were removed, his own pride and sense of honour would not permit him to marry, if he should be reduced to indigence. Gildon and Louisa, however pleased with themselves and pleased with each other, and their fancies kindled by the power of personal beauty and the blandishments of flattery, already swam in visionary bliss. They sat down to a neat, well-dressed dinner, which though little better than that which the table exhibited every day, Gildon supposed manifested extraordinary preparation on his account.

He had spent much of his time in Albany and the city of New-York, and he was forcibly struck with the contrast which he thought he perceived between the house and furniture of his friend's family, and their table and style of living. If the former fell short of his expectations, the latter certainly exceeded them. A canvass floor-cloth, nicely waxed indeed, but with its original colours and figures almost effaced, nearly covered the floor— the chairs were of dark walnut, with high backs, and an antiquated form, with stuffed leather seats. Family portraits of Mrs. Grayson's grandfather and grandmother, in carved frames, and six prints of Hogarth's Marriage a la mode, decorated the walls. On a side-board, whose form and dark ebony colour bespoke its age, shone two well polished mahogany knife-cases; several drinking glasses, and what alone came up to his ideas of congruity, three or four pieces of well kept plate. On the table, however, every thing indicated luxury the most refined, as well as neatness and comfort. The fine damask table-cloth and blue nankin china, set off each other to the best advantage. The dinner consisted of soup; a savoury ham, garnished with young cabbage; a green goose; boiled chicken, and a stew of venison. The drink was toddy, household beer, and Madeira. Gildon showed that he was not insensible to the display of hospitality that had been made on his account. He did ample justice to every dish, but he was seen to prefer both the beer and the Maderia to his favourite beverage; nor did he fail to bear a liberal part in the dessert, which, though it consisted of nothing but baked pears and such dainties as every day affords, and a bit of English cheese, was excellent in its kind.

Gildon, with such substantial reasons for being

in a good humour, was in the happiest vein of pleasantry. Sometimes he amused them with little anecdotes of his college adventures; sometimes he made Edward the subject of a playful raillery, as to his conquests with the ancient maidens of Williamsburg, or his occasional abstraction and absence of mind, or fits of enthusiasm; selecting such topics (for he could have found no other) which under his skilful banter, though they might raise a laugh, were upon the whole calculated to exalt him; so that Mrs. Grayson, for a time, forgot her sorrows and perplexities, and good-naturedly suffered herself to be pleased with the playful gayety of the lively New-Yorker; and Edward, always delighted to see his mother's countenance lighted with a smile, not only forgave, but even invited and encouraged the sallies of his friend.

The agreeable transformation thus wrought on the countenances of her mother and brother, acted anew on Louisa. They gave a richer glow to her cheek, a more dazzling brightness to her eyes; and she felt gratitude for those pleasing talents which could so diffuse the charm of cheerfulness around them, and which were intrinsically so admirable in themselves. She thought she had never seen so agreeable a young man.

"I wonder, brother, you do not retaliate on Mr. Gildon, and let us into some of his secrets," said Louisa, awaiting his answer with eager curiosity, but half afraid of betraying it.

"Oh, I believe I can defy him," said Gildon. "He is too much in the clouds to know what concerns such a son of earth as I am. Whenever he formally sets out on a tour of knight-errantry, I shall accompany him, that I may catch some of the spirit of the mirror of modern chivalry."

"That, I presume," said Edward, "will depend upon whether I direct my course northerly or not."

Louisa felt a degree of uneasiness at this remark, which was almost unperceived by herself; and, with an awakened curiosity, she observed, "why people generally go abroad, and not towards home, to seek adventures."

"True, my dear sister, but though Don Quixotte went abroad in search of adventures, he was not unwilling to return to Toboso."

"Oh," said Louisa, not much gratified with the explanation, though affecting to smile, "I had not been thinking of a Dulcinea."

Gildon, whom the turn the conversation had now taken, at first a little embarrassed, soon recovered his self-possession. "Oh, certainly ma'am, you would not think so unfavourably of me as to suppose me wanting in this necessary appendage to every one who aspires to the honour of chivalry. Yes; I too have a Dulcinea. I have often described her to my friend Grayson, and I will now describe her to you." And he began, and in his happy style of the burlesque and mock heroic, delineated a little fat, blowsy, red-headed girl of

Troy, who had honoured him with a valentine, the poetry of which he recited very ludicrously as follows:—

> The rose is red, the violet blue,
> They both are sweet, and so are you—
> Oh! prove you're not more sweet than true.
>
> As sun-flowers to the sun incline,
> My face still turns to follow thine,
> And hence you are my Valentine.
>
> The rose, when from the stalk 'tis torn,
> Soon sheds its leaves, but keeps its thorn—
> Oh! serve not thus thy Ann Vanhorn.

"You see," said he, "that this damsel of Troy was another Sappho as well as a Helen; and I could do nothing less than vow to her beauty and genius a service of seven years, which, (after a pause and a comic, but significant look to Louisa,) expired last evening."

All this was said with such a careless ease, that Louisa was satisfied her brother's allusion meant nothing serious; and Edward, admiring his dexterity at evading the subject and carried away by his friend's diverting sallies, spared all further attack; especially as Gildon had long since assured him, that the early preference to which Edward had at first alluded, he had entirely overcome.

The ladies soon retired from table, and Louisa said to her mother, "Mamma, do you not think Mr. Gildon very witty?"

"He is very entertaining indeed, my dear," replied Mrs. Grayson;—"but I value him more for his friendship and generous services to your brother, than for those qualities, which, though they may gain the applause of a crowd, do little in procuring solid happiness either to the possessor, or to those who are joined with him in the same family circle."

But, mamma, I have often heard you say, that nothing was more important than good humour in making those around us happy."

"True, my child, but there is a wide difference between the good humour which is the result of a mild temper and contented mind, and the mere exuberance of animal spirits united with a sprightly fancy. The one may dazzle and please at the festive board—the other makes all around us happy at home. We admire the one as we gaze at a flashing meteor with surprise and delight; but in a moment it passes away and is forgotten.—It is the other, which, like the mild rays of the sun in winter, cheers and warms us when every thing around is bleak and dreary. This quality can easily be associated not only with great violence of temper, but with a very cold heart and great selfishness of feeling." But recollecting the pleasure she had so recently derived from Gildon's sprightly powers, she added, "It is, however, an amiable talent, that can cause a smile or a laugh at pleasure, and cheat life of some of its cares and vexations, as I have this day experienced."

Louisa was delighted to find her mother's opinion thus far coincide with her own; but had an undefinable repugnance to herself to let her feelings be known; and without further reply retired to her room, to pursue some one of her usual occupations of reading, needlework, or writing to her female correspondents.

Edward being remarkably temperate at table, and Gildon having done ample justice to the Madeira, the former proposed to take a stroll towards the river, and look at their corn, then in the silk, when (as in animals approaching maturity,) it is in the most rapid state of growth. As they passed along a row of small huts or cabins, somewhat irregularly arranged, with a little garden or truck patch roughly enclosed attached to each, Edward proposed to step in and see old Granny Mott, whose long services and numerous progeny he had spoken of in the morning.

They entered a low cabin made of hewn logs, notched at the ends so as nearly to touch; and the more effectually to exclude the cold and the air, the small spaces between were filled in with mud. The chimney was made of the same materials as the house, except that the logs were smaller, and the inside was also plaistered with a thick coat of mud. The door afforded the only aperture for the admission of light or air. The floor was of the original earth, made hard by long use, and clean by sweeping, which a tidy mulatto girl of fourteen, her granddaughter, regularly performed every morning.

The old woman sat near the door, winding from a reel some hanks of cotton thread which little Milly had spun. She was dressed in a yellow and white striped homespun wrapper, and petticoat, and had a cap tied under her chin that partly discovered her grisly locks, and round her neck a handkerchief, which (as well as the cap,) from its whiteness and fineness, had probably once the honour of belonging to some more dignified member of the family. She was of a yellowish complexion, with features more raised and delicate than belong to the African face, and eyes that still retained much of the fire they had once emitted.

As soon as Edward darkened her door, she turned round her head and said, " God bless my young master—how has he been this long time? I thought you would come to see Granny. I was afraid my poor old eyes would never see you again. And how did you leave them all at Williamsburg?— Master James's family—Miss Betsey's, and your uncle William's?"—running over a long list of names as they suggested themselves to her enfeebled memory, like one soliloquizing.—" Well, my young master, you find old Granny here still."

"And how are you Granny—and how have you been this winter?" said Edward.

"Oh! it was mighty cold—I can't stand cold as I used to do, and the overseer stint me in wood: But my mistress, God bless her, make Joe sometimes take the cart and bring me a load. But this country colder, my child, than where you been."

"Not much, Granny, I think."

"O yes, my master, this place so near the mountains. Snow be there one or two days; but be here upon the mountains all the year. Did you see cousin Phœbe, that belonged to old Councillor Carter?"

"Yes, Granny, I know her very well; she asked after you. She is very fond of talking of old times."

"Why, my master, Phœbe could tell you all about it—Phew," with a sort of half whistle, expressing at once her admiration of the past, and contempt of the present times—" there is nothing like it now days. Yes, Phœbe know what grand doings took place when the Governor drive down from the palace to the capitol in his coach and six, and the soldiers march up and down with their scarlet coats, the drums a beating and colours flying: And then such show and parade at the palace. It was in the time of the great Lord Botetourt, whose image they afterwards had all cut out of marble. And my old master, my mistress's grandfather, was such a grand gentleman, with his great rich chariot and outriders, and his gold laced waistcoat that reach down to his knees—not such little, pinched up things, as you all wear now a days, child; and the ladies with their stomachers and long laced cuffs, and their hoops, and their toupees, and curls, and silks, and brocades—they are all gone. Bristol beer and London porter, were as common then as whiskey is now; and all the gentlemen had their waiting-men in such fine liveries—my old master's was orange and green; and all wore the finest and the best, and all brought in from England every year of their lives. These old eyes have lived to see great changes, master Edward."

"What is your age, old woman?" said Gildon.

"I am eighty-four the tenth day of next October, please God I live so long. My old master of all put down my age, and gave me to his eldest daughter, that is, miss Betsey's mother. I remember when General Braddock march out of Williamsburg, with his soldiers and riflemen, and cannon and all. I was there waiting on my young mistress, and had done had my last child. There was a mighty fuss then about the French and the Indians; and they took up a Frenchman that went about dressing hair, and put him in jail; and old lawyer Randall spoke for him, and got him clear; and the Governor was so mad he would not speak to lawyer Randall. My old master then, your mamma's grandfather Allen, had a great tract of land here that he bought of the Indians; and I have heard my young master, that is your grandfather Harrison, say, that the first quarter he settled here was where Major Fawkner now lives, and which he afterwards sell to the Dutch people; and the father of old Steener come in as a waiting man; and that after he had served out his time, he turned in, and was a mighty sober, hard-working, careful man—bought him a little piece of land, and went on saving while my old master went on spending, until he bought them very Elms—and now they are as great as any body. But I tell Milly they an't quality after all."

"I thought, Granny, the Fawkners, were people of great consequence in old times," said Edward.

"And so they were: Old Councillor Fawkner was one of the grandest people on James River. I know folks talked mightily when his son married the old Dutch grazier's daughter; and they allowed that the old Colonel would never have give his consent if he had not run through his estate. But for my part, I think they are all upstarts now a-days. There is only a few of the old families left, and they can just keep their heads above water."

Edward, to whom this topic was an unpleasant one, by way of changing it said, "Bless me, Granny, what a fine cap you have."

"Ah, Major Fawkner's daughter, that went to school with our little Louisa, and is so fond of her, sent it to me. She is a sweet young lady. She and my young mistress used to come and sit here by the hour, helping old Granny to wind broaches; and sometimes," added the old dame, with a chuckling laugh, "doing Milly's task for her. Milly was always mighty glad to see them here."

Edward felt not a little gratified at her reply, as this act of Matilda's considerate kindness not only evinced a feeling heart, but his self-complacency told him, that possibly it had been partly on his account; as the old woman had been his nurse, and he was known to be much attached to her.

"She is very beautiful then, is she?" said Gildon.

"O yes, master, she is mighty good—pretty enough too; but not so pretty as my Louisa."

Edward smiled and said, "Well, Granny, if they won't bring you wood, or these young chaps refuse to wait upon you, let me know. Now we must leave you—good bye to you."

"Heaven bless my young master," said the old dame.—"Good bye, master," to Gildon.—"He puts me so much in mind of his grandfather, Colonel Harrison;"—said she in a sort of soliloquy, after they had gone.

Having left the cabin, they proceeded on their walk towards the field. Edward told Gildon, that the old woman being naturally an admirer of past times, dwelt with peculiar fondness upon those circumstances of show and expense which had most excited her youthful imagination—and that she still retained all the reverence for every thing English, which was prevalent in those times; and consequently, her predilections for rank and official dignity, had given her a distaste to the equality which now prevails, and to those persons who had newly made their fortunes—upstarts as she called them : In short, she is what is now termed a rank aristocrat ; but one may tolerate in her, ignorant and uneducated as she is, prejudices to which M'Culloch ought to be superior.

Having diverted themselves with the old woman's aristocratic pride, and viewed the crop of Indian corn then tasseling and displaying all the luxuriance that heat, moisture, and a fertile soil could bestow, they returned to the drawing room a little before candles were lighted ; when the firefly is first seen to emit its bright but transient flash, like stars shooting across the firmament, and the whippoorwill commences his monotonous but expressive moan.

CHAPTER VI.

The old woman's prejudices in favour of birth and family, furnished Gildon with a fine subject of pleasantry when he returned to the drawing room, and he said he did not wonder his friend Edward was so high-minded and so much in the heroics when he had been brought up under so aristocratic a nurse. A few lively sallies of this sort, drinking tea, and a little music, filled up a short summer's evening, and about ten they returned to their respective apartments.

Several days glided away at Beechwood, pretty much after the fashion of the one we have somewhat circumstantially detailed, with only that limited variety which a country situation affords—a variety which, however dull in the recital, or to one accustomed to the tumultuous bustle and agitating stir of large cities, is yet, after a while, sufficient to make life enjoyed, and perhaps more thoroughly enjoyed than in more heart-stirring situations.

They usually rode from about two to four hours every morning, after breakfast—sometimes to the fields, where the overseer and the slaves were engaged in some operation of the farm ; but sometimes they crossed the river, and following the public road through Ashby's Gap, found amusement or obtained intelligence from any traveller they chanced to meet. Occasionally, pursuing some small track to the right or left, they were led to one of the many settlements, scattered through the mountains, when, alighting, they entered the humble dwelling, (with the owner of which Edward was in general well acquainted,) and whiled away an hour or two. Or if the place invited, they scrambled to the top of some prominent point or crag, from whence their view was not intercepted by the trees, and enjoyed an extensive prospect of mountain, river, and champaign country, apparently covered with one dark interminable forest, unvaried by any vestige of human improvement, or by any apparent swell in the surface ; and as the distinctness of vision was diminished by distance, and the intervening hazy atmosphere, the prospect to the east resembled, in tint and apparent level, an extensive view of the ocean. The river appeared to meander along the foot of the Blue ridge with the tortuous windings of a snake. Sometimes the sight of it was lost altogether by the shutting in of projections of the mountain, and then it would show its glassy surface some distance beyond, in the likeness of a small lake.

They occasionally tried the sport of fishing, but it suited not the taste of Edward or Gildon ; nor was the situation favourable. Now and then in their rides they would visit some gentlemen of their acquaintance ; and once a week, if the weather was fair, they went to Battle Town or Berryville, (for little towns, like little men, are more apt to have an alias than great ones,) the Post-Office nearest to Beechwood ; where they had an opportunity of reading or hearing the confused statements of the same occurrence, made by the different newspapers, which were the organs of the two great political parties of the day.

It seldom happened that one of those rides did not furnish materials to the ready humour and inventive genius of Gildon, to make some entertaining anecdote or good story on his return. And so inquisitive was he in obtaining a knowledge of facts, and so acute and sagacious in drawing inferences, that it was thought he, in a month, had acquired more accurate knowledge of the people in the neighbourhood, than Edward had acquired in his whole life before. After they returned to Beechwood, they either took up a book and read, in the parlour, or retired to their rooms—then dressed, dined, took a short stroll along one of three or four walks leading from the house ; and passed the evening with the aid of music, reading, and conversation. The scene was further varied by their dining with one or two neighbours, or these dining at Beechwood; some of whom, it may, for the purpose of making this veracious history better understood, be hereafter necessary to introduce to the reader. This life, so far from fatiguing by its sameness, became every day more and more agreeable to Gildon, for all-powerful Love had cast his gay and brilliant tints over the whole surrounding scene.

Nor could the gentle Louisa help bowing to the sway of this tyrant of the heart; and the passion she inspired in the bosom of another, was yet more deeply felt by her own. The circumstances of her education, temper, and situation at the time, peculiarly exposed her to its seductive influence. Treated, from her infancy, with extraordinary delicacy and tenderness, experiencing nothing but kindness and indulgence from both parents, she was all softness, gentleness, timidity, and affection. She had been a great reader of romances, and had thus formed false and exaggerated conceptions of human life—of the elevated and transcendent virtue of lovers—the raptures of sentimental love, and the necessity of loving to fulfil the destiny of every human being, at least of every young person. Forming her notions of excellence from these ideal models, though her beauty and other attractions had, within a year or two, procured her many admirers, yet they all differed so widely from the standard she had created for herself of a hero of romance, that they had served, in a great measure, to keep her heart as yet free and untouched.

But Gildon, whose person was handsome—whose manners were polished and insinuating, and whose conversation was animated and intelligent, evidently possessed qualifications superior to any of her former lovers. His fashionable air, and the tone of superiority he was often seen to assume, were also imposing—and the circumstance that he came from a distant state, with which she associated nothing but gayety, wealth, and splendour, contributed still further to excite her imagination in his favour.

In addition to his personal recommendations, she regarded him as the friend whose prudent counsels and spirited conduct had rendered essential service to her brother, perhaps saved his life—and (what was perhaps, not the least important item in the summary of causes,) the opportunity of seeing one another every day, and of hearing the blandishments of his flattery, in which he was very skilful, and which he began to use from habit, but soon continued from inclination, greatly contributed to the same end. When all these things are considered, it is no wonder that he soon made a strong impression on her susceptible and unoccupied heart, until at length the full-grown passion stood confest to herself, occupied her most secret thoughts by day and night, and prompted and nearly governed all her words and actions.

It had made considerable progress before it was perceived either by Edward or Mrs. Grayson. The affairs of the estate necessarily engaged much of their attention; and the inspection of accounts; the consultations with lawyers, and writing letters, frequently took them away from the parlour; so that the opportunities which Gildon and Louisa had of being together, seemed rather the result of necessity or accident, than to have been contrived by themselves. The anxiety, too, which the investigation of creditors' claims occasioned to Mrs. Grayson and her son, and which events served but to increase, made them both less observing than they had otherwise been. Edward, also, was too much racked with doubts and apprehensions about his own love affairs, to use that vigilance towards his sister, that an unoccupied mind would have permitted. He knew Gildon was an avowed dealer in common-place gallantry, and as his own love had grown with his growth, and been many years in maturing, he had no conception that a residence of a few weeks could have produced any thing more than a little transient flirtation. And if a serious attachment to his sister had appeared probable, he would have had no objection to it, as he had great regard for Gildon—entertained a favourable opinion of his temper and character, and knew that his prospects in life were all that could be wished.

Mrs. Grayson was not quite as unobserving She naturally expected that Louisa would, in time, captivate a young man of Gildon's taste and discrimination ; but his fine flow of spirits and lively rattle, seemed so much like a mind at ease, that she did not think his preference amounted to any thing serious ; and from the unreserved confidence which Louisa had reposed in her on all former occasions of this sort, she was sure that she should hear of a declaration as soon as he had made one. In the mean time, she was more attentive to his manners, sentiments, and deportment, for the purpose of judging how far his character was such as was likely to ensure her daughter's happiness—determining within herself to dissuade Louisa from accepting his offer, though it were in all other respects eligible, if she should form an unfavourable opinion of his heart or principles, and not in the least doubting that her advice would be implicitly followed on the occasion, by her with whom that advice had always been as a law.

Besides, Mrs. Grayson never dreamt that Louisa could feel a lively attachment for any man before he had addressed her, because she had sedulously, and as she thought successfully, inculcated on her daughter's mind the lesson that both prudence and feminine dignity required, that a woman should never feel a decided preference for any man till she was first sure she had inspired one. Yet, not disposed to underrate her daughter's charms, she thought it natural and probable that she would, in time, make a conquest of Gildon; and after a rigid scrutiny, seeing nothing in him to object to, and much to recommend him, she favoured in every allowable way so advantageous a settlement, now doubly desirable, as her daughter was not only an orphan, but likely to be a portionless one. Taking it for granted that he had not yet manifested his views, which his unvarying attentions began plainly to indicate, she waited for the expected disclosure, with all the solicitude of a tender and affectionate mother, whose thoughts often run far more upon their children's happiness than their own.

The little conversations in the parlour, before Gildon and Edward took their morning ride, were insensibly prolonged, and once or twice the ride was declined altogether by Gildon under the pretext of a head-ache, or an appearance of approaching rain. It was the practice of the family, at that season of the year, to drink tea a little before sunset, in the small porch which fronted the river, and which, encompassed with the honey-suckle, sweet-brier, and convolvulus, formed an impenetrable barrier to the rays of the morning sun; but in the evening the bower was recommended only for the beauty of its flowers and foliage, and the delicate perfume they exhaled.

Here, after tea, it was usual to sit till candles were lighted, and when there was no fog from the river, or unusual dampness in the atmosphere, a good while longer. Occasionally left by themselves in this verdant bower, (and bowers have ever been propitious to love,) when the concerns of her household called off Mrs. Grayson, or those of the estate claimed the attention of Edward, the lovers interchanged their sentiments more freely; and Gildon had in such a variety of ways passed compliments on the taste and beauty of the young lady, and had manifested such an interest in all her concerns, particularly as to the state of her heart, and her future movements, that nothing was wanting to convince her of his sentiments but an open declaration of them. Nor would that have been necessary if her own heart had been free from these doubts and fears that love never fails to conjure up in the bosoms of his votaries.

When the moon happened to be above the horizon, the view was enchanting. In front, and to the south, rose the mountain, whose lofty outline was distinctly visible in the heavens, though its sides presented only one uniform dark mass, while the light of the moon, reflected from the surface of the Shenandoah, in addition to the direct rays of that sweet luminary, made the grounds between the house and the river almost as visible, and far more pleasing than they ever appeared by day. Although the lovers praised the beauty of the landscape, and really admired it, they were perhaps still happier when this same lovely landscape was shrouded in utter darkness, save when it was illuminated by the beautiful lightning bug, flitting across the yard in every direction, and enlivening the gloom with his brief, but vivid flashes; or when its stillness was broke in upon by the drone of the unwearied sawyer. Then the world forgetting, with all its toils, and cares, and strife, they drank large draughts of the delicious poison; sometimes manifesting, by expressions of kindness or tenderness, the excited state of their feelings, but more often enjoying in silence a delight which each perfectly understood without words, and which words would have served only to diminish.

There was something so new and delightful in these silent trances of impassioned feeling, that Gildon, though he could not mistake the state of Louisa's heart, felt unwilling to put an end to them by coming to an explanation. Indeed it was on account of this very certainty that he was less disposed to make a declaration, undetermined as he was, which course he should finally pursue. But there soon arose another consideration, which made him doubt whether he might make one at all. To understand which, it is necessary to let the reader into that part of his previous history which has already been slightly alluded to.

James Gildon had, from the days of his boyhood, been remarkable among his companions for being an admirer of the fair sex, and also, (as is the natural consequence,) with being a favourite with them. Thus early invited to the practice of gallantry, he had attained consummate skill in the arts of pleasing; and if his attachments were not very lasting or intense, they had been very easily formed. Among his youthful preferences was one for a distinguished young lady from the city of New-York, whose father (a little while before an eminent merchant,) had, by depredations made on the commerce of neutrals after the declaration of war between Great-Britain and France, become bankrupt; and had sent his family, consisting of a wife and two daughters, to reside with their brother, a gentleman of good estate in the country, until he could wind up his disordered affairs, or chalk out some new line of business.

Emily De Peyster was a very showy and attractive woman, and had been still more so if she had been less conscious of her powers, and less eager to exert them. Naturally possessed of an affectionate, generous heart, her better feelings had been deadened, and almost extinguished by the ambition of conquest, the desire of admiration, and the love of glitter and show. The change in her circumstances mortified her pride, without changing her character—it merely changed her theatre of action—and those charms which would have produced their natural effect any where, if accompanied with modesty and humility, but which required, in a large city, the influence of fortune to temper the haughtiness that had accompanied them, she was determined to show off in the country. She accordingly soon began to look about her for the purpose of seeing for whom her net was to be next thrown, and in a short time selected Gildon from among the sons of two or three of the most wealthy country squires.

He saw in this high-bred city damsel, with her rich wardrobe, in all the extravagance of fashion; her bold and forward, though easy manners, an object more worthy of attack than any he had before met with. He entered the lists, and by his superiority of address, improved as it was under such an instructress, soon gained the victory over all his competitors. What he had begun in sport, he soon found was like to end in downright earnest. He was beaten at his own game, and he at length found himself sufficiently in love. Her want of fortune was, however, a serious obstacle to marriage with him, in whose mind his father, a man of sordid principles, had always inculcated the folly and absurdity of marrying without fortune; and had, by descanting on the advantages of obtaining a wealthy heiress, and judiciously complimenting the skill and success of those who had been thus fortunate, made it present itself to his eye as an object of pride and ambition, and he had been thus brought to look upon it almost as much a matter of honour as of profit.

Whether this bias of education would have been sufficient to have overcome the great bias of nature, is not known, if his calculating father, fearing the worst, had not thought proper to send him off to William and Mary College, in Virginia, after which time, Miss De Peyster, who had not been more interested with Gildon than she had been with others half a dozen times before, directed her artillery against a rich young South Carolinian, then travelling for his health in the western parts of New-York.

Gildon made no serious opposition to this prudent retreat, and in speaking of it to Edward, had called it a boyish preference, which being disagreeable to his father, he had in good time overcome. It had been part of the old man's calculation as well as the son's, that in all probability James would pick up a rich Virginia heiress, in which case it was settled between them that he should turn the lands and slaves into cash, and establish a large mercantile house in the city of New-York, for which, as a place of residence, Gildon had formed a decided predilection. And when accident had brought him and Edward Grayson acquainted, and had enabled him to render the service that had induced the invitation to accompany Edward home, Louisa seemed to him to afford the promise of a good speculation, as Colonel Grayson was known to have a large property in possession, though it was somewhat embarrassed with debt.

Hitherto every thing had seemed to favour his views and wishes, and even to exceed them. The estate of which he had only heard, made more impression now when he was an eye witness of the rich fields and loaded barns—the long retinue of slaves—and when he beheld the numerous household, and very abundant style of living which prevails in the slave-holding states; and when he moreover learnt that a still larger estate was owned by the family in Charles city. Besides, Louisa was far more beautiful than he had expected to find her. This child of nature too seemed to feel a sincerity of attachment of which Miss De Peyster was incapable. The manifestations of partiality which are so captivating in a pure and innocent mind, and which are more studiously concealed as they are more deeply felt, touched him far more thoroughly than the coquettish blandishments of Evelina. The want of serious occupation—that vacuity of mind and pursuit which with young people so often create the *besoin d'aimer*, had also its effect on Gildon, and he gradually gave himself up to the sweet delirium of loving and of being loved, in the full persuasion that he should advance his worldly interests as much as gratify his inclinations,—that the family and fortune of the young lady would make her as acceptable to his parents as her lovely person and tender attachment was to himself.

Hitherto he had learnt nothing of the affairs of the family but what indicated wealth. He had heard and seen enough during his present visit to know that there were numerous debts due from the estate of Colonel Grayson, but he supposed that this was probably the condition of every large landed estate in Virginia, and that the crop of one year might discharge it of these burthens.

But certain occurrences soon undeceived him. After they had been at home about a fortnight, a letter from Richmond evidently gave Edward much uneasiness. He left the room and remained out for a long time, as Gildon supposed, with Mrs. Grayson. That worthy lady soon afterwards complained of a head-ach, and did not make her appearance at dinner, and in the evening was more serious and dejected than usual, though Edward evidently made extraordinary exertions to raise her spirits. The day after, old Hatchett called in the morning, and taking Edward out to a clump of trees in front of the house remained conversing with him a long time; they then returned to the house, and Mrs. Grayson went with them to the dining room, where they continued a full hour; in which time he occasionally heard Edward's voice raised to a tone that showed expostulation and resentment; and the same symptoms of uneasiness were perceived.

By this time Gildon had learnt the character of old Hatchett, and he began to entertain some doubts whether the match would be so eligible, or would be deemed so by his worldly-minded parent.—Sometimes he determined to use caution in the course he should pursue, and not only to forbear making any declaration of love, but to guard against getting his affections too far enlisted to break off, in case he should conclude to do so. At other times, when he witnessed the blooming beauty of Louisa, her easy graceful manners, and her charming sweetness of disposition, and received from her one of those tender but timid glances which so plainly spoke the state of her feelings, he resolved to brave his father's displeasure, and to encounter the evils of poverty, until he could, by his industry and talents, win the means of a livelihood.

But these generous emotions which her loveliness when present inspired, yielded, when it was withdrawn, to the cold suggestions of avarice and ambition; and after vacillating for some time between these conflicting inclinations, he made up his mind to come to no definite conclusion, but to shape his course according to events; though he hoped that the unpleasant suspicions which had been newly awakened in his mind, would prove unfounded. His object was to ascertain the true state of facts, as near as could be, and as soon as possible; though to do so he knew no certain mode without a great violation of delicacy, and giving offence to Edward, for whom he entertained the most profound respect.

In the mean while, the great frequency and the increased length of the interviews between Louisa and Gildon, prompted inquiries on the part of Mrs. Grayson to her daughter; and finding that he continued silent, or had made no open declaration of love, she felt not a little anxiety, lest this gay youth should be merely sporting with the feelings of her child, without entertaining any serious thoughts of marriage. She trembled at the probable effect of disappointment on one of Louisa's enthusiastic temper and feeling heart.

Soon after old Hatchett had gone, and she had conferred with her son on the proposition which Hatchett had made, to receive the amount of his bond by instalments, secured by such a conveyance as Col. Grayson had authorized her to give, she said, "My dear Edward, the conduct of this young friend of yours towards your sister is somewhat strange. He pays her every where the most pointed attentions—he never stirs from her side when he can help it, and he has, as yet, used no other language than that of general and common place compliments. A week ago, indeed, I found upon questioning Louisa, that he had repeatedly used expressions that might have admitted of no other interpretation, than that he meant to address her; but he has seemed for a few days to speak as if he had no such intention. Surely he cannot be one of those odious and contemptible beings, which are called male coquets."

"I am sure, my dear mother," said Edward, "you do him injustice. He has indeed been accustomed to deal in unmeaning gallantry, and, on one occasion, I know he went too far; but he would not dare," said he with emotion—then checking the rising sentiment of indignation he calmly added, "he would not think of such a thing with Louisa."

"But, my dear son, whatever may be his views and intentions, his conduct is calculated to do mischief; for, besides that such marked attentions, when nothing serious is meant, make a girl the subject of ill-natured remarks, I dread lest Louisa, romantic and inexperienced as she is, and evidently pleased with Mr. Gildon, should get her affections entangled."

"I should hope, mother, that a sister of mine, and a daughter of yours, would be in no danger of giving her heart to a man who never asked it. She must certainly have too much pride and maiden delicacy for that."

"I should be sorry, Edward, if I thought your sister wanting in either. But with the opportunities which this young gentleman possesses, and the advantages under which he is introduced, she may, under the guise of esteem and friendship, insensibly feel a more tender sentiment, and the mischief may be done before she is aware that she is exposed to danger. Indeed I greatly fear that this is in a great measure already the case; for I came upon her suddenly yesterday morning in her room, and saw she had been weeping. On the first impulse of feeling, I asked the cause, and finding she evaded my inquiries, I did not think it wise to press the subject further."

"If I thought," said Edward, with indignant look and tone : "but no—it is impossible. He either meditates addressing Louisa, or he has not intended to make an impression on her heart. But if you think it possible that Louisa may draw a different inference from his attentions, or may find his society too agreeable for her peace, she ought immediately to be put on her guard, and he, perceiving a change, will then disclose himself if he means to do so at all. But then, mother, on another account, our honour urges us to have some explanation; for Louisa has, methinks, appeared to Gildon in the character of an heiress ; and if the storm that has been gathering for some time past, should finally burst upon our heads, Louisa will be portionless, or nearly so. And although I cannot think so meanly of Gildon as to believe that this would alter his views towards one on whom he had placed his affections, yet I think it would make a mighty difference with his avaricious father, whose wishes might therefore control those of his son ; at all events, I don't mean that any one should have it to say that we held out false pretensions to fortune. I will then take occasion to disclose to him the disasters which threaten us, to be regarded by him as he sees fit."

It was then agreed by the mother and son, that the one should sound Louisa more closely on the state of her affections, and give her such counsel as the occasion should require; while Edward should let Gildon know, without discovering his motive, the embarrassments in which the affairs of the family were involved.

CHAPTER VII.

An opportunity very soon presented itself to young Grayson's purpose. When he returned to the parlour, where Gildon was looking over some maps, he observed, "that neighbour of yours, Edward, has a most unfortunate physiognomy. Without consulting the rules of Lavater, nature has legibly written in his face, ill-temper, cruelty, and selfishness. If a stranger had lost his way in a town, he would never ask a man with such a face to put him right. If a beggar wanted alms, he would never, from such an one, expect to receive them. Were he one of the jury, in a criminal case, no pathetic appeal would be addressed to him, he looks so much as if he would rather hang than acquit—and yet he has an air of great composure and sedateness and self-satisfaction."

"He is received, too, every where," said Edward, " with respect, and sometimes with seeming kindness. His wealth is a sort of public convenience, as it is at every man's service who will pay for it ; and though he never does a generous action, he always complies with his engagements—for which punctuality, he has the character of being an honest, and in some sort, a just man. Nay, more—although when we consider his motives, it is impossible to feel any regard for one so devotedly bent on gain, and so indifferent to the concerns of others; yet auch people are not without their use, especially in Virginia, where there are so many improvident persons who yet would honourably comply with their other imprudent contracts ; and one can get money from these people when it can be got no where else."

" But," said Gildon, who thought this a good opportunity of getting some insight into a subject which so nearly interested him, " I cannot but wonder how a money lender can find employment for a large capital in this retired part of the country, where there is little or no trade, and where the chief business of buying and selling is carried on with Alexandria, or some other of the commercial towns. Yet they tell me that this old Shylock has fifty or sixty thousand dollars engaged in the business of buying bonds or *shaving*, as I am told they now call it."

" You forget," said Edward, " that you are in an agricultural and a slave-holding country, the inhabitants of which have always been remarkable for spending their incomes before they made them, and for rating them very extravagantly. As the profits of a landed estate come in but once or twice a year, the means of the proprietor are then ample, and if he is not in debt he is likely to become so, by underrating unforseen contingencies, and by getting into habits, formed when his purse was full, which cannot be changed when it is empty. Consequently, in order to continue them, he is compelled to run in debt. Again, brought up in ease and idleness, he has a taste for expensive pleasures and enjoyments—he loves good wine, liberal hospitality fine horses, furniture, and dress. Though he has no money in his pocket, he has a promising crop in the ground, which, by the estimate of the overseer, (who is always ready to put his employer in a good humour, and to compliment his own industry,) he is sure to overrate in quantity. This crop, at the present prices, with the expected rise, from this or that probable event, will bring so much. It would seem not very rash to purchase such little articles as may afford present gratification to himself or his family, by buying on a credit what he can so well afford, and can so speedily repay. He is readily trusted for what he wants, not that the more judicious merchant expects to be paid out of the growing crop, but he knows that the lands and the negroes of his customer will make him eventually safe—that he will get a part of the proceeds of this overrated crop, which will be something, and he compensates himself liberally for the indulgence he gives by extraordinary profits on his goods.

"In the mean time the crop turns out to be far ess in quantity than was estimated, which the overseer ascribes, and in part correctly, to the cutworm or the drought, the gust, or the rust, the smut, or the frost, or the squirrels, or ground hogs, and the other countless casualties to which our principal crops are liable ; which disasters being well known, and visible causes of failure, conceal the deficiency arising from his own mismanagement or miscalculation. Then the prices may have fallen as well as risen. The waste, moreover, and expense of carrying it to market, exceeds all previous estimates in the same proportion ; and lastly when the account of the merchant is rendered, it is always found to be about three times as much as the farmer supposed it to be, trusting as he does to the memory, whose pictures, like those of Hope, always assume more or less the hue we like to give them.

"If he has made a special promise to pay any particular sum from the proceeds of his crop, as the price of a pair of horses that hit his fancy at the last races, or the bill of some carpenter or bricklayer, or the account of his regular merchant, who is compelled to raise a large sum by a certain time, he resorts to one of those convenient reservoirs of cash, such as our neighbour Hatchett, and either sells him a bond he has received for a piece of land he has sold, or gets his own, (given to some friend for that especial purpose,) converted into cash, at a loss of from 25 to 33⅓ per cent.

"Sometimes he runs on in this heedless course of expense every year, cheating himself with the same vain hopes and false calculations, and consequently getting more and more in debt, until finally he gives a deed of trust (mortgages were formerly in use,) on some portion of his land. When that is about to be brought to the hammer for cash, the certainty that it is sold in this way, instead of on a credit of three or four years, induces him, for the sake of preventing so great a sacrifice, to resort to one of those money-lenders. These furnish him with the means of redemption, at the same exorbitant rates, on his securing the re-payment, by pledging the same property, and as much more, until like a horse in a quagmire, in attempting to draw out one foot he gets in the other twice as deep, till he finally sinks the whole four as far as they can go.

"Such is the course of many a landed gentleman in the ancient dominion, and thus are her best estates constantly passing from the hands of those who have inherited them, to those whose frugality, or industry, or rapacity, furnish the means of their purchase. All this is perhaps as it should be, but the change often furnishes subjects of melancholy contemplation to those who can feel for the fallen, and with a good deal of blame on the reckless course of expense they have pursued, and contempt for their deplorable incapacity for business or labour, and their silly pride, there is mingled a lively pity for their humiliation and distress."

" What a picture do you give me of the Virginia aristocracy," said Gildon. " How different had my imagination once pourtrayed it."

" It is nevertheless just," rejoined Edward, as you yourself have lived long enough with us to testify. But there are other occasions than those I have mentioned, which may make such men as old Hatchett convenient, though it must be confessed," he added with some hesitation, " in spite of the temporary relief they afforded— they may eventually lead to ruin. A man is frequently involved in the misfortunes of his friends, by becoming a surety for his engagement, as sheriff, or guardian, or executor—by endorsing his notes, negotiable at bank, or his bills of exchange. My good father, more kind to his friends than prudent to his family, was remarkable for affording this species of favour to his acquaintance, and his wife and children are likely to be material sufferers by his unguarded generosity. Old Hatchett has a bond in which he was bound jointly, with two others, but which he alone of the three, or rather his estate, is able to discharge ; and there is now depending in the general court, a suit on this bond, which, if determined against him, will leave a mere pittance to my mother and sister. As to myself, I value it not, but on their account I feel the most painful anxiety ; and in this state of uncertainty, it will not be prudent in me to remain long in Williamsburg. I shall go into a lawyer's office in a short time, qualify myself for the profession, and endeavour, by my exertions, to render their situations comfortable, if I can do nothing more. A few weeks ago I had other views and hopes; but I dare not now indulge them. I shall try to banish them," said he, with agitation ; and engrossed, at the moment, with the ideas which this topic awakened, he strode with long and hasty steps across the room, and for a time, forgot the first object of the communication he had made.

Gildon listened to what fell from Edward with the deepest attention. Independent of the disappointment of his own selfish views, he felt sincere compassion for the threatened downfall of a family so amiable, so reputable, and living with one another, and with the world, in such perfect harmony ; and he felt the liveliest sympathy for Edward, who was not only about to be suddenly reduced to poverty from affluence, but to give up the long cherished hopes of as pure and ardent an affection as had ever warmed a human breast.

When he contemplated the generous and heroic sacrifice his friend was about to make, and contrasted them with his own narrow and selfish views, he felt his own inferiority ; and the noble elevation of Edward's character, which he had always admired, had never commanded such profound respect as at this time, when he was seen most wanting in that wealth which he himself had been always taught to venerate. In the strain of good feeling in which he was, he would, he thought, have been willing to share his father's fortune with the noble-minded Edward and his lovely sister; and an alliance with such a family appeared to him, for the moment, more honourable and more desirable than mere opulence could ever have made it.

" Perhaps, Grayson," said Gildon, " you overrate the danger—the debt may not be so large—you have in your favour the chances of law, which I have always understood were not inconsiderable ; and if, after the litigation of some years, the cause should be decided against you, the intervening profits of your estate may be able to pay off the debt."

" All this," said Edward, " may by possibility take place ; but if the past profits have not been sufficient to defray the expense of my father's establishment, I cannot expect, that with my little knowledge of such matters, they will be able to discharge those heavy debts with their accumulation of interest, which will be at least equal to any additional profits that I can promise myself by any practicable course of economy. I wish to see Mr. Trueheart, my father's lawyer—as honest a man as he is an able counsellor—and by his advice, I shall be governed. My course is determined—I will devote myself night and day to my profession, until I have earned, if not an independence, at least a competency."

"I do not think," said Gildon, "that Colonel Fawkner would wish such a sacrifice."

"I hardly think he would," said Edward; "but do not mistake me—I do not mean to give up all thoughts of Matilda—I cannot if I would—No, I feel that it is impossible; but I cannot bear to be dependent on her fortune—I cannot submit to the taunts of some of her family, even if their influence and authority were not exerted to frustrate my wishes, as they certainly would be. I shall make known my intention to Matilda; and though my want of fortune would be no objection to her generous and disinterested nature, yet she knows it would be to one of her parents, and she would rather I should become a member of the family with their entire approbation. I know not, indeed, whether she would consent to give me her hand against the decided wishes of her parents. But I shall not test her affection in that way: I shall put it to the stronger proof of time; and I believe her constancy will be as fixed and immoveable as the base of yonder mountain."

"I see, Edward," said Gildon, "you can act as well as talk heroically, when the occasion requires it. I confess I should not be equal to such self-denial, at any rate, not until I found it necessary. I would try the old people first, if they objected the derangement of your father's affairs and your probable want of fortune, you should insist on your prospects of professional success— that a good income was as much the natural product of talent and industry as the soil itself ; and it was of no sort of importance whether a revenue was derived from abundant crops or abundant fees. If they refused to listen to these strong dictates of reason and justice, I would even persuade the young lady to cross the Potomack ; and though there might be a little fretting and threatening at first, the storm would soon be over, and in one month, you would find yourself well settled at the Elms, with money enough to bid old Hatchett defiance, and turn shaver yourself, if you wished it— enough at all events to relieve your father's estate, for the occasions of yourself and your family "

" It is," said Edward, " not a little I would be willing to do or to suffer for them, but I cannot consent to aught which would be a sacrifice of honour. Nor would my mother, who, though mild and gentle as a dove, possesses a loftiness and pride of character of which you have no idea, approve of such a course. I am convinced she would ne ver wish me to ally myself with any family, much less with one that she regards as her inferiors, and which she knows to be purse-proud, against their consent. No, I will pursue a straight-forward and honourable course, come what will of it, and hope for the best."

"Well, my dear fellow, all I can say then," said Gildon, " is, that I wish you the success you so richly deserve."

Since generosity and magnanimity are contagious as well as humbler, and more ignoble sentitiments, Gildon was now half disposed to imitate the disinterestedness of his friend—and added, after a short pause, "I hope it will soon be in my power to lend you some little aid in your praiseworthy efforts, if they should unfortunately prove necessary."

This remark recalled Edward's thoughts to the affair of his sister—and he listened attentively for some less ambiguous disclosure of the course Gildon meant to pursue towards her. As Edward made no reply, Gildon proceeded, (the generous emotion he had felt, dying away almost as soon as it was formed,) " my situation at present, as I have already told you, is altogether dependent on the bounty of my father ; but I have reason to expect that he will soon establish me in business which promises to be profitable, and to an extent that will enable me to render you that aid, which I am sure you would render me under similar circumstances."

Edward would have been better satisfied if his friend had then avowed his partiality for his sister ; but he felt grateful for the kind and generous feelings he manifested, whether they proceeded from friendship to himself or affection for Louisa, of both of which they afforded an evidence ; and he was doubly pleased, for having frankly disclosed that she would be, in all probability, without a portion : as he had thereby not only discharged an act of duty to himself, but it had afforded his frend an opportunity of showing his disinterestedness.

He thanked Gildon warmly for his proffered kindness, and said that there was no other to whom he would sooner owe an obligation ; but his present intention as well as ambition, was to owe his extrication to his own efforts, if possible ; but should they prove abortive, or need the support of a friend, that Gildon should be the first he would apply to.

Thus terminated the explanation which Edward had imposed upon himself as an act of duty ; and though inclined to draw the most favourable inferences from Gildon's friendly offers, he was left in utter uncertainty as to his precise views.

After the ladies had retired from the dinner-table, Mrs. Grayson proposed that she would *** her daughter about a pieced bed-quilt in which she was then engaged, and withdrew to the chamber of Louisa for that purpose. She again renewed her inquiries on the subject of Gildon's addresses, rather for the sake of introducing her advice than to obtain information, as she inferred still more rom Louisa's thoughtful and dejected look than her silence, that nothing particular had occurred between them.

"My dear child," she then added, "I have for some time wished to have a serious conversation with you, on this subject. Mr. Gildon's attentions are very pointed, such, I think, as no man is warranted in bestowing on a lady, except from the honourable view of soliciting her hand; and yet his entire silence makes me doubt whether he seriously has any such intentions. It behooves you, my child, while he pursues this equivocal conduct, to be on your guard; to keep a watch on your affections, and not to bestow your heart when it is not solicited, and where it is not deserved."

Louisa was at first alarmed at the supposition that his sentiments were other than his conduct indicated; and blushed at the consciousness that she had not been as wary as her mother thought she ought to have been. She said, "she hoped she should never forget the respect due to herself; and that she was not sensible that she had acted towards Mr. Gildon, in any way, that did not entirely comport with female dignity and propriety."

"I am sure you have not, my child," said Mrs. Grayson, with her usual gentleness of tone; "but as Mr. Gildon is an agreeable man, I have feared, (to speak without reserve,) that you might feel too lively an interest in his attentions for a mere acquaintance. This, of course, would make you the subject of idle remarks, and what is of much more consequence, endanger your peace of mind. Tell me frankly, Louisa, do you view this young man with indifference? Would it not affect your happiness, to hear that he was about to leave us for his native state, never to return ? and that he was to meet a young lady there, to whom he had been long engaged."

Louisa turned pale at the thought of a successful rival, and, for the moment, believed that under the form of mere suppositions, her mother was communicating facts. In the interest excited by her suspicions, she overlooked her mother's question, and with vivacity replied, "I do not believe it! Who told you, mamma?"

"I was merely supposing a case, child, and your look and manner already answer my question. Well, but if he has that preference for you, without which you would not, I am sure, have entertained your present sentiments towards him, how do you account for his silence?"

"I can't but think, mamma, that he has good reasons for deferring a direct avowal of his preference," said Louisa, "but his favourable sentiments it is impossible to doubt. On this point, no female, mamma, can be mistaken:" thus assuming a degree of confidence to her mother, she was far from acknowledging to herself.

"I agree with you, that no woman can mistake those attentions of a man, which solicit a return of affection, for those of mere kindness or friendship; but, it is sometimes difficult to distinguish between the real and pretended lover. The practice of making love to every pretty face, is the ordinary amusement of some men, particularly in the gay world; and what I wish to guard you against is, that this common-place gallantry, which may be sport to him, should not be fatal to you"

"Oh! I am sure that Mr. Gildon can have no intentions to deceive; he is too much of a gentleman. Brother Edward thinks so highly of him, it is impossible."

"I am far, said Mrs. Grayson, from thinking it probable; but still our confidence may be misplaced. He may be very upright and honourable in all his transactions with his own sex, and have very false and mistaken principles as to ours. He may be a very safe and agreeable companion to your brother, but a dangerous lover to you. I do not mean to prejudge him, I merely mean to put you on your guard."

"What then, mamma, would you have me do? Must I avoid Mr. Gildon's company, and thus betray my weakness, by acknowledging my fears?"

"No, my dear, that is not the course I would recommend; I would have you meet him in the parlour and in the porch, as usual, and behave to him with all the forms of politeness; but encorage no secret whisperings, and be not alone with him, unless he seriously solicits an interview, for the purpose of explanation. If he is a real, and not a pretended lover, he will not be easy under this constraint, but will declare himself; and if, on the other hand, he has been merely playing the gallant, for the sake of whiling away the time, he will see that his conduct is at once noticed and disapproved, and he will change it."

Louisa, who had the most implicit faith in her mother's good sense, as well as affection, and whose own doubts and anxiety about Gildon's conduct were greater than she was willing to confess, promised to fulfil her mother's wishes and injunctions, and to watch narrowly their effect— stoutly resolving to banish him from her thoughts, if his conduct continued longer equivocal; but persuading herself, at the same time, that he was as sincere and honourable, as he appeared to be tender and devoted.

After tea, according to their custom, they all walked out to the little porch, and Gildon, taking a seat by her side, in that low key in which he often complimented her, or conveyed other flattering insinuations of his sentiments, asked her why she looked so serious? for the conversation she had just held with her mother, and the recollection of the new part she was about to act, had impressed her countenance with an air of thoughtfulness.

She, instead of merely listening, as usual, or making some short reply that was sufficient to keep up the ball of conversation, without attracting the attention of those around them, answered in a loud voice, "Mamma and I have been moralizing a little on the affairs of life; but I will try to dispel the cares which so solemn a theme is apt to inspire with a little music."

"Brother, pray join me with your flute," and with the same seeming careless gayety which she had shown on his first arrival, she went into the parlour, sat down to the piano, and played with unusual spirit and effect.

Of late it had been her practice to spend the chief part of her evenings in the porch, alleging in favour of it either the sweetness of the moonlight, or the sultriness of the evening, or the fragrance of the eglantine after a shower, or some other pretext equally plausible, in which females the most ingenuous are at once so ready and so skilful. And here Gildon found his most favourable opportunities of saying those agreeable trifles, which form so large a part of the conversation between youthful lovers, and to which she listened with a continued and still increasing delight.

This new movement, therefore, surprized him, and he imputed it at first to female caprice, which was disposed, for a while, to torment him; but, perceiving something of rather a formal and measured courtesy, both in Mrs. Grayson's conduct and Edward's, he began to suspect the truth, and to apprehend that the time had come when he must either make an open declaration of love, or consent to abandon Louisa for ever. He, too, then became serious and thoughtful; and, as is always the case among parties who have mutual suspicions and come to no explanations, the evening passed off heavily and disagreeably. He passed an agitated and sleepless night, and finally determined to ask his father's consent to his marriage with Louisa, after giving him a representation of the young lady's fortune, which would better accord with the property then possessed by the family, than that which they were long likely to hold; and, in the meantime, to ascertain, if possible, whether the alteration in Louisa's conduct was the effect of a sudden and transient whim, or of a settled course of conduct.

After breakfast, the next morning, he spoke to her on the subject of a new French air, which she had just received from Alexandria, and which he very highly extolled, to give her an opportunity of gratifying him, as she had often done before; but when she retained her seat, and contented herself with remarking that she was not quite mistress of it, he asked her if she would not then favour him with some other piece of music. She begged to be excused, as "she must write some letters that morning."

"The post is not until the day after to-morrow," said he.

"But to-morrow I am to go to Mr. Buckley's,

and I find, when I put off writing to the last day, something is apt to prevent my writing at all."

Gildon now saw too plainly, from these repeated evasions, that she did not wish to be alone with him. He did not doubt but Mrs. Grayson had recommended the plan she was pursuing, and his love, as well as his vanity, were mortified, to find she could so readily and so successfully carry it into execution.

CHAPTER VIII.

The next morning a note from Mr. and Mrs. Buckley, a friend of Mrs. Grayson, who lived about seven miles from Beechwood, invited Mrs. Grayson, and her household over to dinner the next day, to visit a sister of Mrs. Buckley, Mrs. Browne, who, with her husband, was to pass a few weeks, during the months of July and August, in the county of Frederick. Mrs. Grayson excused herself, as she had never since her husband's death made a visit, except in a private way; and indeed had seldom left her own home except to attend divine service at a private chapel in the neighbourhood, which she never missed, or to see some sick person, whom she could assist by her nursing, or cheer by her society. She, however, advised Louisa to make her promised visit to Fanny Buckley, who, as well as Matilda Fawkner, had been to the same school with her in Alexandria.

Edward and Gildon accepted the invitation of course; and the next day the chariot was driven up, with the harness in nice order, and the horses better rubbed than usual, to make some amends, as old Phill thought, for the reduction of the number. Gildon hinted that Miss Grayson ought to have a beau in the carriage; but she gayly said she liked to see her knights on horseback, and manifested a steady adherence to the course she had prescribed to herself.

The road was partly the main highway to Winchester, and partly, for about three miles, a crossroad diverging from it. They had not gone far, before, as they were ascending a steep stony hill, in which the road was washed in deep gullies on each side, so as barely to leave room for a single carriage to pass in safety, they espied a wagon with six horses, at the top of the hill, just beginning to descend. The coachman called out to the wagoner to stop; but he, either not hearing or not heeding the request, still moved on, and Gildon seeing that Edward was some distance behind, put spurs to his horse, and rode up to him, saying, " My good friend, there is not room for two carriages to pass each other, wait a little, till our carriage goes by."

The wagoner, a sturdy fierce looking fellow with a black bristly beard, smiled maliciously, and without answering, still moved on. Gildon then raised his voice, and not being certain but he was a German or deaf, pointed to the carriage and said, more loudly and distinctly, " there is a young lady in the carriage, wait and let her pass." The fellow then said " I am going to market, I shall not stop nor get out of the way for nobody ;" and giving his fore horses a crack of his whip, quickened their motions.

"Why, to be sure, you would not be such a brute as to stop a lady in such a place," said Gildon, with half smothered anger.

" The carriage may drive on one side," said the man of the whip ; and lady or no lady, she has not a right to stop me from going to market. As for you, my young sprout, give us none of your slack jaw, or I will let you feel the weight of my wagon-whip. Gee Jock—ho Devil"—at the same time jerking the wheel horses.

Gildon, having a hickory switch in his hand, instantly replied, "nay, take that, you savage," and struck the wagoner across his eyes, which for a moment blinded him. He then rode up to his adversary and attempted to push him off his horse. But this he found to be not so easy as he expected. The wagoner kept his seat, and having recovered from the smart of the blow, seized Gildon by the arm, and throwing away his whip, by dint of his superior strength, attempted to pull him to the ground ; but Gildon, who was an excellent horseman, making effectual resistance, they grappled each other, and in the scuffle they both came down together, the wagoner being undermost. The wagon all the while slowly descending the hill, by a sudden effort of self-preservation, they both managed to clear themselves from its track, except as to one foot of the driver, which both wheels passed over, pressing his thick leather shoes into the earth, and squeezing the foot until the blood gushed out. The injury had probably been much greater, but the ground was wet and soft with the shower that had fallen the evening before.

This serious accident not only disabled the suffering combatant, but completely disarmed the resentment of his antagonist. The latter attempted to help up his prostrate foe, who smarting under a violence of pain that hardly allowed him breath, requested Gildon to stop his horses.

Edward, who had finished reading the letters which he had received from Primus, on his way from the post-office, and whose presence would no doubt have prevented the accident, from the wagoner's fear of the odds, put spurs to his horse, on witnessing the scene at the top of the hill, and got up just as Gildon had stopped the wagon horses and was scotching the wheels. Seeing what had happened, he proposed to the wagoner, whom he slightly knew, that he would ride back, and get one of his mother's servants to drive the wagon back, while the man himself should go in the carriage to his own house, where a physician should be sent to attend him.

But the man obstinately refused either to go to

the carriage, or to the house, or to suffer them to perform any other service, except to carry him to a little tavern hard by, from whence he could let the owner of the wagon know of the accident, that he might supply his place, and get himself carried home in a cart. He also refused to accept any compensation, which was repeatedly offered to him, but preserved a sullen and resentful silence to all the expressions of regret which Gildon expressed, muttering occasionally that he would see "if a man was to be stopped in the highway by any whipper-snapper in a fine coat; and whether there was not as much law for a wagoner going to market, as for gentlemen and ladies in their carriages."

Finding they could not appease his wrath, nor contribute any farther to his accommodation, they rendered him the only service he would consent to receive, and while they were carrying him to the little tavern, Edward rode on before, to send a surgeon to look at the injury.

Let us now turn to Louisa, who, not anticipating any difficulty at first, was greatly alarmed when she saw a quarrel was likely to arise. She knew the fierce and surly disposition of some of these people, and saw the wagoner's robust form and threatening gestures; but when she beheld the parties engaged in actual combat, forgetting her cautious resolution, she screamed out for help, and urged Phill, the coachman, to run to Mr. Gildon's assistance. She was, indeed, so peremptory in her commands, that Phill seemed in a state of uncertainty, whether he should not leave his horses without a guide, when Edward appeared in sight.

"Oh, brother! brother!" she exclaimed, before he was within hearing, "Mr. Gildon is attacked by a wagoner, for God's sake ride up!"

These evidences of Louisa's lively interest had not escaped Gildon's ear, and had produced on him the same animating effect as the trumpet or bagpipe has upon the warrior, in the heat of battle; and after the conflict was over, the recollection of them was still more lively, (to the shame of his humanity and prudence be it spoken,) than either sympathy for the suffering wagoner, or alarm for the effects of his vengeance.

While Edward was gone for the needed assistance, the carriage drove slowly by the wagon, and stopped at a small distance beyond it, on the level ground, until Edward's return. Gildon went to the carriage door, and Louisa recollecting the extraordinary interest she had manifested, and knowing the source from whence it had proceeded, blushed most deeply, and in great confusion remarked, "I never witnessed such a scene before. I hope the poor man is not seriously hurt."

"His foot is severely bruised," said Gildon, "but I hope not permanently injured. I am truly sorry to have been the cause of so much alarm."

Louisa conscious of having betrayed her feelings, attributed to Gildon's words a sense he did not intend them to convey, and observed, with a serious air and a tone of self-defence, " It would have been strange, if I had not been alarmed, to see two persons in a situation of so much danger, and which has proved so serious to one of them."

" I did not flatter myself," replied Gildon with equal gravity, " that the interest was felt for me, exclusively, or that Miss Grayson could feel more on this occasion, than her generous nature would experience for any human being in distress."

Louisa, perceiving her mistake, and softened by his humility, remarked with her wonted sweetness of countenance and manner, " Yet I trust I can discriminate between strangers and friends. I hope you escaped unhurt."

" I received a slight bruise or two in falling; but if they excite any interest with you, I shall think myself fortunate in having received them."

Louisa remarked, " I flatter myself you are not indeed much hurt, as you have your usual readiness at compliment."

" Do you question my sincerity, Miss Grayson?"

" Not exactly so," said Louisa; " but I am not silly enough to receive literally every civil speech a gentleman may be pleased to utter."

Now when a young man entertains favourable sentiments towards a lady, which, for some reason or other, he does not wish to disclose, or a lady is anxious to conceal the partiality that is springing up in her gentle bosom—let them beware of being together alone—let them beware too of talking of the opinions of each other—and, let them doubly beware of encountering these hazards when their bosoms have been recently agitated by passion, no matter what that passion is. Such was the situation of this youthful pair. The indisposition and subsequent alarm of Gildon, and the lively terrors of Louisa, had not yet subsided when they met, but had left their nerves in a state of tremulous susceptibility to any new cause of excitement, and the flame which had been growing for some weeks, and which had derived strength from the late check it had experienced, received a new accession of force, from the very opposite passions of fear and anger.

"And is it possible," said Gildon with emotion, "that you could not have understood my sentiments towards you? Have my looks and manner so imperfectly expressed the feelings of my heart? or, rather, must I not infer that you are a slow, an unwilling interpreter of what is disagreeable?"

He went on in a species of eloquence, of which he was a great master, and which was, on the present occasion, more the language of passion than it had ever before been; but which, though excessively touching and beautiful in the ears to which it was addressed, would appear very dull in the repetition to the sober reader.

Louisa, much agitated as well as delighted, sought some relief in fanning herself, and by the noise she made, would have prevented his words from being heard by old Phill, if his ears had been better than they were. As it was, he took it for granted they were merely carrying on the conversations which they were seen daily to hold together in the little porch, and which all the servants considered to be a prelude to courtship, if they were not the thing itself.

Encouraged by her timid and blushing silence, he ventured to expostulate on her marked coldness for a day or two. She hinted, as delicately as she could, that it was by her mother's advice, as their private conversations had already attracted notice, and might give rise to reports for which there might be no foundation. Little explanation was sufficient, considering the footing on which they had for some time been, and in a few minutes his love was declared and not rejected. Thus surprised into an avowal of his passion, he briefly intimated that he was dependent on his father, whose opinion as to his marriage he had already been sounding; that he anticipated a favourable result, and he hoped she would in the meantime allow him to assume the character of a decided lover. Louisa, who had no humble idea of the merits and dignity of her family, not having dreamt of any opposition on the part of Gildon's father, and possessing a very imperfect knowledge of the grounds that existed for any, indirectly acquiesced by observing that she should be governed in the affair by her mother.

By this time Edward made his appearance, with the owner of the little tavern, who, divided between his sympathy for his crony, the wagoner, and his unwillingness to give offence to Edward, gave a hearty and uncourteous nod to Gildon, and going up to the wagoner, said, "Oh, Jaque, are you here? you've made a short trip on it. By Jolly, my lad, you've had a narrow squeak for it—you're like old Mike Overhill, who was caught in his own wolf-trap."

"Come, come, I'm in no humour for jokes now," says Jaque, "help me up, and carry me where I can get something done to my foot, and let me see whether I am to be a cripple for life."

They carefully lifted him into the wagon, laying him on the blades of Indian corn with which the upper part was crammed, and the tavern-keeper mounting the wheel-horse, drove on. The wounded man called out, as soon as the wagon lighted on a rut or a stone, to drive more carefully, and not jolt his life out; whereupon the sympathizing Louisa urged that he should be taken into the carriage, while she would walk on, but he still obstinately, and even rudely refused, saying, "he had had enough of their carriage for that day."

The delay which this accident had occasioned, created some anxiety at Mr. Buckley's, about the absentees, for all the other guests had been some time assembled, and dinner was on the point of being ordered in. Mr. Buckley was a plain man, of moderate understanding, prudent character, and a disposition that was friendly, without any pretensions to generosity. His wife was a motherly housewife and matron, fond of busking about, in her house, and dairy, and garden,—of managing, and talking about management. They had two daughters, the youngest of whom had seen her fifth lustre, they both were remarkably homely and fat, possessed of more good nature than protracted celibacy in females is apt to produce.

Mrs. Browne, the sister of Mrs. Buckley, had possessed beauty in her youth, and very sedulously cherished that portion of it which yet remained. Her husband was a thriving, intelligent merchant of Alexandria, and as they had no children, the profits of his business enabled him to live in a style of more than ordinary show and expense; and thus, with Mrs. Buckley and her daughters, "my sister Browne," and "my aunt Browne," was the standard of elegance, taste, and fashion. They commonly passed the summer months, or rather those of autumn, with their relatives in Frederick, and Mrs. Browne's nieces, Peggy and Fanny Buckley, had alternately passed winters with her, without ever having any nearer prospect of what was ill-naturedly conjectured to be the chief motive of their visit, except that Miss Margaret, us she was called when from home, was addressed by a New-London Captain, at a time when flour happened to be twelve dollars a barrel, and her father was reported in Alexandria to be a great farmer—but whether she rejected him, or he getting more accurate information of the extent of her fortune, left her, like another Calypso, to flourish in immortal virginity, is not certainly known, as there are many conflicting rumours on the subject.

Miss Fanny too, the youngest, it was said, had solicited at home, to change her state, by an aged widower; and a Dutch coppersmith had made her several visits, as it was supposed, with a view of paying his addresses, if he was properly encouraged. Saving these offers, all of which were somewhat apocryphal, they had never been tempted to change their life of single blessedness; and this perhaps was the cause, that the thoughts both of themselves and their sympathizing mamma, ran very much in this particular channel. They seemed to think and speak as if it was, and ought to be, the sole business of a female to get " settled in life ;" and being good natured people they were always ready to act as brokers for others, in that sort of business, as they had none of their own to do. They were never so happy as when they were made confidantes of a love affair; were the bearers of the tender protestations of some enamoured Corydon, or the soft-confessions of his gentle Phillis. They knew of every match in embryo for twenty miles round; and sometimes, by their long-practised skill, in such subjects, foresaw them even before the parties themselves had thought of the matter.

When the party from Beechwood entered, they found in the drawing-room at Buck-Hill, besides the family and their relations from Alexandria, the Fawkners, Mr. Wilson, a respectable magistrate of the country, and now a widower with his only daughter, and their old friend Mr. M'Culloch, with his wife and eldest son.

They were received with the same mingled cordiality and respect that they had ever experienced in Col. Grayson's lifetime, by all the company, except Mrs. Fawkner. She returned Edward's bow with a cold and stately salutation, and turning to Louisa, remarked, " I suppose your brother has a mind to introduce Williamsburg fashions among us, by coming so late."

" We had been here more than an hour ago, madam," said Louisa, " but for an unpleasant accident;" and she then narrated all that had taken place, except that which was all the while uppermost in her mind, her own alarm and Gildon's avowal of his passion. She had now recovered from the effects of her fright, as well as of the interview, and giving way to emotions of unmingled delight, she told the story with infinite grace and pleasantry, and bantered her brother about his being in the clouds, meditating a sonnet she presumed, or planning, perhaps, a new constitution for France

Edward, notwithstanding Mrs. Fawkner's haughty airs, made the usual inquiry about her health, and passed on to the other ladies, bowing and speaking to each, until he reached Matilda, who was sitting on the opposite side, between the Miss Buckley's. He bowed to her respectfully, but she, with her usual frankness, held out her hand to him, as if she was determined to make amends for her mother's unkindness. He used a few commonplace terms of civility, but, there was a mixture of tenderness and respect, in his manner, that a nice observer might have easily perceived, and which was not lost on either Matilda or her mother; though it was seen by them with very different eyes.

Old Mr. M'Culloch then came up to Gildon, and said, "So, my young gentleman, you have had a little taste of Virginia play? 'Twas well, he was caught by the wagon wheel, or he would soon have had his fingers in your eyes. I know Jaque Scryder, and a bullying, insolent fellow he is."

"Fanny Buckley," here whispered to Louisa, "Now would it not have been a shame to have spoiled such a face? And besides, (winking significantly,) he could not then have seen you. Indeed Louisa, I never saw you look so well in my life. They say that things go on swimmingly at Beechwood."

Louisa, fearful of this prattle being overheard, endeavoured to check her, but was unable, until finding that Louisa was seriously displeased, she desisted.

Gildon then gave a ludicrous description of the encounter, in which he affected rather to underrate, than to make a display, of his prowess. The ladies were loud in their denunciations of unruly wagoners—several stories were told of their insolence in stopping up the road, upsetting gigs, and preventing carriages from passing them.

" Why, sir, that is a specimen of buckskin independence," said Mr. M'Culloch to Mr. Buckley; " Now I'll warrant you that Jacob Scryder, with his blue painted wagon, and a dozen or more tinkling bells, was as proud as one of your South Carolina dashers, which is being proud enough; or some of your old-fashioned James River gentry"—

" Which is being prouder still," says Major Fawkner. Mrs. Fawkner thought such " low, impertinent fellows ought to be severely punished."

" Softly, my dear madam," said Mr. M'Culloch, "as to punishment, Jaque seems to have had his full share of it this bout, though I should have given him a crack over the pate myself, for his insolence to my little Lilly of the Valley, if I had been present—and as to the matter of making him pay for his rudeness, Jaque has the advantage there, and I am thinking this young gentleman will learn that, to his cost."

This incident furnished the company with conversation till they were summoned to dinner, when they all repaired to a well-spread board—Mr. Buckley being as attentive to his part, in providing good mutton and other meats, as was Mrs. Buckley to hers, in superintending her poultry yard, dairy, and kitchen garden.

Now, while the rest of the company were eying with delightful anticipations, these tempting specimens of their entertainers' good management, and thinking of naught besides, there were four persons of the company, (can ye believe it, epicures?) whose minds, disregarding what was on the table, were occupied solely and exclusively on the places they should occupy at it, and who endeavoured to get as far from the upper end (where the ladies in that day commonly sat by themselves) as they could, without attracting observation. But there not being room for all the guests, and the elder Miss Buckley, with Miss Wilson, betaking themselves to a side table, Matilda insisted on joining them, notwithstanding Mrs. Fawkner told her there was room enough by Mrs. M'Culloch. —Old Mr. M'Culloch's then said, "Nay, these girls shall have a beau—How is this Edward? why you have lost all your gallantry, since you've lived with the Tuckahoes. By Jove—no, by Venus and the Graces, the lads now-a-days have neither taste nor spirit; they are fit for nothing but to talk French politics, and preach mad philosophy."

Mrs. Fawkner now addressing herself to Mrs. Buckley, again remarked, to make her words good, "There was room enough," and was squeezing up to the mistress of the house, but Edward, observing the manœuvre, promptly said, " I can't stand such a rebuke, and must endeavour to retrieve my character." Then turning suddenly round, he seated himself between Matilda, and Margaret Buckley.

Mrs. Fawkner thus foiled, plainly showed internal vexation by her lowering brow, and rather peevishly observed, " For my part, I never have side-tables, they give so much trouble to the servants. The lady of the house good naturedly replied, " That's what sister Browne always tells me; but I could not well help it to-day—and then the young people like to be by themselves," accompanying her last remark with a significant smile and a wink, as she had not yet learnt the new system of politics at the Elms. Mrs. Fawkner still further fretted by Mrs. Buckley's last observation, tartly replied, " Yes, indeed, they are always liking best what least suits them."

"But," said the well-meaning but mistaken hostess, " you can't say that of some young people of my acquaintance," still smiling and winking. But the important interrogatory, "Madam, what do you choose, sir?" " What will you be helped to?" somewhat less in use now than formerly, put an end to the dialogue, as Mr. Fawkner, by way of effecting the same object, was complimenting Mrs. Buckley on her green geese, which, however excellent as they were, and the first of the season, she was unable to enjoy, her thoughts were so engrossed by another subject.

Ever and anon she would cast an eye to the side-table, to watch the movements of Edward and Matilda, and was loud enough in her praises of Gildon to have been overheard by him, if he had not been totally occupied by the short and broken conversation he was holding with Louisa, by whose side he was so fortunate as to obtain a seat. She, gratified and delighted, found in the secret contemplation of the morning's disclosure, a complete substitute for the delicacies of the table, and ate not a morsel. Her lover too yielding to the luxury of his present feelings, banished from his mind all fears of opposition from his father—all his former schemes of prudence or ambition.

The dinner past off with the usual incidents. The company complimented the good housewifery of Mrs. Buckley, the merit of which she was content to share with Peggy and Fanny on this occasion; and they gave by their actions good proof of the sincerity of their language. The wine, which had been selected by Mr. Browne, was first commented on and discussed after dinner, and then the merits of the federalists and republicans became the subject of animated debate, which beginning in good humour, and ending in ill-disguised anger, by way of giving a zest of bitterness to the otherwise pure and tranquil pleasures of the day.

The state of political parties at that period is yet fresh in the recollection of half the readers of this authentic chronicle. After the French revolution had made some progress, and it appeared to be the struggle of a great nation for those civil rights which are justly the pride and boast of this country; the sympathies of a large proportion of our citizens were enlisted on the side of the conductors of the revolutions. And this feeling was so strong that it made many overlook some of the enormities with which that great event was attended, and apologize for those to which they could not be blind. In proportion as they loved the French and wished them success, they hated their enemies, especially the English, with whom they had been in open war, and against whom their enmity was the more inflamed as they had more and warmer friends here than any other European nation, many of them being natives of Great-Britain who spoke the same language, and, accustomed to the same manners, laws, and religion, readily identify themselves with the people of this country.

The attachment of this party to England was supported by those whom they could influence in the character of agents, shop-keepers, lawyers, in short, all those who could profit by an extensive patronage; by many who did not expect a happy termination to a revolution, began in violence, and carried on by cruelty and rapine; and by a few whose sympathies were on the side of the proscribed classes in France. These conflicting causes of our partiality and attachment were lively and intense in proportion to the magnitude of the events which gave rise to them ; and as the revolution advanced, with small fluctuations of fortune, in one continuous career of success, the parties became more distinctly formed and more completely separated from each other.

The British treaty, or Jay's, as it was most frequently called, was ratified by General Washington the year before, 1795, and was then the subject of defence and apology on one side, and of bitter denunciation on the other. The objections to this treaty were argued and repelled in every circle, low or high, from one end of the country to the other. Zeal for the success of the French became louder and bolder, till the friends of the English were finally borne down, and only by cautious and indirect means ventured to oppose their adversaries. Many of our citizens were proud to wear the tri-coloured cockade. The popular songs of the Marsellois, Carmagnol, ça Ira, were sung, not only in private houses, but at public places, and even in the streets, both by young and old, with rapturous enthusiasm. The term of "citizen," often superseded the ordinary titles of respect. One party was branded by their opponents with the name of " jacobins," the other with that of " aristocrats."

Sometimes they were called Frenchmen and Englishmen. And as men embraced their different sides, not according to any great motives of self-interest, but according to the accidental circumstances of temper and character, or the company they had chanced to keep, it was not unusual to see, on opposite sides, those of the same family whose altercations, inflaming them to mutual hatred, destroyed all harmony of social intercourse.

It was now publicly known that General Washington, wearied and somewhat disgusted with these party feuds, and with the censure which began to be very openly cast upon some of his political measures, on the ground that he had abandoned those principles for which he had once fought, was about to return to private life, and seek in the shades of retirement and in the pursuits of agriculture, for that happiness which the highest honours of his country, a nobler fame than mortal man ever before enjoyed, (or aught, it may be added, that this world can afford,) was not able to bestow. Mr. Jefferson had withdrawn from the cabinet, dissatisfied with the course pursued by the administration, and, as his admirers said, had abstracted himself from active politics, and passed his time in building, in experimental agriculture, and the cultivation of letters. But he was the rallying point of opposition, and those who were in the secret knew that he was engaged in an extensive political correspondence, and that A——

B——, from New-York, was then on a visit to Monticello for the purpose of marshalling their hosts, and taking the field as soon as the veteran chief had sounded his retreat.

The dining party at Buck Hill happened to be all federalists, except Edward, Gildon, and Mr. Wilson, a plain, honest man, who had been once a colleague from the county of —— with old George Mason, and who, (as most of those opposed to the adoption of the constitution, were also now opposed to its administration,) had continued his attachment to the same party, through their successive denominations of anti-federalists, jacobins, and democrats. But as he was a man of few words, and not so zealous as most of his associates, he proved a weak ally to the young collegians against the ardour of old M'Culloch, and the shrewd, well-informed Mr. Browne.

Mr. Madison having been given as a toast by Edward, the President's proclamation of neutrality soon came under discussion, and was loudly censured by the small band of democrats. Driven from that ground, the British treaty was then vehemently condemned; but unable to reply to the arguments of an experienced and intelligent merchant, they filed off, as political disputants often do, into general declamation against the policy of the government—their manifest partiality to the English, and aversion to the French, until Edward (whose temper was ardent, and impatient of contradiction,) and old M'Culloch had the field of controversy to themselves; the rest of the party being wearied out with their own efforts.

Passing from the subject of controversy to the person of his opponent, each of the disputants charged the other with being the slave of prejudice—of forming his opinions under some bias of interest or accident, or of yielding to the influence of some particular individual; and the dispute growing more and more warm and personal, there was no saying how far the young man would have forgot the respect due to his senior, or the old one the respect due to himself, and both, the respect due to the company, if Mr. Buckley had not proposed to drink a good afternoon—the customary signal for rising, and joining the ladies in the parlour.

After they came out into the cool air they strolled a while under some shady locusts that grew in the yard, and then rejoined the ladies. Good humour seemed to be completely restored, at least on the part of old M'Culloch, though Edward's violence of temper, when once roused, could not so suddenly subside. M'Culloch, going up to Louisa, said to her, in his wonted jocular style, "my little lilly, or rather, my rose-bud I may call you, for you have a fine colour to-day, these youngsters are such furious democrats I know not what I shall do with them. And if the lasses don't reform them, they will prove as arrant jacobins as citizen Genet himself."

" I will willingly put myself under the tuition of Miss Grayson," said Gildon with a smile, " whose discipline will be more efficacious, as it will be not quite so rough and ungentle as Mr. M'Culloch's."

" I never meddle with politics, said Louisa, but I confess I have always been taught to place unbounded confidence in the wisdom and patriotism of General Washington."

" And well taught you were, my little mountain daisy," said M'Culloch ; and now, young man, I trust that you and Orlando Furioso there," pointing to Edward across the room, " will hardly venture to attack me again when I have such a reinforcement."

" Indeed, Mr. Gildon," said Mrs. Fawkner, "I should not have thought you had belonged to the democratic party—I thought," hesitating, as if doubtful of giving offence, " I somehow always considered the federalists the genteelest party. Oh, I beg pardon, Miss Wilson ; I mean that there were more people of fortune and family on our side."

" I don't know how that can be," replied the young lady, who, though diminutive and of a sickly appearance, seemed no wise deficient in spirit, " there's our member of congress, and the governor of the state, and the Nelson's, and the Pages, and"—

"Stop, ladies," said M'Culloch, who hated to see the flames of war so soon kindling again, and who, in fact, seldom engaged in controversy, except when prompted to it in defence of a favourite, or some other generous motive; "forbear, I pray you, I've had enough of this sort of wrangling in the dining room, till Edward and I liked to have had a quarrel, and it must not set you pulling caps. If you must have an argument, let it be about who has the largest brood of young turkeys, or the greatest quantity of homespun; in which contest I think my old woman there will be likely to eclipse you all. What think you of my new coat, ladies?" inviting their attention to some remarkably fine gray homespun, by drawing it across his breast and looking at himself in a small mirror with the most good-humoured self-complacency.

The conversation very readily took this turn, it being not only better understood, but also more relished by most of the company. By this time, however, the ladies were preparing to return home, and Louisa, who had had some thoughts of passing a few days with her friends, the Miss Buckley's, having changed her mind for the purpose of communicating the most important occurrences of the day to her anxious mother, also ordered her carriage.

Before the party broke up, Major Fawkner, having first whispered to his wife, asked Mr. Browne and the young gentlemen to dine with them the next day, and Mrs. Fawkner, not with the best grace in the world, extended the same request to Louisa, and not content with her husband's invitation to Gildon, she gave him one herself, without noticing Edward. Matilda, hurt at so pointed a slight, handed Edward a sprig of myrtle, as he led her to the carriage, and in a low voice said, I trust we shall see you to-morrow. Mrs. Fawkner's flaunting yellow coach, with two large black horses, came prancing up, having in a brisk trot, passed the more unpretending, but genteeler looking chariot of Miss Grayson. Old Phill would willingly have disputed the road, if Louisa first, and then Edward, more peremptorily, had not ordered him to give place, which he did with a most reluctant and mortified air, and thus terminated the visit to Buck Hill.

Louisa went to her mother's room about sunset, and with more embarrassment than she had ever before experienced in addressing her, communicated the events of the day, especially the one which had exceeded all others in interest. Mrs. Grayson, whose generous, unsuspecting nature could no longer allow her to entertain doubts of Gildon's sincerity, was truly delighted, and was at no pains to conceal the pleasure she felt. But after indulging a while in those felicitations, she reminded her daughter that, as it was yet possible that Mr. Gildon, the father, might be opposed to the match, it would be prudent to prepare for such a result, and to observe the same reserved conduct as she had lately done.

"But, mamma," said the disappointed Louisa, "what objection *can* he have? He cannot object to the connexion."

"I presume, my dear, he will not. But if he should be a mercenary man, as your brother thinks he is, I fear he will object on the score of fortune."

"Supposing he is so narrow-minded, I never knew my father considered to be a poor man," said Louisa, looking apprehensively at her mother.

"My child, I hate to communicate any thing which will give you pain; but it is now become necessary. Know then that the debts and claims against your poor father's estate, of which you have sometimes heard me speak, are far greater than he was aware of; and that some are hanging over it, which, if they prove well founded, will leave us a very moderate fortune. Knowing (with a long drawn sigh) that sufficient for the day is the evil thereof, I have forborne to make this unwelcome communication until it was dictated by something like necessity."

"I cannot think, my dear mother, that Mr. Gildon will allow himself to be influenced by such mercenary considerations. I am sure he is too generous—too noble."

"I hope he is, my dear, and I am the more encouraged to think so because your brother has felt it his duty to make a frank disclosure of the fact without making known his motives, and it seems that a knowledge of the true state of things has not prevented him from addressing you."

"You see, mamma, he has given a proof of his generosity and disinterestedness. I knew his nobleness of soul was not to be swayed by such sordid considerations."

"I trust not—I believe not, my child. But old men and young men see this matter very differently, and a lover chooses his mistress by another rule than that by which a father chooses his daughter-in-law. If such a diversity should unhappily exist on the present occasion, I trust, my daughter, you know too well what is due to yourself and your family to need my suggestion. You will not readily consent to intrude yourself into any family an unwelcome member of it; and you would not be the means of alienating the man of your choice from the countenance and regard of his relations—of reducing him from affluence to poverty—of converting his preference for you into an instrument of his destruction."

"Never, never, my dear mother," interrupted Louisa;—"I would never consent to that which would put his happiness to hazard by losing him the affections of his family, and impairing his standing in society."

"In such a determination, my daughter, you act like yourself, and as I expected. I see that candles are lighted. Let us go into the drawing-room."

Gildon, who thought that now the previous impediment was removed, he should have the happiness of an uninterrupted *tête-à-tête*, was disappointed at learning from Louisa that she meant to retire early; which she did with a heart much less elated and buoyant than it was before she had heard the prudent suggestions of her mother. The other three, from different causes, were all in low spirits, and not being in a humour to enjoy each other's society, soon followed the example of Louisa.

CHAPTER XI.

The next morning, just as Edward and Gildon were about to take their customary ride, a tall young man with a pair of leather saddle-bags on his left arm, entered the passage, and being recognised as Mr. Cruise, one of the acting sheriffs of the county, he informed them, with a smile, that he had a warrant to summon them before a magistrate, the one as a party, and the other as a witness, on the charge of Jacob Scryder, who had sworn the peace against Mr. Gildon for stopping and assaulting him on the highway. The young men being both inexperienced in these matters, were somewhat disconcerted and vexed at first, until the nature of the proceeding was explained by the deputy sheriff. They mounted their horses and rode over to Mr. Buckley's, who, being the nearest magistrate, had issued the warrants, and who, as a matter of course, recognised Gildon to appear at the next county court, held in the town of Winchester, and Edward was the surety for his appearance.

The official business being despatched, they took leave without waiting to see the ladies.

"That was an uncommonly civil peace-officer," said Gildon. "I see that the courtesy of Virginia extends even to her sheriffs."

"They are, indeed," replied Edward, "in general very civil in their demeanour, and discharge their disagreeable functions in a way to give as little offence as possible. For most of them look upon the office as a stepping-stone to future promotion. And as their official duties give them access to every man in the community, they avail themselves of the circumstance to court popularity, which they afterwards turn to good account. I have little doubt that three or four years hence you might see that young man transformed from a supple and accommodating deputy sheriff, to a delegate from the large county of Frederick to the general assembly."

"I fear," said Gildon, "that the same court is paid every where to sovereigns, whether the sovereignty resides in one or many; and that flattery is always the instrument by which cunning manages power."

"But flatterers are a contemptible race," said Edward haughtily, "whether they aim to cheat a prince or people; and yet," continued he, "the ambition of political advancement on the part of our deputy sheriffs is not without its advantages to the public. It makes them more indulgent and accommodating in levying executions and collecting taxes. It often prevents them from practising those petty frauds and unconscionable extortions which their office invites them to, and which are familiar to many of the tribe. The difference which exists between this class of public officers and the clerks of our counties, strongly shows the intimate connexion between morals and habits. Our clerks, not exposed to the same temptations as our sheriffs, but having their quiet duties plainly marked out by law, habitually become methodical, correct, and honest in all their dealings."

"You know," said Gildon, "the Romans used the same word to express morals and habits."

A little black boy, with no other clothes than a shirt and pantaloons, or overalls of hempen cloth, without any covering on his head but his own knotted and sun-burnt wool, but whose appearance indicated that he was plentifully fed, though scantily clothed, came riding up to them, in as brisk a gait as a tall, lean, ragged-hipped sorrel gelding could be made to bring him. He brought a note from Mr. M'Culloch, saying, that the next day being the first of August when, the powers that be give us permission to eat venison, he proposed to start a buck, and should expect Edward and his friend to be on the ground at his house, by dawn the next morning, if they wished to share in the sport, and that he had a gun for the young New-York democrat; that Edward must bring old Thunder and Juno, and might also try his two young black tans, and that, if they meant to join in the chase, they must meet him then on the other side of the river, at the forks of the road, near the shoemaker's, by day-break.

Edward, who had often accompanied the old sportsman on these parties, had no objection whatever to obeying the summons, especially as he reproached himself for some expressions the day before, that were not only intemperate, but unbecoming the respect due to the years of his opponent. Gildon, too, promised himself the gratification of novelty. Arrangements for an early start were made over night, and orders were given to have the horses saddled before day. Accordingly, before the least appearance of dawn could be perceived by an unpractised eye, Primus came to call the young gentlemen to their intended sport. Edward was already up and dressed, and lost no time in seeing that his orders of preparation over night had been complied with; but Gildon required to be repeatedly shaken by Primus, and coaxed to rise before he could make the requisite exertion ; and he might yet have decided to forego the pleasure of the sport, and have fallen again into slumber, if the ready-witted Primus had not said, " Dr. Manifee start a buck before this; Mr. Gildon lie and sleep like Mr. Bolmain, from Carolina, the day Master Edward kill the old buck at the river."

The reproach of effeminacy, and the wish to take part in the sport, perchance to distinguish himself in the eyes of Louisa, roused him from his lethargy, and he was soon dressed with the ready aid of Primus, who continued to retouch the string which he had found to vibrate so readily. Mounted on a spirited and well trained hunter, (knowing the keen impatience of M'Culloch,) they set off at a round gallop, and got to the house a little before sun-rise, just as the old man was loading his last rifle.

" A pretty pair of sportsmen," said the veteran, " you are truly. Why, Edward, before you became such a democrat, you would be here before cock crow, and now we have been waiting for you this half hour. Meinwether and Sandy have reached the starting ground by this time, and we must be quick and get to our stand. Jack Martin, don't let these dogs out unless the deer should take to the river. Here Slut—Ringwood—Leader— where are you? Mr Gildon, as you are a young huntsman, you shall have my favourite stand, and my best shot gun, (handing him a long clumsy fowling piece.) Edward, I shall place you at the Walnut tree, and I shall stand myself at the hazle thicket, near the mouth of Bull Branch. Dick Mole and Whittle have gone across the river, in case the deer should come down Poplar ridge. Come on, my lads, come take a julep, before you start."

As some of my read rs may mistake the meaning of this beverage, and think the worthy mountaineer meant to recommend some peculiar medicine by way of preparing them for the enterprise, he must be informed that nothing more nor less was intended than a morning dram, consisting sometimes of spirits and sugar, with an infusion of garden mint, but at present of peach brandy sweetened with honey. The hunters all partook of it, some of them repeatedly; and Gildon would not be singular. They left their horses at the house, and also the hounds, as they were too late to join the rest of the pack, and each one set out with a rifle or fowling-piece, properly charged.

The mode of hunting deer in that part of the country, then, and no doubt at present, is for a party who are well acquainted with the localities of the woodlands, and the haunts of the animal (and who are commonly well mounted) to set off to the places frequented by the deer, as early in the morning as possible, taking the hounds with them, for the purpose of starting the game. And as it is known by experience, that those creatures, when pursued, have particular tracks, commonly leading to the river, other hunters are posted in ambush, near the line of the tracks, where they remain idle and unoccupied, until they hear the opening cry of the hounds. Then, knowing that the deer is some distance in advance, they keep a close look-out for him, and as soon as he comes within reach of their guns, a noise is purposely made by the one he is nearest to; on hearing which the deer invariably stops for a moment to see whence it proceeds, and to change his course, if necessary. This pause, if the hunter is prompt, and a good marksman, is often fatal; but sometimes the animal bounds off before the piece can be discharged, and is shot at, and often hit, running. Where there are several tracks, all equally likely to be taken according to the known habits of the animal, only one of the stands on the same side of the river is likely to have a shot; but where there is but one favourite track, the stands are placed on each side of it, and the deer is fired at by several, as he passes them, in regular succession.

The freshness of the morning air at this season; the novelty of the scene; and the lively anticipations of the experienced hunters, producing their usual contagious effect on Gildon, raised his spirits very high, and he began to feel some foretaste of that warm enthusiasm which field sports so often excite, and which are beyond the comprehension of the uninitiated.

They had to walk about a mile and a half from M'Culloch's house before they came to the stands usually occupied by the hunters in the intended drive. Each one was then posted at his stand, about three or four hundred yards apart. They had waited upwards of an hour near the river bank without hearing any thing but the dull murmuring sound of the gentle Shenandoah, as it flowed rippling over the rocks or bars in its channel—the occasional cooing of one or two wood-pigeons—or the cawing of a flock of crows, when Gildon began to think it but a dull business, and to regret that he had not been with the party which were more actively employed in starting and pursuing the game. He would indeed have found the long interval of fruitless expectation wearisome in the extreme, if the lovely image of his mistress, in some past scene of endearment, did not always present itself to the youthful lover, and keep him company in the wildest solitude. While both he and Edward were indulging these luxurious meditations, and the rest were supported in their patience by this keen love of the sport, the hounds were heard to cry. In a moment they were all attention. The sound was then lost, and again was heard, something plainer than before. As the intervals of its return grew shorter, the cry became louder and more distinct. Suddenly they were heard in full chorus, in the bosom of the wood, making that music which is far more symphonious, in a sportsman's ears, than would be the divine warble of Madame Catalina herself, and were evidently drawing rapidly near. Gildon was in breathless expectation. The pulsations of his heart were so strong he thought he could almost hear it beat. He listens—he hears a rustling sound in the woods in a rather different direction from the cry of the hounds; he turns his head and sees a large and beautiful buck, with his branching antlers thrown back, and his nose in the air, make lopes and bounds through the wood, more as if in sport than to avoid pursuit. After one moment of surprise, and another of admiration at the beauty of the animal and the grace of its movements, he recollected his lesson and made a noise. But it was too late; for the deer, with his usual quickness of sight, had discovered him on his first movements, and diverging a little on one side, had darted like an arrow in the direction most likely to avoid both his new enemy and his first pursuers. He fired, nevertheless, though the deer was two hundred yards past him, and had then reached the river. The discharge of the piece was a signal to the hunters to run to the river side, by which time the buck was nearly on the opposite bank. Two rifles were however discharged, one of which seemed to check the animal's progress as he ascended the bank of the river. Whittle, who, as well as Moles, had been keeping a sharp look-out, as soon as he heard the hounds, and was some distance above Gildon, took him in the flank, as he was ascending the hill, and Moles, who was nearer, endeavouring to get before him, fired nearly at the same time, and evidently crippled him. The animal suddenly wheeled about, and, by one or two almost supernatural bounds, again took to the river, and endeavoured to follow its downward current. By this time the hounds had reached the river into which they all, except two or three young yelping curs, readily plunged, when old M'Culloch, whose cries could be heard above that of all others, bawled first to the hunters and then to the hounds. Those who were at the lowest stand levelled the rifle which had done so much execution in its time, and lodged a ball in his neck just as old Thunder, as if to make amends for being out of the way in the morning, seized him by the haunch—though the deer had received his death wound, he did not yet surrender. By a sudden effort he disengaged himself from old Thunder's fangs, posting himself in a shallow part of the river, and presenting his bristling front to the old hound, kept him awhile at bay until a reinforcement came up. The hunters then plunged into the river from both banks, until the buck, overpowered by fatigue, loss of blood, and superior numbers, ceased to make resistance, and was seized by three or four hounds just as the hunters came up in time to prevent them from tearing him to pieces.

Such was a sketch of the scene as it presented itself to Gildon. But ten times the space would not be sufficient to give in full the various details which each actor reported of what had been done, or seen, or heard. The qualities and activity of the several hounds—the minutest movements of the deer; the particulars of each shot as to time, place, and effect, were narrated, commented upon, and repeated, until they returned to M'Culloch's, and the operations of the breakfast-table suspended the talking faculty by employing that of eating. Nor did they, in the midst of their joyous exultations, forget to spare Gildon, whose awkward *debut* was the subject of unceasing raillery. He was much mortified that he could take no share in the glory of the day, but was at length consoled to learn how common a thing it was to fail in the first essay of deer-hunting; and several others of the company became in turn the theme of banter on their blunders, or want of self-possession on some former occasion.

Another julep was thought to be a proper preparative for breakfast, and they sat down with keen appetites and gladsome faces to the plentiful and hospitable board of one who, though not without his share of perplexities, was at that moment the happiest man in christendom. Mrs. M'Culloch was a silent, placid, meek-hearted woman, who accommodated herself in all things to her husband's humour; and while that love of sport and jollity which had made such inroads on his estate, were not thwarted by her, a course of industry, frugality, and thrift, if such had been his nature, would have met with equal countenance from her, and a support more congenial to her character. She was one of those happy and gentle natures which suffer themselves to be moulded by the circumstances in which they are placed, and which, though not exactly fitted for the firm and rugged duties of the warrior, or statesman, or legislator, are admirable in the character of a companion or wife.

It was often the humour of her facetious spouse, to affect to be under her government, and to say that for all her seeming mildness and gentleness, the little woman had a high spirit, which she more effectually refuted by her silence and contented smile, on a face that was still pleasing, than she could have done by any direct contradiction. When he would descend to particulars, and give some distorted and extravagant account of how she had scolded the servants, quarrelled with her weaver, and even hated him, he would sometimes succeed in calling up a slight emotion of displeasure, and a flush into her cheek; and even in provoking her to-day, " Mr. M'Culloch I am surprised at you—what will people think of me?" On which, exulting at his success, he would exclaim, ah, the little woman's mettle is up—I see it rising—I must stand clear now—which ungenerous teazing commonly excited (such are our vicious tastes,) the diversion of the by-standers rather than their pity or indignation. But though fond of thus wantonly plaguing his patient unoffending wife, he did it without any real malignity of disposition, and was known to be most truly and devotedly attached to her. Sandy was a rough, good natured, two-fisted youth of eighteen; an unbroke, untrimmed, uncurried colt; blest with a good appetite, robust, healthy, an easy temper, and a good conscience; his two next children were daughters at boarding-school, and his four youngest were three boys and a girl. All healthy, bluff, and good-natured, none of them evincing sprightliness of mind even in a parent's eye, except the youngest boy, on whom his father's hopes were fixed, who was intended by him for the bar, and was called Hamilton.

Gildon, on casting one of his inquisitive glances around, saw at once evidences of the liberal thoughtless disposition, as well as the bad management of his host, and the easy good nature of his wife. The house was a framed one, and had once been painted; but every vestige of this ornament and defence was nearly effaced. Most of the windows required glazing; in some, wooden panes had been put, in others, a pillow or great coat, or whatever else was at hand, had been used by the servants to keep out the cold or the rain. The yard and garden were surrounded by pales, many of which had fallen off, and whole pannels were leaning on this side or that, and in some instances would have fallen but for the support of some prop or forked stick. The gate was a pretty good one, (being comparatively new,) except that the upper hinge, having been broke, it required so much time and trouble to open and shut it, that the most active members of the family commonly got over the fence. Most of the chairs had something wanting; either the back had been broken, or some of the legs were loose, or the seat was split across. A new carpet, lately purchased at Attick's, covered the floor, and some tolerable prints in gilt frames hung around the room. Their occasional display of luxury, together with the abundance with which their table was supplied, with a fare rather substantially good than remarkably nice, removed the impression of poverty, which the exterior of the house was calculated to convey; but left that of bad management in all its original force. Mr. M'Culloch was constantly deluding himself with the hope of making better crops, as the casualty which had disappointed him this year was not likely to recur the next. But to his vexation and surprise, some new disaster was ever befalling him, no wise inferior to those which had preceded it. Finding his situation growing worse and worse, and that his land and slaves were gradually slipping from him, in casting his eye around for future relief, he looked to the west, (the *el Dorado* of all bad managers,) as the place of his final retreat, and in the full confidence that he should, at last, find a comfortable asylum there, he continued on, the same reckless course of expense and waste as ever. By thus constantly recurring to the probability of removing to the western country, the idea had become familiar to the whole family, though at first very repugnant to Mrs. M'Culloch and her daughters, and was considered, like death, as an event which was certainly to take place, though nobody knew when.

"You see us, Mr. Gildon," said the old man, a little out of order, "but if the Hessian fly will let me alone another year, I mean to furbish up, and will stick to the old hunting ground a little longer. Yes, if the cursed fly will keep away for a few years, and Edward, your friends, the French, continue to keep them busy in Europe, I hope to kill as fine a buck in your mountain, twenty years hence, as that we have just killed. I sometimes talk of going to Kentucky, but the old woman protests she won't stir a foot; and I am sure, my boy, I shall never meet with a place that I shall like as well as these mountains—nor friends," he added, with evident emotion, "I shall love as much as those I am used to, though (endeavouring to disguise his feelings,) some of them *are* such vile democrats."

The painful ideas which these remarks were calculated to raise, produced seriousness and silence in the company, when his second son came running in and told him Mr. Slop's hogs were in the corn-field. "Set the dogs after them, Wash—I wish old Slop, his hogs, and distillery, were all at the devil together."

"I see, sir, you have one bad neighbour then," said Gildon.

"Bad, yes d———n him—he buys my grain of my negroes—then corrupts them with his whiskey—is trying to cheat me out of a piece of my best land, and, to crown all, he wants to fatten his hogs in my corn-field. I verily believe he has a slip-gap in my fence." The dogs were promptly let loose by his son Washington, and they as promptly drove out the hogs, wounding some and killing others; for which the Dutchman afterwards sued and recovered damages, having proved that the fence was not a sufficient one according to law, and that he had even offered to assist M'Culloch's overseer in repairing its breaches.

CHAPTER X.

AFTER the little interlude of hog-hunting was over, Mr. M'Culloch, whose passion for sport was now excited to the utmost, proposed they should take a turn round the corn-field with their rifles, and see who could in an hour kill the greatest number of squirrels for a dozen of porter, of which article he had just got up some very good. Edward and Gildon excused themselves, as being desirous of receiving some letters they expected, they would ride to the post-office at Battle-Town, before dinner. Though the bet was declined, old Mr. M'Culloch, Sandy Whittle, and Moses accepted the other part of the old man's proposal, to make war on the little animals which threatened such destruction, this year, to the growing crop. On their way, Edward expressed his regret at the improvident course his old Scotch-Irish friend was pursuing, and his fears that ere long his debts would so accumulate, that he would be entirely broken up; and that his mother, as well as others, would lose a most kind-hearted neighbour, as well as merry, facetious acquaintance. "But to say the truth," he added, "I don't know we shall not choose to go with him, for it is painful and difficult to descend from the style of expense and mode of living which one has been accustomed to, and that seems now to be almost inevitable."

Gildon, who was one of those mixed and imperfect characters, which though seldom found in novels, are very commonly met in real life, had had his mind in a constant state of oscillation and doubt, ever since the avowal of his passion. When in the presence of Louisa, her beauty and sweetness, and artless affection, made him forget the cold dictates of prudence and ambition, and think only of the happiness of calling such a lovely creature his own ; and he moreover thought that he had gone too far to recede. But when out of the immediate influence of her beauty, selfish and worldly considerations acquired the ascendancy over him, and he sometimes even called in the assistance of love to plead their cause; for he thought to himself—if my father was so decidedly hostile to my marrying Miss De Peyster, merely because she was without fortune, he will not be less opposed to my union with this young lady, especially as his cautious temper will apprehend that I shall be involved in the embarrassments of the family ; and, indeed, how could I forbear to assist Edward, in his difficulties, when he became my brother-in-law, and in so doing, I should involve myself in ruin without materially benefiting him. And again, ought I to wish to marry a woman who has been accustomed to every indulgence and luxury the country affords, and consign her to poverty? If I were rich indeed, and independent, I should be happy to make her my wife, without a penny; but circumstanced as I am, I ought to stifle my rash and ill-placed affection, or, at any rate, before I give it further indulgence, wait and see if I can provide for her, in a way suitable to her condition. Prudence, duty, honour, and even love itself recommends this course, and allows of no other. Such had been the character of his reflections the evening before, and such his determination. The subject then of Edward's remarks was somewhat awkward and embarrassing to Gildon, as in his late interview with Louisa, he had encouraged the idea, (and he was himself deluded by what he really wished at the time,) that his father would not long withhold his consent, and he did not doubt that Edward had been made acquainted with these his expectations—knowing, therefore, Edward's frank and honourable character, he dreaded entangling himself in any course of disingenuousness or duplicity. He contented himself, however, with expressing his hopes that Edward's affairs were not so irretrievable as he seemed to apprehend, and asked him if he had received any late information on the subject. Edward told him, that in the morning he had quitted his own stand and gone to Mr. M'Culloch's, before the deer was started, and he had then learnt from his neighbour that old Hatchett had been invited to purchase the claim that was litigated, and that he had been shown the opinions of two of the ablest counsel of the Richmond bar, that the claimants must eventually succeed, on the strength of which the usurer was disposed to become the purchaser; and he, accordingly, advised my mother and myself to make proposals of compromise to the creditor, as we might thereby save something handsome;—and we are waiting for the advice of Mr. Trueheart, my father's trusty counsel, who will call at Beechwood on Sunday evening, on his way to August court, before we determine on the course we shall pursue. Gildon, who had at first intended to confer with Edward, unreservedly, on the subject of his own prospects and views, now considered he had better put off the eclaircissement until he learnt the result of the advice which Edward expected, and until he himself heard from his friends, in New-York, replied, " And I too am expecting letters from home, on a most important subject, on which I wish to communicate with you."

" I presume I am aware of the subject," replied Edward ; " and as things are likely to turn out, I must say, Gildon, that I think it unlucky, and I sincerely regret, for your sake, that you ever thought of linking your fortune with our ill-fated house; but I shall insist that you abandon all idea of such a union, except with your father's entire approbation."

Gildon was not displeased at this advice; but, merely remarked, that "he had flattered himself his father would not obstinately oppose his wishes, without signifying what would be his ulterior course in case he did." He then inquired of Edward, in a delicate way, "What he meant to do in his own love affair?" who at once declared, with emphasis and emotion, "that he was more and more confirmed in the course he had prescribed to himself, when they last conversed on the subject; that he would render himself worthy of Matilda, not only in her eyes, but in the eyes of her relations, and of the whole world, or he would surrender his pretensions. And such being my fixed determination," said he, "I am not sure that I act rightly, in putting myself in the way of seeing her often; for though it may not swerve me from my purpose, it will naturally increase the difficulty of my own struggle—and perhaps—but as soon as I have rendered all the assistance in my power to my mother, towards settling my father's perplexed affairs, I shall set out for Williamsburgh, as I told you, and not return but with a license in my pocket."

Gildon felt that the manly course of his friend was the one that he ought to pursue, and he secretly extolled the extraordinary self-denial he exhibited, especially when it had the additional motive of gratifying and assisting a parent;—but what he so much admired, he was not able to imitate, and he could neither forego the delight of Louisa's society, nor frankly avow his weakness, nor boldly, at all hazards, pursue the course of honourable inclination; but acted upon, first by one impulse, and then by another, and able to adopt no plan that he approved, he suffered greater anxiety, at times, than Edward, whose passion was far stronger and deeper, but who was supported in his purpose by self-approbation.

"You act like a hero, Edward," said Gildon, "and I trust your reward will be in proportion to your sacrifice."

As they entered Battle-Town, a gentleman of a middle age, on a handsome horse, having a valise behind him, who proved to be Dr. Manifee, overtook them, and after an interchange of civilities and an introduction to Gildon, he informed them that "he had seen Jaque that morning, and that he was able to walk with a crutch, and might walk without one in a week; but he still threatened the vengeance of the law on the tam'd Yankee, for so he called Gildon."

This village contained about a dozen houses, built irregularly on each side of a street, which was a continuation of the main road leading from Inisken's Gap to Winchester; and though denominated Berryville, by act of assembly, the people perseveringly call it by its old name of Battle-Town, which is derived from the circumstance of its being the scene of many a fierce rencontre between different parties of wagoners, often made this a place of rendezvous; in which violent conflicts old General Morgan, then a mere wag oner, used to distinguish himself, andafford a presage of the same impetuous valour which he afterward displayed in the war of the revolution. They reached the Post-office soon after the mail had arrived, and already five or six of the neighbouring gentlemen, as many servants, and most of the inhabitants of the village had assembled, in the store or shop in which it was kept, for the purpose of hearing the news, foreign and domestic. The Philadelphia papers were most in request, some taking Fenno's Gazette, and a few the Aurora. Without quitting the store, each one eagerly seized a newspaper, wet as it was, and began to read, occasionally giving to the company such paragraphs as happened to favour his own party. The replies which these would produce, would sometimes give rise to an argument, which commonly extended itself to others of the company. Some, however, took no part in the discussion, either feeling a contempt for their adversaries, or believing from past experience such disputations were more likely to confirm the parties in their respective opinions than to change them.

The number of letters was then much smaller than at present; that of the newspapers something larger. There was little of domestic politics, at that season, except some scurrilous abuse of the great political parties, as either could bestow on the other, or on its leading politicians. Moreau and the Arch Duke Charles were then fiercely contending for victory; but the price of of wheat was, with all the zeal in the cause of liberty and France, first looked to. After those who were before them, had been waited on, Edward inquired for letters for Gildon and himself. He received several, as usual, most of which either contained accounts, or related to claims on his father's estate, and two only were from debtors, one from a merchant, who yet owed for a quantity of flour, purchased some time before, informing him that the writer had been unfortunate in business, and was not able to pay his creditors, which he greatly lamented; but such being his desperate situation, it was unnecessary to bring suit against him. The other was from an honest boot-maker, who wrote that Col. Groyson had, a little before his death, ordered a pair of boots, for which he had paid at the time; that supposing, after the Colonel's death they would not be wanted, he had disposed of them, and he then returned the money, not having certainly known, until he saw Edward's late advertisement, who was his representative.

All his other letters, to those who appeared to

be debtors, on his father's books, in which he had urged that there was pressing occasion for the funds belonging to the estate, remained unanswered. Two letters were handed to Gildon, one from his father, expressing his surprise at his thinking of a matrimonial connexion with a woman without fortune, brought up in habits of idleness and luxury, and accustomed to be waited on by slaves; a circumstance he said, "by-the-by, very little favourable either to a wife's obedience or good temper—that he was disposed to share with him what he had, which, with prudence, might give him a good start, but which would not be sufficient to support a high-bred Virginia dame in her southern notions of style. But if he was determined to throw himself away, then he must understand that what little he had, he had made by industry and strict economy, and he could not see it fooled away in fine horses and fine clothes;—that, in short, if he married, he must not count upon any aid from him; for, if his wife should turn out to be rich, as he seemed to hope, he would not require it; and if poor, she would have no right to expect it, so that he had better give up the silly notion at once, and return to his own state, where he would find women that would please him quite as well, and suit him a great deal better." The other letter was from Livingston, his confidential friend, who told him that his father was seriously displeased; but his letter had better speak for itself—it was as follows:

"*My dear James,*

"You are fated, it seems, to be ever entangled in the snares of beauty. Scarcely are you extricated from one danger of this character before you are involved in another. In flying a Charybdis in New-York, you run upon a Scylla in Virginia. Who could have thought, that in those wild and rugged mountains, you were to meet with a person of such perfection as you describe? I think, however, that some part of your extravagant encomiums is to be ascribed to the absence of rival attractions ; and you see elegance and grace in this little wood-nymph, in her own native wilderness, which you would be scarely able to discern in Broadway or Wall-street. But a truce to badinage. Your father was out of all patience at this truant humour of yours, and I believe would have given you up in despair when he first got your letter, but for the fast hold you have on his heart, by being his only son. His objection to Miss G——n is yet greater than it was to Miss D——r, as he is prejudiced against her for being a Virginian, in addition to her being without fortune, though I think, but for those losses and debts you speak of, the first objection might have been overcome. But this is not all; six months have made great changes in the commercial world here, and with no one more than with Mr. W——m D——r. His claim against the Marine Insurance, which compelled him to stop payment, has, contrary to the general expectation, been decided in his favour, and he has been able to begin business again with a respectable capital. Commerce was never so profitable as at present; and should his mercantile skill and experience be rewarded with success, would it not be better for you to forget this romantic attachment, and return to your first love, or rather, I may say, to your fourth or fifth, all will go on smoothly. Emily, I've good reason to believe, with all that disposition to coquetry which fine women are so apt to possess, is still attached to you, and I cannot but think that in manners, accomplishments, and understanding, she must be very superior to this little Virginia rustic, and more fitted to shine as Mrs. Gildon in the fashionable circles of the city. My advice to you therefore is, to extricate yourself from this unfortunate connexion, as I understand you it is yet in your power to do with honour, and seek safety in flight, if you can save yourself in no other way. Sharpe is again seeking to play the agreeable; but a word of encouragement from you would no doubt put an end to his hopes, or, at any rate, would make her defer them. Your father's friends amuse themselves greatly at his expense, and say that you have fairly jumped out of the frying-pan into the fire ; and that if you were now sent into exile to the farthest west, the first letter from you would bring accounts of your sighing at the feet of some 'lovely and interesting dame.' Excuse the freedom of this letter, and believe that it proceeds from the interest taken in your welfare by your friend,

John A. Livingston."

Gildon read these letters with less of surprise than chagrin. It seemed to him as if his attachment to Louisa was stronger now that he knew it was disapproved by his father, whose cool irony displeased him more than Livingston's lively *persiflage*. There was, indeed, in the letter of his friend, more than one passage which gave him pleasure, and after a while awakened new and flattering trains of thought. It gratified his vanity to hear that the gay, the elegant, the volatile Emily, still discovered a preference for him; and the charms which had once fascinated him, did not lose in his recollection of them by the great probability that they would soon beam with the additional lustre of fortune, like a diamond, which shines all the brighter for being tastefully set.

After the first feeling of disappointment, and the value that one is apt to set on every good in proportion as it is more out of our reach, he was again thrown back from his generous and romantic resolutions, and brought down from his air-built castle to be a mere son of earth. But yet he had not the ingenuousness, or the firmness to disclose the true state of things to the open-hearted, unsuspecting Edward, who, perceiving the mortification of his first looks, and the perplexity of those which succeeded, observed that "he hoped he had received no unwelcome intelligence."

"It is very far from being such as I expected," said Gildon. "My father has greater unwillingness to my marrying than I had anticipated, and," hesitating, "seems particularly unwilling that I should marry in a southern state. I believe I have mentioned to you some of his prejudices on this subject; and a friend writes me to the same effect. But I yet flatter myself, his objections will yield to my firmness. if not to my arguments."

"Indeed, Gildon, I think you had better give up the thoughts of a connexion which is so much disliked by your friends, and which may prove a source of future misfortune and regret. My sister, I believe, is not insensible to your merits, but she has, with warm feelings, great good sense, and unbounded generosity ; and she conld now, in the present stage of your acquaintance, consent to surrender you up for your own benefit, and make a sacrifice, to which, by-and-by, she may not be equal. Leave a family which too much appreciates your worth, and is too sensible of the distinction you bestow on it, to consent to do you an injury. Leave us to descend in silence from that state of prosperity and happiness in which you once saw us, and do not embitter our feelings by the consciousness that we have involved one of our best friends in our misfortunes."

Gildon, whose instability of purpose was the

sport of every new gale, began to yield to his admiration of Edward's disinterestedness, and to the unseen operation of love, said: " How happens it, Grayson, that you give me advice which you do not take yourself? You are not willing to surrender Matilda; but are merely willing to postpone the gratification of your wishes until present impediments are removed—not to give them up altogether—allow me then, my friend, to do the same."

" I have not been unmindful of the similarity of our situations," replied Edward; " but the inconsistency of which you speak is rather apparent than real. I wish my sister to take the same course that I have prescribed to myself; and I ask you as a friend, to aid in carrying it into effect. It is true, I propose to you to break off the connexion altogether; but female delicacy and dignity require that this should be done ; though should you hereafter be able to renew your addresses, with the consent of your father, and Louisa should be still disengaged, you cannot doubt that you would be received with the same cordial welcome as ever. Besides, the ties which bind you together, are but as of yesterday, while those which link me with Matilda, have grown with our growth and strengthened with our strength. They have been cherished and encouraged by our families, and can be now rent asunder only with those that bind us to life."

Though Edward was then arguing in support of a

proposition which favoured Gildon's secret wishes, and which he had a few minutes before almost resolved to pursue; yet he felt more repugnance to it, when it was so strongly pressed; and still more to let his real inclination be seen. He told Edward that he underrated the force of his attachment to Louisa; that when the heart was exclusively filled with one adored object, it could gain no accession of strength from time; and that it was no more practicable or proper for him to abandon or forget his sister, than it was for Edward to renounce Matilda; and while he was willing to release Louisa from the obligation of an engagement, he must be allowed to continue his entire devotion to her, and wait in the hope that the present difficulties to their union would not prove insurmountable. He added, that if his father should remain obdurate, he also had his prospects and chances of making himself independent, in which case he should hope Louisa's scruples might be removed.

"I cannot answer for my sister," said Edward; " but if she were to take my advice, she would never become a member of your family, or any other, against the consent of the heads of it. And this makes the difference in our situations. I have hopes of one day being able to remove the objections of Matilda's family, but you have no prospect of removing the repugnance of yours; as Louisa's lot is, I fear, lasting and hopeless poverty. But on this subject, Gildon, my sister must judge for herself; and if you do not overrate the strength and constancy of your attachment; if your purpose is fixed, I cannot further object to it. I felt myself in duty bound, however, to advise you otherwise."

When they reached the house of their Scotch-Irish friend, they found him with his coat off in a little porch on the north side of the house, with a string of seven or eight squirrels hanging over the rail of the porch. He had been returned some time, overcome by the intense heat of the day, and was then regaling himself with a drink of cool toddy, in company with Mr. Buckley and Mr. Browne.

"What news, young gentlemen? Come, open your budgets," said he; "but first wet your whistles with the toddy. Any new tidings from your friends the French? How is wheat in Alexandria?"

Edward threw down a bundle of newspapers, saying, "I'll thus answer all your questions at once. I believe, however, there is nothing material on any of the subjects of your inquiry." Each one then took a favourite newspaper and began eagerly to read.

"Why, what a lying unprincipled scoundrel is this Bache," exclaimed M'Culloch; "he is here endeavouring to prove that General Washington is a public defaulter."

"While I appreciate Mr. Bache's services very highly," said Edward "I really wish they would let the old General remain in peace and quiet the remnant of his days. If they were to succeed in establishing that he had forfeited his integrity after his long course of public service, the people of the United States would feel like the husband who had discovered the infidelity of a beloved wife."

"And in encouraging these slanders," said Mr. Browne, "we act about as wisely as a husband would, who should listen to false accusations against his wife; for though they may not have the effect of corrupting her purity, they are very likely to sour her temper and alienate her affections, and he is sure to share in her disgrace. This scurrilous attack, in my opinion, had some effect in making him form the resolution from which no persuasions of his friends have been able to shake him, of retiring from public life at the end of his present term of service. Mr. Lear, his private secretary, dined with me the other day, and told me that the old gentleman had been for some time past engaged in preparing a farewell address to the people of the United States, which is to appear in the course of this year, and which, he says, will be greatly admired both for its political wisdom, and its good taste in point of composition."

"I wonder who will succeed him?" said Mr. Buckley, taking the cigar he was smoking from his mouth.

"Mr. Jefferson, to be sure," says Edward; "New-York, as well as all the southern states, will support Mr. Jefferson, and nobody else will get a vote in Virginia, I should think."

"I am not so sure of that," said M'Culloch. "We choose here by districts, and not by the legislature, or by what they call a general ticket in some of the states, and I'm thinking that John Adams, the Vice-President, will get several votes in this state. I think we shall choose federal electors here."

The gauntlet was now thrown, and the merits of these candidates and their respective probabilities of success were bandied to and fro, until they were summoned to dinner, when M'Culloch put on his coat, saying, at the same time, that if it were not for fear "of the old woman," he should waive ceremony, and dine without it. They found, among several other dishes, the fruits of the morning's toil, served up in a variety of ways. Gildon could not help remarking that the same air of disorder and waste was exhibited at the dinner-table as was manifested about the rest of the establishment. But the substantial comfort of the entertainment, and yet more, the kindness and hearty welcome of the entertainers, counteracted every unfavourable impression from aught besides. The venison was very good, and was highly relished by the company, though they were compelled to wash it down in toddy, porter, and some indifferent muddy wine, which had been purchased that day at Battle-Town, in compliment to the stranger guests. The adventures of the morning's chase were reiterated, and they naturally introduced other hunting anecdotes, with which M'Culloch, availing himself of the privilege of a host, exclusively entertained them; but the subject being rather dull to all the company, except the narrator, they soon rose from table, and in a short time afterwards, Edward and Gildon took leave of their warm-hearted and jovial entertainer.

Returning early in the evening, they found Mrs. Grayson and her daughter in the porch. The rays of the setting sun decking the western horizon with crimson and gold, glimmered here and there through the thick foliage of the vines which were planted on each side of the porch, and shed a rich and mellow light within their verdant bowers, without imparting any of his heat. Mrs. Grayson welcomed them with her usual serene benignity, and after inquiring into the success of the day, she read the letter which Edward handed to her. Louisa cast an anxious and inquiring look towards Gildon at the mention of letters; and Mrs. Grayson and Edward having retired to confer on those they had received, he drew near to her, and told her he had indeed heard from his father, who, he said, (endeavouring to soften his opposition as much as he could,) was unwilling he should marry until he was settled in business; saying nothing on the subject of Miss De Peyster. According to the promise she had made to her doubting anxious mother before their return, Louisa, with a reluctant and somewhat embarrassed air then said, that she feared he had been precipitate in the step he had taken in making a tender of his affections, and that it might lay the foundation of much future regret—that she begged him to weigh these things, and wait until a more auspicious moment should arrive for the expression of his regard; or—hesitating, and unable to stifle the rising sigh—perhaps as there was no probability that the present obstacles would be soon removed, he had better forget he had ever known her.

Louisa had been dressed that evening with unusual taste and care. Her fine, silky hair, hung in careless profusion over her neck and forehead, and the walk she had taken, together with her mental anxiety, had, by raising a colour in her cheek, given to her face all that it wanted. The seriousness, not to say sadness with which these sentiments were expressed, and the sighs and tears of tenderness which so plainly contradicted them, drove from him all his previous selfish resolutions, and he gave himself up, for the moment, to the enthusiasm of love.

"Oh! Louisa, could your own heart teach you rightly to judge of mine, you would see how impossible it is for me to comply with what you propose. Leave you, my angelic Louisa? No—so long as life and sense remain, I shall cherish my passion as that which makes existence dear; and indulge the hope that it will one day meet its just reward."

"It would be in vain to deny," said the artless Louisa, "that my request is founded more on a sense of duty than on my own wishes. I have not disguised from you my feelings; and, had I wished it, I fear my actions have sometimes expressed them a little too plainly."

"Say not so, my lovely Louisa: your frankness and sincerity of manner is a thousand times more captivating than the most studied graces of art; and of all your attractions this has ever pleased me most.—Do not, then, try to divest yourself of any portion of this amiable simplicity;—this absence of all artifice and dissimulation—this pledge of innocence and purity; and be assured you can never appear so lovely, or make me so happy, as when you favour me with expressions of esteem and regard."

"But, my friend," said she, "ought I not to be more reserved while matters remain thus uncertain?"

"Why so, my beloved Louisa? My heart is as wholly and truly yours as it can ever be; and you, who are the soul of generosity and ingenuousness, can you refuse to afford such affection as mine some portion of the reward it covets—something to solace and support it when compelled to taste the bitterness of hope deferred?"

"I cannot reason with you," said Louisa, half playfully, "but I have told you enough already; and if—you must guess the rest—until—but mamma expects me in the porch."

"O do not leave me yet, Louisa. If you will not favour me with expressions of kindness, do not treat me thus distantly—cruelly I may say."

"Ah, Mr. Gildon, we know not what is best for us. I am guided by the counsels of the best and kindest of mothers, and she has prescribed my course."

"You have indeed an affectionate mother; but parents always apprehend the worst. Your mother's imagination takes a tinge from her own domestic misfortunes; and she magnifies the difficulties that oppose our union. She, however, knows me not. Could she appreciate the strength and purity of my affection, she would not require of you to withhold from me the happiness of your society, and treat me with the distance of a stranger, instead of the confidence of a lover or even of a friend. I trust, Louisa," taking her hand, "you know me better; and I expect more justice from you. Do not refuse me.—Sit here with me, or in the parlour as you were wont to do, when, thoughtless and happy, you were kindling in my bosom the passion which it depends upon you to make a blessing or a curse."

"If mamma approves it, I will grant your request.—Do not insist further."

"Oh, Louisa, how coldly prudent you are! I deceived myself—my too flattering hopes deceived me. You would never bring yourself to refuse me a boon so easily granted, so reasonable in itself, if I had been able to inspire you with one spark of that affection which I feel."

"Believe me," she said, "you do me injustice. But I have passed my word to my mother, and you would not have me forfeit it?"

"Well, I acquiesce; but I shall not despair of convincing you of your error."

The rest of the evening passed in general conversation, somewhat restrained on the part of Mrs. Grayson and Edward, from a knowledge of the continued opposition of Gildon's father; and, on the part of the lovers, because all other society appears dull except that which they have with one another; and even that, when had in the company of third persons, compared with the perfect interchange of thoughts and feelings, and overflowings of the soul which take place when left entirely to themselves.

They had not been many minutes in the parlour before Primus came in, and told Edward there were two gentlemen at the gate. "I hope," said he, "one of them is Mr. Trueheart."—And so it proved. The other, a Mr. Hardy, was also a gentleman of the bar, going from the county of Rockingham, with Trueheart, to Winchester, to attend the quarterly court for the county. Gildon, who had formed his ideas of an eminent lawyer from what he had seen in the city of New-York, was surprised to see two middle-aged men, clad in gray homespun coats, some light summer wear for waistcoats and breeches, and long white-top boots, each with a pair of leather saddlebags on his arm, resembling those carried by the deputy sheriff.

They both were well acquainted with the family, and were very cordially greeted; indeed, Trueheart had been left one of Col. Grayson's executors, and although he had not qualified, he seemed to feel the same interest, and to render almost as much service, as if he had. He was a stout, square-built man, of a healthy complexion, and a countenance naturally good natured, but marked with traces of thought, and, occasionally, of severity. The other was a small man, about forty, of a lively, acute, and rather satirical cast of face; he was very talkative, and his whole air and manner indicated great confidence in himself, which amounted often to an oppressive self-sufficiency. In answer to Gildon's inquiries, Edward told him they both belonged to the republican party; were men of high standing in their profession, as well for integrity as talents; but the elder was still more distinguished for his rare generosity and benevolence.

They had been in the habit of calling here on the evening before the quarterly courts, during Col.

Grayson's lifetime, but these visits had been partially discontinued since his death. The table was now ordered to be set, and a light supper prepared, suitable at once to the season, and to those who were fatigued with travelling. Mr. Trueheart was disposed to converse with the young gentleman on the miscellaneous subjects of literature, politics, and the present state of William and Mary College, which had been his own *alma mater*. But Hardy, who was a man of less general information, though a more able advocate, would frequently speak of some litigated case in court, which had recently occurred, or which they expected to meet with, and commented on it in a tone of dogmatism, and somewhat of defiance, and seemed at all times cocked and primed for argument, not always indeed from the hope of obtaining a triumph, or with a view of displaying his learning, nor yet from a parade of business, (motives which had once operated on him with great force, but had now lost much of their influence,) but by the mere dint of habit which these motives had greatly contributed to form. But, finding all his efforts at discussion parried by Trueheart, who, though " cunning in fence" himself, good-naturedly endeavoured to direct the stream of conversation into that channel in which they all might bear a part. Hardy then addressed himself to Gildon, and inquired of the relative standing and probable profits of business of Burr, Harrison, and others, eminent lawyers in

New-York, of whom he had heard. Gildon, whose thoughts were otherwise occupied, and who wished to continue his conversation with Louisa, made as brief answers as politeness would permit. But, being then pressed to give an account of the organization of their courts, with their respective powers and jurisdictions, a subject with which he had but a limited acquaintance, and in which he felt no interest, he became impatient, and by way of ridding himself of his persevering querist, began to inquire, in his turn, of the system of jurisprudence in Virginia, in the hope of starting some game which his tormentor, and the rest of the company, might pursue, and leave him to that most delightful of all employments to a young man, of conversing with the woman that he loves.

Hardy readily took the bait, and at once gave a rapid detail of the whole system of Virginia jurisprudence, beginning with the county courts, and ending with the court of appeals. He proceeded then to speak of the mode of appointing the county-court magistrates, which he vehemently deprecated as an odious feature of aristocracy.

At this word Trueheart and Edward pricked up their ears, and the former, who approved what Hardy so denounced, and had frequently argued the matter before with him, not liking that a stranger should be prejudiced against the constitution of Virginia, and fearing lest a young man of Edward's promise should receive such a wrong bias, undertook the defence of this part of the institutions of his country, and a dialogue, or rather argument ensued, in which Gildon and Edward took little part, not only because they were less competent to discuss its merits, but because the vehement earnestness, and ready fluency of the disputants, allowed of no interval of time for them to put in a word. But, for the convenience of my fair readers, for I expect these pages to be honoured with their perusal, from the Atlantic to the Pacific, I shall insert it in a chapter by itself, to be passed over by the lovely creatures, hating, as they do, what is serious and dull, but to be read with some interest by those minds which, at once patient and inquisitive, are not averse to dry speculations,

CHAPTER XI.

"Yes, sir," says Hardy, addressing himself to Gildon, until finding his attentions engrossed by a very different object, he turned to his old adversary, and him whom he wished to make a proselyte, "yes, gentlemen, I am sorry to be compelled to use so harsh a term in speaking of the constitution of the old dominion, which, in the main, I am very proud of, and very highly approve; but I repeat it, the justices of our county courts constitute a sheer aristocracy, and for aught I know, the only one in these United States."

"I little expected," said Edward, "such a charge against the constitution of Virginia. I had thought——"

"I will explain," interrupted Hardy; "you must, kind sir," again making an effort to engage Gildon's attention. "These courts are composed of the magistrates or justices of the peace of the county, consisting commonly of from twenty to fifty, according to the size of the county. Vacancies are filled by the Governor and Council, on the recommendation of their own body; and thus they have the means of perpetuating themselves for ever, independent of the people, or of any of the representatives of the people."

"I believe," said Edward, "that the Governor and Council, whose offices are elective, have exclusively the power of making the appointments, and of course they have that of rejecting the recommendations."

"That is true, but this has become a matter of mere form; magistrates are wanted in a county to try little neighbourhood disputes, under forty shillings, that is, sir," again turning to Gildon, "six dollars and two thirds of a dollar; to take depositions and affidavits, recognisances, and that sort of out of door business; and although the persons recommended may not be such as the people, or any other unbiassed electors would choose, yet indifferent magistrates are preferred to no magistrates; and public opinion, on which all our other functionaries more or less depends, insists on an appointment, which must accordingly be made. Now the natural consequence of giving to these magistrates the right to perpetuate themselves is, that the office is apt to be kept always in the same families—so that three or four parties, or juntos, will engross the whole political power with which they are invested, (and a formidable array it is,) as I shall show you by-and-by. Sometimes two of these families more numerous, or ambitious, or intriguing than the rest, fall out in a squabble for some office of honour or emolument, or perchance from mere emulation and jealousy of influence, become opposed to each other, and form two rival parties under which all the others enlist, and thus disturb the peace of the county, and sully the pure stream of justice, by their intrigues and their feuds. This is more especially the case in the smaller counties—but, in the larger ones, there are commonly too many of these petty nobles, and their power is too much divided to be thus melted down into two divisions; and every family has a weight and influence, in proportion to its numbers and talent for intrigue, which numbers it is constantly trying to augment. Occasionally, some one family has obtained such an ascendency that it controls the county, without a rival, and without resistance. But the worst consequence of this mode of appointment is, that it lays the foundation of a future aristocracy. A few families, accustomed to monopolize all the civil honours of the county, will gradually begin to think themselves better than the rest of their fellow-citizens. The people, too, under the like influence of habit, will be brought, in time, to acknowledge their superiority; and when once this feeling of inferiority becomes engrafted on public opinion, the chief support of our political equality is removed, and the laws themselves, which take their form and colour from the sentiments of the people, may be moulded to confer superior *privileges* on a particular class, in conformity with that superiority of *rank* which public opinion had already bestowed. Power will invariably command flattery and respect: make the power permanent, and limit it to one or a few, and you virtually prepare men's minds for a monarchy or oligarchy."

"But," said Edward, "I should not suppose that the power possessed by these courts, could ever become formidable. It is the humblest tribunal of that department of civil powers, the judiciary, which is commonly considered the weakest of the three."

"True," said Hardy, "but the powers possessed by our county court are not merely judicial, though these, subordinate as they are, give them great weight in the community. Our magistrates not only unite common law and chancery jurisdiction to an unlimited extent, as to property, but they also have jurisdiction in a numerous class of small cases, from which the superior courts are excluded. The power of deciding small disputes, without appeal, is felt by a much larger number of persons, than the power which has cognizance of more important controversies. Their courts sit every month;—in the character of examining courts, they have a portion of criminal jurisdiction, which also gives them the greater influence, as it is complete as to acquittal, and restricted only in the power of producing conviction. They can absolve the worst offender against the laws, from punishment; which is more than any judge can do. But this is not all. They have ample powers relative to the police of the county; they can tax the people *ad libitum* for certain specific objects, such as repairing roads, building bridges, jails, and court-houses. All apprentices, and poor orphans, are under their exclusive cognizance. They recommend to the executive all militia officers, below the rank of brigadier-general, which is virtually the same as appointing them. The sheriff and coroner are always members of their body, recommended by themselves; and thus possessed of these large powers and means of popular influence, they may use them to become members of assembly, or of congress, from which neither the constitution nor laws have excluded them."

" But how does all this operate," said Gildon, who did not wish to seem altogether inattentive to so animated a discussion; " does not this accumulation of powers create a jealousy on the part of the people? and the magistrates who are eligible, I presume, are seldom elected."

" Quite the contrary, sir," said Hardy. " The means of influence which they possess, produce their natural effect. I would observe, sir, that the general results of moral causes are as uniform as those in the physical world, though they may not be calculated with the same precision. At least one half, and sometimes more than half of the members of the legislature, are justices of the peace, that is, members of the county court; and the number would be yet greater, if many of the profession to which I happen to belong, profiting by their extensive personal knowledge of the people, and having superior qualifications, were not often their successful rivals. But this superiority is but temporary; and when our county-court magistrates shall become more intelligent and capable, as they will no doubt be in time, their number in the legislature will be probably still greater than it now is. This change in their qualifications, so naturally to be expected by the general progress of wealth and improvement in our country, and especially in a class that possesses so many means of advancement, will make a fearful addition to their power. At present, there is nothing like general concert or combination, among them—nothing of an *esprit du corps*, I believe the French call it; and if there were, they have not the talents that would be requisite for success, in any conspiracy, against the liberties of the people, or for the extension of their own privileges. But when the union of powers legislative, executive, and judicial, which, by-the-by, our bill of rights pronounces to be incompatible with free government, shall be wielded by abilities capable of turning them to the best account, we shall see the pernicious effects of this strange anomaly in our constitution. Our present safety consists in their ignorance, and that security is every day growing weaker."

Hardy having made a pause here, Trueheart, who had sat patiently watching for an opportunity to reply, occasionally smiling at his companion's vehemence, but sometimes showing emotion when he thought his adversary had used a plausible argument, then took up the subject, and said, " I dare venture to assert, Edward, that you never expected to hear such bitter denunciations against any part of the constitution of Virginia, by a good republican, nor to hear from any quarter whatever, her institutions charged with being of an aristocratical tendency. Virginia, who was one of the first, if not the very first, to aspire to national independence—presented in the revolution which ensued, a firm, undivided phalanx of patriots and whigs—who, with one voice, has hailed the dawn of liberty in France—whose extreme jealousy of power, and attachment to republican principles, has erected the standard of opposition to the most illustrious of her sons—and who is considered as the fountain-head of the spirit of liberty and republicanism ! You must attribute the strictures of my friend Hardy, to an excess of this very spirit by which our state has been so distinguished. But when the subject is looked to, with that sobriety and moderation which are indispensable to just reasoning, I think a great part of his censures will be found unjust, and his fears visionary. It is true, that our county court magistrates have the right of recommending persons to fill up vacancies in their own body, and that they often select those who are related to themselves; but it will commonly be found that they are guided by the public wishes, in the discharge of this duty. Such is that resistless sway of opinion which Hardy speaks of; and if they were to attempt to make any recommendations of persons decidedly incompetent, the executive would be quickly apprized of the fact, and bowing, as (from the mode in which it is constituted) it may be expected to do, before the public will, it would refuse to make the appointment, and the censures of the community, which wanted new magistrates, would fall where it was due, on those, whose character, or corrupt motives, were the real cause of their disappointment. But let us test this part of our system by its effects; let us judge of the tree by its fruits. Are there any more upright, pure, impartial, and independent magistrates on earth than those which compose our county courts? They have large and various powers, but they as rarely abuse them as any class of men we have, to whom power has been confided. Compare their decisions with those of the superior court. In a late conversation with the venerable Pendleton, he told me, that their judgments were more often confirmed, in the court of appeals, than those of the superior courts. No one ever heard of bribery or corruption among them—and we never knew a magistrate to sit on any judicial question, in which any, the remotest connexion, had an interest. Their powers are great, to be sure, but great by their number and variety, rather than in any one subject or department; and in thus cutting it up into small portions, and distributing it among some thirty or forty persons in each county, the power, that, concentred into one hand, would be formidable, is divided into fragments, harmless and insignificant. It is, moreover, almost always subordinate to other powers. If they do wrong, or refuse to do right, they are liable to be controlled by appeal, by mandamus, or prohibition, so that their judicial functions, the most important they possess, are limited to doing good. As instruments of mischief, or oppression, they are utterly feeble and unimportant: it is true, they are often elected to the assembly, but it is by precisely the same means, the same arts of winning popular favour as other citizens; and we know that there is also among the people a lively jealousy against them, on this very account, which counteracts their official influence, and is sometimes sufficient to defeat their election. This salutary check, like every other *vis predicatrix*, will, no doubt, become stronger, as the occasion calls for it; and the people, who have the power, will also have the inclination to correct the evil, as soon as it needs correction.

" As to the office being limited to a few families,

I admit there is some force in that objection—but there is connected with it, an advantage which ought to outweigh a good deal of inconvenience. From the manner in which the county courts are constituted, they are likely to have a uniform and consistent character—and amidst the perpetual fluctuations of party, and changes of popular opinion, it is desirable to have somewhat in our institutions that is permanent and unchanging. The county courts eminently possess this advantage; they are our political sheet-anchor to keep the vessel of state steady, in all the storms of civil faction and sudden veerings of popular caprice. They guard us against the imperceptible operations of time. We have nothing in this state, or in any of the states, so far as I am acquainted, that is

equal to them for giving steadfastness to the character of the nation, or endurance to its policy—and hence you see us the same people now that we were twenty years ago—that our state has been disgraced by no insurrection or internal commotion, and that it never pauses, or waivers, or deviates, in its party politics. For this singular advantage, which republican constitutions are apt to want, I am willing to put up with a good deal of inconvenience, some of which I allow to exist, though my friend here has greatly overrated them."

" I have," replied Hardy, who had long manifested an impatience to speak, " often heard you insist on this advantage, but I neither admit, that it is as great a one as you claim it to be—nor that it is attributable to our county courts. It is true, our state has been remarkable for its internal tranquillity, and its obedience to the laws. But we are a more homogeneous population than most of the other large states—New-York, or Pennsylvania, for example. We are not only the same people now that we were twenty years ago, but we are also the same that we were before the revolution, which was before such large powers were given to the county courts, and even before the courts themselves were organized. We owe our tranquillity, our love of order, our submission to the laws, to the circumstance that our yeomanry are people of property, and commonly of education. As the labouring class are slaves, those who are free must be of a superior character—and the same self-respect, the same regard to the rights of property, or whatever it may be, whether a generous or selfish motive, or both, which kept us quiet, during the trial of Callender for sedition, in 1800, made us loyal supporters of Charles I., against the Parliament, a century and a half before. No sir! annihilate the county courts, and you would still find in us the same sobriety, and, I may say, dignity of character, which has ever distinguished us. But if the agency of these courts were as great as you suppose, I confess I would run a little risk of disorder, and change rather than incur that of a privileged order—I mean no pun, sir, (seeing Gildon smile)—and when our country is constantly undergoing such rapid changes in its physical circumstances, and some of its political, ought not its laws and constitutions to be capable of being moulded to suit them? As we increase in numbers and in wealth, and improve in science and art, our habits and manners change, and our laws and civil institutions ought to change with them. You think, friend Trueheart, too, that the popular jealousy of their great power will prevent any mischief from their eligibility to the legislature, whenever that power becomes dangerous; but you forget that public opinion is itself the creature of our institutions—and in the silent, unseen operation of the county courts on the public mind, consists their greatest danger. The ambition and love of power of individuals is always awake and active—but the jealousy of the people may perchance fall asleep. You speak of their present moderation in the exercise of power, and of their personal respectability. So far as respects their judicial functions, I readily pay them that tribute of praise—but they are kept from intrigue, and in a faithful discharge of their duty, partly by their ignorance of the powers they possess, and partly by their conscious inferiority to those lynx-eyed and jealous sentinels of public freedom, the members of the bar. Let there be a considerable portion of able, well educated men among them, incited to ambition by the possession of all the means of gratifying it, and, see if the course of justice would flow in the same placid and unpolluted stream as at present. If the power of adjudication would not be as much abused then, as the power of appointment often is now. If self-interest, and intrigue, and corruption, would not manifest themselves in all their acts ; and, naturally extending from the public functionaries to the mass of the people, sap the principles of republican government to their foundation—believe me, sir, we can have no safety for the permanence of our democratic principles, until by a change of the constitution, the body politic is rid of this foul excrescence, and restored to a healthy action."

Mr. Trueheart, manifested more of impatience than he had done before, and evidently showed that he was prepared to answer the arguments of his opponent with some hope of success. But Primus entering with his wonted brisk step and bow, that would not have disgraced a preux cavalier, announced that supper was ready, upon which he contented himself with saying, he should take some other opportunity of vindicating the most favourite part of the constitution of Virginia, from the ingenious attacks that had been made upon it.

They then joined the ladies at supper, in which Mr. Hardy attacked the ham, and boiled chicken, and tea, and buckwheat cakes, with even more keenness than he had done the county courts, and Mr. Trueheart proved the goodness of his own constitution as zealously as he had done that of his country. These worthy limbs of the law, having discharged a goodly cargo of argument, and taken in a more substantial one of provisions, set sail for the land of Morpheus, which they soon reached in a pleasant voyage. In other and better language, they retired to rest in one of the best furnished lodging rooms of Frederick, where, at that period, a mattress was a rare luxury.

CHAPTER XII.

The next morning the gentlemen of the long robe, invigorated by their comfortable night's rest, paid their respects to Mrs. Grayson's excellent breakfast, particularly as she, ever kind and considerate, in addition to muffins, and wheat bread rivalling ivory in whiteness, had provided buckwheat cakes and honey, of which her guests were known to be very fond. After they rose from the table, Edward invited Mr. Trueheart, to walk with him and his mother into the office, while Mr. Hardy, Gildon, and Louisa, withdrew to the parlour. When they were all seated in the little office, Edward disclosed the particulars of their situation, and of the offer that had been made to old Hatchett, and asked his friend's advice about the suggestion made by M'Culloch of compromising with the creditor.

This worthy man looked very serious after he heard Edward's statement, and told them that if it were advisable to compromise, a matter he could not positively decide without further consideration, and communicating with the counsel for the estate in Richmond, he feared they would not be able to offer any terms which would probably be accepted. He admitted, however, that there were many uncertainties in the law—that securities were always favoured suitors—and that in all new and doubtful cases, both courts and juries were sure to lean in their favour. He then with the foresight which long experience had given, and that benevolence which he had derived from nature, adverted to the situation of their affairs, in the different events of the compromise, or its failure —and set before them (with a frankness which, however, disagreeable, he thought the occasion called for,) the difficulty of their situation. He was pleased, however, to find that Edward had considered the worst, and that he felt a confidence in his own exertions, which augured future success —and that although Mrs. Grayson had not taken so desperate a view of their affairs, as he was compelled to do, she found consolation and support in the piety she had always cherished.

The worthy counsellor, then, with equal delicacy and feeling, recommended as much economy as was practicable—advised them to call in the debts due to the estate, pay off all claims against it, and to save if possible the house and a small portion of land adjoining. He further intimated that he had a sum of money lying idle which might be used until their intended sales could replace it, and that a small but comfortable farm in the adjoining county of Shenandoah, might afford them an asylum, at a low rent, if the worst consequence he had predicted should ensue. He also promised to take the negotiation of compromise into his own hands, if that course should be determined on, as he had often done business for the creditor, and had some influence with him—and recommended them to have nothing whatever to do with Hatchett, who, rapacious and unfeeling, would show them no favour, and would expect to get their property lower by heightening their distress and precipitating its crisis.

"I trust, my dear sir, that Heaven will reward you for your goodness, as I cannot."

"Say nothing on that score, madam," said he; "I do no more for Colonel Grayson's family, than I am sure he would have done for mine—nay, what do I say? for any little services I may be able to render you, and which you greatly overrate, I have been long paid in advance. I can never forget that when I moved to this part of the country from Hanover, I was an entire stranger, and by the patronage and aid of Colonel Grayson, I soon got into very extensive business, and some of it of a very profitable character, which I could not have possibly got otherwise. He treated me like a brother. His house was always open to me, as well as his counsels, and his purse. I should be then a monster of ingratitude, if I were to act otherwise than I propose. Yet, my dear madam." said he, with a benevolent smile, "if you are too proud to receive favours from one who has received so many from you, you must allow me to discharge a debt —and if my friend Edward can profit by reading in my office, and learning something of the machinery of the profession, after he returns from the law lectures in Williamsburg, he must pass some months with me—unless, as report says, he means to take up his residence a little nearer to you." Edward replied that there was no probability of his being able to find shelter under any roof that would be more acceptable than his—and he would gladly accept his offer.

They all now set out for Winchester, as it had been arranged, that, at this court, Louisa should choose her mother as her guardian. The ladies rode in the carriage, while Edward, Gildon, and the two lawyers attended them on horseback. The distance was about fourteen miles, and the roads being very good at this season of the year, they got to the town by eleven o'clock. Mrs. Grayson drove to the house of Mrs. Stewart, a widow lady of great respectability, who kept a private boarding-house, where Trueheart, and two or three other lawyers put up, when attending the courts.

After some slight change in their dress, the ladies proceeded to the court-house. The yard was thronged with people from the remotest parts of the county—they presented a most motley and grotesque collection. Here an old German with a long black beard, dressed in red and blue striped homespun—not far from him, a stout, hale, rawboned, ruddy farmer, evidently of Scotch-Irish origin—in one corner, an old woman with a little table spread with cakes, and early apples, and a boy or two to replenish her table when required— wagons were also near the court yard, containing different species of rude ware of country manufacture—some with hempen cloth, some with whiskey—and coarse pottery—spinning wheels— slaies for weaving—and other household implements. They were all neat and clean in their dress, which, was of cotton cloth, manufactured by themselves, and striped yellow, red, and blue, in infinite variety, but producing in the *tout ensemble* the character of uniformity.

The mother and daughter, each, rested on Edward's arm, and as he was personally known to many, and to still more by his resemblance to his father, it had been easy for an observing spectator to perceive in the looks and manner of the throng the innate respect which the people have for goodness, and that the homage voluntarily paid to a virtuous man is transferred in some degree to his family. The crowd readily opened, and made way for them to pass, as they walked up the little green before the court. Their voices were unconsciously hushed to a whisper—some took off their hats—a few spoke, but most of them showed their respect and the interest they took in the fallen fortunes of the family, (which were now becoming matters of notoriety) by a silent reverence, and looks of heartfelt sympathy.

Colonel Grayson had been a member of the court, and had deservedly possessed great weight among his brethren. Several of these magistrates approached Mrs. Grayson, while they made their way through the crowd in the court room, to enquire about her health—and invited her to take a seat on the bench until her business could be executed—old Trueheart had sent on a messenger to the Clerk, to prepare the necessary papers, that the ladies might be detained as short a time as possible in such a scene of confusion, and he intended to accompany them into court—but he was so assailed on all sides by his clients, "Mr. Trueheart, I want to have a word with you"— "Colonel, stop a moment"—"well here's Major Trueheart, I'll leave it to him." "Stop Major," "stop Colonel," that though he disregarded many of their applications and put off others—yet, he was laid hold of by some with so much violence, that he was at length separated, not without reluctance and some sallies of anger, which were regarded like the harmless flashes of the Aurora Borealis. He soon followed them on the bench, puffing and blowing, and telling those who were still calling to him not to pester him at that time.

The Clerk who was very nimble with his pen, and who felt the highest respect for the ladies, soon prepared the necessary papers, and Louisa, led into court by her brother, was asked who she chose as her guardian; and as soon as her choice was declared, several members of the court immediately tendered themselves as sureties; but Mrs. Grayson politely declined their offer, as Trueheart and two or three others had been before them.

These ladies attracted the eyes of the whole assembly—their standing in the county, as well as their dress and appearance, being superior to that of the females who usually show themselves in court. The regard they had for Col. Grayson, but more than all, the beauty of Louisa, set-off as it was, by artless innocence and virgin modesty, commanded their reverential homage. Gildon, reading the inquiries of some, and the eager gaze of others, the success of those charms which had at once won his regard, and acknowledged him as their sovereign, felt somewhat of the intoxicating triumph which we may suppose a victorious General experiences, when on a parade, ten thousand voices proclaim his victories and his popularity. Several members of the bar were particularly struck with Louisa's appearance, and one more than the rest kept his eyes fixed on her face, until he seemed lost in reverie. He proved to be one of her discarded lovers. This general homage to her personal appearance, was not altogether lost on the timid Louisa—and the consciousness of being the focus on which so many eyes concentred, heightened her blushes and augmented her beauty.

As she and her mother were retiring from the court, the attorney for the commonwealth told the sheriff to call James Gildon, who, animated by the admiration she had excited, could not forbear the enviable gratification of approaching her, and attending her out of the court-house. The name of him who was ever present to Louisa's mind, being thus proclaimed, in a voice of thunder, in such a crowd, overwhelmed her with confusion. She thought every one knew her sentiments, every eye read what was then passing in her bosom; and the blood might be seen to come and go in her delicate cheek like flashes of distant lightning in a summer evening. She would fain have asked why he was called, but timidity restrained her. Her lover, however, remarked, "Now I am to answer for my misdeeds towards my old friend Jaque; but I must first see you to your lodgings."

Mrs. Grayson was insisting on his return, when old Trueheart, who had been again trying to join them, came bustling out, and told Gildon his presence was wanted immediately in court.

They returned into court, and Trueheart stated that the person whose name had been just called then appeared, in discharge of his recognisance, and was ready to answer the complaint against him. Jaque was seen standing within the bar ; and although he had been walking about his farm for more than a week, without assistance, he was then supported on the crutches which he had, at first, been obliged to use ; and his foot was swathed in wrappings six inches thick.

As Trueheart was an experienced advocate, and had the ear of the court, as the phrase is, and the commonwealth's attorney was a man of but ordinary talents, Jaque had employed lawyer Worricourt as an auxiliary, a veteran renowned for his deep knowledge of the law, for unbounded zeal in behalf of his clients, and the untired perseverance with which he was wont to assail court, jury, and antagonists.

The testimony was now heard, which was that of Jaque himself, who gave an artful and exaggerated statement of his going to market, and just as he got to the brow of the hill, he saw a carriage near the bottom, where the road was wide enough for them to pass each other, and expected they would remain there; but they moved on, as much as to say, a wagon must get out of the road for a fine carriage. "I thought," said he, "I would frighten them a bit ; but up rites a young fellow, the same that's in the par there, wid that horse collar rount his neck, and called me prute, and tamned scoundrel ; when I told him if he tid not get out of the way, he should feel my wagon whip; upon which he struck me, and while I was trying to defend myself, he served me a yankee trick, and canted me off my horse, and town I fell under my wagon-wheel, that run over one foot, as you see here, and might have run over poth, or my pody; and I does want to know if these Yankees are allowed to come here and impose on a wagoner, pecause he has not a fine coat on his pack."

Trueheart then called on Edward, who was not present at the beginning of the fray, but who, on coming up, had heard the matter stated by Gildon, and not denied by Scryder; after which, some interrogatories put to Jaque, and a stout resistance on the part of Worricourt, Gildon was discharged. But as he was about to seek Louisa, he heard the Clerk proclaim the unwelcome sound of "the Commonwealth against Gildon, a true bill." Trueheart advised his young client to plead to the indictment immediately; by which means the case might, with the consent of the counsel for the commonwealth, be tried without further delay. He did so, and the case was agreed to be argued in the morning. Gildon then went in search of his friends, and to his great regret found that Edward had returned home with his mother and sister; but leaving a message, that he would be again with him in the morning.

As he was acquainted with no one but M'Culloch and Trueheart, both of whom were very much engaged, though in different sorts of business, he endeavoured to find some amusement by observing the course of proceedings in the court. He saw numbers thronging round the Clerk's table, for the purpose of proving deeds and wills, or to execute bonds, as guardians, executors, or administrators. He heard various motions made for judgments on bonds, which had been given by debtors for the delivery of property taken in execution, and had been then forfeited, and one or two attachments against runaway debtors, tried: but unable to understand the technical language of the bar, which appeared to him a barbarous jargon, he soon became wearied of the scene. "Is it possible," thought he, "that questions of right and wrong should be involved in so much doubt and difficulty; and if all these subtelties and nice distinctions are unavoidable, is it also necessary that they should be veiled in a language that none but the initiated can understand? The law is said to be a rule of action, and a rule of property to the citizen, yet these rules it is impossible he can know; and those who make a business of interpreting, do not seem to agree about."

While these reflections were passing through Gildon's mind, as he was sauntering idly at the back of the bar, he lighted on Trueheart, in company with the young lawyer who had gazed with so much interest on Louisa. The barrister immediately accosted him with " where have you hid yourself? I have been searching for you in the crowd this half hour. Let me introduce to your acquaintance a young friend of mine, and a member of the bar. Mr. Fanshaw, Mr. Gildon."

This was a young man of a genteel appearance, with a face that indicated genius, of a grave and rather melancholy aspect.

Having learnt from Gildon what had occurred with regard to Jaque's suit, he abruptly left them, saying to Gildon, "I must now go into the bar, and leave you with my friend Fanshaw; and I am sure you will find no difficulty in entertaining one another."

Gildon now, according to his habitual practice, began to converse with his new acquaintance on the subject which he presumed he best understood; and communicated to him some of his thoughts on the profession of the law, which had been passing in his mind a little before. He found that Fanshaw, (whom indolence and false delicacy, as he afterwards understood, had prevented from succeeding at the bar,) while he vindicated our systems of jurisprudence, thought more unfavourably of the practice than Gildon himself had done: it was, indeed, a favourite theme of declamation with him.

"The law, as an occupation, Mr. Gildon," said this young man, "has little to recommend it. You must be surrounded by a set of ill-mannered, low-minded people, who are either rapacious, unfeeling creditors, or knavish, fraudulent debtors, seeking to evade their contracts; savage bullies on one side, or contemptible cowards on the other; and slanderers endeavouring to screen themselves from the effects of their malignity, or those who meanly seek to make those slanders against his character, which every man believes, at least in part, a source of profit. In short, he is familiar with every form which violence, injustice, meanness, or crime can assume. Then, too, you must put up with grossness and vulgarity, breathing their pestilential breaths, impregnated with the fumes of whiskey or tobacco, into your lungs; uttering their low suspicions, or no less offensive jests; and giving you a taste, in defrauding you of your fees, of that knavery they want your aid to practise on others. You must dance attendance, in this dirty court-house, at all seasons; in winter without fire, and in summer without air: wedged in with a crowd of cold-hearted, contentious rivals, who envy you every fee they are not able to intercept; and who listen to your speeches only to cavil at your logic, or to laugh at your mistakes: and when you have been fortunate, and get employed by a bad man, in a bad cause, (as is the case nine times out of ten,) you are compelled to identify yourself with him, and to tax your memory, and fancy, and invention, for arguments, and law, and embellishments to support what you know to be unreasonable and unjust. Besides, you must not only sell them your words, and learning, and ingenuity, but body and soul in the bargain. You must bellow, toil, and sweat, be angry, and indignant, and pathetic, or you are charged with ignorance or stupidity; and ten to one but you are also suspected of being bribed by the opposite party.

"Such is the profession which I have foolishly selected as the means of acquiring fortune and fame; but which no man ever yet acquired in this way, unless he was goaded by necessity; for nothing less would be sufficient to carry him through the direful probation I have mentioned."

While Fanshaw was thus speaking, a stout, rough-looking man, in a blue hunting shirt, came up to him, and said, "is your name Fanshaw?"

"It is."

"I have been recommended to you by old George Trueheart. Are you at leisure?"

"Perfectly, sir," said the other, his face assuming an expression of lively pleasure; and making a slight apology to Gildon, he suddenly withdrew with his client, and showed that, amid all his denunciations against his profession, he was not without a due relish for its delights.

Thus again left to himself, Gildon took a stroll over the town, which he found to consist principally of industrious, thriving mechanics, and some shops of dry-goods and groceries. There was an air of stir and bustle in the streets and the shops, and the public houses, which he correctly attributed to the court being then in session. A few handsome carriages paraded the streets, of which he found the chief part belonged to the country, the gentry of the neighbourhood taking this opportunity of displaying their equipages, and of supplying themselves with the finery of the shops.

When sufficiently exercised with this ramble, Gildon returned to the tavern, and sat down to the ordinary with about forty or fifty persons, who said little, but ate heartily of the meats, and the various species of fruit, pies, and other articles of pastry which succeeded. He observed that every man began with bacon and cabbage, and ended with milk, the *ova* and *mala* of Virginia. He returned to the court-house in the afternoon, and found the scene little changed, except that many of the country people were flustered by the liquor in which they had been indulging; and some were mounting their horses, and others harnessing and preparing to return. He found himself more solitary in this crowd, than if he had been entirely alone; but the irksomeness of his situation, which he imputed to his being a stranger, was, no doubt, still more that which every lover feels, when he is first separated from his mistress. He returns to the tavern, inquires for a room, and with some difficulty gets one in which he is free from interruption; and there, between writing to his friends in New-York, and reading the newspapers, he makes out to get rid of a long summer afternoon.

In the evening Trueheart walked over to the tavern, and insisted on his returning with him, and passing the evening at Mrs. Stewart's. He readily complied, for he was not of a temper to relish solitude long. Supper was over at an early hour, and the lawyers, assembling in Trueheart's room, found in the pleasures of convivial society, some amends for the fatigues of the day. The dry and unintelligible jargon of the courts was exchanged for wit and humour at once, lively and delicate. Political subjects were discussed with ingenuity and ability; though with rather too much pertinacity. Pleasant stories, particularly such as hit off the characteristics of the Dutch, the Irish, or the Yankees, by turns, entertained the company—two or three of them sung good songs, and amongst others, the Marseillois Hymn, at which time they all stood up, and, taking hands, joined in general chorus. The sprightliness of their wit, the acuteness and depth of their reflections, the felicity and good humour with which they bantered one another, made them appear, like another set of persons from that which their care-clouded brows, their sharp and even morose altercations exhibited them in the morning, and Gildon almost thought himself in the green-room of the New-York Theatre, with the cleverest actors, who had laid aside the dresses of the parts they had been performing, to pass the remainder of the night in mirth and jollity. They appeared to be the happiest fellows in the world, and he felt his respect greatly increased for the profession. Fanshaw too was there, and forgetting the picture he had drawn of the miseries of the profession, partook of the reigning hilarity; but it was easy to see that his discerning associates attributed his unusual flow of spirits to the fee, which Trueheart had procured *for him* in the morning. Among other things which struck Gildon, was the vast sum of intelligence they collected, of all that was memorable or worthy of note in the adjoining counties, and even of some of those that were remote. They knew every man's private affairs intimately; and freely communicated to each other, not only what they had personally seen and known, but what they had learnt from those lawyers they had met in their distant circuits. In this way they are a sort of living telegraphs, to transmit over the state intelligence that never finds its way to the newspapers, and which by the echoes of popular rumour is greatly distorted and exaggerated.

It is no wonder, thought Gildon, that this class has obtained such an ascendency in our country. Their talents, their activity, and their intimate knowledge of men and their concerns, must give them infinite advantages over every other class. It seemed, too, as if the knavery and frauds of their clients, had passed through their minds like smoke through the atmosphere, without staining its purity. They appeared to be, for the most part, men of honourable feelings, and elevated sentiments;

of great integrity in their dealings, and prudence in the management of their affairs. If now and then some unworthy member came among them, who endeavoured, by dint of cunning, to supply the place of talents, he was soon put into Coventry; and continued there by his brethren, he could obtain no lasting respect among the people.

The next day, about ten o'clock, Edward Grayson returned to Winchester, and they forthwith repaired to the court-house. They no longer saw there the crowd of yesterday. All was comparative stillness, and quiet, and order; for no one was present, except the officers of the court, the suitors, the witnesses, and a few loungers of the town. Trueheart had interest enough with the states-attorney, whom he occasionally assisted, both with his pen and advice, to get his case taken up before it was reached in regular order. Worricourt made no objection, as he was impatient to get a further fee from Jaque Scryder.

The case was accordingly called, and Jaque appeared, as the chief witness:—he stated the principal facts correctly, but gave them all the colouring the extent of his art would permit. Beal, the tavern-keeper, proved his condition when he arrived; and Dr. Manifee stated the nature of the contusion, though neither with the brevity or plainness which the occasion demanded. He spoke of the meticarpel bones, and the tendo-Achilles, of extravasation, suppuration, and antiseptics, with great learning and self complacency, as well as of his own attendance, and the bill which he had rendered. The case was opened by the commonwealth's attorney, who said the assault was proved, that it was without provocation, and had been attended with great bodily injury, much loss of time and expense, and that an exemplary fine should be imposed on the wrong doer.

Trueheart followed in behalf of the defendant, as Gildon was called. He spoke of the privilege of juries, carried further in this state, than by the common law of England, or in most of the other states, since they had the power of fining for misdemeanours. That they were thus the guardians of the people's rights, and the shield of the poor against the rich, and the well-born. Having thus secured their confidence, he cautioned them against the prejudices to which they were exposed. He reminded them that, on one side, was a poor man, and on the other one who was said to be rich. That the prosecutor was indeed a countryman, and the other a stranger; but he trusted that a liberal and enlightened jury would be as ready to do justice to a citizen of another state as to one of their own, though he should happen to be rich; but of that he knew nothing, except that he had just returned from the college in Williamsburg, where he had been to finish his education, and he should be sorry he should return to his own state, with cause to complain of the severity of our laws:—that it was true, it had been clearly proved, that his young client had done an act of violence, but they must consider the circumstances of justification, or excuse which accompanied it. That he was attending the daughter of the late Col. Grayson, whom they had all known, and on a visit to a neighbour, when about to meet the prosecutor's wagon, on a hill side, where that and the carriage could not pass at the same time; that a regard to the safety of his charge, made him insist that the prosecutor, who was at the top of the hill, where he could easily stop, would wait a few minutes, till they could get by, which request the prosecutor brutally and unfeelingly refused. The defendant, finding him determined to persevere in a course that would have endangered the safety of a helpless female, endeavoured to detain the horses for two minutes; when the prosecutor threatened to make use of his whip against the defendant, and was in the act of raising it for that purpose, on which it seems, said the barrister, my client struck him. This, gentlemen, was the beginning of the affray, and what followed was pure accident, which might have befallen either party. Now, I lay down the law under the correction of the court, that an offer to strike, by one party, justifies an actual assault by the other; and so far from blaming the young gentleman for the part he acted, I commend him for his gallantry; and he would have deserved to be not only fined, but to be followed by the execration of every generous spirit, if he had done less, for the defence of the innocence and beauty which yesterday graced that bench, and which so strongly reminded us of him who was once one of its proudest ornaments. No, gentlemen, I cannot believe that an honest jury of Frederick, will require a youth of spirit to stand by with folded arms, and see any man, whether he be poor or rich, threaten the safety of a defenceless female, though she were not the pride of your county, and an ornament to her sex, and not make an effort to arrest the purpose of the unfeeling savage, who would attempt it, nor yet to wait until the meditated blow should put it out of his power to render assistance.

He, amid the manifest, but silent approbation of the whole audience, sat down, and several of the jury rose, with an involuntary impulse, to retire and bring in their verdict. But Worricourt got up and said, "Gentlemen of the jury, it is our right to conclude. Be pleased to take your seats." He then delivered a studied and formal harangue, which he had spent some hours of the evening before in preparing. He began by a formal dissertation on roads—noticed the laws appointing surveyors, and their various duties—the changes they had undergone from time to time—the difference between public ways and private ways—and how turnpikes differed from other public highways. Before he had got through this tedious introduction, one of the jury, who had taken more than the proper quantity of julep that morning, fell asleep; two of them stood up leaning on one shoulder against the rail, round the justices' bench, and the rest showed great impatience. Having, at length, perceived it, he hurried to the evidence, which he misrepresented, where he could, and distorted and twisted where he could not, as would best suit his purpose, and having taken equal liberties with the law, he concluded by saying, that it was one of the plainest cases he had ever been concerned in since he had had the honour of a place at that bar, and he had no doubt they would teach these fine-bred gentlemen a lesson, that should cure them of assaulting honest wagoners, on their way to market, especially when going down hill.

The jury who, for the last hour, had been internally abusing his tedious clink, as they called it, and had paid no attention to his argument, which was equally a perversion of law, evidence, and common sense; withdrew for a moment, and returned a verdict of not guilty, to the great satisfaction of all present. Gildon, elated with his triumph, again offered through Trueheart to make Jaque satisfaction for the injury he had unintentionally done, and somewhat cooled by his failure in the indictment, he readily accepted fifty dollars, in full satisfaction for the injury.

While Gildon was waiting till Mr. Trueheart

could come out of the bar, for the purpose of making his acknowledgments to him, and of taking leave, a tall, gawky man, of a saturnine cast of countenance, rose up, and addressed the court. He made such prefatory remarks, as are usual with those who wish to command particular attention. He said that he would avail himself of that short interval, to propose to the court to correct a proceeding which had continued too long, to the reproach of those principles of liberty and equality which were the best fruits of the glorious revolution. He called the attention of the court to the first sentence of the Bill of Rights, "All men are by nature free and equal."

"Except negroes," whispered Gildon to Trueheart.

"And they too, by nature," replied Trueheart, "but not by the law of the land, nor yet by the great law of necessity."

The orator then spoke of the rise and progress of privileged classes in the civilized world; of titles, and other artificial distinctions. He said, that if we wished to preserve the equality of which we are now so justly proud, we should guard against every thing that squints at these odious features of aristocracy and feudal barbarism. He then adverted to the style of addressing the court and jury, which had continued, with other odious and heterodox customs of the regal government; that so long as these badges of our former servitude remained, we should never have the noble sense of equality which became the citizens of a free commonwealth. He fortified these remarks, by the practice of the Greeks and Romans, and the modern French republic; and concluded by proposing that hereafter, in that court, those barbarous usages should be abolished, and that both magistrates and juries should be addressed by the title of citizens, for they were nothing more, and which, indeed, he added was the most dignified of all titles.

A profound silence prevailed for some time after he sat down, and the court, then consisting of five members, looked around and seemed to expect that, according to custom, other members of the bar would say something, either for or against the proposal. The fraternity, however, remained silent, (which some may regard as not the least remarkable part of the occurrence.) Some of them smiled, but the greater part, especially the younger members, gave signs of cordial approbation.

The court then consulted with one another; and one member openly expressed his unwillingness to the change. He said he was an enemy to innovation—and he had no idea of following the French in all their wild, new-fangled notions. Said he, "By-and-by, we must have the names of our counties changed; beginning with King

George, and King William, and King and Queen, and coming down to Frederick, and Berkley, and Loudon, and all for what? to imitate the French, who I'm thinking will, in catching at the shadow lose the substance of liberty. I'm then for sticking to old customs, and old names, unless there is some real advantage in the change." A majority of the court were of a different opinion; and one or two of the young attorneys immediately rose, and addressed motions to the court, for the purpose of trying the new style of citizens justices. As soon as they sat down, the presiding magistrate, who was a fat, good-natured, heavy-looking man, formally promulged from the bench, that hereafter the style of addressing the court and jury, should be " citizens justices," "citizens of the jury," all others would be pleased to take notice.

A case was then called, and the sheriff was directed to summon a jury. He accordingly did so, from a written list, or pannel, which he held in his hand, and when about to direct them to go to the book to be sworn, he said, " Gentlemen of the jury! Oh! I beg pardon of the court for calling the jury gentlemen."

" This unintended hit, which was the happier as most of the jurors made but a sorry appearance, produced a peal of laughter from every part of the court-house, and threw such a ridicule over the proposition, that during the whole court, afterwards, it was observed that the lawyers managed so as to avoid both the new and the old style, and at the succeeding court, by a silent and general concurrence, it fell into disuse, and might have passed into utter oblivion, but for this authentic and circumstantial history. Gildon was highly amused with the incident, so suited to his laughter-loving humour, and in the cessation of business, which this merriment occasioned, took leave of his faithful advocate, as well as those whose acquaintance he had made the evening before, and set out, with Edward, for Beechwood, which they reached a little before dinner.

On his arrival there, Gildon was so delighted at finding himself again in the presence of his lovely mistress, that he could scarcely persuade himself he had been absent but a single day, and he looked forward with unaffected pain to the time which approached, when he must leave, probably for ever, the scene of such pure joy, and where he could find, but for one single consideration, such lasting happiness. These disagreeable reflections hung on his mind, like a dark threatening cloud, in a sky elsewhere serene, to check his present bliss, and they became more painful when he learnt from Louisa, as he soon did, that she was to set off, in a few days, for Fredericksburg and the Northern Neck, on a visit of some months. He looked back on the few weeks he had passed at Beechwood, as on a pleasing dream, from which he had just been awaked—and when he retired to his pillow, his mind was so disturbed, that in spite of the fatigue of his ride, he passed an almost sleepless night.

CHAPTER XIII.

The next day they all prepared to set out for the Elms. Gildon was very pressing for an interview with Louisa, in the morning, for the purpose of persuading her to defer her visit to the lower country ; or, if that was impossible, of obtaining her promise to write to him; but Mrs. Grayson had been so much influenced by the prudents counsel of Mr. Trueheart, that she afforded her daughter no opportunity of a private conversation. He flattered himself, however, that he should be more successful in the course of the day.

Mrs. Grayson said, that as she was so soon to part with her daughter, she would accompany her to the Elms, especially as Mrs. Fawkner had complained of being neglected of late; but, without doubt, the wish to keep up the same course of maternal vigilance influenced her, and made her impose a task on herself that was, on more accounts than one, truly painful. Edward, without examining into his mother's motives, was much pleased to hear of her intention, for it always delighted him to see the two beings he most loved on earth together; and such was the purity and refined nature of his attachment, that he felt almost as much happiness, in seeing his mother in company with Matilda, as he derived from her society himself, under the restrictions which circumstances had imposed upon him.

They reached the Elms at an earlier hour than usual, and found Matilda and her mother ready to receive them. Mrs. Fawkner was apparently glad to see them, but showed a marked difference in her reception of Gildon and Edward, to the last of whom she was formal and reserved, except when chance afforded her an opportunity of saying something sarcastic or ill-natured. Matilda met her friends from Beechwood with her usual sweetness. She was overjoyed to see Mrs. Grayson again at the Elms, and kissed her so often, and embraced her so affectionately, that Mrs. Fawkner observed, " Why, Matilda, one would think that you had not seen Mrs. Grayson for a twelve month."

" Indeed, madam, it seems almost as long to me—I used to see you so often, you know," turning to Mrs. Grayson; " and I am so much obliged to you for coming early:—It looks so like old times."

Mrs. Fawkner frowned a little at this remark."

" Matilda, child," she said, " you will fatigue

Mrs. Grayson. Come, madam, walk into the chamber, and rest yourself before dinner. Mr. Gildon, you and Mr. Edward can amuse yourselves with the newspapers, till the major returns from his ride. He has gone to see his new purchase, where he talks of building. Come, madam," motioning to the ladies, who walked on to her own bed-room. Edward would have been more mortified at the chilling reception he met with from the mother, if certain sly looks and sweet smiles from the daughter had not afforded him ample consolation; as the comfortable fire of our hearth, within doors, makes us regardless of the bleak north-wester which rages without; nay, we are the more sensible of our safe and snug situation within, by reason of the contrast.

Indeed, Matilda had made more unreserved display of the kindness she felt towards every member of the Grayson family, on account of the change of sentiments on the part of her mother; a change which, she was sure they must observe, in spite of the restraints which the forms of politeness, and the wish to save appearances, imposed upon her mother. But the unaffected meekness and sweetness of Mrs. Grayson's behaviour were such, and they were accompanied, moreover, by so much real dignity, that it was impossible for any one long to feel ill-will towards her, or to treat her with disrespect.

" I wonder at your fortitude and self-denial,

Grayson," said Gildon, after the ladies had left the room—" When I see so much beauty, and intelligence, and grace, so entirely devoted to you, I think the resolution you've rashly formed would be ' more honoured in the breach than the observance.' "

Gildon, whose mind had been occupied with the pain of a separation from Louisa, ever since he had heard it, had some faint hope that if Edward would change his course, it might prevent, or at least delay, his sister's purposed visit.

"So far from it," replied Edward. "I never see that heavenly face, but it animates and supports me in the sacrifice I am about to make. The devotion which fills one person with melancholy and gloom, exalts another to the highest pitch of enthusiasm."

"And yet," says Gildon, "every one would choose, I should suppose, to be near the shrine of his devotions."

"That ought to depend," said Edward, "upon where he can best serve the holy cause to which he has devoted himself. No!" he continued, "the hand that I offer Matilda, shall be deemed by others, as well as by herself, worthy her acceptance. I know, too well, the efforts the occasion requires, but I am prepared to meet them."

Gildon, finding he had not been able to make any impression on Edward's purpose, and knowing the inflexibility of his temper, changed the subject, and observed, that as Edward would, no doubt, accompany his sister to Fredericksburg, he must prepare to take his leave, though he had not yet determined whither he should bend his course, whether to the Springs, or to New-York. But, if he were to consult his own inclinations, he should attend them to Fredericksburg, provided there was no objection on the part of Miss Grayson, or her friends.

"While there is any thing like uncertainty, in the result of your attachment to Louisa, it should be made as little the subject of public observation and remark as possible. I am confident that my mother, and I should think my sister, would be decidedly opposed to your making one of her escort."

"But, I presume, there would be no objection to my being at the races?" said Gildon.

"I should think not," answered Edward; "provided you were not particular in your visits or attentions. On this condition, I can see no objection, except it may be imprudent in you both, thus to encourage hopes that may never be realized."

"My dear fellow," said Gildon, "we have already argued that matter. You have your own way, and you must let me have mine. But here comes the Major; and who is that dashing blade with such a well-dressed servant behind him?"

"I imagine," said Edward, "it is the young South-Carolinian we have heard of."

"I was told yesterday," said Gildon, " he was on his way to the Springs, and comes to renew his visit to your sister, I suppose?"

Major Fawkner now entered, and introduced Mr. Belmain, a young man of a slender figure and delicate and effeminate appearance, dressed in the extremity of the fashion, and wearing a pair of hussar boots, with large tassels dangling from the top—his hair turned up behind, and fastened with a small comb; one of that class who are viewed with a mixture of envy and contempt by the men, by great admiration by the women, and who are commonly designated by some cant appellation of the day. Then they were called Jemmy Jessamies, and at present dandies. He was very volatile: had some natural generosity, which was almost choaked by the weeds of vanity and selfishness, that had been suffered to grow around it undisturbed; and a good genius, which had been so little improved that he was devoid of all information, except on matters of dress, fashion, and etiquette.

At the mention of Grayson's name he made a theatrical strut—" The brother of Miss Grayson, of Beechwood, I presume? I had often the honour of hearing your sister speak of you, sir. I hope she is well, and Mrs. Grayson? I should have done myself the honour to pay my respects this morning to the ladies, if I had not heard I should have the happiness of meeting them here;" taking out a fine cambric handkerchief, whose perfume of double-distilled lavender filled the room.

"The ladies are now in the house, sir," said Edward, "and are very well."

"Ah! they have arrived, have they? Early, upon my honour. I became quite used to your early hours, sir, last summer, when I had the honour of passing some time in Virginia. Four is our hour in South-Carolina."

"You are not before us in every thing I see," said Gildon, who felt not what precisely amounted to jealousy, but an irresistible desire to amuse himself at his expense.

"Oh, sir, said Belmain, we yield to the old dominion in most things"—but with an air that showed how little his opinion agreed with his words.

The Major gave the young gentlemen a cordial welcome, and Edward thought there was a warmth and a kindness in his manner towards himself, which he had not experienced for a long time before. He told them he had returned a day or two previous from the western parts of the state, where he had been attending a large survey of lands, on the Kenahwa, and with the fertility of which he seemed greatly pleased.

He spoke of the rapid growth of the Western Country—and thought if the citizens of the United States could ever secure to themselves the right of deposite at New-Orleans, free from molestation or duty from Spain, there would, in less than a century, be an immense population, and a very active trade on the Missisippi. He did not know a mode in which money could be so advantageously used—and he wondered that more capital from New-York did not take that direction. Gildon thought their lands could never be valuable, without the benefits of commerce and navigation, which the strong current of the Missisippi would prevent their ever enjoying. Edward agreed that they might not be very rich—but thought they might continue to increase in numbers—and that they could, by sending horses, cattle, and hogs, into the Atlantic states, procure as much money as their circumstances required, with most of the comforts, and even some of the luxuries of life. He reminded them, that cattle constituted the first medium of exchange with the Romans, (whence their money was called pecunia,) and he believed they now formed the chief instrument of commerce in the Western Country—the merchants receiving cattle in exchange for their goods, until they procured a number sufficient to make a drove.

The South Carolinian, finding this conversation very dull, walked up to one of the prints, humming a new tune, and at length inquired who was for the springs.

" I hope, sir, (addressing himself to Edward,)

Miss Grayson will honour them with her presence."

"My sister, sir, intends to go to Stafford, in a few days."

"Ah, I am very sorry for that, upon my honour."

In this miscellaneous chit-chat, an hour or more passed away before the rest of the company arrived, when they beheld a large cavalcade coming down the avenue of aged elms, consisting of Mr. and Mrs. Browne, and Mrs. Buckley, in a handsome chariot, with a splendid new hammer-cloth, and a servant in livery behind. The Miss Buckleys in a plain neat carriage, drawn by two large fat horses, and some distance behind, Mr. M'Culloch, and Mrs. M'Culloch, in a ricketty reddish coloured coachee, with the curtains torn, rattling and clattering like a mill-hopper, and drawn by two horses differing in colour, height, and form, and agreeing only in being very poor, and in their unwillingness to quicken their pace, in time to overtake the other carriages before they reached the outer gate. But the frequent lashes from the vigorous arm of Jack Martin, Mr. M'Culloch's *fac totum*, were unavailing to this end; and poor Jack felt like the gallant captain of some dull sailing frigate, who seeing all the rest of the fleet getting into action before him, while he is toiling in vain to join the brave squadron in the van, fears his own character will be called in question by the tardiness of the ship. He finally reached the place of deposite, to the great relief of all parties concerned, as well those who were in the vehicle, as those who were compelled to draw it, when Edward and the Major came up to hand out Mrs. M'Culloch, and Miss Tabb, her niece.

By this time old M'Culloch himself arrived, and bellowed out, "why Jack, what has come to you, driving at such a Jehu rate? I could not keep up with you. Take it coolly, man; don't push your nags this weather"—and certainly the condition of the poor animals dripping with sweat, and tottering with weakness, showed that their powers had been put to a severe test.

The ladies were all ushered into Mrs. Fawkner's bed-room, and the gentlemen into the parlour, where M'Culloch's arrival infused new life in the party. The ladies made their appearance in the parlour before dinner, seated around with great primness, and they would have been very dull but for the independent careless humour of old M'Culloch, who occasionally said something that diverted the whole company, and on whom their eyes were generally turned with the expectation of hearing something diverting, good humoured, or blunt."

"They tell me, my little Lily," said he, addressing himself to Louisa, "that you are going to leave your native valley—pray how long will you stay?"

"I do not certainly know, sir; perhaps I shall pass the winter below."

"That depends upon circumstances I suppose," said he, winking and chuckling.

Louisa blushed. "It depends upon mamma's wishes," she said—

"I am glad to hear, however, you do not mean to leave the state." She blushed more deeply, and Mrs. M'Culloch, who sat by her, and whose quicker perceptions saw that the conversation was, for some reason, particularly unacceptable, mildly said, "you are such a favourite with Mr. M'Culloch, that he never likes to hear of your going down the country;" then turning to her husband, she added, "how can you teaze her so?"

"See there," said he, to Louisa; "the old lady's jealous, I must hush"—and turning to Matilda, "pray my little stag-eyes, where do you go this summer?"

"I stay at home," she replied.

"Yes, Mr. M'Culloch," said Mrs. Fawkner, "home is the blest place for young people, these hard times: but I have had some notion of taking Matilda to Bath, if the Major would get me an additional pair of horses, as he has been talking of—but he is always buying land, land—I am sick of so much land. Are you going to trust Louisa with two!" to Mrs. Grayson. "I never mean to keep more than a pair again," said the other. "What do you say, Mr. Gildon, would you not like an excursion to Bath?" "It would give me great pleasure, madam, if I was not compelled to bend my course in another direction."

"Do you return to New-York?"

"Not immediately, madam, as I now think."

"I suppose you would have no objection, Mr. Belmain?"

"It would delight me to make one of the party, madam. Suppose, Miss Grayson, you alter your course, and visit Bath before you go to Stafford— you will make some charming acquaintance there. I know several very agreeable people from South-Carolina, Baltimore, and Alexandria, who intend to go to Bath this season."

"Her cousin expects her, said Mrs. Grayson, in Stafford, or I should have no objection to her going to Bath, or any other of the Springs, in company with Matilda."

Dinner was now announced, and Mrs. Fawkner, ever on the alert to further her purpose, said, "come, Mr. Gildon, hand one of the ladies," pointing to where Matilda and Peggy Buckley sat. He accordingly selected Matilda, while M'Culloch took the hand of the other, saying, "let us little people go together."

"Mr. Grayson, Mrs. Browne is by you," continued the lady of the house, thus endeavouring to separate Edward from Matilda, at table. But Belmain exclaimed, to Louisa and Fanny Buckley, "I protest, ladies, you must allow me to part you

—it is quite too cruel." "I think it is rather barbarous," said Gildon, and moved down between the young ladies. Edward, who had hesitated to place himself according to his inclination, from the fear of some rebuff, which he regarded more on Matilda's account than his own, now said, "allow me to follow so good an example," and moved up to the chair between Matilda and the elder Miss Buckley, before Mrs. Fawkner had time to practise any new left-handed manœuvre. As, however, that lady had made an extraordinary effort at display to-day, and her thoughts were necessarily occupied in attending to her company, she did not manifest her wonted impatience at being foiled.

The table groaned with a profusion of meats and vegetables; and all her plate, cut glass, and china, were exhibited, even to the smallest article. But it was in the dessert that her chief art and skill had been expended. There, custards, and syllabubs, trifles, and floating islands, and tarts, and puddings, and jellies, and sweatmeats, set out in a handsome service of cut glass, distracted the choice with the variety, and gratified her pride of wealth as well as of housewifery. Edward, happy in being placed by the side of Matilda, and fearful of rousing her mother's displeasure, ventured to speak to her only on general subjects; and so divided his attentions between Matilda and Miss Margaret, that a careless observer would have supposed he regarded them with equal interest; but a practised eye might have seen that when he spoke to Miss Buckley, his manner was more hurried, and, at the same time, more scrupulously polite; but that his air was more serious when addressing Miss Fawkner.

"Is it true," said Matilda, "that you do not return to Frederick with Louisa?"

"I think I shall not," said he. "I wish to have an opportunity of consulting with my friends before I set out. Do, Miss Buckley, let me help you to an ice cream."

"Have you an ice house yet, madam," said Mrs. Fawkner to Mrs. Grayson, "I wonder how you do without one—they are so convenient."

"I have never been accustomed to the convenience," said Mrs. Grayson.

"Positively, I had as lieve be without a smokehouse," said Mrs. Fawkner.

"Oh, they must be so fine for milk and butter," said Mrs. Buckley; "my sister Browne says every family in Alexandria is supplied with ice at three cents a pound."

"Well, give me a good spring-house," said M'Culloch, "with the old lady, there, to scold the dairy maids, and I'd wish for nothing cooler. Every thing in season. There's a time for all things, as the wise man says; and I care as little for ice in summer, as for cucumbers in winter.

Mrs. Grayson, shall I join you in a glass of wine? that is always in season."

Gildon was pretty well occupied with the little compliments and expressions of tenderness with which he would dexterously contrive to address Louisa, and with parrying the questions and good natured fiddle-faddle of Fanny Buckley.

" Oh, Mr. Gildon, I heard such a piece of news, that Frederick is to lose one of its greatest belles."

" What! are you going to be married?" said he—

The lady gave one of her good-humoured titters, and said, " you are such an odd man, Mr. Gildon—you know what I mean."

" Sometimes I am so fortunate ma'am," said he. But as her habitual laugh was not so hearty as before, he promptly added, " shall I have the honour of a glass of wine, madam? That young gentleman looks this way very often—I verily think, Miss Fanny, you've made a conquest; he is a great admirer of new fashions."

" Louisa," said she, leaning a little back, " you never told me how you like the pattern that aunt Browne brought up."

" I never saw it," said Louisa, heedlessly.

" This is one I am wearing. Do you approve of it?"

" Oh, very much; it is very becoming."

" Well, I am glad to hear you say so—you have so good a taste. But Mr. Gildo 's mistaken; that young gentleman is looking towards another person, winking significantly to Louisa; they say he is immensely rich. But I don't think him handsome; he has such a finical look."

All this while, young Belmain, who, by the dexterous retreat of Gildon, had been placed between Mrs. Buckley and Mrs. Browne, and was the only one who had not profited by his own suggestion, sat throwing his eyes across the table, envying the happiness of Gildon, and lamenting that he had no opportunity of showing his self-importance, by reason of the unceasing garrulity of Mrs. Buckley. That good lady had been giving him minute details of her household, the notable qualities of her daughters, the oracular decisions of her sister Browne, and some of her arguments on family matters with Mr. Buckley, till he fairly wished the whole family at Jericho. It was in vain that he endeavoured to break the thread of her discourse by asking for the honour of drinking wine with every body at table; no spider was ever more nimble and dexterous at closing up a breach in his web. "And so, sir, as I was telling you, sister Browne said to me, or said to Mr. Buckley."—He at length put on such a half-beseeching, half-despairing look, that he afforded infinite amusement to Gildon, who also contrived to make Louisa partake of his sly pastime. But, saving this mortified gallant and Mrs. Fawkner, when her eye, glaring around the table, lighted upon Edward, speaking with a pensive air to Matilda, who was listening with evident interest and pleasure, it may be safely said, that there was not a more pleased or joyous company that day in all Virginia.

The ladies rose from table soon after the cloth was removed, and the gentlemen, at least the seniors, appeared disposed to do honour to their guest's wine, which was the best that Alexandria could afford, and they had the benefit of ice, rather a rare luxury at that time. The skill which each of the guests happened to possess on this fertile theme, was first brought forth. They then conversed on different topics of farming, which appeared to Gildon to be inexhaustible, but in which he was able to bear little part. The wonders of plaster—the benefits of deep ploughing—the remedies for the Hessian fly—the best plan of a threshing machine—of curing clover—of saving its seed—the various species of meadow grasses, and the advantages and peculiarities of the May wheat, (then first getting into use,) all were discussed in succession, and furnished two sides, and sometimes more, to an argument.

At length the merits of a plough, which Mr. Jefferson had lately recommended, being mentioned, the conversation seemed immediately about to become political, when M'Culloch, who saw that Edward was prepared to accept the defiance which he had unwarily thrown down, and remembering their former altercation, said: "Now, when I was of your age, lads, I should as soon have thought of making my will, as of staying so long with a parcel of gray-beards when there were pretty lasses in the house. But ye are a degenerate race, and I will not own you for Virginians, much less for mountaineers."

Gildon and Edward, who had been some time watching for an opportunity of stealing away, immediately profited by the hint, and rose from the table; and Belmain, who had been in purgatory all day, since he could neither make love nor talk of himself, was little less pleased at the release than they.

"I have been most delectably entertained upon my honour," said he, "with my sister Browne, and my daughter Margaret; and how happily too we were located !"

"It is no uncommon thing," replied Gildon, "for those who introduce great improvements to reap the least benefit from them."

They found the elder ladies in the drawing-room, and the younger in the portico or the garden. Edward caught a glimpse of Matilda, setting in her little bower with his sister, and he felt a strong impulse to join them, but the presence, and ever watchful eye of Mrs. Fawkner restrained him. Matilda had probably somewhat of the same apprehension, as they soon returned to the house.

Miss Fanny Buckley had proposed to take a walk, by a public road running along the bank of

the river, for the purpose of visiting the seat of a
French gentleman about two miles above the Elms,
the taste, and expense of whose improvements had
become the subject of general conversation in the
neighbourhood, and consequently of exaggerated
description. Mrs. Fawkner objected to the length
of the walk, and the dampness of the ground, for
it had rained the evening before, and Mrs. Grayson also discouraged it; but finding that the young
people promised themselves so much pleasure from
the visit, she ceased to make further objection,
and finally became an advocate for it.

They accordingly had on their bonnets and
gypsey hats in a trice, and set off. The party
consisting of five young ladies, the two Misses
Buckley, Louisa, Matilda, and Miss Tabb,
escorted by Gildon, Edward, Belmain, and Frank
M'Culloch. Belmain, who seemed determined
to make up for the time he had lost at the dinner
table, stuck close to the side of Louisa, whose good
breeding and natural sweetness of disposition were
thus put severely to the test. Anticipating rivalship, he had been very prompt in offering his arm
to Louisa, and Gildon had, on his part, been restrained, by way of giving an earnest of his forbearance and self-command, and of showing that
he was not unmindful of his promise to Edward.
He therefore made a virtue of necessity, and seeing that Edward and Matilda kept at a distance
from each other, he offered his assistance to the

latter. The younger Miss Buckley, who was greatly attached to Louisa, and did not like her company the less for being attended by a gay and fashionable young man, put herself in such a situation that Belmain was obliged to ask her acceptance of his other arm. Edward walked with Miss Peggy Buckley, the least attractive of the company, and Frank M'Culloch with his lively hoydenish cousin, whose free and frolicksome humour seemed to have made a strong impression on him.

It was about six o'clock on a fine summer's evening, at the latter end of August, when the heat of the season and of the day had so abated that one could not pronounce the temperature too hot or too cold. The road ran along, and we presume still does, the banks of the river, on a black sandy soil, which is neither miry in winter nor dusty in summer, but is at once level, smooth, and firm, and is for the most part defended from the rays of the mid-day sun by the sycamore, birch, walnut, and elm, growing luxuriantly along the banks of the river, and on the borders of the fence that encloses the flat lands. Sometimes the hills approach so near the river as to have made it necessary to cut out the road, and in these places it is somewhat rough and stony—they serve, however, as marks to divide the distance in one's mind, and to make one more sensible of the goodness of the other parts of the road. The order of the line of march was not exactly such as some of the party would have chosen, but they were within sight and hearing of the objects of their affection, and they all enjoyed the mildness of the evening, the beauty of the scenery, and the sweet murmur of the river, then very low, but clear as rock crystal, and reflecting the rays of the declining sun through the thick foliage of the trees, and the vines on the bank.

When they reached the place they set out to visit, those who had seen it before, found it indeed greatly improved and embellished, but far short of that spot of fairy enchantment, and costly decoration, which their youthful fancies had depicted. It was, however, really a pretty place, and although the improvements would not rank very high with those who have seen the beautiful and finished pleasure grounds of Europe, yet, art had here been sufficiently successful in embellishing nature, without disguising her, to make it seem a very pleasant spot to any taste however fastidious, and to excite great admiration with the inexperienced. The proprietor happened then to be absent on a trip to the north, and the servants, according to the directions they had received, very civilly asked the ladies and gentlemen to walk into the house, as well as to view the grounds.

A long piazza, overlooking the river, runs from one end of the building to the other, and here the party sat to rest themselves from the fatigues of their walk, and from the eminence on which the house stood, to view the tasteful improvements that had been finished, or were then in execution, as well as the more magnificent beauties of nature, in the woody mountain before them, stretching away to the south-west, until its dark sides growing of a lighter and lighter hue, melted into a pale bluish gray ; and in the lovely Shenandoah, washing the base of the blue ridge, and bearing its limpid waters in a gentle stream to mingle with those of the Potomac.

A very civil swarthy old Frenchman dressed in clothes that were neat and clean, but quite threadbare, with his long hair queued behind, was foremost in doing the honours of the place. He took particular pains in showing the young folks his flowers, among which were some rare exotics. Most of the company, impatient to see all that was new and curious, flew from bower to parterre—from the summer-house to the green-house—or looked at the pictures, or prints, or casts, or new and stylish furniture of the mansion. Matilda and Louisa seemed inclined to withdraw from the rest of the company, which they found not very easy, as Belmain, elated with his past success, and nothing checked by the coldness of Louisa, which was more than counteracted by the ever ready civility and compliments of Fanny Buckley, still insisted on being at her side. But Gildon, perceiving this, observed that the ladies had probably much to say to each other, as they were so soon to part, and taking him by the arm, half forced him to look at a fish pond, made in a little brook that emptied itself into the river about two hundred yards from the house.

Edward then joined them privately, and said to Gildon, "would it be possible for me to have ten minutes' conversation with Matilda, without attracting observation?"

"Certainly," said Gildon, "you can go in pursuit of your sister, who is with her, and she can keep sentinel at the door of the summer-house, while you and Miss Fawkner are within, or I can pretend to have discovered some new wonder in this elysium, and in their eagerness to see it, they will never perceive that you are absent; and when they return they will of course conclude that Miss Fawkner is examining some of the old citizen's curious flowers."

"Well, I will mention it to my sister, who can propose it to Matilda, but I much question if she will consent, she is so averse to every thing like artifice."

The proposal was accordingly made to Matilda, who immediately said, "my dear Louisa, you know my sentiments towards your brother; I have never disguised them even from him, but I feel great repugnance to any interview with him against the knowledge of my parents, and at this time it would have too much the air of trick and management. I may sometimes be disobedient to them—I fear I am so too often; but I will not deceive them. Tell your brother to ride down to the Elms some morning before he leaves Frederick; I will mention to my mother that he wishes to converse privately with me, and she will, when thus consulted, probably consent. But if she objects, I will then determine whether we had better communicate our sentiments by letter."

Louisa made a faint endeavour to change her purpose, but knowing her inflexibility, soon desisted. She returned to her brother with Matilda's answer, and he immediately expressed as much surprise and indignant complaint, as if he had entertained no doubt of her compliance.

"Yes, I see how it is," said he; "Matilda is already cooled in her affection, or she would never have refused so reasonable a request. Did you intimate to her my purpose?" addressing himself to Louisa.

"I did—and she entirely approves it. She said if any thing could exalt you in her eyes, it would have been such an act of self-denial and disinterestedness; indeed, brother, you do Matilda injustice; she really loves you, and her attachment is now stronger than ever."

"But this is such refined and fastidious prudence," said he. "Such scrupulous caution is inconsistent with that warmth which genuine love inspires."

He thus went on, with the inconsistency of vehement tempers, under the influence of disappointment, imputing her refusal to any thing rather than the same sense of self-respect, which supported him in the course he himself was taking. Louisa, moved by the distress which her brother seemed to suffer, and thinking, moreover, that there was something of prudery in Matilda's scruples, good-naturedly promised that she would still endeavour to procure him an interview. She mentioned the matter to Fanny Buckley, to whom she confided all secrets but her own, and many of those too; when that good-natured damsel very promptly agreed that it was a most unreasonable, cruel, and ridiculous refusal on the part of Matilda, and insisted that they should contrive Edward an opportunity of conversing with her on their way home, if not before.

Edward, in the meanwhile, gloomy, and vexed, and disappointed, sauntered about the garden by himself, and withdrew from the rest of the company, though he endeavoured to make it appear the effect of accident. Matilda was distressed at the refusal she had been obliged to give, and when she saw him apparently musing and abstracted, when she recollected how different his situation and feelings now were from what they had been the year before, and that he was, under the pressure of the change, about to exile himself from his family and friends, she felt for him most keenly, and almost relented. She, however, maintained her resolution, though she did not withhold her pity, and in her lively sympathy could not refrain from tears. Taking Louisa's arm, she endeavoured to approach him, but he still avoided them. When being near her, he turned off, she called aloud, "Mr. Grayson," and offering him a sprig of mignonette, said in a whisper, "Edward, if you could read my heart, you would pity, rather than blame me." Edward was greatly moved at this proof of tenderness and humility, and was mortified at the part he had acted.

"Forgive me, Matilda," said he, "I have been unreasonable;" upon which she held out her hand, and smiling through the tears which she had not been able to conceal, she proposed to join the rest of the party who were examining a small obelisk, in a retired part of the garden, surrounded by cypress and yew, and which the proprietor had erected to the memory of his deceased wife.

By the time the party had run over the garden and surrounding grounds, and surveyed all the improvements, finished or unfinished, the sun had sunk behind the western hills, and warned them it was time to return.

As they were preparing to set out, Monsieur La Porte insisted on their doing him the honour of tasting one of his cantelope melons, which they could not refuse, and he further begged Matilda who had shown herself most of a florist, to accept a bouquet of the choicest flowers he had then in bloom. They then took their leave, having, with some hesitation, prevailed on him to accept a small gratification for his attention. When about to return to the Elms, Gildon made some overture to assist Louisa; but on Belmain also claiming his right, she said, "Excuse me, gentlemen, Miss Fawkner must be my beau this evening;" and Belmain, finding his entreaties unavailing, proposed to take charge of Miss Fanny Buckley; but she, having another object in view, had put herself under the protection of Edward. Frank M'Culloch and his cousin had started off at the first talk of returning, saying, "We shall all be in the night, and father is a spluttering mightily before this."

Mr. Belmain was not a little piqued to find himself thus excluded, and seemed about to walk by himself, when Miss Fanny, who always hated to give offence, particularly to so fashionable a gentleman, said, "Sister, I transfer my beau to you, while I'm talking secrets with Miss Grayson," upon which Miss Peggy smiled, and appearing nothing loath, he was forced to offer his assistance, saying, "Madam, shall I have the honour"—but showing by his manner that he thought he was conferring one.

Gildon, unable to have Louisa's society, at first strolled sullenly on by himself; but soon sought to gratify his taste for the ludicrous, by joining

Miss Peggy and the South-Carolinian; Matilda and Louisa brought up the rear. The former, who was not so occupied with her own distresses as to be indifferent to the concerns of her friend, in quired of Louisa of her prospects with her lover; and when she understood the actual state of things, she recommended to her friend the greatest circumspection in her conduct, and urged her to object to Gildon's attending her at the races. "If he was sincere in his attachment," she observed, "and was worthy of her affection, as she trusted he was, such discretion would but exalt her in his eyes, and stimulate him in his efforts to procure the consent of his father; and if any thing should happen"——

"Oh! do not mention it, Matilda—my imagination turns from that picture with horror. I must hope for the best, and I more and more feel that in such a state of things, I should certainly lose my reason."

"There are events in life, my dear Louisa, to meet which we have need of all our fortitude. Recollect what you owe your excellent mother, what you owe to yourself. Accustom yourself, moreover, to contemplate what is disagreeable sometimes; since they who only look to the bright side of things, lay up for themselves a good store of disappointment, heaven knows!" and the sigh that escaped her, on recollecting how different were her feelings when they last conversed on her then happy love, and unclouded prospects, reminded Louisa that she was not the only one who needed sympathy.

Remembering then her promise to Edward, Louisa again interceded with Matilda to grant him an interview that evening; when Fanny Buckley, turning suddenly round, according to an ingenious scheme she had been some time planning, insisted that Matilda should not monopolize Louisa Grayson any longer; that she would make her as grave and serious as she was herself. "Only see, now," said she, looking under Louisa's gypsey, "if she has not been crying. I shall leave you, Mr. Grayson," disengaging herself from his arm, " and try to raise your sister's spirits. Matilda, I cannot let you have Louisa altogether to yourself, when she is to leave us next week," and, as she spoke, seized on the unresisting Louisa as a kite seizes on a chicken, and bore her off in triumph. Nor was it until Edward, seeing Matilda alone, said, " he hoped she would not now object to accept his assistance," that she suspected the whole to be a piece of contrivance of the accommodating Miss Buckley.

Matilda thought it would look like prudery and affectation to make further resistance, when her resolutions of prudence and propriety were thus frustrated, and she yielded to the necessity with a good grace—with more pleasure, indeed, than she was willing to allow, even to herself. At first she kept close to the two young ladies, in spite of Edward's gentle endeavours to detain her, and of their quickened pace. But as her lover's conversation became more animated, and he spoke with greater feeling, their gait insensibly slackened, and ere they had proceeded a mile, they were more than a quarter behind.

After renewing those professions which lovers are never tired of making or hearing, he proceeded to detail to her the particulars of his several plans of qualifying himself for the bar, of settling his father's estate, and of providing an asylum for his mother and sister. He spoke of his anxiety about Louisa, as he had doubts about the firmness and the prudence both of Gildon and his sister, whose sanguine and enthusiastic temper, if longer indulged, would render a disappointment worse than death—which opinion Matilda confirmed, and urged him to insist on Gildon's immediate return to New-York, that absence and her own prudent counsels might restore her mind to its proper tone. He then obtained a promise from her to write to him, though she refused to carry on any correspondence which she should find it necessary to conceal from her family.

By this time they had reached a part of the road where the hill juts in towards the river, and at once limits the domain of Major Fawkner, and the view of the road from the Elms; when the young ladies who were before, stopped to wait for the lovers, who, in the interesting conversation they had carried on, had not perceived that they were very far behind the rest, and that it was past sunset. Matilda now began to fear she should incur the displeasure of her mother, and what she hated still more, be suspected of management—but she thought she could not quit the arm of Edward, without giving some colour to the suspicion.

Fanny Buckley, however, soon relieved her from her difficulties, for, when they came up, she said, "Well, Matilda, as you have been a good girl, and have purposely kept back until Louisa and I have talked all our secrets, I will now give her up to you, and take my beau again," thrusting her arm into Edward's. Matilda smiled, saying, "Go on, Fanny Buckley, you are an odd girl," and gently disengaging herself from Edward, took Louisa by the arm, and followed on.

They now quickened their pace, and saw Frank M'Culloch and his cousin going into the house, and Belmain, with Miss Buckley and Gildon, near the gate, walking slowly, and looking behind.

When they reached the Elms, the carriages were drawn up at the gate, and waiting for orders to drive in, Mrs. Browne's showy equipage in the van, and M'Culloch's modestly hanging back in the rear.

"Why Bess, you baggage, where have you been for this hour?" said he to Miss Tabb— "You have kept your aunt a waiting till she is out of all patience—and her beasts are not like your town-pampered jades. I make every thing work with me Mrs. Browne—Jack Martin, as the other ladies an't ready, drive up."

"How, Mr. M'Culloch!" said his wife with more quickness than usual, though still with meekness—"Don't be in such a hurry, Jack, I say!" raising his voice.

"Would you have me," said his helpmate, a little more animated than before, "go without taking leave of Matilda?"

"Pshaw! wife, you'll be an hour taking leave, and the moon will be down before you get home. Jack Martin!" calling with the voice of Stentor, "that fellow always likes to go in a crowd."

"Mr. M'Culloch," said Mrs. M'Culloch, with a more beseeching earnestness, the efficacy of which she had, no doubt, often experienced before, "do let me take leave of Louisa before she goes down the country. I shall have no chance of seeing her again."

"Ah! my lily of the valley!—why, I want to shake her by the hand, and give her a piece of advice myself."

By this time Jack Martin, who had disregarded the first commands of his master, no longer having the pretext of not hearing, was by a few flourishes of his whip, and some sly cuts, which he endeavoured to make effectual, with as little noise as possible, endeavouring to take the post of honour, when M'Culloch called out, "You may wait Jack, your mistress isn't ready yet," a command which the horses seemed to understand quite as well as their driver, for they did not move an inch from the spot.

"You see, madam," turning to Mrs. Browne, who stood foremost in the parties, the ladies will always have their way."

"I wish," said she, "I could get Mrs. M'Culloch to give me a lesson."

"Some have the art, my dear, of ruling, and never seeming to rule," said Mr. Browne.

"Thank you, my dear," replied Mrs. Browne. "You call it three miles to Mr. Buckley's, I think, madam," turning to Mrs. Fawkner, who stood looking down towards the gate, apparently so much abstracted as to give no attention to what was passing around her,—"Madam, I beg pardon." "Yes, madam, it is two miles—long miles I always think them. It is so imprudent in these girls to stay out so late on the river bank—Matilda already has a cold."

The second party now came up.

"And what has become of Matilda and Louisa?" and she had liked to have said, Edward.

"Oh! they walked so slow, we were tired of waiting for them," said Miss Peggy; "but Mr. Belmain is almost as slow a walker as they."

"I endeavoured to support you, madam," said he, "as well as I was able"—laughing.

"Girls are so thoughtless and imprudent!" said Mrs. Fawkner. "The dew has already begun to fall."

"They will soon be here," said Mrs. Grayson; and just as she spoke, the tall slender figure of Edward was seen walking with the younger Miss Buckley, who was known by the lowness and rotundity of her form.

"Here they come," said M'Culloch, "after all the world like a great I and little o—but where are my little blossoms, my lily and my rose of Sharon? Oh! I see them now."

Mrs. Fawkner said in a tone of more good humour than she had manifested for some time before, "Matilda and Louisa will always be the last of all—they have so much to say when they meet"——

"I'll order your carriage up, madam," said M'Culloch to Mrs. Browne.

"Do, if you please, sir," said Mrs. Buckley, who having hauled Major Fawkner in a corner, had been giving him a detail of her manner of making cream-cheese.

Gildon said, "I will go and hurry the young ladies," and springing off the steps, ran to meet them. Belmain was disposed to follow his example, but could not break off the conversation in which he was engaged with Mrs. Browne, on what were the most fashionable riding carriages, in which it so happened that his description coincided with nothing then at the gate, in form, colour, or style of decoration—to the evident chagrin of Mrs. Browne, who had been deriving no small consequence from the superiority of her equipage to all around her.

"We are plain people in Virginia, sir," said she, endeavouring to disguise her pique under an assumed air of indifference; "we merely make use of carriages as things of convenience. If they are strong and neat, it is all I require," glancing her eyes towards her own showy chariot, whose saucy mulatto driver, from his elevated seat, was looking with the same contempt on the humbler vehicles near him, as a young officer on a parcel of ragged recruits, and whose elegant bays were champing their bits, and pawing the ground, with impatience to start.

"True, madam," said M'Culloch, "it is all vanity and vexation of spirit—as I tell the little woman there, when she wants to make a show."

"Show, indeed," said his gentle rib with a smile—"If I can get along, it is all I wish."

By this time the ladies and their escort had arrived, and the usual courtesies were observed on taking leave. But M'Culloch shook Louisa very cordially by the hand, and said, "Take care of yourself, my sweet girl; don't let any of the Tuckahoes run away with your heart, until you are sure they deserve it," thereby meaning to give her a hint respecting Gildon, whom it began now to be generally understood was addressing Louisa, avowedly against the wishes of his father—" and come back to us soon, the same little fresh and sweet floweret as ever." Again shaking her hand and giving her lips a smack, while a tear, had it not been twilight, might have been seen in his eye. Matilda pressed Mrs. Grayson to let Louisa stay that evening, and she finally consented.

The rest of the party then rode off, generally taking precedence according to the dignity of the equipage, except that Mrs. Grayson, having but a short distance to go and a good road along the river, compelled Phill reluctantly to take the rear, though, but for that, he would have contended with Mrs. Browne's driver himself for precedency. He had been accustomed to attach to his master's family some vague notion of superiority, compounded of fortune, and style of living, and rank, which right of precedence he had always asserted, and it had been commonly yielded, until the growing wealth and ostentation of the Fawkners, had contested the point with him.

Belmain accepted the proffered hospitality of the Elms the more readily, as Louisa was to remain there, and in doing so, found some amends for the penance he had undergone during the day. Edward returned with a heart disburdened of half the load of care that had oppressed it, and he relished, more than he had done some time before, the humorous account Gildon gave of his dialogue with Miss Fanny—and the caustic satire with which he ridiculed the fopperies of the ricebird, as he called Belmain. They reached their quiet mansion as the new moon sunk behind the hill to the west ; and both were buoyed up with the hope of seeing their charmers the next day, as Edward had now a sufficient pretext for returning to accompany his sister home. Mrs. Fawkner, exhausted with her exertions, and still more her anxiety to make a display worthy of her imaginary consequence, retired early, and the young ladies, for the sake of being together, and of ridding themselves of young Belmain's fulsome adulation and incessant egotism, followed her example, while the Major and his young guest were left to pass a dull drowsy evening by themselves.

CHAPTER XIII.

The next day Edward and Gildon rode over to the Elms, to accompany Louisa home. They found the young people assembled in the drawing room, where Belmain, who was a good performer on the flute, was accompanying Matilda and Louisa on the piano. He seemed to be in high spirits, and met Gildon with rather a triumphant air.

"The ladies say, they have not had so fine a concert this many a day."

"There was a sweet concord of opinion with the whole party, then no doubt?" said Gildon, with a sneer.

"Mr. Belmain," said Louisa, "is a charming player indeed; would you not like to hear him, brother?"

"Certainly, if Mr. Belmain will so far oblige us," replied Edward; and taking up a song of great tenderness, which Matilda had often sung to him, he requested his sister to play it. The words so well accorded with Louisa's feelings and situation that she was greatly pleased, and expressed her delight with her usual warmth.

"Is it not a sweet thing?" said she, turning to Gildon, who convinced as he was of the undivided affection of Louisa, yet felt pain in hearing her praise another, and express pleasure from his performance—and he felt it the more, as that other was her undoubted admirer.

"It is like other love ditties," said he coldly.

"You are not a performer, I believe, sir," said Belmain.

"I am sorry you do not play," said Louisa, who at the moment felt a slight regret that they did not have a sympathy in every thing.

"I should be very happy indeed, Miss Grayson," said he formally, "if I could do any thing which could afford you as much gratification as that music seems to have given you."

She cast on him a look of tender reproach, and began to suspect the truth, that he thought she was playing the coquette. She soon rose from the instrument, and sat down, mortified and hurt at the unjust suspicion; while Belmain, not understanding from this short dialogue more than met the ear, was showing, by all the quavers and shakes he was master of, how well he was entitled to the encomiums he had received. After a few minutes of awkward silence, Louisa proposed to Matilda to visit her bower, and take a last look at it for the present year. They both withdrew, and Belmain, who was soon tired of being in one place, and never continued long in the same house, the same room, or the same part of the room if he could help it, went out, and in a little while his servant, an ill-favoured black boy, very showily dressed, came in and told him the phæton was ready, upon which he said, " he was going to pay his respects to the ladies at Mrs. Buckley's," and added, " I want to make my peace with Mrs. Browne, who I quizzed a little last evening about her carriage, which she thinks is the tip of the mode. But I'll make up for it to-day. The young ladies, though a little in the Dutch style of beauty, seem to be women of sense and good taste—don't you think so?"

" I thought," said Gildon, " *you* seemed to their taste."

" Oh! sir, you flatter me. But I'm off, ' *au revoir, citoyens.*' " As he drove off he spied the ladies in the garden, and, kissing his hand, most reverently bowed, and pushed through the avenue at as brisk a trot as his horses could carry him.

Gildon, looking over the garden pales, said, " Ladies, would you admit two of your humble followers to approach your bower, though they are not able to entertain you with music."

" Certainly," said Matilda, " open the gate and come in."

The permission was no sooner given than accepted, and the youths were within the little bower in a twinkling.

Gildon, going up to Louisa, gaily said, "I had no idea that rice-birds were so musical."

"I suppose you mean Mr. Belmain; he performs very agreeably."

"I think you seemed to admire him very much," said he.

"You rather overrate my admiration, which was caused still more by the words than the air, though I found myself affected by both, when I recollected how soon I was to part with all I hold dear"—and her heart was filled.

"I wonder, Louisa, you can consent to go when the idea seems so to distress you," said Gildon, who had ventured to take hold of her hand as he spoke. In the meanwhile Edward had seated himself by Matilda, at the opposite corner, and began a conversation, which would have been heard, if any but lovers had been present.

"How often," said he, "has this enchanting spot been present to my mind, in some of its pleasing day dreams—and when shall I see it again? with the same careless gayety of heart as formerly. Don't you remember that sweet brier, which in helping to set out, gave you a scratch on your arm?"

"I have your impromptu now."

"Yes," says she, "and I believe I have your impromptu now with me," drawing out a little pocket-book, from which she took a paper containing the following lines:

> Of Love's mishaps, too sure, I fear,
> All soon or late complain :
> And as each rose its thorn must wear,
> Each pleasure has its pain.

Underneath, Matilda seemed to have recently written, " Alas! That which I once regarded as a mere poetic fancy, every day proves to be a sad reality."

" And yet," said Edward, looking at her with extreme tenderness, " who for the sake of avoiding its thorns would forego the beauty and fragrance of the rose."

" But there are many thorns for one rose on yon bush," said she.

" True, Matilda, but it is in our power to avoid most of the one while we are gathering the other."

" That depends on our prudence," said she.

" No, Matilda, the true secret of happiness consists in our fortitude to bear the ills of life, and on our sensibility to relish its joys. What would induce me to forego some of the recollections occasioned by the sweet passion whose misery delights. Amidst all my present perplexities, and dark views of the future, the memory of former joys come over my soul like the refreshing breeze that gives new life to the fainting traveller. You remember the day you were near falling out of the swing at the upper end of the garden. How often has that scene been present to my mind with all the freshness of an occurrence of yesterday. Will you let me see the trifle I sent you the next day by way of atonement? I think I could improve it."

"I would not have it altered," said Matilda; "you know it was our treaty of peace."

"Nay, but let me see it for a moment."

"It is put away," said Matilda.

"Ah! you've lost it," said Edward, greatly mortified at the supposition.

"Stay," said Matilda, "I will convince you to the contrary," and from the same little pocket book, she drew the original, which was as follows:

> From Myra's lips of rosy hue,
>   I snatch'd a balmy kiss:
> But soon my heart had cause to rue
>   The cheating, short-liv'd bliss.
>
> For when the indignant, lovely prize,
>   Reluctant I resign'd,
> Away the airy pleasure flies,
>   But leaves a sting behind.
>
> Those lips, where smiles so sweetly play,
>   Act but the traitor's part,
> For with their nectar they convey
>   Love's poison to the heart.

> Perhaps they, like Achilles' spear,
>   May heal the wound they give;
> Deign then, in pity, lovely fair!
>   To let me kiss, and live.
>
> But if, alas! a second kiss
>   It would be death to try—
> Then! grant once more the heav'nly bliss,
>   Oh! let me kiss and die.

On looking at it he perceived the initials of his name in a large cypher, tastefully coloured and ornamented; and in a very small hand at the bottom, hardly discernable, she had written, by the Flower of Frederick. He then discovered why she had been unwilling for him to see the paper, and with equal delicacy on his part, he did not make known his discovery.

"And ought not our treaty to be renewed," said he, approaching her with a mixture of tenderness and familiarity, and she yielded, for a moment, to his embrace—but in another, recollecting herself, she said, "Edward, let us be prudent; after all that I have said, you want no further proof of my sentiments. You know I'm yours in heart and soul; that my hand will, probably, also be yours, but until then, whatever tenderness we may feel, let us at least *act* as mere friends."

"Ah, Matilda, you know not your own heart—you deceive yourself—if you really loved, you could not always be thus coldly prudent."

"Edward, you ought—you must know me better. But do not ask me for proofs of affection, which, as things now stand, I feel to be every way improper. Indeed, Edward, if you loved me as you ought, you would never ask me to do that, on which I could look back with regret."

"My dear Matilda," said he, "listen for a moment——"

Now whether the cold water thus thrown on the fire that burnt within him, would have extinguished it, or, as sometimes happens, make it blaze the fiercer, can never be known, as Mrs. Fawkner, going into the parlour and finding no one there, and concluding that Matilda and her friends were in her favourite retreat, had followed them for the purpose of putting an end to one of the *tête-à-têtes* which she, with such good reason, anticipated.

She was now heard to call out: "Matilda, child, where are you? always in that unwholesome place"—and certainly never could word of magician be supposed ever to have ended an enchantment more suddenly than the appearance of this lady put to flight the romance of the four lovers. Then, endeavouring to disguise her motive for following them, she added, "I'm told Mr. Belmain is gone. Why didn't you tell me he was going? To be sure you did not leave him in the parlour by himself, and come off here to your flowers and nonsense."

"No, madam," said Matilda, colouring; "Mr. Belmain has merely rode over to Buck Hill, and means to return I believe. Louisa proposed to me to take a walk in the garden."

"And I," said Gildon, who saw how the land lay, and first recovered his ease, "ventured to solicit a peep at this little temple of taste and beauty."

"Indeed, Mr. Gildon," said the lady, (her features relaxing from their first severity,) "Matilda has bestowed pains enough on the place to make it handsome. But you had better return to the house, as it was very foggy early this morning, and I'm sure the ground must be damp. I'm told you will be absent some time from Frederick, Mr. Grayson," (for so she always now addressed Edward.)

"I do not expect to return, madam, till I am ready to commence the practice of the law," said Edward, gravely.

"I think you are right," said she; "the law, however, seems to be a more uncertain business now than it used to be. Barbawl says they have a very crowded and clever bar at present in this part of the country. I heard Major Fawkner say the other day that the western country holds out great inducements to a young lawyer."

"I shall, madam," said Edward, "make choice of the place that shall seem most likely to advance the interests of myself and my family."

"I was sorry to hear that you meant to sell Beechwood."

"We have come to no determination yet madam." Desirous of waving a subject which was always a painful one, and more particularly when it was pressed by the mother of Matilda for the purpose of mortifying him, he added, "I believe, ma'am, we shall not be able to keep it."

But the lady, who had, besides wishing to humble Edward, the additional motive of endeavouring to discourage Gildon in his views on Louisa, was not so easily checked.

"Will your mother continue in Frederick?"

"She will continue here, madam," he replied, with as much impatience as his regard for Matilda would allow him to show.

"I did not know but she might have removed to Charles' City, though I heard that Easton was also to be sold."

"It is, madam—but when all is sold, an asylum has been provided for my mother and sister," with an anger he could no longer disguise.

"Oh! I did not mean to be inquisitive. But one naturally feels an interest in a neighbour's welfare."

In reply to this speech, Edward gave her a look, in which pride, anger, and scorn, were most manifest, but said nothing. Matilda, who (as well as Louisa) had been on thorns during the whole dialogue, felt abashed, and motioned to Louisa to return to the house, which they all did in that awkward silence which takes place between persons who are not only conscious of their unkind feelings towards each other, but also that they are mutually known.

The carriage from Beechwood now drove down the avenue, and Louisa, whose softer and more unresisting nature had indulged Gildon in those little caresses that are at once so tempting and so dangerous to youthful lovers, and who had, in addition to other causes of vexation, that of self reproach for not adhering to the course she had prescribed to herself, took a hurried leave of Mrs. Fawkner, and when she came to bid farewell to Matilda, that tide of enthusiastic feeling which had been suddenly checked, burst like a torrent, and she hung on the neck of her friend and wept.

Edward, whose own breast promptly told him what had been passing in that of Louisa's and her lover, now reproached himself for having been instrumental in affording his sister an opportunity of adding fuel to a fire that might consume her.

"Do not distress one another," said he, and taking Louisa by the hand conducted her to the carriage.

A half hour brought them to Beechwood, where the quick eye of her mother readily perceived the agitation her daughter's spirits had lately undergone. When they had retired, and she had inquired into the cause, Louisa merely spoke of her distress on taking leave of Matilda, but said nothing of her conversation with Gildon. This was the first breach of that confidence which had ever subsisted between them from her earliest infancy. The mildness of Mrs. Grayson's manners, and her affectionate disposition, had inspired love unmingled with fear, on the part of her children, and she had formed them to the habit of imparting to her all their thoughts and wishes, by abstaining from any thing like bitterness or severity of rebuke, and by not overloading them even with advice. A favourite maxim being with her that they would not be likely to act very much amiss so long as they did not practise concealment, and that faults were half cured when they were once freely confessed.

"Have you had any private conversation, my dear, with Mr. Gildon this morning?"

"He conversed with me some time madam, when he and brother were with Matilda and myself in the summer house;" and she felt her cheeks tingle as with the consciousness of practising a deception on the best of mothers, though she was not telling an untruth.

"And what did he say of his returning to New-York?" inquired Mrs. Grayson, set at rest by her daughter's answer.

"Yes—madam—he—he said he should not be at the races, or if he did, he should not stop more than a day or two."

"I could wish he had abandoned it altogether," said Mrs. Grayson. "And what said your brother?"

"He," stammered Louisa, turning her head

aside to conceal her increasing confusion. "He said nothing, madam."

"Well, I wonder at that, but he, poor fellow, was no doubt thinking of his own difficulties. They sometimes seem to absorb him so entirely, that I feel miserable about him, and fear he will not be able to prosecute his studies to advantage. He must speak to Mr. Gildon again on the subject, and point out the impropriety of his further attentions in still plainer language."

"He has already done so," said Louisa, "I believe. But will it not seem strange, mamma," said Louisa, now recovering herself, "to object to his merely passing through a place because I happen to be there?"

"There can surely be no objection to that my child, but only that he should not pay you the attentions of a lover, which he will be very apt to do if he is near you, and which I fear you cannot help showing that you are pleased with. If this should be the case, had he not better stay away?"

Louisa's conscience told her that there was but too much truth in her mother's supposition, and said: "Perhaps so, madam; but yet he wlll soon leave us—leave the state, I mean."

"That's true, my child, but as he is to go so soon, I think he had better take leave of you here, until he can return under more favourable circumstances."

Louisa made no reply, though she still thought

her mother's fears and objections carried too far. Her little maid Bella now came running into the chamber, and announced that a gentleman in a fine carriage with a waiting man behind him were coming up the lane. This gentleman they rightly conjectured to be Mr. Belmain. The mother and daughter then returned to the parlour to receive the honour of the visit, which he soon gave them to understand was intended for them.

He came back charged more highly than ever with that subtle and animating fluid which is called self-approbation in one man, and self-conceit in another, in consequence of the compliments and civilities he had received from the good-natured Misses Buckley. He played off his airs with unusual spirit, and, contrary to their natural effect, they happened on the present occasion to be much more annoying to Gildon than to Edward, who often found Belmain's little fopperies, joined as they were with great gayety and liveliness of temper, to be very amusing. While Gildon, with an evident feeling of dislike, never lost an opportunity of saying something sarcastic, or of paying him some ironical compliment. And he was disappointed to find that his wit did not produce the effect he thought it merited on any of his auditors. Mrs. Grayson's good breeding would have prevented her encouraging his raillery if her state of mind had allowed her to relish it. Louisa took no pleasure in seeing Gildon fretted at a rival, and was withal too generous and good-natured to laugh at the expense of one who admired her. And Edward neither relished what he called the *pesiflage amère* of his friend, and was not often in a mood of merriment. The young gentleman never once perceived the drift of his rival, so artfully was Gildon's raillery disguised, and his self-complacency was slow to suspect that he could be an object of ridicule in a place so inferior in point of wealth and fashion to others in which he had been a leader of the *bon ton*.

After pressing Louisa to play and sing some of her last songs, in which he accompanied her, (for he never travelled without his flute,) and receiving a new tribute of praise, he took his leave, as he had engaged to dine with Mr. Buckley, but promised to do himself the honour of seeing Miss Grayson again several times before she left the county. He said he would even call in the morning if she would be at home, and practise one of her last sonatas by Pleyel. She could say no less than that she should be at home, and would be happy to see him and his flute.

"Now, Mr. Belmain," said Gildon, with affected gayety, after the Carolinian had left the room, "is a happy man, to have, in addition to a handsome person and a stylish equipage, that which can take the ears captive."

"Do you think," said Louisa, "that these things are sufficient to confer happiness?"

"I know not any so likely to make one agreeable, and nothing so likely to confer happiness as the power of pleasing."

"I think," said Mrs. Grayson, "you overrate this young gentleman's powers in this way."

"I imagine not, madam, but I will leave the matter to Miss Grayson."

"I am not sure," said Louisa, "how you really do rate them. But I do not estimate them very highly. I merely think he has a good taste in music, and that though vain, he has a good heart at bottom."

"Nay, that I deny, madam, for I am sure he has lost it"—and by this sally Gildon closed the conversation, in which, however, he appeared to less advantage in the eyes of both mother and daughter than he had done before since his arrival, though the latter found an excuse for his pique in its cause.

This young man's skilful performance on the flute, and the common place praises it procured, furnished indeed one of those topics of complaint which lovers are ever ready to seize on, and which, with the little bickerings to which they give rise, and the reconciliations that follow, seem as necessary accompaniments of the tender passion; and to be as essential to its growth as exercise is to that of the body. After Louisa and her lover had, by such snatches of explanation as Mrs. Grayson and Edward's presence permitted, gone the usual round of lover's quarrels, they met the next morning in a forgiving humour, and were soon better satisfied with each other than they had ever been before; so that when Primus came to the door to tell the gentlemen, according to custom, that the horses were ready, it was with some difficulty that Gildon could tear himself away to take his morning ride.

CHAPTER XIV.

They had not been gone long before young Belmain in his phæton, followed by his liveried valet, appeared in sight, and in a moment he entered the parlour in a fashionable blue frock coat with doeskin pantaloons and hussar boots. He found Louisa at her piano, not expecting him so soon, or, rather, not having thought of him at all.

"You see," Miss Grayson, said he, "I am punctual to my engagement, and I am delighted to find that you have not forgot it."

"What engagement?" said she, sir, for she had regarded his proposal like so many other things he said, as mere common-place, not worth remembering, and not intended by him to be remembered.

"Why, to practise that difficult sonata by Pleyel, to be sure."

"Oh, I remember, sir," and she immediately began to look for it among a number of loose sheets, when he said, "my dear Miss Grayson, chance favours me with an opportunity that I have long prayed for to discover my sentiments to you, if my eyes have not already spoken a language that is not to be misunderstood." He then went on in the style of rhapsody common on such occasions, and drawing a favourable inference from the embarrassment which such explanations seldom fail to occasion, he pressed his suit with more vehement protestations, and with the air of one who was confident of success. Louisa, collecting all the resolution she was mistress of, declined the honour he intended her in terms so strong and decisive, as to put an end to his hopes at once.

His looks showed that he was quite as much astonished as hurt; and in no very indirect terms he spoke of his situation and prospects, and gave some intimation of the disparity between them in this particular. But finding that she held the same positive, unqualified language, he gave her to understand that he could account for her conduct by a prior engagement which he had heard of, but had not credited from what he had seen. To which she could not forbear replying, that strange as it might seem, it was possible he might not be to the taste of every female, though her heart should be unoccupied. He then ventured, in the course of his expostulations, to insinuate that she had given him encouragement, especially the day before, upon which, with some indignation, she told him, that if such was his mode of interpreting a lady's conduct, she must leave him, lest he should consider her hearing such assertions with patience, as encouragement. And finding she was bent on quitting the room, he made a half-way apology for the uncourteous charge, and bowing formally and profoundly, took leave without practising the difficult sonata by Pleyel.

The truth is, that his feelings were rather those of mortified vanity, than of disappointed love. Having a lively susceptibility to female beauty, and an exalted idea of his own qualifications to please, he was in the habit of falling in love, and of making love to every pretty face he saw. But as Louisa's was a beauty of no ordinary stamp, and she had the eclat in the preceding summer of being an heiress, he had been more than usually taken with her, and had determined that after making the tour of the northern and western states in the winter, if he saw no lady more to his taste, he would return and pluck the little mountain rose, as he never doubted that he would be as much superior in Louisa's eyes to the rural swains whom he saw around her, as he excelled them in his equipment, skill in points of etiquette, and matters of fashion. On returning to Virginia this summer, finding that her prospects of fortune were entirely blasted, he had abandoned at first all thoughts of offering her his hand. But such had been the influence of her beauty, which a year had improved and matured, and such the unaffected sweetness of her manners, which he construed into personal partiality for himself, that he was insensibly drawn along to think of her seriously as a wife, notwithstanding she had lost the recommendation of fortune, though that circumstance was not without its refrigerating effect.

In this state of mind where the conflicting motives nearly balanced one with another, his rebuff was not a cause of suicide, and he was seen the following week at the warm springs dividing his attentions between his own spruce and dapper little person, and the pretty faces which are annually transported thither for the kind purposes of cheering the low-spirited and comforting the sick.

The little mortification which Belmain appeared to suffer, and the offensive insinuations of his vanity, had enabled Louisa to discard him with great indifference; for her good nature and tenderness of heart had commonly made her feel a great deal on such occasions. She immediately went to her mother's chamber, and communicated to her all the particulars, not even suppressing his last hint of the cause of his failure, and in doing so she persuaded herself she was conforming to a secret resolution she had made never more to conceal from her mother any incident of her life. Mrs. Grayson congratulated her on being rid of one who had proved himself so unworthy of her, and superadded further injunctions on the necessity of circumspection, drawn from the seeming notoriety of Gildon's attachment.

Louisa then took a walk down to see Granny Moll, as she usually did after returning from a visit, and patiently answered the old woman's minute inquiries about those subjects that had chiefly occupied her mind—the different dishes at the dinner-table—the servants who waited—and the style and character of the whole establishment at the Elms.

"Ah, the lord bless, you my young mistress," said the old woman, "how times are changed! I can remember when old Steener, Mr. Fawkner's father, was overseer to your grandpa—my old master—and now they are at the top of the pot—and Phill tells me that Mrs. Fawkner is not willing for Master Edward to marry her daughter, and that he an't rich enough. But I tell Phill if he hadn't a rag to his back he would be a match for are a young lady in Frederick. Alack-a-daisy! I never expected to live to see the day when one of old Fritz Steener's grand-children would be thought too good for any of my master's family. But honey, I suppose little Randal, that is Chloe's son, was one of the waiters. They tell me they have taken him in the house since he's grown up, and he's now head waiter."

"He is so," said Louisa.

"Well, my old master give that Chloe's mother and another girl named Patty, for a pair of horses. I remember it as well as if it was yesterday—and honey, the horses were puffed up, and made very sleek and fat, and in two months time they baulked and got good for nothing, and old master let Ben, Sal's father, have them for his wagon; and Major Fawkner owns now more than thirty negroes from these girls. Phill and I counted up twenty t'other day, and we could not count half of them, for there is a good many at the upper quarter."

"Well, but granny, how does Rachel behave to you now; does she wait upon you, and bring you wood?"

"Ah, Miss Louisa, after you talk so to Rachel, and shame her so, she did little better for two or three days. But she soon get in her old way again. Last week my Dick brought me four roasting ears out of his patch, the first I'd seen this year, and if you'll believe me, Rachel eat three of them. She's a monstrous greedy girl. Ah, Miss Louisa, young folks will go their way. But tell me, my young mistress, is it true that this young gentleman that Master Edward brought home with him is a courting you?"

"La, granny, who could have told you that?"

"Rachel, honey, told me so t'other day, and I thought as much before. But Phill says his father that is away to the north, an't willing for him to have my young mistress. God bless the folks! What has come to them? I remember the time when the grandest and richest young gentlemen in the land would have been proud to have married into my old master's family. Now money makes the mare go, as the saying is. But is it true that he is courting my young mistress?" and without waiting for an answer she proceeded: " well, I must say he's a mighty clever gentleman. He comes down here with Master Edward, and sits with the old woman by the hour, and asks me about old times when I lived in Williamsburg, in Lord Botetourt's time; and he always remembers the old woman. I didn't use to like the yankees, though they say they act like what they was in old times, when they used to come up York River in their little vessels, with their onions, and potatoes, and wooden dishes. But is he courting you, child?"

" You musn't believe all you hear granny. I don't mean to marry."

" Ah, Miss Louisa, I know better than that; you can't cheat the old woman so, and I'm thinking you have got the man in your eye already.— Primus says he's more of a gentleman to servants than the little man from Carolina, for all he makes such a show."

Louisa listened with pleasure to these praises of her lover, as every woman does, however humble the quarter, or doubtful the motive from which the commendations proceed, and thought that his kindness to the old woman manifested a very amiable disposition. She was disposed to continue the conversation in the same channel, without seeming to wish it, and added, "I suppose when this gentleman—but he's not a yankee, granny, he's a New-Yorker—asks you about old times, you tell him what fine doings you used to have in those days: of the coach and six, and green and orange liveries, and so forth."

"Ah, let the old woman alone for that. I told him my old master and family were the grandest people in the land, and would be so if they had an acre of low grounds, or a negro to work."

"And what said he to that?" trying to disguise the interest she took in an affected carelessness.

"Oh, he laughed mightily, and said, 'I think so too granny.' He sets a heap of store by you all, you may depend upon it."

In such chit-chat Louisa passed a full hour, after which she was observed to be more particular in catechising Rachel about neglecting the old woman, and not content with giving directions, she herself often went to see that they were obeyed. At these times she seldom failed to hear something relative to Gildon, which gratified her, as evincing either his amiable disposition, his generosity, or his attachment to her, to which last, indeed, she principally ascribed his visits.

As Gildon had expressed a wish to see Harper's Ferry before he left the country, Edward and he concluded to ride there this morning, the distance being but about sixteen miles. The high-wrought description that had been given of this celebrated spot had had the common effect of producing disappointment—that is to say, the gratification derived from the grandeur and variety of the scene, had not been as great as they had expected, though, without doubt they, would have felt no less admiration than he who has described that scene so eloquently, if they had viewed it under less disadvantages of preparation.

They did not discover those clear marks of an abrasion of the mountain, where the united waters of the Potomac and the Shenandoah find a passage through the Blue Ridge into the level country lying east of it. But the tongue of land which separates the two rivers being very steep and high, enabled them to look down on both the streams, which, hemmed in on each side by high and abrupt mountains, appeared to the eye above to be greatly diminished in their dimensions as they meandered in the bottom of their respective vallies.

They looked at the wild scenery around from different points, but no where was it so varied and picturesque as in the very gap of the Blue Ridge, on the Maryland side; for here they could trace the course of both rivers from the South and the West, for a considerable distance; and follow with their eyes the Blue Ridge, gradually softening into a paler hue, until it sinks in the horizon. To the South they saw the section of the mountain which made in one side of the gap an abrupt and almost perpendicular cliff, and to the East the river Potomac, now enlarged by the accession of the Shenandoah, running through a woody and seemingly level country, till both river and country were blended into a pale misty surface of vast extent, resembling a magnificent view of the ocean. These grand and picturesque features of nature were rather interrupted than embellished by the arsenal of the United States, where smoke, and hammers, and workmen moving to and fro, broke in upon the repose of nature, and raised a new and uncongenial train of ideas.

An old man, who was standing with a gun in his hand, near the narrow path which they were ascending, very readily undertook to conduct them to the jutting rock in the gap, to which they had been recommended. He was very communicative, and informed them that he had been a soldier of the revolution, which his erect figure, firm step, and union of a respectful deference of manners with great rigidity of features, all plainly bespoke he had served in the continental line in the Northern campaign—was at the battles of Princeton and Brandywine—and afterwards in the South under the gallant young La Fayette—that he had a cottage at the foot of the mountain, though he had no employment under government. He was then taking a turn on the mountain, and always carried his gun with him, in case he should see a wild turkey, or deer. The young men were delighted to meet with a war-worn veteran in such a spot, and Edward who had inherited from his father a great predilection for the character of a soldier, questioned him very closely about his several campaigns; and when he mentioned serving in the 21st regiment, he said, " the same, I think, in which my father commanded a company."

" His name, sir, if I may be so bold?"

" Edward Grayson."

" Is it possible! and are you a son of Capt. Grayson of the horse? But I see you are the same flash of the eye when he was pleased—I must shake you by the hand, sir; and this is not your brother?"

" No, a friend from another state."

" Well! a braver man," said the veteran, " never drew a sword—nor one who had more feeling for a soldier. Sir, I knew him to give five hundred dollars for a side of leather, (to a Quaker tanner in Pennsylvania, who was a d——d tory, I believe,) and distribute it among his soldiers— for, my young masters, you must know we suffered in the revolution more for want of something to wear, than something to eat, though sometimes it was tough work to forage for provision. I enlisted for a second tour in another company, and was sent to the South under Col. Covington, and never saw your father again till after the war, when I met with him at Winchester. Take the right, sir, by that old pine. Now you, who are possessed of large estates, and are now enjoying the fruits of our independence, have little idea of what those underwent who fought for it; and yet I can't say but that in the midst of our hardships we enjoyed ourselves a good deal at times, when seated around a good fire, with a turkey or goose, or may be a mutton that we had robbed a tory of, and now and then some of our people; for a soldier, young gentlemen, is not very particular in these things. We never thought of the march we had made in the snow, with hardly a shoe to our foot, or expected to make next day. The women, too, were every where mighty kind to us. They often helped us to clothes. They gave us the best their kitchens and dairies afforded—and what is something more than all, my masters, to a young soldier, they gave us kind looks and fair words."

The veteran, who had been a lad of gallantry in every sense, gave them some details of his personal adventures and successes, in which it is not improbable that an active imagination supplied the deficiencies of a declining memory. But they found the communicative old soldier a very entertaining guide, and he, on his part, was so much pleased with his new acquaintances, that he pressed them very much to call and partake of such fare as his little cabin afforded. But they excused themselves, as it was out of their road, and prevailing on him to accept a small gratuity, which he at first refused, they proceeded to the tavern to dinner, which they had previously ordered, and taking a hasty look at the public arsenal then recently established, and the arms that had been there manufactured, they rode back to Beechwood, which they reached a little after sunset.

In the evening, Gildon observed to Louisa, "that he was afraid she would not attempt any of her new music without her late accompaniment; but if she would favour him with one of her old fashioned songs, it might be quite agreeable to the hearers, if not to herself."

"Nay, I please myself most when I please them," said she; and played and sung with more grace and spirit than he had ever before heard her. The song that had been selected, being also one of Matilda's favourites, reminded Edward so strongly of the happy moments that were past, which were so different from those he then saw in perspective, that he felt a heaviness of the heart which he could not repress nor conceal.

The affectionate Louisa perceived it, and going up to him said " Brother, I have something to raise your spirits," and took from her bosom a pacquet she had received that afternoon from Matilda, containing a short note, in which she had requested Louisa to give the enclosed letter to Edward, after they had left Frederick. She then added, in a whisper, " I intended to comply with Matilda's request, though I know it is only some little piece of her prudery; but you looked so disconsolate, I could not help trying to comfort you."

"You are a sweet girl, Louisa; it is the only request from the same person which I could be obliged to you for denying." He withdrew into the next room, and breaking open the seal with impatience, experienced that delight which can be known only to those whose feelings have been refined and ublimated by sentimental love, on finding a little glass locket, with a plain gold rim, in which was to be seen one of her beautiful dark curls, and to the ring of which she had fastened a pale blue ribbon. The paper enveloping it contained the following short note—" Louisa is requested to deliver you this paper, when you will be far distant, and when I am sure the keepsake it contains, will be most acceptable. May the heart which is about to warm this little remembrancer, be also inspired by it with courage and hope, prays your faithful, M——a."

He kissed the little present again and again, with the most rapturous joy, and it was some time before he would forego the luxury of his feelings, to join the party in the parlour. The change in his air and manner, when he entered, was so striking, that Louisa seemed to have wrought a miracle.

"I had no faith in love-powder before," said Gildon, " but I think there was some in that pacquet, and I thought I knew the hand of the physician. It must have been a powerful prescription to have produced so sudden a change."

"It is indeed," said Edward, " and I must take another dose."

" And I, for my part, feel some curiosity to see it administered," says Mrs. Grayson, following him into the dining room, for her maternal solicitude was now diverted from Louisa to Edward.

" What an enthusiast my brother is," said Louisa.

" And may I inquire," said Gildon, " what has occurred to excite his enthusiasm ?"

" A keepsake from Matilda, I believe," said she.

" It is no wonder," said Gildon seriously, " that for such a favour, at once unexpected and unsolicited, he should feel a transport of delight !—Ah, Louisa ! if I could ever hope to inspire you with such sentiments, how happy should I be ! But you are so cold and so prudent—so unwilling to indulge in that enthusiasm which is so interesting in your brother."

" I wish," said she, in a low, trembling voice, " I was as free from all other faults as from coldness of heart."

" And think you," said he, " that you have that fervour of feeling which distinguishes Miss Fawkner ?"

" It is difficult to judge of ourselves," said Louisa, with a mortified air ; " but I know I feel too much for my own peace—though I may appear very dull and inanimate to others."

"My dear Louisa, you misunderstood me—I was only doubting whether there existed any adequate cause to excite you to enthusiasm, and rather meant to express my distrust of myself than of you."

Mrs. Grayson, whose watchful interest in the concerns of her daughter had been for a moment suspended, now returned to the parlour, and her inquiring eye saw, in the suffused cheek, and fluttering manner of Louisa, that her lover had made the best use of the few precious moments afforded him. She then asked her daughter to play a favourite hymn, in which the Deity is fervently besought to inspire us with good resolutions, to pity our weakness and to uphold us in our wavering course—for she was habitually fond of church music, and since her husband's death had never been seen to take pleasure in any other.

Louisa's previous hurry of spirits, and the consciousness of how much she needed that support which she was then invoking, gave uncommon expression to her performance; and when she came to the last stanza, the humility and contrition she really felt got the better of her self-possession, and she was unable to proceed. Her tender mother deeply affected with more than one lively emotion rose, and taking her by the hand, "My child," said she, "you exert yourself too much. You are not well, and had better retire." Then wishing Gildon a good night, she led her daughter into her chamber.

When there, Louisa, no longer under any restraint, threw her head on her mother's bosom, and without uttering a word, burst into tears.

"Has any thing happened, my child, to distress you? speak."

"No, mamma, nothing at all;" yet such is the strange inconsistency of human nature, she felt the stings of self-reproach more keenly than when she had committed a far greater transgression.

"I have been imprudent, my beloved mother; can you forgive me?" She then detailed the hurried conversation which had taken place.

"It would be better for you, my dear child," said Mrs. Grayson, "to be explicit with Mr. Gildon, and refuse to converse with him on a subject which every thing convinces me is not only improper, under present circumstances, but highly dangerous—and if you are fearful of giving him offence, you may plead my commands."

"Oh, my dear mother, I will endeavour to do all you wish me," said Louisa, relieved by having confessed her fault, and by her mother's abstaining from reproof.

Thus calmed in spirit by the gentle treatment of her indulgent and considerate parent, and by more of self-approbation than she had for some time enjoyed, they passed an hour in conversing on indifferent subjects, particularly on the prospect of her intended visit; and by way of confirming the frame of mind in which Louisa then was, Mrs. Grayson, whose heart was ever alive to sentiments of piety, and who never forgot the efficacy of religion, desired her to read aloud Tillotson's excellent sermon on the regulation of the passions; for she preferred his vigorous sense, and rational devotion, to the more polished compositions of the present day; after which Louisa retired more tranquil, and even cheerful, than she had been since she had first experienced the feverish agitations of love.

The next day, which was Sunday, she rose fresh from a sound and untroubled sleep; and according to their invariable practice, attended an Episcopal chapel, which a wealthy gentleman had built in the neighbourhood on his own estate. It was a small building of stone, finished with great plainness and simplicity, and it stood in a narrow bottom, almost surrounded by low hills, covered with thick wood. The congregation which was commonly seen here were mostly people of fortune, who had removed to this county from below, and a few of the neighbours who frequented it merely because it was the nearest place of worship. Gildon was surprised to see the number of carriages, many of them elegant, in attendance on this humble temple of Christ; and on entering he found a very genteel and well-dressed congregation. The preacher was a man of a mild prepossessing appearance and manner, though the earnestness of his exhortations showed that his zeal was of a warmer character.

Louisa entered this place of worship in a frame of mind more than usually prepared to profit by the wholesome doctrine and pure spirit of devotion, which was inculcated. The seeds of religion had been early planted in her breast by her pious mother, and without being an enthusiast on this subject, she was very sincerely devout. But in spite of the resolutions she made in secret to herself, her eyes would often wander towards the seat on which Gildon sat—and then, aware of the impropriety of this interchange of glances, and conscious of the terrestrial character of her thoughts, she would cast her eyes on her prayer-book, and there steadfastly continue them, until her watchfulness relaxed, and the predominating feeling of her bosom gained the ascendency. Thus her whole time in church was spent in a struggle between duty and inclination—between grace and passion: and when the congregation, many of whom were good singers, raised their voices in a hymn or psalm, her feelings of mingled love and devotion overpowered her—and while her devotion was the more fervid, from the sentiments of tenderness which filled her bosom, her love in turn was purified and refined from its earthly dross, by the spirit of devotion. At such times her mind, as pure as that of an angel, regarded her lover only as one of a nobler class of beings in the image of the Creator, for whose happiness she most devoutly prayed, in common with that of her beloved mother and brother.

After service was over, some minutes were passed in an exchange of greetings among the neighbouring gentry, and many were the invitations that Louisa received to dinner—but as she expected to set off on the following Tuesday, they were all declined; and, indeed, the idea of parting with him who more and more engrossed her whole thoughts and mind, produced a sadness of the heart which made company extremely irksome and dull.

Gildon attended the carriage back to Beechwood; and rode off to take leave of the family at Buckley, where he was received with their wonted cordiality, and a profusion of kind expressions of regret at his leaving them so soon, it being understood that he would attend Louisa as far as where the road to Mr. Hawkins's turned off from the main road. After dinner, he escorted Miss Fanny to Beechwood, where she proposed to bid farewell to Louisa, and to remain some days after her departure, to help to cheer Mrs. Grayson's spirits. They found that good lady afflicted with a severe head-ach, which confined her and themselves to her chamber the whole evening.

The next day being spent in packing, and in those various little arrangements which are always made when one is going to be long absent, Gildon and Louisa met only at the breakfast and dinner table. In the evening Louisa walked down to see Granny Molly for a few minutes, and as she was returning, Gildon, who had been informed of it by Miss Fanny, and had been waiting near the spot, approached her, and profiting by the veil which the shades of twilight threw around them, he snatched from her trembling lips the kisses she had not strength enough to refuse, until she heard Primus say, " Miss Louisa, tea is ready," when she had time to recollect her indiscretion, and the inefficacy of all her resolutions.

She persuaded herself that Primus, whose noiseless step had given no intimation of his approach, but who, with a natural curiosity, had stood a while to witness the caresses of the lover, had not witnessed her imprudence, and excusing herself on the ground of surprise, and promising to herself more circumspect conduct for the future, she walked on to the house, and, as soon as tea was over, retired to pass the evening with her mother and her friend.

While they were engaged in rather a melancholy conversation, Bella came up to her mistress and said, " uncle Phill wants to see you, madam."

" Tell him to come to the door. Well Phill, what is the matter?"

" I'm thinking, madam, that the two bays will

hardly do to travel so far—Romulus is getting old now."

"Why, what will you do?" said his mistress.

"I was thinking, ma'am, that Jenus and Stribling would match very well, and we had better put them in, as the overseer is not yet ready to sow wheat."

"Oh, mamma," said Louisa, "we had better take them—uncle Phill is such a good judge."

"I am afraid, Phill," said his mistress, "you want two more horses as much for the sake of making a show as from any necessity."

"Why, to be sure, madam, when I am driving my young mistress, I would rather she should travel as she has been used to travel; but I think the old bays are hardly sufficient, and besides, they go so much better when I have horses before them. They were very near stopping the other day when we were coming up the hill by the new ground."

"I will speak to the overseer about it first—ask him to step here."

"By-and-by Mr. Slade made his appearance, and being questioned as to the propriety of two additional horses, he assured Mrs. Grayson that the bays were in excellent plight, were never stronger nor truer than at this time; that Phill had endeavoured to impose on *him*, as he wished to do on his mistress—and that although he was not ploughing, he wanted the horses to finish getting out the wheat. It was therefore settled, that, for the first time, they meant to travel with but two horses.

Tuesday was a day of tribulation to the amiable and grief-worn Mrs. Grayson. To whatever side she turned her eyes she saw nothing but sorrow, and disappointment, and danger. Her property was about to be taken from her, or rather her children. Her son was blasted in his fairest hopes and was endeavouring to struggle against poverty, and unsuccessful love—and her beloved and helpless daughter, was exposed to similar disappointment, with all the aggravation that her extreme sensibility, and want of firmness exposed her to. Every thing was ready by seven o'clock, though that was later by an hour than they had intended to start. Bella was taken into the carriage with her young mistress, and when Phill drove off, with a loud crack of the whip, the sound of the lash seemed to go to the worthy matron's heart.

The Valley of Shenandoah

Volume II

# THE

VALLEY OF SHENANDOAH.

CHAPTER I.

To enable the reader the better to understand all the considerations which operated on Gildon's mind, it may not be amiss to make him better acquainted with the character and views of Nathaniel Gildon, the father. Having, by a long course of successful industry, amassed a large fortune, he conceived the wish, not only of transmitting his wealth, and the faculty of increasing it, to his son, but also the ambition of bringing him up a fine gentleman, and a man of weight and importance in society. He had once, indeed, an idea of making his son a lawyer; but the distaste which James's volatile genius had for that dry and laborious study, and his inclination for travel, had so strongly resisted this desire, that the old man was finally persuaded to abandon it in favour of mercantile pursuits; and he was the more reconciled to the change, as some of those who figured most conspicuously here, in the circles of fashion, and even in the political world, had been commercial men. At that very time, the showy style of living of one merchant in Philadelphia, whose marble staircase, and mirror doors, and crowded routs, were common topics of admiration, and the yet greater magnificence which another exhibited in perspective, by the palace he was then building, were as attractive and imposing to ordinary minds, as any political reputation whatever.

The son was therefore intended to become a merchant on a large scale, as soon as he had acquired a complete college education, and had been initiated in the arcana of his intended profession, in the counting-house of some eminent merchant in New-York; and when the quick susceptibility of his heart, united to the vanity of being admired, had induced him to become a dangler after the gay Miss De Peyster, the father saw, in that unpromising connexion, his whole fabric of ambition overthrown at once, and bethought himself of the expedient of sending James to the distant college of William and Mary.

Hearing, soon afterwards, that his son had entirely overcome his imprudent attachment, his hopes revived, and he looked for him back, after graduating the following session, to fix himself in New-York. But when he heard that he had contracted another attachment, still more imprudent than the first, he lost all patience, and had determined, if he should marry, to let him taste the folly of his course, without relief or mitigation.

He had requested a nephew, who, to a sprightly genius and much gayety of temper, added a good deal of his own worldly prudence, to write to his son, and, exerting the influence over him he had always possessed, endeavour, if possible, to break off the match. Hence was the letter written, which has already been given to the reader; and the circumstance, on which much stress was laid in that letter, that is, the improving condition of Mr. De Peyster's affairs, was not without its effect on Gildon's mind, whenever he was not under the immediate influence of Louisa's personal attractions—brought up, as he had been, to consider wealth as essential to happiness, and one of the surest instruments of procuring respect and consequence in society. But, as we have seen, such was the magic power of beauty, that these cold dictates of prudence and ambition occasionally melted before it, like snow before the rays of an April sun. And yet, as when the rays of that luminary are withdrawn from above the horizon, the freezing power of ambition would soon resume its sway.

At this time, he was so much under the influence of love, that he was determined to use all the skill and address he was master of, to obtain his father's consent; and if that should fail, to marry Louisa, and trust to the chance of his parent's returning affection; conceiving that his being an only child was as much in favour of that result, as his father's avarice and implacability were against it. If Louisa's friends, of whose pride and disinterestedness he had a very exalted idea, should oppose the match under such circumstances, he flattered himself the interest he had in her affections would finally enable him to win her consent; and it was this standing with her which he was anxiously endeavouring to attain.

But while beauty, and sweetness, and ardent affection, were thus producing their legitimate effects, the unremitted success of Miss De Peyster's father in business was counteracting it. That gentleman, from being a bankrupt but two short years before, was now in a more extensive business, and more rapid course of prosperity, than any merchant of New-York; and the ill fortune of young Gildon, or his folly, in letting such a prize slip through his fingers, was a common theme among their mutual acquaintance. The letters he received from his friends always mentioned this circumstance, and it sometimes excited in him a wish to convince them that what he had thrown away he could at any time resume; and at other times he formed the desire of trying his talents at pleasing with Miss De Peyster, for the purpose of obtaining this triumph to his vanity, and then sacrificing all at the shrine of love. Such were his sentiments when he left Beechwood, to attend Louisa as far as he was permitted, before he set out for New-York, on the plan of conciliating his father.

Though Phill had not been able to procure an extra pair of horses, to go the whole length of the journey, he had succeeded so far as to get the use of them until they should cross the ridge at Ashby's Gap, where the two leaders were unharnessed, and sent back to the treading yard. They stopped at the little village of Salem, in the upper part of Fauquier; and while the horses were fed at the stable of the little ordinary, Bella brought out the store of refreshments with which the provident care of Mrs. Grayson had filled the pockets of the carriage, and which, not relying on the fare they might chance to meet with at the humble places of entertainment on the road, they had always been in the habit of carrying in their journeys. There was a neat's tongue, cold chicken, sliced ham, pickles, and a loaf of such bread as is seldom seen out of the United States, and not often there, except in a few private families, together with cake, Naples biscuit and gingerbread in profusion. But the pain of leaving her beloved mother, and the further and perhaps yet greater pain she anticipated, deprived Louisa of all appetite. Edward and Gildon, who also had their share of mental anxiety, experienced not the same effects from it, but partook of all that was before them, with the keen appetite that belongs to young men at three and twenty. The fragments, after taking as much as would satisfy Phill and Bella, were left as a perquisite to the house; and were eyed, that is, the sweeter portion of them, with great good will by two little bluff-looking urchins in the back room.

The mistress of the house, a silent, decent-looking, stirring woman, came in with a waiter covered with excellent peaches, which had now attained their full perfection, and asked Louisa if she would not like to rest awhile on her bed while the horses were feeding. She readily accepted the offer, and found the little chamber far more neat and comfortable than the outer room had led her to expect. After resting about two hours, they set off at three in the afternoon, with the intention of stopping at the house of Mr. Hawkins, a distant relation, in Fauquier, on whom they had long been in the habit of calling, in passing to and fro. Though Edward had been better satisfied if Gildon had left them at once, yet as they were going the same road some distance farther, when they must necessarily part, he thought it would be fastidious to object to his continuing with them, and accordingly offered to introduce him to the house of his kinsman, where he would be sure of a cordial welcome.

It was past twilight before they reached Mr. Hawkins's, owing, as Phill said, to their having but two horses, as he had predicted; but he might more easily have accounted for the delay, by his turning out of the public road, and missing his way, for a short time, in consequence of having rather too freely indulged himself at the sign of the Cross Keys at Salem. They were received with the kind welcome they ever experienced, though to those who did not know the family, there was a formality in all they said and did, that scarcely comported with that goodness of heart they really possessed. " Cousin Louisa," and " Cousin Edward," were asked the usual round of questions about " Cousin Grayson." Mr. Gildon was formally welcomed to Hawkinsville ; and Mrs. Hawkins told him, she had " had the pleasure of hearing his name frequently mentioned since he had visited Cousin Grayson's ; that is, since he had returned from Williamsburg with Cousin Edward."

About nine they were asked to sit down to a supper, in which every thing was arranged in due form, as it had been prepared with the most scrupulous care. Mrs. Hawkins pressed all of her several little dainties on each of her guests in regular succession, accompanying each solicitation with regret that she had nothing better to offer—and that travelling had given them no better appetites ; though this was correct with no individual of the party ; as the freshness of the night air, and long fasting, had restored even Louisa's appetite. This worthy lady had four children, the eldest of whom, a girl of thirteen or fourteen, was a devoted admirer of " Cousin Louisa Grayson," but was held in mute silence by the presence of a stranger ; while Gildon's rattle took so kindly with her, that she laughed at every word he said. The younger children were very shy of the whole party; running to the door, peeping in, and then starting back, the moment their mama called to them "to come in and speak to their cousins and the gentleman, and to behave pretty."

"I tell Tommy, cousin," she said, "he will never make a lawyer, for you must know Mr. Hawkins talks of making him one when he grows up; but Mr. Hawkins tells me there's Mr. Shalmar, the great lawyer in Richmond, who was raised in this county; he was once a mighty bashful man, and could hardly open his mouth when he first went to the bar. Many people, I am sure I may say several, think he favours you, cousin Edward."

By this time, the little urchin again made his appearance. "Come here, Tommy, and speak to your cousin Edward; you know you're going to be a lawyer—cousin Edward's a lawyer;" on which, he again darted off laughing.

In this way they were entertained by these amiable simple people, in a style of kindness which was at once laborious to the entertainers, and oppressive to the guests. In the lodging rooms every thing was exact and in place; the water, and glasses, and towels, laid to the square; the beds were the nicest and most inviting that were possible; the sheets, to be sure, were of cotton, but spun and wove with so much firmness and compactness, as to have the feel of linen, and they were of the most dazzling whiteness. They were also highly perfumed with roses. The little window curtains were also of domestic fabric, decorated with handsome cotton fringe. Every thing, in short, indicated good management, industry, and neatness. The servants were all clad in homespun, and perfectly clean; with their wool combed almost straight.

Mr. Hawkins was absent in Alexandria, where he had gone to make sale of his crop, and to purchase some necessaries for his family ; which, his wife said, he always did, three times a year. An early breakfast was provided by their considerate hostess, protesting, however, most vehemently, that it was " not with any view of getting rid of them ; she would be very glad if they would spend the day with her, or even several days ; and Mr. Gildon, too, though she had not known him before; but that was no reason they were always to be strangers." And here she cast a significant look towards Louisa, and put on the countenance of one who had said a good thing, but was somewhat doubtful how it would be received ; and inferring some disapprobation from the silence of Louisa, who had not perceived her allusion, said, " Cousin, you must not mind my jokes ; I tell Mr. Hawkins sometimes, friends must be allowed to joke with one another measurably ; don't you think so, Mr. Gildon ?"

" Certainly, madam ; I like always to be joked myself, and am particularly fond of jesting with those I like best."

This he said by way of salvo to one or two little sallies, in which he could not forbear to indulge, when such tempting occasions presented themselves, and for the purpose of securing some stock of good will and friendship beforehand, for what he might be further tempted to say.

When the travellers resisted all her entreaties, Mrs. Hawkins then told her cousin, that as she had been afraid she could not prevail on her to pass the day, she had put up something cold for her to take when they stopped to feed : and ordered the trim, neat looking girl, who was in the room, to bring it out of her closet, where this motherly housewife had provided almost as much as Mrs. Grayson had done the day before.

"Cousin," said Louisa, "I am sorry you have taken this trouble ; Mama has given us an ample supply of cake. But do not let us take your napkins. Grace, ask Bella to wrap up those articles in one of her own"—

"No, cousin," said Mrs. Hawkins, interrupting her, "don't disturb them ; Phill can bring them back as he returns, and I want him to call to let me know how you get down."

Little Tommy, having eaten and drank at the same table with the visiters, and finding Gildon full of jokes and pleasantry, had now overcome his shyness, and seemed as unwilling to leave them as he had been to approach them at first, and eyed them with the intense gaze of curiosity and admiration. Though Mrs. Hawkins had hurried breakfast for them, when they were about starting, she again feared she had driven them away, and even asked them to sit a while longer, as the day was pleasant. She insisted with each in succession, that they would never pass Hawkinsville without calling; and hoped Mr. Gildon, when he travelled that way again, would favour them with a call, and there was no knowing but he might visit Virginia once more. " Cousin, you know you must excuse my jokes."

" Ah, madam," said Gildon, " you must remind Miss Grayson of that duty very often, or she would be apt to overlook it."

The mock gravity with which this was spoken so overcame the air of strangeness Louisa was affecting at Mrs. Hawkins's allusion, that she could not help laughing outright ; and then she felt alarmed lest she should give offence, and vexed with herself for being amused at the little peculiarities of one so amiable, and so studious to oblige her. By way of putting an end to the exercise of a talent, which, though she strongly relished, and often admired, she could not at times help thinking a little unamiable, she wished her kind friend a good day, after, however, the usual length of conference that commonly preceded all leave taking between Mrs. Hawkins and her friends. They set off in a bold trot, according to Phill's practice, (who said, unless his horses started off in good spirit, they were apt to be dull all day,) until they reached the main road they had left.

The next day they travelled on without accident,

till they met with a family moving to the west. It consisted of a middle aged man, his wife, about thirty-five, and eight children, the oldest not fourteen. The man, woman, and the largest children, were all walking, and the youngest were in a little covered cart, driven by the eldest son. He told them he was moving from Westmoreland county to Kentucky, where he could more easily provide for a large and growing family. Gildon seemed disposed to sympathize with so many indigent beings, condemned to exile from the scenes of their early attachment; but he found, on entering into conversation with them, that they were not only reconciled to the necessity of removal, but even full of lively hope, from the plenty they expected to enjoy, and the favourable expectations we naturally form of the future, where the imagination is free to shape it out.

The man told them he had been for many years a tenant on a piece of poor land, and finding it hard, after paying his rent, to support himself with so large a family, and alarmed at the prospect of a crop for the present year, he had sold out all he could spare, crop and all, and with the proceeds purchased the little cart, and retained money enough, with economy, to carry him to the west; after which he expected to rent or settle himself on some piece of good land, not occupied, of which, he was told, there was abundance in that country. They had their little vessels for cooking and eating, and commonly slept on the road side. Louisa presented the woman with a shawl not half worn, and gave the children some pieces of muslin and riband, which had been put away in her trunk, and wished them a prosperous journey.

" One of those little fellows," says Gildon, "will some day be coming to Philadelphia, or to the new federal City, if the seat of government shall ever be removed to that place, as member of Congress."

" Stranger things than that," said Edward, " happen every day in our country, where the avenues to public honour are open to all; and though this man has that extreme poverty, which, in some places, is proof of great indolence or intemperance ; yet, judging from his air and manner, and the compactness of his little fixtures, it probably is not so with him, but the mere result of his being situated on a piece of land too poor to enable him to pay his rent, and support his children while they are young. But in the country to which he is going, his children will, in a few years, be a source of wealth to him, and he will become rich, unless the facility of providing for a family makes him indolent, as I have known to be the case with some who have removed from the poor sandy lands on tide water, to the fertile soil of Frederick."

They now left the road which Phill was accustomed to take in their visits to Col. Grayson's estate in Charles City. Edward had a great facility in losing himself, and Phill was in a road which he had never before travelled. They had not proceeded far, before they came to the fork in the highway, where a guide-post had once stood, for the information of the traveller, but which, with a disinterested love of mischief, (what Mr. Bentham calls the pleasure of malice,) had been struck down.

They took the right hand, the one which seemed most in the proper course, and followed a road on a barren ridge, on which there was neither house nor plantation to be seen for several miles, until they overtook a man from the western part of the state, with a small drove of horses, going to Fredericksburg and Richmond, who, in answer to their inquiries, informed them that he was not well acquainted in that part of the country, but he believed they should have taken the left hand. At length they saw a small log house on the road side, in a bottom, and there they learnt that they had travelled a considerable distance out of the way; and directions somewhat intricate were given by the man whom they saw. He directed them " to take the first two right hands, and then to keep strait forward till they came to a big road, and after keeping down that half a mile, to turn short to the left, and keep that until they crossed a branch, after crossing which, they were to take the right, and then the left in an old field, which would bring them into the main road they had left."

They endeavoured to follow these directions as closely as they could; but sometimes they came by roads leading to neighbouring houses and farms.

which their informant had not thought worthy of notice, but which appeared to them not likely to have been overlooked, and gave rise to much doubt and uncertainty. On one of these occasions they took the wrong road, and after several vain attempts to get right, they fell into a large road, which they presumed was the one they had left, and keeping on for some distance, looking out for the house they wished to reach, they at length spied a small building about two hundred yards from the road, where Primus was sent to inquire the way. He soon returned, with the unwelcome intelligence that they had again mistaken the road; that the house they inquired for was at least five or six miles off, over a rough, hilly way, and that there was no place of entertainment near; but that a gentleman lived a mile and a piece before—a Col. Mason, who was in the habit of accommodating travellers that happened to be benighted, and had lost their way. They accordingly proceeded on with some alacrity; for though the gentleman was unknown both to Edward and his sister, yet they had often heard of his hospitality.

In a brisk trot, which the horses, now wishing to get to their night's quarters, readily struck into, they came to a large gate on the road, and, by the aid of the moonlight, saw a large white house about a quarter of a mile from it. Primus was despatched, with compliments to Col. Mason, and to say, that Mr. Grayson, his sister, and a friend, would take it as a great favour if he would accommodate them for the night, as they had lost their way. "Tell them," said Phill, "the son of Col. Grayson, of Frederick," whose name he thought was a passport to a welcome every where.

Primus soon returned, with a message, that Colonel Mason would be very happy to see them, and before they drove up to the second gate, they saw lights in the front rooms, and a maid with a candle in the passage. A large and venerable old gentleman came out to meet them, and stood at the bottom of the steps which led to the little porch in front of the house, and, handing Louisa out of the carriage, led her up the steps, and introduced her to his wife and daughter, who stood there ready to receive her. Edward introduced himself and his friend to the old gentleman, who in turn announced their names to the ladies of his household, and in a little time our travellers felt as much at home as if they had been among old and intimate acquaintances.

Colonel Mason having a good estate, and living near a road much travelled by persons passing between Alexandria and the western country, and on which there was no inn or house of entertainment for several miles, was frequently applied to for quarters, and his hospitable doors were always open on such occasions, not only to the wayfaring traveller, but also to the wealthy families of the lower country, who sought pleasure or health at the watering places across the mountains. His wife, a friendly, good-humoured little woman, was also well pleased, at these times, to second the kind disposition of her spouse, to show her talent at housewifery, and to hear the news of the leading families of her acquaintance, their recent, births, deaths, and marriages, as well as the matches then on foot, in which she took particular interest.

As neither Louisa nor Gildon were willing to excite the observation or suspicion of strangers, under existing circumstances, no opportunity was afforded him of a long conversation with her while at this hospitable mansion; but as he had contrived to be seated next her at the supper table, he could not forbear touching on what had been, for some days, ever present to the minds of both—their separation the next day; and in spite of the strong effort she made to hide what was passing in her bosom, the rising tear might have been seen in her eye. Without turning her face towards him, she begged him to desist from further conversation on the subject; and, as if to compensate him for the seeming harshness of the request, she slipped into his hand, unperceived by any eye, a small paper, which he found afterwards to contain a topaz ring, on the inside of which was inscribed "Louisa," and which she had intended to give him on the following day.

The next morning they took leave of their kind entertainers, who did not fail to insist on their guests all promising that they would never pass that way without calling on them; and after travelling about an hour, they came to the road where it had been determined that Gildon was to leave them. He had been in hopes that Edward would have given him an opportunity of a private conversation with his sister at the door of the carriage, though but for a few minutes, and as he himself rode at a slackened pace, he frequently, by way of hint, reminded his friend that he was about to take leave of them. Finding, however, that Edward's sense of propriety did not accord with his wishes, he took a hurried and abrupt adieu both of him and of Louisa, and turned his horse's head towards Colchester, on his way to Mount Vernon.

Louisa did not attempt to conceal her grief at parting with her lover; but no longer striving against the feelings which agitated her, she yielded to all the violence of her emotions, and, as the carriage proceeded, sobbed aloud. Edward, who knew what she felt, sympathized with her most truly, but avoided as much as possible seeming to observe her distress; and thus the day passed in gloomy silence—both the brother and sister lamenting their cruel fate, and the crosses and obstacles which opposed them on their first entrance into life. Gildon, too, rode off with a heavy heart, for he loved with a real affection; but his love was of a less pure and disinterested character than theirs; and, besides, he had a buoyancy of spirit that bore him up under misfortune, and which almost always made him look forward to some more favourable future, when the clouds which then hovered over him would be dissipated, and leave a clear sky and comfortable sunshine. He felt the existing disappointment most keenly, but he was supported by an entire confidence, that, sooner or later, his love would be successful and happy.

His present plan was to visit Mount Vernon, Monticello, and the Natural Bridge, to attend the races of Fredericksburg, and then return to New-York, and use all the address he was master of to procure his father's consent; but if he failed, to return, insist on the hand of Louisa, and trust to his father's forgiveness, and the chances of fortune, for the rest. Yet it must not be supposed, that this was the settled determination of a firm and decisive mind, who, deliberately weighing all the arguments for and against a particular measure or course of conduct, and ascertaining what is best in a choice of difficulties, makes his selection, and thenceforward pursues it with steadiness and earnestness. No, it was rather the impulse of feeling than of judgment— the predominance of one inclination over another. He had frequently vacillated between this course, and that of forcibly breaking off from Louisa, and then returning to New-York, for the purpose of renewing his addresses to Miss De Peyster. Indeed, after he seemed to have made his determination, he had considerable misgivings about the propriety and even practicability of his course. His father's obduracy, the opposition of Louisa's friends, and the desperate plan of marrying without the means of supporting a family in comfort, much less in the style he wished, seemed at times to be insuperable objections to the gratification of his wishes. But when he saw Louisa, conversed with her, perceived the warmth of her affection, in her whole look and manner; and received her enthusiastic yet innocent assurances of regard, his fears and his prudence both gave way, and he yielded only to the suggestions of love. He had been on the point of insisting, as his hints to that purpose were not regarded by Edward, on being permitted to accompany them to Stanley; and he perhaps had done so, if it had not in some measure thwarted his plans. Besides, he had prevailed on his father to give his consent, that before he returned to New-York, he should avail himself of the only opportunity he might ever have, of visiting the seats of the two most conspicuous personages in the state of Virginia, as well as its most celebrated natural curiosit —and he had not more time than was sufficient for these purposes.

Edward and Louisa reached Stanley, the seat of Colonel Barton, in the county of Stafford, about noon. The mansion house is pleasantly situated, on an eminence, about half a mile from the Potomac, whose broad stream it overlooks for seven or eight miles up and down the river. As their visit had been announced by letter, they had been anxiously expected for several days; and Miss Barton, the eldest daughter of their entertainers, about the age of Louisa, was overjoyed to embrace her friend, after an absence of nearly two years. Two of her sisters were married, one of whom, with her husband, Mr. Jones, was then on a visit to pass the summer at Stanley. There was also in the house a brother of Mr. Jones, who was an admirer of Miss Julia, and a young Scotchman, the schoolmaster of the younger children; so that the family ordinarily consisted of fourteen or fifteen. The extensive low grounds, stretching in a perfect level towards the river, and gently undulating on the north side of the house, formed an agreeable contrast (from its novelty) to the mountainous and woody country they had just left, though they were inferior in point of fertility. The house was of brick, and consisted of a wide passage through the middle, with two rooms on each side, both above and below stairs. There was, besides, a small building near the main one, in which there were two lodging rooms that were occasionally occupied by young gentlemen and other visiters. The known hospitality of Col. Barton invited a great resort of company in that part of the country, where visiting, and junketting, and merry-making, were at that time followed as the chief business of life. It was indeed in the neighbourhood of Choptank, called Joetank, whose inhabitants have from time immemorial been remarkable for their love of barbacues, fish-fries, cock fights, horse races, and balls. They were great epicures at the table—fond of dress and dancing, and every species of sport and revel. Frank Barton, Col. Barton's eldest son, had long been one of this fraternity of *bons vivants*, and he spent the most of his time from home with his gay companions of King George, Westmoreland, and the neighbouring counties, in hunting, fishing, shooting, dancing, or fiddling. The Colonel was a hale, hearty looking man, of about fifty-five, of a fair character, and with a pleasing urbanity of manners, united to great frankness and ease. It was impossible to treat him with disrespect, and yet the deference shown to his age and worth was entirely free from awe. Mrs. Barton was about six years his junior, but her face being fat and free from wrinkles, she appeared to be still younger. She was a very lively, laughing old lady, and never was better pleased than when she saw the young people happy and making merry.

It scarcely ever happened, in the summer or winter, that some two or three families, commonly their relatives, but sometimes others, were not domesticated with them. Living in a county abounding with fish, oysters, and crabs, wild duck, and other water fowl, and surrounded by woods furnished with deer, and hares, and squirrels, or by pastures, tolerable for cattle and excellent for sheep, they always had a good table. The old gentleman imported his wine from Madeira, and his porter from England. Cider, of the Hughes' Crab and Royal Wilding, he made from his own orchard. A very large garden, containing several acres, in which the gratification of the eye was a secondary object, furnished every variety of vegetable and fruit, produced in the country, in the greatest abundance. A boat, equipped with an awning, oars and sails, was always ready for the accommodation of those who either wished to cross the river, to go on a fishing excursion, or to sail or row up and down the river on a party of pleasure. Besides, as a further provision against *ennui*, there were also backgammon, shuttlecock, chess, and cards, an old harpsichord, a flute, a violin, and two or three book cases of books, which were exclusively those that had been of greatest celebrity when Col. Barton was a young man. With all these means of getting rid of time, it yet seemed sometimes to pass on heavily, in the intervals between breakfast and dinner, and dinner and supper; but at these times, it must be confessed, there were few sorry hearts or sad faces. Mrs. Barton's loud and good humoured laughs, the Colonel's lively jests and urbane suavity of manners, and their excellent fare, made every one cheerful and happy.

Julia Barton quickly perceived the alteration that had taken place in her once gay and almost volatile friend. Instead of that incessant lively prattle which formerly distinguished her, she was now silent and reserved, seldom laughing, and never in that careless joyousness of manner for which she was once so remarkable. Perceiving that she manifested a wish of being alone, and was frequently absent and abstracted when in company, Julia that evening made the inquiries which friendship dictated; and, after some little hesitation, she brought Louisa to disclose every thing. Indeed, Miss Barton had known of Gildon's attentions to Louisa, and that they were favourably received ; but she had not been apprized of the difficulties in the way of their marriage. Louisa, after this frank disclosure, found in the sympathizing bosom of her friend, the greatest consolation that affliction of any kind can know, but more especially the anxieties of love. From this time, her attachment, and the difficulties which attended it, and the hopes it held out, formed the principal theme of conversation with these young friends, and would have occupied them often the whole night as well as the day, if Julia had not been so much more disposed to sleep than her guest. When, however, she was wide awake, she took a lively interest in her cousin's affairs; and amidst all the sufferings which touched her sympathy, she saw in Louisa's fate as much to admire as to pity.

Brought up in ease and affluence, and indulged in all her whims, Julia Barton had somewhat of that proneness to discontent, which unvarying prosperity is apt to produce. Devoting the chief part of her leisure to novel reading, she saw every thing through the false medium, which these delusive pictures of life are apt to create; and nothing interested her much, except as she thought she could discover in it a resemblance to these same ideal pictures. The height of her ambition was to be a heroine of romance; and she often deplored her wayward fate in secret, that her life should glide on in one dull unruffled quiet, exempt from those tender distresses, and delicate sorrows, which constitute the charm of so many romantic tales. All had gone with her too smoothly and too soberly, and she saw no prospect of her meeting with any more remarkable adventures, or perplexities, or interesting incidents, than her mother and grandmother before her. It was owing to this frame of mind, that the young gentleman then in the house, and the brother of her sister's husband, had been kept in a state of suspense for nearly a year. Nathaniel Jones, or Nat Jones, as he was called in the neighbourhood, possessed the solid recommendations of a good estate, a respectable understanding, a fair character, and an amiable temper; but having known him from his infancy, and seeing in him nothing more than she saw in most of the young men of the Northern Neck, except more moderation and sobriety of character, she could not bring herself to regard him as a lover, though before he took upon himself that character, his uniform propriety of deportment had made him a great favourite. His name, too, so little like that of a hero of romance, was a great damper of his success; and the cordial approbation which his suit met with from Julia's friends, was a further disadvantage. She did not, indeed, dislike Mr. Jones, and she always treated him with civility, as she did every other person, but she could not readily bring herself to look upon one as her lover, whom she had known from her infancy; who was not a foundling, nor even an orphan, and whose suit went on in the plain every-day course that all the matches in the neighbourhood were made. Had there been any opposition on either side; had there been any mystery, any singular circumstances, connected with his suit, there is no doubt, that the esteem she already felt for him would have soon ripened into love. She found in the affairs of her cousin, all that sentimental distress and difficulty of situation, which she so much coveted, and she could not but view Louisa, in the midst of her misfortunes, as an object more of envy than compassion. When she disclosed her own love affairs to her friend, she even felt ashamed, that every thing connected with them should appear in so homely and rustic a style. She was agreeably disappointed, when Louisa congratulated her on the bright prospects of happiness before her, and wondered she could for a moment hesitate about accepting a man, who to an agreeable person and amiable disposition, added all the qualifications, which her considerate friends deemed necessary. Louisa indeed at first suspected that her heart must be pre-engaged; but finding that was not the case, she expostulated with her, and forcibly contrasted Julia's happy lot with her own.

We will now leave these young ladies, so differently the victims of sentiment—for the one was afflicted at the obstacles in the way of her attachment, and the other lamented that she had no obstacles to encounter—let us leave them to attend Edward, who, after he had rested himself and his cavalry for two days, set off for Richmond, where he proposed to have an interview with his father's counsel, and, after remaining there, and at the old family mansion in Charles City, till the sickly season was over in Williamsburg, to go to that place, for the purpose of attending the law lectures.

He passed through Fredericksburg, which he reached the following night. He stopped at a much frequented tavern there, and found several young men smoking cigars, and discussing the merits of General Washington's farewell address, which had been published a short time before. Some of them greatly admired it; some found fault with its sentiments, though they approved the style; and one or two condemned both. In the course of the evening, the company was composed of half a dozen different sets, most of whom were dressed in the extreme of the fashion, either smoked cigars or chewed tobacco, were zealous republicans, and commonly addressed one another by the title of " citizen."

One young man, more neatly, but less fashionably dressed than the rest, rebuked another, who, in offensive and indecorous language, was reviling the character of the president; and observed that if we were sure that we were right, and the president wrong, no one could doubt his upright intentions, and that for a single cause of dissatisfaction, (the ratification of Jay's treaty,) we ought never to forget the services he had rendered the country. Upon which a small man, wearing a calico gown, and who had several times attempted to make himself heard, now stepped forward, and in a tone and manner that commanded attention, said, nay, sir, if gratitude for past services should make us swerve from present duties, or hinder us from doing justice, it is a vice and not a virtue. He proceeded to demonstrate his proposition according to the doctrines of Godwin's political justice, then getting into vogue, and zealously propagated by a few enthusiasts in that section of the country. The young philosopher was fluent, ardent, and specious; and those whom he did not convince, he confounded, until he drove from the field of dispute every antagonist. Edward, who felt an extreme repugnance to the doctrines he then heard, was strongly inclined to express his disapprobation of them, if nothing more; but, being a stranger, and more than that, not liking the politics of those whose moral doctrines he agreed with, he became neutralized, and remained silent.

The next morning he arose early, and, having visited the house in which the illustrious Washington had once lived, and where his venerable mother then tottered on the verge of the grave; he set off for Richmond, and in the evening reached Hanover Court House, where the self-created orator, Patrick Henry, began his career of eloquence, and where our traveller was very well accommodated, and the next day he reached the Swan tavern in Richmond, to dinner. He passed the evening in walking along the bank of the river, and about Mayo's bridge, then building, and in writing to his mother and sister. In the morning he called on his lawyer, Mr. ———, at that time in the zenith of his reputation. He told Edward, that the case in which his father was sued as a surety, would be argued at the succeeding term— that there was little chance of his being able to get clear of paying the debt, and he recommended a compromise, if one could be effected. In the afternoon he walked down to the Brick Row, now E. Street, to the billiard table, and to his great surprise he there saw the same eminent counsel, busily engaged at play, and betting very freely. He was easy and familiar with every one; and if there was not a great deal of the forms of respect paid to him, their place was amply supplied, with the affection and good will they evidently bore towards him. Edward expressed some surprise at what he saw, to a young man, with whom he was slightly acquainted, and learnt that this distinguished advocate was devoted to billiards, dice, and faro-bank; that he often spent the best part of the night at some noted gaming-house, where he lost a large portion of the gains which his fame and talents had acquired.

During his stay here, Edward was introduced to a society of young gentlemen in this town, consisting principally of students of law, where legal, moral and political questions were discussed with a good deal of ability and ingenuity. Most of its members, who have not found a premature grave, have obtained a distinguished standing in society, and some of them have filled the highest honours of the country. At first, Edward's haughty reserve prevented their seeing and knowing his worth, but after a while he became a great favourite with them. By these means, he was introduced into several genteel houses, and saw females whose charms he could not have beheld with indifference, if he had not been fortified with a previous attachment.

Parties were more distinctly formed and more widely separated here than he had seen them in Frederick; and there was but little intercourse, certainly none that was cordial, between the leading families of the two parties. The merits of the British treaty had been busily discussed throughout the preceding winter and the current year, and it still formed a very common topic of abuse for one party, and of apology for the other. The party to which Edward belonged, was the strongest in numbers as well as talents; and he would have found the place and its inhabitants very much to his liking, if the condition of his affairs had permitted him to remain there.

After staying some eight or ten days in the metropolis, he set off for Easton, the place of his nativity in Charles City. If he had never visited this spot in the height of his prosperity, without a feeling of melancholy, which an appearance of decay and desertion always inspires, how must it be now that it was about to pass into strange hands! Formerly, the sadness he felt arose from the vague impression of the uncertainty and instability of all human possessions; but now, the sight of this venerable seat of his ancestors reminded him of the fall of his family from their former opulence and consequence to the most absolute poverty; and the tender and not unpleasing melancholy he had formerly experienced, was exchanged for a bitterness of feeling, and soreness of the heart, which had nothing in it consolatory or agreeable.

The house was a large one for the time and country in which it was erected. It consisted of a quadrangular building in the centre, and two wings, to each of which the different offices were attached, so as that the whole extended to a great length. It stood within two hundred yards of the river, to the banks of which, the ground, well coated with turf, had a gradual and regular slope. On one side of the house, was an extensive garden, running parallel to the river. A wide plain, stretching to a great distance back of the mansion, was divided into large fields, which were every year shifted from Indian corn or wheat, to extensive pastures covered with horses and cattle. But on the other side, a tongue of woodland ran within a quarter of a mile of the house, and furnished it with fuel. Near this point, and a little behind it, "the Quarter," as it was called, was situated, on which the huts of the negroes were arranged nearly in a line, to each of which was attached a little garden. In front of the house, covering the way, were two rows of catalpas, and behind, several very large oaks, some of them in a state of decay from age, gave a venerable air to the building. The house was of brick, and had suffered from the natural injuries of time before Col. Grayson came to the possession of it. He had, however, as long as he lived in it, kept it in tolerable repair. Since he had removed to Frederick, he had by degrees suffered it to be neglected, and it was now in a state of evident dilapidation. Most of the windows wanted some panes of glass, and in a few, the sashes themselves were broken out. Several of the outer doors had rotted at the bottoms, as had also the threshold and window sills. Moss had grown about the steps, and the stones of which they were made, had either sunk in, or, by the gradual action of frost and vegetation, had been moved from their original places, and afforded between their interstices nourishment for the plantain, the dock, and dandelion, and underneath them, an asylum for lizards, frogs, and toads.

An old man, who had long since been past labour, but whose tried fidelity recommended him for such a duty, had the charge of airing the house, and keeping it in order for the reception of such of the family as occasionally visited it. One wing had been for some time occupied by the overseer, or manager, a smooth, plausible, voluble man, who had got the blind side of Col. Grayson in his lifetime, and had maintained himself in the good opinion of the family ever since. Old Bristol, or Bristow, as he was commonly called, was engaged in cobbling his shoes, with the aid of a pair of spectacles, in the kitchen door, when Primus, opening the gate, called out, " Uncle Bristow, Master Edward is come."

The old man laid down the implements of his industry, and came tottering with age to welcome his young master.

" How goes it, uncle Bristow," said Edward, offering his hand, with a more mournful feeling than he had ever before greeted the old man—" and how are you all ?"

"Oh, master, I am up and about, thank God! Aggy has been complaining of pains in her bones. There is several of the people at the Quarter that have agues."

" And where is Mr. Cutchins ?"

" He is gone to Petersburg to engage the wheat."

" How are the crops ?"

" I heard the overseer say the wheat would not turn out well. We had a wet harvest, and the weevil got in it before he found time to tread it out. I told him it was always our rule, in Mr. Ward's time, to get out our wheat before the full moon in August. Most of the corn is mighty bad, but it is pretty good on the river."

Thus the faithful old servant went on detailing all the particulars relative to the estate, as far as he remembered, and had been able to procure information from the younger and more active part of the slaves. A smart lively boy now came in, and bowing to Edward, said, "Mistress bid me ask, sir, if you have dined."

"I have not," said he. "What boy is that, uncle Bristow?"

"That's a boy Mr. Cutchins bought this summer."

"I wonder Cutchins lays out all his gains in purchasing negroes, and does not buy land."

Bristow smiled. "I believe Mr. Cutchins' got money enough to buy land and niggers too."

"How can that be?" said Edward.

"Oh, master, Mr. Cutchins' a mighty money making man. He rents a little plantation of old Col. Cocke, he make fine crops, and sell wheat and corn; and he make good crops whether we do or not."

"Ah, uncle Bristow, I see you have still your old suspicions. I am afraid Mr. Cutchins and you are on no better terms than formerly."

"No, master—Mr. Cutchins use me very well, absept that he take Aggy's cow when she had a calf, and give a good chance of milk, and give Aggy another. Absepting this, Mr. Cutchins use me very well; but I don't think it right for overseers to make so much money out of their employer. He's gone now to Petersburg to sell wheat, and Dick says he means to have it ground into flour."

"Well, if he does," said Edward, "I have no doubt he will render a just account of it. I believe him to be very honest, as well as fit for business; but we shall not long have occasion for his services, Bristow."

"Well, thank God for that, master," said Bristow.

"I mean," said Edward, "there is every reason to believe, that the debts which have come against my father's estate, will make it necessary that the plantation should be broken up, and every thing sold."

"What! niggers and all?" said Bristow, with an accent of alarm.

"I fear so," said Edward.

The old man shook his head. "I was afraid it would come to this. I told Aggy I was sure from the way things were carried on here, that every thing would be sold. And what is to become of my poor mistress?"

"My mother is reconciled to the change. I am in hopes there will be enough left to make her comfortable," endeavouring to cheat himself as well as this faithful domestic.

"And will the people be sold at public sale?"

"No, uncle Bristow, I will never consent to that. They shall be sold with the land to some good man, so that their situation will be no worse than it has been."

"Well, thank God for that. But did ever I think to see the day when this place was to go from the Graysons?"

Edward, whose family pride, and attachment to the residence of his ancestors, were sufficiently excited before, heard these lamentations of this affectionate slave, who had grown gray in their service, with great pain; when the little mulatto again made his appearance, and told Edward that dinner was ready.

Mrs. Cutchins received him very kindly, and he found her greatly improved in dress and appearance since he saw her the year before, and several new articles of furniture indicated a correspondent change in their condition. He sat down to a broiled chicken and fried ham, with several dishes of vegetables—the whole served up in the same style of neatness, for which Mrs. Cutchins had ever been remarked and praised, but in one of greater expense. She gave him a melancholy detail of the sickness of the negroes, and the various mishaps of the crops of wheat and corn—the death of horses, and cattle, and hogs; adding, that her husband had gone to make sale of the wheat, but it was so injured, he feared it would not turn out much.

"He means to have it ground, I hear."

"Yes, sir, he said he should see which would prove the best for the estate. He is always planning, Mr. Grayson, how he can manage every thing to the best advantage, especially as the wheat turned out so badly. But you don't eat any thing, Mr. Grayson—you cannot put up with my plain fare."

"Your dinner is very good, Mrs. Cutchins, and I have done justice to it."

"Won't you taste my preserves? I made them expecting to see some of the family," said the dame, putting a nice white loaf before him, with one plate of butter, and another of preserved raspberries.

Having finished his repast, he walked into the garden, that was endeared to him by the recollection of his boyish days—where he had purloined the earliest figs, the ripest pears, or the best melons—or had run races with some of his boyish companions. He found the gravelled walks grown up with weeds and grass, the beds broken down, the espaliers in decay, some inclining towards the ground, and others actually down. Two or three large fig trees that had been annually trimmed, now in unpruned luxuriance, wore a more flourishing appearance than he had ever seen them. The vines were loaded with grapes, some of which were now ripe. The lilachs and altheas had grown very much, and the latter were just losing their rich bloom. In the corner, next the house, two or three squares, negligently cultivated, furnished the overseer with cabbages, pulse, and other common vegetables. The late flowering shrubs appeared here and there, brightening the scene with their gay hues; but showing, by their diminished size, and irregular dispersion, that art had had no hand in their production.

In the farther division of the garden, there had formerly been a choice collection of fruit trees, many of which were in full bearing, but for want of pruning, they were overloaded with fruit, or had been the prey of some destructive insect. A few apricots appeared to be ripe, and he plucked one and tasted it ; but it appeared to him a different fruit from what it had been six years before, for it had been so long since he had been here at this season.

He went down to the bank of the majestic James river, there upwards of two miles wide, and walked along the beach. He had a lively recollection of his boyish feelings, when he had searched in the rubbish which the tide had cast up for something curious or valuable, and found nothing but a chip or refuse piece of carpenter's work. He remembered the buoyancy and elasticity of spirit with which he used to run along the beach of soft white sand, at this season of the year, when the air was neither warm nor cold, and when the bare consciousness of existence was a source of lively pleasure ; or when he would jump into the boat which his father kept, and would assist in putting any one across who had missed the neighbouring ferry, or had not time to reach it ; or would join the parties which hooked the sturgeon, or hauled the seine ; or go on board the vessels that appeared to have come from sea, for the purpose of purchasing oranges or cocoa nuts. All these early adventures came fresh into his mind, as he viewed the scenes where they had occurred, and added new poignancy to his regrets at parting with a spot so endeared to him. How different, it often seemed to him, would have been his lot, if he had been able to call Matilda his own; when, blest in mutual affection, he could have walked with her along the beach, and recounted to her some of his boyish adventures or rash exploits: he then recollected that all this might easily have taken place, and that the same untoward course of events which compelled him to sell his patrimonial estate, also thwarted his love. He involuntarily censured his father; and he was emphatically of opinion, that prudence was the first of virtues.

In this melancholy musing, he saw a boat rowing towards him, and in a little while he descried Cutchins, with his horse, on his return from Petersburg. This adroit politician, who felt none of that extreme delight at seeing any of the Grayson family which he pretended, shook Edward by the hand most cordially, and said he had been looking for him for some time; that he had been endeavouring to dispose of the wheat, as he thought he could do better with it in Petersburg, though it was a little further to carry it than to Richmond; that he had been dissatisfied with the merchant at the latter place, both on account of the weights, and in settling the price.

"But I thought," said Edward, "you meant to turn it into flour."

"Why, no—yes, I meant to turn a part into flour,

by way of trial. And how is Mrs. Grayson, and all the family? You look very well, Mr. Grayson. I wonder we had not seen you when you was in Williamsburg last winter."

Though his account of the disposition of the wheat did not agree with that of Mrs. Cutchins, he perfectly coincided with her in the quantity and quality of the crop, and of the great loss in horses, hogs, &c.; in the frequent sickness of the negroes, and of the quantity of salts and tartar and ipecac. he had used—he averred he was as good a doctor as any body, and could not bear to see these gentry running off with all the profits of an article; that if he had sent for a doctor as often as they had been accustomed to do when Doctor Riker used to attend, it would have swallowed up half the estate. Edward, imposed upon by these professions of zeal and fidelity, thanked him for his prudence in managing the estate, but cautioned him against relying on his own skill, and enjoined him to call in a physician whenever the disease was out of the common way, or at all violent.

Cutchins then remarked, that he had been wishing to see him, or his mother, for some time, to speak with them on an important subject, and he hated to do it too, but he had a growing family, which he was obliged to provide for. After more of this sort of prelude to a request which one expects may be refused, or rather which he knows ought to be refused, he said, that great as was his regard for the family, it would be impossible for him to continue there, unless his salary was raised. Edward felt unaffected surprise at this declaration, as he had always heard that his father had been very liberal with this man, and he knew that the profits of the estate would not justify a greater stipend. He therefore told him that he was sorry, on his account, to learn, that he did not find his present situation profitable, but he had understood he often purchased property. He replied, that he had bought one or two negroes lately, but they were great bargains, and all the money had not been paid yet. Edward repeated his regret, and then told him that in all probability the estate would soon pass into other hands. This news, of which some vague rumour had reached Cutchins before, gave him more concern than surprise; he knew that he could never meet with persons so easily imposed upon, even if he could be sure of being employed. He was sincere then in the sorrow which he expressed, and made particular inquiries when and how the sale was to be made; and when Edward told him that the whole would be sold together, he urged on him most earnestly the great sacrifice he would make in such a sale; told him the land, by being divided into three or four parts, would bring twice as much; and that the slaves might be sold in families, if he did not wish to separate them. He even inquired if he would not sell him a small part of the land, which he named, running from the river, and taking in all that poor land on the hill. Edward looked at him with a mixture of surprise and suspicion, remarking, that he had not supposed him in a situation to purchase. He very promptly said, that he had a friend who had money, and who had promised to befriend him, in case he should not continue longer at Easton.

The confidence of Edward, thus finally shaken by the repeated attacks which had been made on it, was not so speedily restored; and he contented himself with saying that he expected the whole of the tract would go together, if a purchaser could be found. Cutchins was dissatisfied, observing, that one man's money was as good as another; and, as if resenting ill treatment, was evidently less respectful to Edward than he had ever before been.

They then went to the part of the house occupied by Cutchins, who gave an account to his wife of his expedition, and of his endeavours to make the most of his crop.

"I tell Mr. Grayson," said Mrs. Cutchins, "you are always planning how to make the estate profitable."

"Yes, I have been doing my best, day and night, for nine years come Christmas, and I don't know that I shall get any more thanks than them that do nothing."

"Why, what's the matter now," said his wife, somewhat perturbed, "has that old hypocrite been trying to make mischief with Mr. Grayson? He threatened me the other day, because I would not let him have the best cow on the land, that he would take satisfaction."

"How you talk, wife," said Cutchins; "do you think I care what old Bristow tells? Mr. Grayson has too much sense to be listening to negroes' news; and if he was, thank God, I am a free man, and can shift for myself. But the matter is this—Mr. Grayson tells me, the estate, land, negroes and all, is soon to be sold to pay his father's debts, and I wanted to buy a scrap of low ground, with the poor ridge, and the worn out old field joining it. I could borrow the money, and he don't seem willing to divide it."

Mrs. Cutchins's first sensation was surprise, that Easton was to pass from the hands of those who had owned it from her earliest recollection; but soon having an eye to her husband's interest, and taking his cue, said, "why to be sure, John Cutchins, you would not want to buy broom straw? If I did buy land, I would buy some that would produce—though may be you expected, that poor land poor price."

"The place is not worth much, to be sure," says Cutchins; "but I thought that if it was taken off, it might help the sale of the rest, and that may be I might make out to purchase it."

Edward said he should be governed by the advice of his friends, but as he was determined not to separate the negroes, he did not think the tract was too large. He might not have had his eyes so easily open to the selfish views of these narrow-minded people, if they had not too plainly shown, that they regarded him very differently, when seen as the heir of a large estate, and when, stripped of his patrimony, he, like themselves, had his fortune to make—so much more sharp sighted are we in detecting the faults of those who chance to displease us.

The next morning Cutchins, who had recollected it was still to his advantage to keep on fair terms with Edward, resumed his habitual smoothness and courtesy, and extolled the value of the estate, and of the negroes, and gave advice about the most advantageous mode of disposing of the cattle and stock. He laid before Edward his accounts of disbursements and receipts for the estate, all of which he explained and accounted for, with a wonderful glibness; and although he was not able to restore the former confidence of Edward, his explanations were too plausible, for one who was both liberal and inexperienced, to detect their errors. The result of the whole was, that before the sale of the present crop of wheat, he was, by the purchase of negro-clothing, the payment of taxes, blacksmith's work, and other necessary expenses, and the few orders he had discharged, in advance for the estate.

Edward then rode over the land, and visited the negro quarters. He found them more uncomfortable in clothing, and in their little dwellings, than he had ever before seen them. Several were sick with agues; these were badly nursed, and ill supplied with medicines, and their little articles of diet, which are of still more importance in slight diseases,

Throughout the whole body of them, an air of sadness, and sometimes of sullen discontent, manifested itself in their behaviour towards him; for the news that they were to be sold, had flown like wild fire, as soon as Bristol had told Aggy, and Aggy had told all she met with. "So you are going to sell us, my young master—and we are all to be sold," said first one and then another; while some were too proud to give utterance to their complaints. Edward endeavoured to soften the unwelcome intelligence, by telling them of his resolution, not to separate them, for which act of kindness some warmly thanked him, while others looked incredulous. He found the crop of Indian corn a very small one, the blame of which, both Bristow and several others threw on the overseer, though, to say the truth, the chief cause was in the unusual drought they had experienced in July and August. He found the horses to be greatly diminished in number, and deteriorated in value; all of which disasters, Cutchins accounted for in the most prompt and satisfactory manner.

Edward rode back, still more dissatisfied with the manager than before; but he soon found that he had no good reason to complain of Mrs. Cutchins's management, whatever he might of her husband's. They had taken especial pains to give him a nice dinner, and Cutchins remarked, that his "old woman" would send up to Sam Hook's for a piece of sturgeon, as she supposed it was a rarity to him; in addition to which, they had procured for him a dish of soras ; and if the truth must be told, the sight of this well known rarity made him, for a moment, forget his vexations and suspicions, and even Matilda herself. This delicious little bird, a species of the rail, is taken about the month of September, in great numbers, in the swampy grounds of this and the neighbouring counties. Figs, peaches, grapes, apricots, water melons, and musk melons, all were produced, to tempt the palate and win the favour of their guest; though Edward could not help fancying, that they did not treat him with the same deferential respect which they had formerly done.

The next day, with the assistance of the ready and convenient Mr. Cutchins, he took an inventory of all the slaves, stock, and farming utensils, as well as the furniture, an operation in which he was assisted by old Bristow and Aggy, to whom it seemed to be even more painful than to himself.

" Will you sell the pictures too ?" said the old man, in a tone, still more of complaint than inquiry, and pointing to several family portraits, which hung in the dining room and parlour.

" No, uncle Bristow, we shall not part with them ; but it may be necessary to go through the formality of selling them."

"That," said the old woman, " was my old master's mother, counsellor Grayson's eldest daughter. I remember the day she was married, as well as if it was yesterday. Don't you remember, old man, that Governor Dunwooddy was at the wedding?"

"I believe I do," says the old man; "and that was your aunt Betty, that married counsellor Nelson. She opened the ball at the Raleigh, with Lord Botetourt, and they all said it was the grandest minuet that was ever seen."

"Ah! there was a gentleman for you, Master Edward," said the old woman; "my old master was always thought great at a bow, but he could not bow like Lord Botetourt. You see that little man in a red coat, with the cocked hat under his arm; that was your uncle Carey, who had such a quarrel with the governor." And thus they went on, through all the rooms, taking an account of old chairs, bedsteads, presses, and tables, most of which brought to their minds some past occurrence, or piece of family history, or moral reflection. The newest and handsomest furniture of the house, had been sent to Frederick in Colonel Grayson's lifetime, though he was unwilling to remove the pictures of his family from the walls on which they had slept more than half a century. Edward having discharged this painful duty, and written to his mother, Mr. Trueheart, and Matilda, he visited his old neighbours, with whom he passed a few days, rather from a sense of propriety, and in gratitude for their past civilities, than any relish he found in the society of the cheerful and happy. He then set out for Williamsburg, which he reached the last day of September.

CHAPTER III.

There are many persons now living, who remember what Williamsburg was twenty-five or thirty years ago, and who can bear testimony to the rare union of good breeding and good fellowship which that place then exhibited. Here one met with the most cultivated minds, free from either the pedantry or rust that a life of study is apt to superinduce—the greatest simplicity of character, joined to the greatest polish of manners, and a style of delicate and even luxurious living, unaccompanied with that love of show and rivalry, which so often poisons social enjoyment.

There were at that time, among the residents of this town, some fifteen or twenty families, who were in sufficiently easy circumstances to live well, but not to throw away money in ostentatious expense. They all, or nearly all, kept their carriages, gave dinners occasionally, and drank wine; and, following no occupation that engrossed their time, the pleasures of society were at once more necessary to them, and more relished. There being no political contentions among them, no emulation among the ladies as to their furniture, their equipages, or their parties, they exhibited the harmony of one family. This happy circle consisted of judges of the federal or state courts, professors of the college, lawyers, physicians, and two or three gentlemen of fortune, who resided there for the sake of society, or of educating their children; the town containing not only the ancient college of William and Mary, but a respectable female boarding school. They had all been well educated, and some of them were persons of learning and genius. In addition to the inhabitants of the town, those of the students who brought letters of introduction, or who were recommended by their own merits, always partook of the hospitality of the old city, and added the graces of youth and everchanging variety to the social circles. Visiters too came there from distant parts of the country, and often passed weeks, and even months, in a society which they found so fascinating.

The inhabitants possessed great advantages in furnishing their tables. The bays and creeks from James river on one side, and York river on the other, afforded them a variety of the best fish; rock, perch, sturgeon, sheepshead, boneto, with the best oysters in the state, and a variety of wild fowl; crabs, soft and hard, when in season, were abundant; venison was always to be procured from some of the large tracts of forest land in the neighbourhood, that continued in their state of original wildness. As to other things, the neighbouring farmers had been in the habit of resorting to the market of

Williamsburg, when it was the seat of government, and they retained much of the neatness and skill which the former encouragement had produced.

Thus amply possessed of the materials of good living, they did not churlishly nor stoically slight the bounties of nature, nor did they mar them, as is too often done, by bad cooking. Their tables might have satisfied the most fastidious epicure, provided his palate did not desiderate French cookery. These dainties of the table were diffused around by a generous hospitality. There never was a week, that two or three dinners were not given, to some three or four families of the circle that has been mentioned, and a few favoured students. And here might be really seen, what is so rarely seen, " the feast of reason, and the flow of soul."

Never was a little place so free from scandal and detraction. Their subjects of serious conversation, were generally politics, literature, science, the news of the day, foreign and domestic; and they bantered each other, with great freedom, on those little foibles or peculiarities, which, though somewhat ludicrous to others, were either thought pardonable, or were redeemed by some associated good quality of the possessor. Nor was their mirth ever stimulated by wine, or adulterated by gaming. Now and then, when the tide of hilarity was at its height, and there were none but the most intimate friends present, they would partake of the little plays of forfeit with the young people, in which the gravest among them, in the lively recollection of the days of their youth, would take a part ; and on these occasions there was a rivalship of wits in imposing the penalties. At other times, where the circle happened to be more literary, they employed themselves in making extemporary charades, or epigrams, or filling up *bouts rimés;* and at their *petit soupers*, one might, sometimes, hear unpremediated effusions of wit, that would have discredited no grade of talent or course of preparation.

While party politics was poisoning social intercourse in other parts of the Union, and arraying the son against the father, and brother against brother, in this happily constituted society, they only served to give a little zest and variety to conversation, or to furnish materials for good-humoured raillery. It even happened, that those who were most nearly drawn together by the cords friendship, were of different sides; and the difference served, like the acid in punch, to make the mixture more palatable. The parties were nearly balanced in numbers and talents, and politics seldom were treated as a serious business, except during the time of electing a delegate to the assembly, or voting for a member of congress, when individual efforts were exerted in proportion as they were felt; and at which times party zeal produced somewhat of the hostile and bitter spirit, which is its natural fruit; but which, however, was certain to fly off in an invisible vapour, at the first dinner at which the adversaries met. The little love affairs of the students, their balls and parties, and their nightly riots, in which they removed garden seats, pulled up horse racks, and now then broke two or three panes of glass, for some unpopular inhabitant, were incidents of note, in this peaceful happy village, and formed topics of discussion in every circle. Such another place, perhaps, does not exist, where the pure pleasures of society can be enjoyed, without those banes which ordinarily attend it. For here one saw the advantages of wealth, without parade or rivalship, learning without pedantry or awkwardness, frankness without rusticity, refinement without insincerity or affectation, luxury unattended with gaming or any excess, and a free intercourse between the sexes, with the most perfect innocence and purity of manners.

There might be other places in which they lived equally well, though that was not easy; but then one would be sure to find a good deal more of formality and punctilio. Richmond, being much larger, afforded more of talent and intellectual cultivation; but the literary men in that city were absorbed in the duties of their avocations or professions, and they were, besides, divided into two hostile political sects. As to the state of manners in Williamsburg, there was a mixture of courtesy and ease, of frankness and politeness, of simplicity and delicacy, which partly resulted from its having been the former metropolis of the state, and in part from the peculiar circumstances that have been detailed; and as there was no theatre, no gaming in private houses, no public places or amusements, and no intrigues of any sort, society was cultivated and relished for its own sake. There is not one of those who composed that happy community, who does not look back on the period of which we have been speaking, as the sunny spot in the dreary field of existence—on which his memory dwells with peculiar complacency, and who does not feel a melancholy regret, that those days are gone, never more to return!

Such was Williamsburg, in October, 1796, when Edward Grayson arrived at the Raleigh, a long, low house, with many little confined attic bed rooms, and two or three large ones below, in which the students gave their balls—or met to play billiards—or the daily ordinary was kept. As soon as a young man was seen to stop at the door, over which stood, exposed to all weathers, the venerable bronze bust of the gallant knight who gave his name to the tavern, inquiries immediately ran through the village, " what new student has arrived?" " what is his name?" " where is he from?" " who is he?" And they were repeated until satisfactory answers were given. On this occasion, as Grayson had been there the year before, it was merely said, that " Edward Grayson had returned to attend the law lectures."

He found two or three students in town who had remained there all the summer, rather than return to their distant homes, and one or two others who had just arrived, and had not yet selected their lodgings, (as by the regulations of the faculty they were not compelled to live in the college,) and still continued at the Raleigh. They were all in the long piazza of the tavern when he arrived, anxiously awaiting the stage from Richmond, in which they looked for a reinforcement to relieve the dulness which always exists when one is in a town with nothing to do, and still more, when one sees a long street, in which there is neither business nor people.

The students of the preceding session gave him a cordial welcome, though they had commonly thought him a proud and rather eccentric young man. They introduced him to the new comers, and in the course of an hour, they all became well acquainted with each other ; and, disregarding their immediate pursuits for the present, undertook to settle the affairs of the nation.

After looking about a day or two, Edward engaged lodgings with a respectable widow lady, living not far from the college, who had two maiden daughters, one of whom had passed the prime of youth, but the other was young and handsome, and they both were sensible and well bred. This house was recommended to him by its privacy, and by its having but one other boarder, who was also a student of law.

Having provided himself with lodgings, and engaged the washerwoman and hairdresser which he had the preceding year, he prepared to attend the lectures on natural philosophy, then delivered by the venerable Bishop Madison, who, to great industry in acquiring the discoveries of modern science, and much taste and judgment in combining them into a series of well written essays, added grea mildness and amenity of manners ; and yet, so delicate is the relation between teacher and pupil, he was not popular among the students.

Leaving Edward to the quiet prosecution of his studies, let us now turn to the gentle, but highminded Matilda. Possessed of a great portion of good sense, and uncommon fortitude, she soon reconciled her mind to the long separation from her lover, which she seemed about to experience, and she determined to wait with patience the result of the experiment he was making to obtain the consent of her family; and she so judiciously disposed of her leisure, that it was always employed to her profit or amusement.

She divided her time between books, music, drawing, decorating her bower, and cultivating her flowers. Nor was she inattentive to the active duties of life. She bore little share in the duties of housekeeping, but she occasionally executed some nice piece of needlework ; and in these innocent and laudable occupations, a good constitution, and the reward of self-approbation, cheered, too, by the hope of the society of him whom her heart worshipped, she probably enjoyed more unmingled happiness, than if all her fond wishes had been realized. She also took particular interest in two little orphan children, whose mother, the wife of a former overseer, had lingered some time before her death, and whose premature fate had excited her commiseration. She had given to these children, when first bereaved of their parents, the attentions their helpless situation required; and what she had begun under the influence of lively sympathy, habit, and the pleasure which always attends active benevolence, soon made agreeable. She taught little Ruth and Sally Hodges to read, write, sew, and knit, and endeavoured to give them a taste for gardening. Aware, too, that it would be a mistaken and pernicious kindness to give them an education, and ways of thinking unsuited to the walks of life in which they were destined to move, she always endeavoured to give them a taste for those pursuits and occupations in which they would probably be conversant; and in thus guiding her young *protegées*, she acquired a knowledge of many of the arts of housewifery, of which she had previously been almost totally ignorant—such as spinning, weaving, making soap, cooking, and other arts, so essential to domestic comfort and economy.

She found such real satisfaction in these employments, that she conceived the plan of extending her eleemosynary efforts, and of opening a sort of school, in which the children of the neighbouring poor might be instructed in the same manner as her own favourite orphans; but her mother was so much opposed to it, and urged so many well-founded objections to its feasibility, that she soon abandoned the idea.

Mrs. Fawkner had flattered herself, that after Edward had left the county, Matilda might by degrees be brought to give him up as a lover, now that she must be sensible he was not a suitable match for her ; and, under that expectation, she more readily yielded to her daughter's plans of passing her time, some of which were not exactly to her taste. She also had hopes that Frederick Steener, who had been for some time past at the college of Lexington, would make a more favourable impression on Matilda, with her own well-timed assistance, now that his rival was away. But in this expectation she made a false estimate of her own powers, and her daughter's firmness.

A few days after Louisa and her brother had left the county, Matilda went into her mother's chamber, and asked her to walk into the garden. "What new contrivance are you making now, Matilda? you are always doing and undoing, till you'll spoil your bower after all."

"I wish, mama, to speak to you on a subject of more importance than the bower," said Matilda, seriously.

"Why, what's the matter now? It is time, child, for you to be reasonable," said Mrs. Fawkner, anticipating from her daughter's serious manner that it was on the subject of Edward.

"I shall endeavour to be so, madam." She then

told her mother her promise to Edward to write to him; that she would not consent to do so clandestinely; and that she held it her duty to let her mother know her intentions.

"And I never can consent that you shall be keeping up a correspondence with a young gentleman, giving rise to ill-natured reports and observations, and encouraging hopes that Edward Grayson ought now to abandon."

"Can you think, mama," said Matilda, "that the partiality which I have so long felt for him, and which you yourself have contributed to create, can be so easily laid aside?"

"No, not at once, perhaps," said her mother, mistaking her meaning; "but if you are continually writing to one another, it never will be laid aside; you may be sure, that the readiest way to get the better of your childish preference, is to have no further correspondence, and to banish him from your thoughts."

Matilda looked at her mother with surprise and concern. "I never can do that, madam, whether I write to him or not, and I should hate myself if I could. The esteem and friendship which I have felt for him from my infancy, I never can eradicate; and if I could, it would be an act of injustice, I might almost say, of meanness, in me to do it, now that he has been unfortunate. I have encouraged his attentions; I have not concealed my sentiments from him; I have given him promises, when they had your sanction, which I am not now able to violate."

"You surely have not been so imprudent as to engage yourself," said Mrs. Fawkner, " since his return ; and I never considered what passed between you before as an engagement."

" My heart has long been his, wholly and unchangeably ; I have told him so, and thus far we may be considered as engaged. But he has not the promise of my hand, except with my father's and your consent. He has, however, my promise of writing to him ; and as I have done him injustice enough in the conditions I have imposed on him, I could not refuse what would afford him an innocent gratification."

"Do you call that innocent," said her mother, not relaxing from her purpose, though pleased to find she had not given a promise of marriage, " which may injure your character, and make his disappointment more severely felt ? You say you have assured him you will not marry without our consent ; and as your father, (as well as myself,) is utterly opposed to your throwing yourself away on a man who is now reduced to beggary, how can you wish to keep up a correspondence with a man whom you have no prospect of marrying ?"

"That man, my dear mother, might justly claim a great deal more; and because I refuse to comply with my promise in a greater matter, is it any reason that I should not comply with it in a less ? Or because I choose to be unjust, as my conscience too plainly tells me I am, ought I also to be ungenerous and unkind? No, mama, do not wish to see me so degrade myself; let it never be said, that we courted Edward Grayson for his fortune, and as soon as he lost this recommendation, we neglected and despised him. I have no wish to marry him, while the match would be imprudent; and whatever you may think of Edward Grayson, he himself would not wish it. But as it is very possible that his situation may change, he cherishes the hope, that all opposition will in time be removed; and I cannot seek to repress it; nay, more, it is beyond my power to make the attempt; and do not, my dear mother, ask it."

"You were always, Matilda, the most self-willed, headstrong girl, I ever saw," said her mother, trying another tack, (as the sailors say,) "and I see that in following your own wild humour, you will bring yourself to ruin, and your father and me to an early grave."

Matilda was distressed; but soon recovering herself, and recollecting her predetermined course, said, "I would do any thing to promote my father's happiness and yours, that honour and conscience would permit; but I cannot do what they forbid. I am sure my kind, indulgent father, will be satisfied with the pledge I am ready to give, to remain as I am until I have his sanction, and will not ask of me a greater sacrifice—a sacrifice I must not, I ought not, I cannot make."

Mrs. Fawkner, finding her immovable, withdrew,

saying, as she went away, that her daughter would see her folly when it was too late, and declaring that she had overrated the extent of her father's indulgence.

Matilda had screwed up her resolution, before the interview, to the occasion; and though she was somewhat staggered during the dialogue, her natural perseverance, supported by her love, finally prevailed. But after her mother left her, with something like a malediction, and the reproach of inflicting pain on those for whom she felt the greatest filial reverence and love, her courage ceased to support her, and, bursting into tears, she felt the severity of the conflict, which every well regulated mind experiences in the struggle between inclination and filial obedience.

The agitation Matilda had undergone produced a violent head-ach, which prevented her from appearing at dinner; and this in turn softened her mother's resentment so far as to induce her to recommend and to administer the customary remedies. But the silent aid of her mother, while it soothed her agitated spirits, and made her feel very grateful, did not so fill her heart as the overflowing tenderness of Major Fawkner, who ever showed kindness and affection in all that he said to her, but who manifested the most tender and anxious solicitude whenever her health was in the smallest degree affected. And had not Mrs. Fawkner, who knew his softness of heart, and his devoted affection to his daughter, used some address to conceal from him the real state of things, he might, on these occasions have abandoned all the schemes of prudence and ambition, which his wife was building up, and have been as eager to further the match as she was to prevent it.

Frederick Steener had been sent to Lexington college, at the earnest recommendation of Mr. M'Culloch, though Major Fawkner was disposed to give a preference to William and Mary; but his clannish neighbours insisted that it was better for a mountaineer, to be educated on the west side of the Blue Ridge, and that they ought, moreover, to encourage their own institutions; in addition to which, his arguments were seconded by the opinion of Mrs. Fawkner, who wished to have her nephew more under her eye, than he could be, if he was sent to Williamsburg.

About a week after the conversation that has been detailed, between Mrs. Fawkner and her daughter, one evening, about 4 o'clock in the afternoon, Frederick, and his old friend, whose house lay near the road he had travelled, made their appearance at the gate. The good natured old man had always liked Frederick, as an honest well-disposed youth, and, considering him now to have improved as much in learning, as he evidently had in appearance, he was desirous of returning with him, and of taking the credit of his own sagacity.

Frederick was a stout, square-built, full-faced

youth, of about twenty; always ready to join in a laugh, a great eater, a good judge of a horse, and very indifferent to women, at least to that portion of the sex which is best worth knowing, and much of a sloven in his dress, going commonly without a cravat in the summer, and often in the winter. Such was the youth, whom Mrs. Fawkner, regarding with the partial eye of kindred blood, and mindful of his valuable estate, wished to become her son-in-law.

Major Fawkner, with his usual good natured indifference, said, he thought Frederick would make a kind husband, and as he had a fine estate, if Matilda could be brought to fancy him, he should not object to him; though, to be sure, he should have liked a man of a little more polish, for one who had so much taste and delicacy as his daughter.

Frederick himself was merely passive in the business; he was willing to marry his cousin, because he had always been told he was to marry some one, and every body said she was a fine woman. Yet he would have had the same indifference in letting it alone; nay, more, there was a young lady, the daughter of the man at whose house he had boarded in Lexington, who had seemed to take a violent fancy for Mr. Steener, had so often provided something nice for him in the long winter evenings, and so generally been his partner, at the balls given in the village, that he began to grow fond of her; and if he had not considered that he was to marry as his Aunt Fawkner chose, he would have had no objection to make a match with Susan Tidball. He had often been heard to say, that "Susan was one of the nicest girls he had ever seen. She gave herself no airs, and did not require so much waiting on, as most of your high-flying dames. She was a fine hearty girl, and would not require nursing, like your chalk-faced chits, who cut themselves in two, like so many wasps."

Susan was not without rivals in that little village: but, partly owing to her greater experience, (she having for the five preceding sessions regularly made a conquest of some good natured man of estate, and as regularly lost him,) and partly from the advantage of opportunity, she fairly eclipsed them all. Frederick then was, at least, in as much indifference as ever, with regard to his beautiful cousin; or perhaps it would be more correct to say, he had rather an unwillingness to the match.

Mrs. Fawkner was delighted to meet her nephew, and to perceive that he looked remarkably well. "We had been expecting a letter from you, ordering your horses, a fortnight before you wrote. You were in no great hurry, Frederick, to see us."

"Why, aunt, you know I never hurry myself, and they live mighty well at old Tidball's; we had a famous hunt or two after the session was over. I had a fine shot at a spike buck, but Joe Cheatham's powder is not worth a bawbee." Matilda, who had been summoned by the nimble-footed Bella down stairs, on the arrival of the new comers, having now entered, Frederick gave her a hearty shake of the hand; " how goes it, coz ? always poring over your books; you'll study all the colour out of your cheeks. There's Susan Tidball, that's as fresh and as plump as a mayduke cherry, she never looks into a book, and yet she talks as well as any body, for all that I can judge."

"I'm glad to see you, my rose of Sharon," said M'Culloch; "there's ne'er a girl in Lexington to compare with her, let my friend Fritz say what he will."

"Frederick is his real name, Mr. M'Culloch," said Mrs. Fawkner, who disliked this vulgar diminutive, because her father had commonly borne it when he was in indigence. Mrs. Fawkner eyed the young persons closely, and was rather pleased than otherwise, to find they seemed glad to meet with each other. The truth was, that Matilda regarded her cousin as a friend and relation, but never for a moment harboured the idea of his assuming any other character. And in the first moments of meeting, he recognised his amiable cousin, who was always ready to part with a large portion of her cake or gingerbread, or to put a string to his watch, and whom he had loved, as we always love one with whom we have lived, who has been friendly and kind to us.

Mrs. Fawkner, speaking to Mr. M'Culloch, said, "I'm really glad you've had your way; I never saw Frederick look so well."

"Yes, madam, Lexington is worth a dozen of old

Williamsburg. How much better is it to come home with such rosy gills, as Fritz—I beg your pardon, madam; old habits can't be readily changed—than such tallow faces as Edward and that New-Yorker brought from the lower country."

"One would think, Mr. M'Culloch," said Matilda, "from what you say, that the young gentlemen went to college, as the ladies go to the springs, to get a complexion."

"No, my little sharp-shooter; but because a head is well lined, it is no reason why it should not also show a good face—no more than it is an objection to a rifle for being well mounted; and it little becomes.you, Matilda, to be undervaluing pretty complexions."

After so direct a compliment, she could not farther contend, and she inquired about his family.

"All after the old sort. The old woman is now busy with her cider, her dried apples, peaches and preserves. My house is like some grocer's cellar, and I dare not say a word, or the little woman's back is up. I hope that now you have got such a protector as Fritz—as Frederick—I beg your pardon, Madam—you must come and see the old lady. She has some fine water melons, from her own patch."

"Ay, Matilda," said her mother, " you wished to make Mrs. M'Culloch a visit, and you and Frederick can ride over at any time."

"I hope your'e a better horseman, coz," said

Frederick, with a loud chuckling laugh, " than you were, or I shall be apt to leave you in the lurch. There's Susan Tidball, that can ride in a man's saddle as well as she can in her own, and can spring upon my horse Alligator at a leap."

"I am afraid, cousin Frederick, you will find me both a clumsy and a timid rider, compared with this Lexington belle of whom you speak."

"What Susan's that you talk so much about?" said Mrs. Fawkner, in a tone half scolding, half inquiring.

"Only the tavern keeper's daughter," said Frederick; " but a fine jolly girl she is—she'd weigh two of coz here, though she's not quite so tall."

"Pshaw! I thought you were speaking of somebody of consequence."

Frederick, to whom his aunt's wishes had been before plainly indicated, not choosing to say any thing more in praise of Susan, turned off whistling. Immediately addressing himself to his old friend, he said, " But when, uncle Mac, shall we start a deer? I'm told they are fine at this time."

"In excellent plight, my boy. Tom Lockhart killed one two days ago, that cut two inches on the ribs. He was as blue as a razor."

"Next week, then, next week, we'll be at them. But where's uncle?"

"He has taken a ride to Battletown."

Mrs. Fawkner now saw, that however Frederick might have improved in appearance, he was not altered in taste or habits, unless, indeed, this fair equestrian, of whom he so often spoke, had taken that place in his vacant heart, which she had wished to fill with another.

He now walked out into the yard, and inquired into the condition of all the horses, calling them by their stable names ; but, becoming impatient, he ran off to the stable to satisfy himself, and, soon returning, he gave an account of their state and condition to M'Culloch, whom he found in the garden, admiring the neatness and taste of " Rosamond's bower," as he called Matilda's favourite arbour. A hunting party being then arranged for the following week, the old man left the gate just as Major Fawkner was entering it.

" Fritz is come back," said M'Culloch, " and the same jolly dog as ever. I was so pleased to see him, that I rode over with him, and his aunt and cousin are making much of him."

Major Fawkner pressed him to return, but he declined, lest a shower should come up before the wheat he was treading out, should be covered over.

Mrs. Fawkner so often reminded her husband of Frederick's great improvement, that as he was commonly too indolent to be at the trouble to examine any subject for himself, he was persuaded that he saw it. The next morning, Mrs. Fawkner told Frederick, she wanted to see him in her chamber ; and when, soon after breakfast, she repaired there, and found he had not come, she sent Bella to inquire for him, and learnt that he had heard the cry of some hounds near the house, and immediately jumped upon the first horse he could find, and had joined the sportsmen. He returned before dinner; and on being reprimanded for the neglect of his promise, he told his aunt how it had happened, and said, "that if he had been even going to be married, he could not have helped pushing off with the hounds. But I have got that," added he, "which will make my peace, aunt. You may have as fine a venison steak as ever smoked in the Valley."

"Your thoughts, nephew, seem to run a good deal on being married. Have you any notion of changing your state soon?"

"Not I—I don't want to give up my liberty yet a while; but I suppose I must be noosed by and by, as well as other people."

"It is time, Frederick, that you should be a little more staid, and leave off that rattle-pated humour. You are now almost of age, and one of your fortune ought to get married, and settle himself down on his own estate. It is the only thing that will give you respectability."

"What! you would have me, like a racer, quit the turf, and set up for——" laughing heartily at the supposed wit of his own conceit.

"I would have you behave like a man of sense, and a gentleman," said Mrs. Fawkner, sharply, endeavouring to awe him into seriousness.

"And how, my good aunt, would you have me set about it?" said he.

"How? why, look out for some woman whose character and standing is suitable to your own, and then lead a regular and rational life."

"I shall do that a year or two hence, aunt; but I don't see any occasion for being in such a violent hurry. I want to look about me."

"I'm afraid you have been looking too much about you already. Did you meet with no young woman in Lexington that you would be willing to make mistress of Hempfields? Come, tell me now—what would you say to Miss Susan? I have a little bird which tells me all that's passing."

"For the matter of that, aunt," said he, "Susan Tidball is a fine girl; and if I was wishing to put the marriage halter round my neck, and it was agreeable to all parties, and no objections were made on account of the old man's keeping tavern, and such as that, I don't know but I might go further, and fare worse."

"Why, surely, Frederick, you are not serious— to suffer yourself to be wheedled by the first young woman you happen to board with."

"Serious! Oh no, madam—marrying is what I've no notion for as yet."

"Frederick," said Mrs. Fawkner, in a more solemn manner, "my poor dear brother made me promise never to desert you. I have ever considered you as a child, and I have looked forward to the time when you would, in fact, be one. I know, that your poor dear father, who's dead and gone, always intended you for Matilda ; and there is not a young man in the country who would not be proud of her."

"As to that, aunt, nobody can say ought against Consin Matty, (as he often called her,) but I know I am not good enough for her. It is as if uncle was to send his Cleopatra filly"—

"Pshaw—will you never learn to behave like a gentleman?" said Mrs. Fawkner, interrupting him.

"But aunt"—

"But what?" repeated Mrs. Fawkner, emphatically.

"I don't think that Cousin Matilda will have me."

"Why not?" said Mrs. Fawkner; "it is but trying. Girls are of one mind to-day and another to-morrow, as to that matter. If you will court her, and follow my advice, I'll engage she shall marry you."

"But, aunt, she used to like Edward Grayson, when every body thought it was to be a match; and I'll wager she likes him still, for when once she takes a notion in her head, she's mighty apt to stick to it."

"Oh, that's all at an end. She has promised me, solemnly, never to think of marrying Edward Grayson without my consent, and that I'm sure she'll never get. But if there was any danger of her marrying him, that is another reason why you should help to prevent her from throwing herself away. You know the Graysons are head and ears in debt, and all their property is soon to be sold to pay the crediters."

"I heard," said Frederick, "they had fallen through. Well, pride, they say, will have a fall."

"I always thought," said Mrs. Fawkner, "they would bring their nobles to nine-pence; and now that they are about to suffer for their pride and extravagance, they never shall be supported out of my substance, if I can help it. Frederick, my dear nephew, my son, I may say, you must help to save us from this danger. It would break my heart to see Matilda married to that conceited coxcomb, who is prouder, if possible, than ever, and gives himself as many airs as if he was worth the Indies."

"As to that, aunt, I must say, that Edward always used me well, though he's proud enough, that's certain. He ought not to expect to marry the richest girl in Frederick, when he's got his fortune to make by pleading the law; and, rather than Cousin Matilda should throw herself away, as you say, and bring the family to ruin, and you should be so much distressed, if you can get Cousin Matty to consent, I'm her man, though, to say the truth, I had rather been my own man a little longer."

"Poh! poh! your own man indeed! Why, when you are married, you may not only do as you please in your own house, but have a wife to obey you too. The wife of one of your fortune, will have nothing else to do but to humour your fancies, dress your venison as you like it, and provide nice things for you."

"Say no more, aunt," said Frederick, whose imagination was fired with this picture of matrimonial bliss; "it is a bargain; and now I'll thank you for the bit of advice you promised me; for, let me tell you, aunt, Cousin Matty's a little queer at times. When her spirit's up, I'd as soon undertake to gentle a two year old filly—she's a chip of the old block."

"Why, then, you must use the same means as if you were breaking a young filly, since your thoughts always will be running on the stable. You must try coaxing and gentleness, which is the only way that women of spirit can be managed; pay her little attentions; take more pains with your dress—I see you are getting into your old slovenly ways already;— help to weed her flowers; don't indulge in those coarse jokes you are so fond of; refrain from all horse play; and you will, in time, do a good deed for yourself, and make us all happy."

Frederick, who had a fund of good nature, and was not without some of the saving knowledge of the family, was in earnest at the time, in intending what his aunt proved to be every way so desirable, and the impression that Miss Tidball's comely person, and well managed flattery, had made, was for the moment obliterated.

He accordingly began at once to execute his part of the late treaty with good faith; and, going into his room, he put on a cravat, which was some trial of his patience, as it was a sultry afternoon in August; and he then went into the garden, where he found his fair cousin reading, in her favourite retreat. Frederick would rather she had been occupied with her flowers, in which employment he could have lent a ready assistance, in watering or transplanting, or in trailing the vines; but he had an instinctive aversion to books, and knew that he must appear to some disadvantage whenever he was brought into contact with them. He came to the door of the summer house, however, and rather abruptly said, " cousin, can I lend you a hand in any thing about your flowers?"

"No," said Matilda, somewhat surprised at the offer.

" What a fine stock of crysanthemums—and these daisies, I believe you call them."

"China-asters," said Matilda, looking off her book.

" But I see," said he, " I'm interrupting you; shall I take this watering-pot and water your flowers?"

" Oh no, I thank you, it is too soon; but if you would do it about sunset, I would be extremely obliged to you," said Matilda, resuming her reading.

" I'll be sure to do it," said Frederick, going off, and glad of so good an excuse to be relieved from a duty, he found himself but ill qualified to perform.

He was soon heard bellowing with stentorian

lungs, for Ben to saddle Alligator, as he wanted to see how neighbour Stubbs came on with a new rifle. He returned about sunset, and with great assiduity gave the flowers a better watering, as Matilda told him, than they had had throughout the whole summer. The next day he performed the same duty, for which he was again thanked by his cousin; and there is no telling what might have been the effect of his continued exposure to so much sweetness and beauty, as his cousin possessed, when he was assiduously attending her, for the express purpose of pleasing her, if, when he had been thus employed for about a week, he had not found a letter for him in the post office at Battletown—an occurrence, which, never having happened to him more than two or three times in his life, excited no little curiosity. He eagerly broke it open, and found it to be from the fair Susan; and it ran in these words, though we have somewhat improved the orthography:

"*Lexington, September,* 1796.
"Mr. FREDERICK STEENER,

"*Dear Sir*—The report has come here, that you are paying your addresses to your cousin, Matilda Fawkner. I always told you, your aunt would not let you marry out of the family, and you persisted in denying it, and said you was your own man, and not to be led by the nose : and you were so partiklar in your attentions, that every body here has been plaguing me about you; and, although I told them

I knew your aunt would object, even if you had
no objections, yet they all said they could see how
it was; and one tells me I have fallen away twenty
pounds, since you left us. I know I ought not to
have received such partiklar attentions—as a girl's
character is her fortin; and people are so apt to
talk. We all miss you mightily. We had a fine
piece of venison yesterday, and mother was wishing
for you. Let me know if the report is true; and if
you are coming back, as you promised; and whether
you think as much of us as we do of you. You must
not show this to a living soul; and you may be sure
I should not have writ to you, if you had not been
such a partiklar favourite—but mother tells me that
I can think and talk of nothing but you. I often
walk towards the old school-house. No more at
present, but remain your sincere and most partiklar
friend,

"Susan Tidball."

He read this precious epistle again and again,
with renewed delight, and said, "Why, as sure as a
gun, the girl's in love with me; I see it plain in
every word she writes, and she's jealous of cousin
Matilda, and the poor thing is taking her solitary
rambles, where we used to walk last spring. This
is unlucky—and yet not so mighty bad neither, to
have such a nice tit bit dropping into one's mouth,
as I may say. But here I am engaged in a chace of
the game, that I see no chance of catching, while a
plumper and nicer doe is within the reach of my

rifle. But so it has always been, as Milton, or the Spectator, I forget which, says, 'True love never yet ran smooth.' And yet I don't see why it should not, if I like Susan as well as she likes me. But how to give the slip to this aunt of mine, whose eye is as sharp as a hawk's, and who is a nonsuch for match making and match breaking—that's the question—I must think on it." Such a revolution had this well timed stroke of diplomacy made in Frederick's sentiments.

After cogitating on the subject for some time, he determined to mention the matter to Matilda herself, who, he plainly saw, regarded him in no other light than as a relative, and as every way her inferior. Accordingly, the next evening, when engaged in his usual occupation of watering her flowers, he said, "Coz, come this way a little, I have a secret to tell you;" and perceiving that she hesitated and looked disturbed, he added, " don't be uneasy, it is not what you suppose, it is quite another thing." She then followed him, and he said, " Coz, I want a bit of your advice, what I ought to do. I got this letter the other day, and you must give me your word not to mention it. Susan would never forgive me for showing it." He then handed her the paper, which she read.

"And what do you mean to do?" said Matilda.

"Why, that's what I am puzzled about. I like Susan well enough. But aunt won't hear of it, and you know, cousin, she's looking another way," said he, putting on an awkward and sheepish air, and laughing.

"You might make yourself easy, if that was all the difficulty," said Matilda, " for it would be affectation in me to pretend not to understand you, but that can never, never be. I esteem and regard you, Frederick, as a cousin, but never could do more; and I am delighted to find that my determination in this matter will cause you no disappointment. But as to this young lady, to speak frankly, her letter does not say much, in favour either of her prudence or her understanding, and she may be a mere female fortune hunter."

"You think, cousin," said Frederick, still more chagrined at her throwing cold water on his wishes, than mortified at her insinuations, " that because I'm not to *your* taste, I can be to no other person's; but they say, many men many minds ; and I suppose it is the same with women too. If aunt would give up her project, which it is clear she might as well do, and Susan Tidball would marry me, I'd be willing to run the risk of her loving me, and making me a good wife."

"You like her well enough then to marry her ?" said Matilda.

"Why, to speak the honest truth, coz, I do, and I expected when I asked your advice, you'd have been as much in favour of the match as I was. But a man never can tell which way the fox is going to run, until he has started, and so it is with women.

Matilda could not help smiling at her kinsman's simplicity, and said, " if I were to consult my own inclinations, Frederick, I should encourage you in your wishes. But as I have doubts about this young woman's motives, and she is a mere stranger, I could not be tempted to withhold from you my honest counsel. This is, to wait and see a little more of her, and ascertain whether she is really attached to you, or only to your fortune; for such things sometimes happen, Frederick, to persons every way worthy of inspiring love. But if you think yourself certain of her affections, you must act as you think best. I think, however, you should disclose the affair to my mother."

" No, not yet, cousin ; I never shoot until I'm ready. I shall not consult aunt until I have Susan's consent, and until I'm of age, which will be the thirteenth day of next October, and I will then try to make fair weather with aunt, and get her consent. But if she refuses, I'll marry without it, and take my wife to my own house at once, that's what I'm resolved on."

" And if you're resolved, cousin Frederick, I see not why you wanted counsel. But I have a favour to ask of you, and that is, to forward a letter to Mr. Edward Grayson, and receive such as he may hereafter address to me ; for I promised him to write, and I do not wish to excite observation."

" So then, coz, you want to hoodwink the old folks too ; and you are sure that *your* swain is not a fortune hunter." Matilda coloured at this double reproof.

"The gentleman I alluded to, Frederick, you know, as well as I do, is all that is noble and disinterested; and you are mistaken, if you suppose the correspondence I am about to carry on is clandestine. I have informed my mother of it, though, as she does not exactly approve of it, I cannot expect any aid or facility from her—but, perhaps, I ought not to trouble you."

"Oh, I ask your pardon, my sweet cousin, I meant no offence; I merely wanted you to know by experience, what it is to hear the person you love reflected on, that's all. I will forward your letter with all pleasure in life, and I hope I shall live to dance at your wedding; and now, my pretty cousin, let us be friends," holding out his hand. Having given her's a cordial shake, they parted, mutually satisfied with the explanation which had thus taken place.

Frederick then proceeded to answer the epistle of the fair Susan—a work of no small labour to his unpractised pen. He had seen, among the books in his aunt's bureau, or on the mantle piece, a tattered volume, called the Complete Letter Writer, from which he had been formerly made to transcribe, by dint of some coaxing, and more threats, and he thought he would consult it for assistance in his present dilemma. He found in it a letter "from a lover to his mistress," which he thought might serve as a foundation, on which he might add what particularly required an answer, or was suited to his own situation.

After spending two mornings in this labour, which he was on the point of abandoning once or twice in despair, he at length produced the following piece of literary patchwork, in which the Complete Letter Writer formed the ground, and his own sentiments were occasionally inlaid.

"*The Elms, Frederick County, Sept.* 3, 1796.
"Dear Miss,

" Permit, divine charmer, the humblest of thy admirers to throw himself at thy feet, and pour out the sad tale of those afflictions, which thy peerless beauty has caused. I duly received your letter, Miss Susan, and note the contents. Love has not, believe me, a votary more fond and devoted than him who now addresses you. They are mistaken if they suppose I'm to be ruled by my aunt. I'm not for petticoat government, any how ; and if I knock under to a woman, it must be a young one. Couldst thou see the havoc thou hast made in that heart which beats only for thee, I am certain it would incline thy tender bosom to pity. Never mind their plaguing you, Susan—why should you mind them ? Let them laugh that wins. Your loved image is ever present to my excited fancy, whether waking, or when my exhausted spirit is lulled to rest. You make my mouth water at the thoughts of the venison, but I trust there are as fat bucks in the forest as ever come out of it. You ask me if the report is true—I tell you it is a lie, every word of it. I mean to choose for myself ; and if you love me as I love you, never did a couple love so true. I cannot give utterance to the feelings which the sweet idea inspires, when I recollect that thou hast, in thy gracious condescension, bid me not despair. I shall post off to Lexington as soon as I am of age, and bring a parson and a wedding ring, if you can take such a shabby fellow as I am. With sentiments of the truest tenderness, and most heartfelt devotion, I am your own faithful, and, but for the hope of your favour, despairing lover,

"FREDERICK W. STEENER."

When this rare composition (whose orthography we have also ventured to improve) was completed, he read it again and again, not a little pleased with so scholar-like a performance, and sealing it up, sent it to the post office, together with the one which Matilda had given him. In this letter, after informing her lover of Frederick's attentions, and their subsequent eclaircissement, she endeavoured to encourage him in his efforts and resolutions; besought him to bear patiently the pains of absence, and even to forget her when engaged in acquiring a knowledge of his profession. She reminded him that their future happiness would be more complete, for the sufferings and self-denial they had previously undergone. She asked him for a more minute account of the incidents which befell him, and of the society he met with—informed him of the health of his mother, who, she said, appeared to be more cheerful than she had lately seen her, when she was last at Beechwood; and she advised him to forward his letters, under cover, to Frederick Steener.

Every week brought or carried a letter from this fond and virtuous couple, striving to console each other under the obstacles which opposed their pure and fervid attachment. Friday evening was the most important event in the quiet, uniform life of Matilda. Frederick was sure to be at Battletown by the time the post arrived, and, with his uncle's letters and papers, to receive the one from Edward, which he secretly conveyed to Matilda. This concealment she acquiesced in, for fear so exquisite an enjoyment should be interrupted by her mother, or, at any rate, excite her displeasure, and as she had satisfied her conscience by the open declaration she had made, of her intention to write. Mrs. Fawkner, however, seeing that Frederick was regular in his attendance on his cousin, considered that her plan was in a fair train of success, and that all was going on as she wished

CHAPTER III.

We will now return to Gildon, whom we left on a journey to Mount Vernon. After gratifying himself with seeing and hearing the most illustrious man his country had produced, and one of the very few persons, who did not suffer in the estimation that was previously made of him, on a near approach, our traveller turned his course towards Monticello, for the purpose of seeing him, who was then fondly looked to by the zealous republicans, as the successor of the present chief magistrate; and who, with a popular character in New-York, was expected to receive the suffrage of his own state, for the office of president and vice president.

When he reached Colchester, a small village on Acquia creek, an arm of the Potomac, he found at the public house at which he stopped, two young men, genteelly dressed, lounging in the porch, and engaged in careless conversation, which they did not think proper to check on his account.

"Is she really very handsome?" said one, dressed in a neat suit of homespun.

"She's a beauty," said the other, in a green frock with sherry vallies; "old Grayson was once very rich, but I believe he had nearly run through his estate." Gildon here pricked up his ears, and listened with the closest attention. "I expect she has gone down to set her cap for her cousin, Frank Barton."

"She'll hardly catch Frank," said the other; "he's got a new pair of ponies, that he wouldn't give up to marry the finest girl in Virginia. I wonder if he's at home now. He was to have been at Carter's last week."

"He must now be at Dumfries, where Sam Fox is to give him a chance of winning back what he lost at the court house, on the fourth of July."

"But they say the girl's engaged to a young South Carolinian, whose father's unwilling to the match," said the one in gray.

"And when are Julia Barton and Nat Jones to be married?" said the one in green. "She's playing fast and loose with him, and keeps him dangling, to see if she can get a better offer. If I were Nat, I would bring the matter to an issue at once—Lee has gone over to Stanley, and if he does, he'll be sure to court either Julia Barton, or that little mountain girl you speak of, if it is only to keep his hand in. But here the landlord has brought in the toddy; Mr. Minter, is your toddy cool? let us taste it."

They then came into the room, and invited Gildon to join them. "Warm riding, sir."

"Yes, sir, though not more so than we may expect at this season."

"You are travelling to the south, I perceive."

"Yes, sir."

"Are your crops good there this year."

"I don't know, sir," said Gildon."

"Oh, you have been to the north."

"No—yes, a little way, sir." Gildon showed, evidently, such an indisposition to be communicative, that his interrogator desisted from further inquiry; and they sat down to a nice dinner, at which Gildon preserved a guarded silence, partly because he did not wish to make himself known, and partly for the purpose of hearing their unreserved sentiments, on what so nearly concerned him. He was, however, able to glean nothing more. The young gentlemen arose immediately after dinner, and mounting two elegant horses, paced off in an easterly direction.

"Those gentlemen live in the neighbourhood, I presume?" said Gildon to the landlord.

"One does; the other's home I don't exactly know, but I believe he lives in King George county."

"They have good estates, I should suppose."

"The one in the Virginia cloth coat, once owned a very fine estate, on the Potomac; but he has nearly run through it all by gambling and extravagance; and the other in green, they say, has won a good deal of it. He is a sharp, wary chap, who always knows what he is about. The tall one has lately sold a piece of land, and is full of cash at present; and I'll bet a horse, that Dick Scapin will not leave him, till he strips him of every penny."

Gildon was somewhat surprised, to find that one, who was a professed swindler, should be deemed fit company for a gentleman, and should so much possess the manners and appearance of one. But the landlord informed him, that Scapin was himself a man of reputable family, and left very much to his own guidance, by the early death of his father ; he had been soon cheated out of his own little patrimony, and was now making reprisals on the community for his own losses ; in which he had been but too successful.

The conversation of these young men made a lively impression on Gildon, and confirmed him in that, to which he was previously much inclined ; which was to throw himself in the neighbourhood of Stanley, and get introduced to the family, if possible, for the purpose of having opportunities of conversing more uninterruptedly with Louisa, whose society seemed now indispensable to his peace. And when he contemplated her, exposed to the gallantry of an insinuating young man, jealousy added new force to his love, and he at once determined to turn his horse's head in that direction, and in the first place, to aim at forming an acquaintance with Frank Barton.

He got to Dumfries early in the afternoon, and expressing himself, in the public room, pleased with the situation, and fatigued with the journey, he took occasion to say, he would remain there a day or two, to rest himself and his nag. He was shown into a room, for the purpose of changing his dress, and learnt from the waiter, by a careless question or two, that Mr. Barton was then a lodger in the house, and that he had been there with his servant and two horses for several days; that he was then out, and would not probably be in that night, till late, if at all. The boy, conceiving it would be no harm to open his budget to a stranger, told him all that he knew, or heard, or imagined, relative to Mr. Frank Barton; his love of sport of every kind, his wasteful expense, and above all his princely generosity to servants. Gildon, having extracted all that the boy knew, while he only seemed to be listening to a strange tale, in which he felt no particular interest, dismissed his informant, and then took a stroll through the little village. His handsome person, and fashionable dress and air, would have been sufficient to attract attention, if the look of inquiry he threw around him, had not marked him for a stranger; and more than once a pair of sparkling eyes, or rosy cheeks, or a mouth, disclosing two rows of orient pearl, appeared at some window, by which he happened to pass, and seemed to indicate a lively curiosity, and to say, they had no objection to a further acquaintance. Yet seeing no symptoms of the party he was in search of; he returned to the tavern, and resolved to wait until Barton came home, be it when it might.

The next morning after breakfast, Barton, who had returned during the night, made his appearance in the public room. He had a florid complexion and good features, but a very haggard look, from keeping late hours, and still more from the mental agitations to which he was exposed. He appeared to be about five and thirty, though Gildon knew him not to be so old by seven or eight years. After a slight inclination of the head to Gildon, he called for a mint julep, and ordered breakfast, which was served up with despatch, and in good style, as his habits and taste appeared to be well known to the house. Gildon sat anxiously waiting for an opportunity of introducing himself. At length, the landlord having pronounced the other's name, audibly, he said, " are you Mr. Barton of Stanley?"

" The same, sir, at your service."

" I have the pleasure of knowing a friend and relative of yours, Mr. Edward Grayson."

" Of Frederick," said Barton; " yes, we are distantly related. And how is Ned; is he as great a bookworm, and as much in the heroics as ever?"

" He is now a student of law, at Williamsburg," said Gildon. " I have often heard him speak of you."

" Why I wonder at that; we never took much to one another; our walks lay in different directions— he was for fame, and I for pleasure."

" In which," said Gildon, " you have this advantage, that you are sure of running down your game, while he may never get in sight of his."

" You are not from Frederick?" said Frank,

with an air of courtesy, which showed he was pleased with this specimen of the stranger's judgment.

"I have lately been in Frederick, sir, but am just now returned from a visit to Mount Vernon; my name is Gildon; my home is in New-York; and I have some idea of going to Williamsburg, where I should be happy to be the bearer of any commands to your relation, Mr. Grayson."

"Oh, none at all, I thank you," said Frank; "but you may tell him, I'm going on after the old sort, considering women and wine, cards and dice, horses and dogs, all that are worth living for."

"I see you allow yourself some latitude in your tastes," said Gildon; "and in your list of meritorious objects, there are some items which the wisest and gravest do not disdain. Perhaps, sir, you can give him some intelligence about his sister, who, I believe, is now with her friends in this part of the country."

"I'll be shot if I can," said Frank. "I have heard she was at Stanley, but I have not been at home since her arrival; as, however, you are going across the country, suppose you call at Stanley, and take a letter from her—they are monstrous people for writing letters to one another."

"If I had the honour of knowing any of the family at Stanley," replied Gildon, "I would do so with pleasure."

"You need not be so particular here, sir; we

are an unceremonious people; our houses, in the Northern Neck, are always open to our acquaintance, and to strangers—and the latter are always the most welcome; at least, I think it is the case with our women. I shall set off to-morrow for Hobbes Hole; and, as I shall go within ten miles of Stanley, we can travel that far together, if you have no objection."

"It will give me great pleasure to accompany you," said Gildon; "and I consider myself extremely fortunate in having stopt here last evening."

The business being thus satisfactorily arranged, the conversation turned on indifferent subjects, particularly those that Frank best understood; during which, Gildon lost no opportunity of insinuating himself into the confidence of Barton, by agreeing with him in opinion, and adroitly flattering his ruling propensities. He succeeded so well in ingratiating himself with his new acquaintance, that, learning from Gildon he sometimes played, but was not very skilful, Frank proposed to carry him to the house of a friend, where a party of jolly fellows were to have their last meeting at loo that evening. Gildon would have excused himself, as he had no great partiality for cards, and played well at no game, except whist; but he did not wish to impair the favourable footing on which he stood with Barton, and he consented.

They proceeded to a respectable looking house

on the side of a hill, bordering on the little village, where he understood a widow lady lived. They were politely received by a young man, his mother and sister; and they also found there two other gentlemen, from the neighbouring country. The early part of the evening passed rather heavily—most of the party, by their loud yawning, showing either the want of rest, from the frolic of the past night, or present lassitude. In the course of the evening, two other residents of the town entered—one of them considerably older than the other.

After tea, the card table was set out, and immediately the countenances of all brightened up; a saucer, containing grains of Indian corn, as counters, was set on the table, from which every one helped himself to the prescribed number; and the rest were put aside. Gildon excused himself from joining the party, as there were five without him; and they began the game of little loo, at which each player had but three cards.

The ladies, with whom he conversed awhile, soon retired, and the master of the house again urged on Gildon to take a hand. He would again have excused himself, both because his company seemed not to be solicited by all the party, and because he was not in the humour for playing; but Barton, against whom the cards had been running unfavourably, insisted so peremptorily on his joining them, that he sat down; and as, at the rate they were playing, his finances might have been easily exhausted, he played, at first, with great caution, and with nearly equal fortune. But after some time, luck began to run in his favour, and he won pool after pool, in so rapid a succession, that he became, at length, the object either of envy or suspicion to the whole board.

"This is d—d surprising," said one; "the cards all seem to go in one hand."

"It is always so," said another, "when the set I begin with is changed "

"Gentlemen," said Gildon, "I fear I have spoiled your sport; I cared not about joining in it, and will quit now if you will permit me."

"Keep your seat," said Frank, "and don't mind these fellows."

"The gentleman," said one of the townsmen, "won't think of quitting, now that he has won all our cash."

"I will play, or leave off, as you wish, gentlemen," said Gildon, evidently somewhat piqued.

"Keep your seat, I say, Mr. Gildon," repeated Barton; "and lend me ten, if you please."

"Do, sir," said the other, "allow me to be your banker."

Gildon now played more unguardedly; yet the same good fortune continued to attend him. He won, until he had greatly increased his loan to Barton, and two of the others were also his debtors. Not feeling easy at such extraordinary success, and not wishing to appear in the character of a skilful gamester, he set all the rules of prudence, and the little skill he possessed, at nought, and endeavoured, by playing on the worst hands, to reduce his winnings; but fortune, in one of those insolent freaks, which she occasionally assumes, defied him, and he continued to win, whether he was bold, cautious, or careless. At length, galled with such a vexatious and perverse course of ill luck, they seemed to unite to play against him, and did somewhat check his success; but when the day began to dawn, the servant, who had been alternately waiting and nodding all night, whispered to the gentleman of the house, that the cocks were crowing, and the day breaking. Upon this, the elder townsman, who was the only winner besides Gildon, affecting great alarm and surprise, and declaring that he expected a man at his house that morning on an important business, they finally consented to settle their accounts. Gildon found himself, nominally, a winner of upwards of three hundred dollars; but, as they all continued to shift their debts on Frank, either because he was owing them, or they could pay him more easily than Gildon, his winnings added nothing to his stock of cash. The worst of the matter was, that the elderly man had lent Gildon, when he happened to have lent to others all that he had won himself; and now, though Gildon was so large a winner, he was required to pay twenty dollars to this gentleman, who persisted in seeming not to understand the delicate intimations which Gildon gave, that those who were in the same county, and even in the same town, might more conveniently settle with each other, than for him, who was a stranger, to pay away his money, and yet go way a creditor. But Frank Barton observed what was passing, and said, in an authoritative tone, " damn it, Thornton, let Seymour, who owes Mr. Gildon, pay you the twenty dollars, instead of my settling it with Mr. Gildon, to whom I've enough to pay already."

" Oh, very well," said Thornton, unable to parry such a direct attack, " it is the same thing."

The party then broke up, each one sneaking to his bed with blunted faculties, exhausted spirits, and bodies chilled with the morning damp, though it was then early in September. How different were they then, from what he had seen them eight or ten hours before ! Gildon, regardless of his success, reproached himself for being a party in so disgraceful a scene, and he thought, had he been previously devoted to the amusement, the spectacle he had witnessed that night, must have cured him. Their frequent bickerings and altercations, their degrading suspicions of each other—which sometimes, no doubt, were warranted by what they felt themselves capable of—their inward fretting and impatience at their own want of success, which was further aggravated by their envy at the good fortune of others ; their superstitious faith in signs of the most trivial character ; and, last of all, their bitter self-reproach for thus wasting their time and health, in the hope of gaining, at the expense of an intimate friend, and then finding the injury they meditated on others, retorted on themselves.

Gildon's mind was so filled with these reflections, and the agitations of the past night, that it was some time before he could compose himself to sleep; and, just as he had fallen into a doze, he was summoned to breakfast. He refused, however, to rise, and remained in bed till nearly noon, when he awoke, considerably refreshed, and partook of some soup, which Frank had provided.

They set off about three in the afternoon for Stafford Court House. Gildon lost no time in endeavouring to put Barton at his ease, on the subject of the money he owed him, observing, that he should act on the occasion as he would have expected of Barton, and give him an opportunity of winning it off.

"And perhaps," said Frank, "of doubling your winnings. I should not have lost what I did, if I had not been trying to win off; and I verily believe, that if I had won, I should have been obliged to take those fellows' scrip, instead of getting back any of my own cash. Did you watch their manœuvres when we broke up?"

"I did not think," replied Gildon; "they seemed to stand in good credit with each other, at least with the gentleman, who was the only winner except myself."

"Ay, Ned Thornton—an old hand. He has been the guide and instructor of all you saw, and he knows that they're slack enough in paying. He's a merchant of the place, and a thrifty fellow too ; but he has a strong itch for gaming, and he carries the same coolness and shrewdness to the card table, that he has behind the counter ; and the consequence is, that he seldom fails to win. He has outlived, or impoverished, two or three successive generations, I may say, in that town ; and I think, from the symptoms manifested last night, this set are nearly worn threadbare."

"I wonder, Mr. Barton, that you would venture your money with a party, of which one is likely to out play you, and the rest are not able to pay you if you win. It is like throwing cross and pile whether you shall keep your own money or not."

"I confess it is a foolish business," said Frank. "I see it plain enough now, but I never see it till after the game is over ; besides, I lost a few hundred to two of these men at Stafford Court House, at a ball on the 4th of July ; and I took it for granted, that if I had won of them, they would have been able to have paid me back my own—for you know your luck might have been mine. By the bye, the purchase of these bays, and my loss together, have drained me completely, and I must give you my note ; but as soon as I can get my crop to market, I will discharge it."

"Make yourself easy on that score," said Gildon

"If you will not take a chance of winning it off at backgammon or picquet, allow me to continue your creditor; for, as I have incurred so many obligations in Virginia, I don't wish to carry away your money too. You may next year buy me a gelding, if you chance to meet with one."

"I think I have some that will suit you; and I believe I must even go with you to Stanley; from thence we can ride over to my estate, where I can match you with such a horse as you like, and thus, both of us be accommodated."

Gildon congratulated himself on his good fortune at loo, as it had brought about what he so much wished, a regular introduction to the family, in which Louisa Grayson then resided, by one of its own members. It was night when they reached Stafford Court House, where Frank Barton was received with great deference and respect by the landlord and his servants, not only because his father was a man of wealth and consequence in the county, but because he himself was a liberal guest, who spent his money very freely.

Barton insisted on Gildon's playing a few games of backgammon, by which he somewhat reduced the debt he owed; and they set off, after an early breakfast, the next day for Stanley.

CHAPTER IV.

They reached the venerable mansion about one the next day. Frank Barton was so irregular in his movements and absences, that his coming or staying away never excited much surprise in the family; and the father, finding that his hints to his son, about pursuing a more regular and rational life were entirely disregarded, had ceased to interfere with him, and he held his eccentric course without let or molestation,—except when he had occasion for extraordinary subsidies, to open a new campaign, or defray the expenses of the old one, in which case, he generally met with some advice from his father, and sometimes a gentle paternal censure, which was neither agreeable at the time, nor long remembered afterwards.

His father had not long returned from his morning's ride, when the travellers arrived. He was sitting in the wide passage which ran through the middle of the house, enjoying the southwestern breeze, then pleasantly passing through it. After the customary greeting between Mr. Barton and his son, Gildon was introduced to the old man, who immediately gave the young stranger a most cordial reception.

"I'm glad to see you, sir. Have you lately come to Virginia."

"No, sir. I have been here more than a year."

"A resident of Alexandria or Fredericksburg?"

"No, sir," said Frank, "Mr. Gildon has been a fellow student of Edward Grayson at Williamsburg, and, returning from Mount Vernon to college, I have prevailed on him to call by, and he has consented to do so, under the hope, that Louisa may wish to write to her brother."

"I'm very happy to see you, Mr. Gildon, and hope you will pass some weeks with us. We consider our situation to be much more healthy than Williamsburg at this season."

"I hope the family are all well, sir," said Frank.

"Tolerably so, I believe ; but I think you look badly. Have you been sick, or only raking, Frank?"

"I was up late last night, sir, at a party at Dumfries," said Frank.

"And somewhere else the night before, I presume," said the old gentleman ; "and the same the night before that. Our young Virginians, Mr. Gildon, live as if they could never get rid of their constitutions or estates soon enough ; and yet many of them contrive to wear out both before they are thirty. You are more prudent, I believe, in your state."

"I do not perceive much difference, sir," replied Gildon, "except that there are a greater number here, who have both the leisure and the means of indulgence."

"And how does your state receive the President's resignation?"

"It seems to be very generally regretted; but I believe it had been expected. I think he is more reverenced and beloved in our state, than he is in his own."

"You know," said the Colonel, "no man is a prophet in his own country; but if ever there was an exception, it is in the case of Gen. Washington; yet, not a few regret, (and, I confess, I am one of the number,) that he had not either refused the office of president, or resigned it before he had lost any portion of the regard which his countrymen entertained for him. It had been better for his glory, and perhaps also for his happiness."

"Of its effect on his reputation," said Gildon, "I am not competent to judge; but it does not seem to have affected his spirits, as they are remarkably good, and so is his health. I left Mount Vernon three days ago."

"I am glad to hear that he is cheerful," rejoined the Colonel. "I never can be brought to believe that he is under British influence, as some of our violent newspapers would persuade us; and if he has erred, as, I confess, I think he has, on several important occasions, his errors have been those of the head, and not of the heart. It is impossible that he could be regardless of the interests of that country, whose glory is identified with his own—in whose service his whole life has been spent—his best efforts directed—his own fame established ; and he never would be tempted, by flattery, or any arts of seduction, to give up either his present popularity, or the promises of future reputation, for any other advantages this world could present."

Gildon was surprised to hear this worthy old gentleman labouring to prove that General Washington was honest and patriotic, which seemed to him like "gilding refined gold," or any other vain and ridiculous excess ; and he saw a specimen of the conflict, which many a worthy citizen in Virginia felt in those days, between former veneration, and the distrust which political rancour was then engendering against the pride and ornament of his country.

In the midst of this conversation, Mrs. Jones and Julia Barton made their appearance with Frank, and Gildon was greatly disappointed at not seeing Louisa. He had abstained from mentioning to Frank Barton, that he was particularly acquainted with her ; but as Louisa had been unreserved in her communications to her cousin, and she had often mentioned him to the family, his partiality was known to them all. She was therefore not a little embarrassed how she should receive him—whether she should, like an obedient daughter, undertake to remonstrate with him for this violation of his compact, or affect not to notice it, and meet him as a passing acquaintance. But, whatever might be the appearance she should assume, she was delighted beyond measure on hearing of his arrival ; and the agitation she betrayed would not have escaped more observing eyes than those of Frank Barton and his mother, who were the only persons in the room when he announced the name of the gentleman he had brought with him.

Anxious to see the object of her waking and sleeping thoughts, him whose society she remembered with inexpressible fondness and regret, she yet hesitated. She dreaded the gaze of the family, amiable as were its members, and long as she had been acquainted with them ; and amid all the tumultuous delight which filled her bosom, she trembled and was alarmed at the thoughts of the interview. She was again and again called down, before she could move, and did not forget to go several times to her glass, and adjust her hair, or neck dress, (less, it must be admitted, for the purpose of decorating her person than to gain time.) On its being mentioned, on the last summons, that dinner was coming down, she sent for Julia Barton, to accompany her down stairs ; and she would hardly have been able to support herself in going down, if she had not leaned upon her cousin's arm. Fortunately Gildon was in the south portico, (then getting to be the shady side of the house,) when she came into the passage, upon which old Mr. Barton exclaimed, "Mr. Gildon, here is an old acquaintance of yours, I believe;" at which Frank stared, but Gildon ran immediately into the passage, and seeing Louisa, forgot the course he had prescribed to himself, and seizing her hand, which she, by a similar but more subdued emotion, readily held out, he bowed to her at once respectfully and tenderly.

He inquired about her health, her journey, and whether she had heard from Frederick, in the week since he had left her; to all of which questions she answered with timidity, and the greater embarrassment for her unsuccessful efforts to conceal what she felt. Perceiving her emotion, and secretly delighted when he reflected on its cause, he turned to Miss Barton, and told her he presumed they were now both very happy, as he knew Miss Grayson's sentiments towards her friend, and Miss Barton's sentiments he could conjecture, because he knew Miss Grayson. Although this was said in a low voice, and with that easy, assured air, for which Gildon was remarkable, Louisa blushed exceedingly.

"I am indeed truly happy," said Miss Julia; "and I wish, sir, you would join me in persuading my cousin to pass the winter with me."

"I hardly know whether I could consent to do that, Miss Barton, if my entreaties would have any weight, in justice to my friend, Mrs. Grayson, who could never brook so long a separation."

Louisa, in spite of her virgin timidity, gave him a

look of kindness and gratitude, for thus remembering and speaking of her dear mother.

"And so, cousin," said Frank; "you and my friend here, turn out to be old acquaintances, while I thought he knew only your brother; and would you believe it? I had some difficulty in persuading him to call by, on his way to Williamsburg."

"Are you then going to Williamsburg," said Louisa.

"I probably shall," replied Gildon; "but you know my movements have been irregular, and they may still so continue."

They were now asked out to dinner, where Gildon saw the same nice cookery he had commonly met with at Beechwood, and that far greater variety which the lower country affords. Mr. Barton was a specimen of that class of old fashioned persons, (the Virginia gentlemen,) which is now nearly extinct. They were remarkable for their urbanity, frankness, and ease; a nice sense of honour; a hatred of all that was little or mean; more fond of hospitality than show; great epicures at table; great lovers of Madeira wine, of horses and dogs; free at a jest, particularly after dinner; with a goodly store of family pride, and a moderate portion of learning; never disputing a bill, and seldom paying a debt, until, like their Madeira, it had acquired age; scrupulously neat in their persons, but affecting plainness and simplicity in their dress; kind and indulgent, rather than faithful husbands, deeming some variety essential in all gratifications of the appetite. There was enough of frankness and ease in their courtesy, to prevent disagreeable restraint in others, and so much warmth in their hospitality, as to insure gratitude and good will. The luxurious and social habits in which they were educated, gave them all that polished and easy grace, which is possessed by the highest classes in Europe. Indeed, the higher classes of society, every where, have the same manners, which are the joint result of their leisure, education, the cultivation of social pleasures, and above all, a high sense of self-respect. And from the equality which existed there, as well as in other parts of the United States, there were none of those forms and ceremonies, invented to preserve the distinction of rank and titles to precedency, all of which naturally give rise to stiffness and restraint in society.

There is more intelligence among the best informed classes of the present day, but it is commonly associated, either with pedantry, or coarseness, or a careless ease, which does not disguise its indifference for the accommodation of others. Wherever the same refinement of manners was found in other countries, one could seldom meet with the same frankness and cordiality; for these qualities would beat down the barriers, which the institutions of society had erected, to separate the different classes from each other. Nor could it exist in such countries, as perfectly, even among equals, since habits of formality, produced in the intercourse between those of different ranks, would be naturally extended to those of the same rank. The manners of the females, with us, have not deteriorated in the same degree, if at all. They have gained, generally speaking, in mental improvement, without losing in delicacy or purity.

Louisa did not feel sufficiently at her ease, to wish to be placed at the side of her lover; and profitted by the practice which then prevailed, of the ladies sitting at the upper end of the table, and the men below, to place herself at a distance from Gildon, who, however, was seated by the side of her friend. And so assiduous was he in his attentions, and so graciously were they received by Miss Barton, that Louisa would have felt ill at ease, had she not, by the words which occasionally reached her quick ears, perceived that their conversation turned altogether on herself

He inquired how they past their time, of their visiters, neighbours, and acquaintance, and soon perceived, that this young lady was yet more a child of romance than the gentle Louisa; so fondly she dwelt on their solitary walks by moonlight in the garden—along the banks of the Potomac—in the grove near the house—so praised the sweet notes of the mocking bird, and expressed such lively regret that our country could boast of no nightingales; in all of which Gildon affected to agree in opinion, and sympathize in feeling. In answer to his inquiries concerning their beaux, he had a detailed account of each one, except of her own lover, Mr. Jones, whom she comprehended under the general description of "some few others." He learned from Miss Barton, that Louisa's charms had made great impression, in her attendance on the church of the parish, and with such of the neighbouring young gentlemen as had visited at Stanley, which information he very readily believed, and as readily deprecated.

After the ladies had retired from table, Gildon having manifested his fatigue, as it was, in fact, a dull party, between the father, son, son-in-law, and himself, they soon went out into the south portico, fronting the Potomac, smoked cigars, and looked over the newspapers, until tea, when they repaired to the drawing room, to join the ladies. After tea, Julia Barton proposed a walk to her cousin ; and the usual rules of politeness paired Frank Barton with Louisa, and Gildon with her cousin—an arrangement that was disagreeable to all the parties, except Miss Barton. The lovers pined for the conversation of each other, and Frank had very little relish for female society ; but, after going some distance, Miss Julia, turning round to her brother, who was behind, said, "brother, I have a secret to tell you ; I must make Louisa give you up awhile, and I must lend her my beau." Louisa, who would have been delighted if the exchange could have been made without attracting observation, felt an invincible repugnance to yield to her wishes on the occasion, and objected to giving up her cousin : and, while they were debating the matter, young Mr. Jones came up to them, walking very fast, and, having bowed to the ladies, was introduced to Gildon.

"Here is one who will settle this dispute," said Frank; "and, as there is a beau a piece, ladies, I must go and see my sick horse, and wish you a good evening;" and turned off, without waiting to see how his abrupt departure would be received.

Jones then took Julia Barton under his arm, and Gildon, with yet more eagerness than respect, seized on Louisa, who made no further resistance. They soon fell behind, though Jones manifested some disposition to dispute with him that favourite post of lovers in a line of march; but, finding it as tenaciously maintained as it had been promptly occupied, he seemed to make amends for the time he had lost, by quickening his pace; so that there was soon so long an interval between them, that had they been far less engrossed than they were, not a word of the other's dialogue could either party have heard. Gildon detailed, with ready eloquence, his regrets and anxieties, his hopes and fears; told her, that finding longer absence insupportable, he had determined to throw himself in the neighbourhood of her, whose looks and smiles alone could make life supportable; and then stated how far chance had favoured his designs.

Louisa listened with delight to this detail; her own bosom responded to every sentiment he expressed; and she said as much as she dare trust herself to say, in the overflowings of her heart; but the softness and inexpressible tenderness, which love can infuse in the whole air, and look, and manner, of a delicate female, told him that which her words failed to express. So sweetly glided away the precious moments, that when, about dusk, they met their friends returning, they wondered at the shortness of the walk.

Louisa did not communicate to Julia all that had passed between Gildon and herself; for love, particularly first love, feeds on the secret recollection of its mysteries, and feels as if the luxury of its sensations would be diminished by communication: yet she, in general terms, told her cousin of their mutual attachment, but that they did not wish it known, until Mr. Gildon could see whether he could obtain his father's consent; and that they wished still to maintain the appearance of lovers in the first stage of courtship—all of which, having the air of romance, and being, at all events, a love secret, was exactly to Miss Barton's taste; and she took great pleasure in planning walks and interviews, by which the lovers could have free conferences, and yet appear only to have that sort of intercourse which ordinarily takes place between two young persons, who are merely forming an intimacy. So completely did her cousin's more romantic attachment, thwarted by difficulties, and wrapped in mystery to all but the lovers and herself, interest her, that it occupied her mind still more than her own safe, easy, common-place engagement; and she envied Louisa all the delicate distress which her situation seemed calculated to call forth.

There never was an evening that the two pair of lovers did not walk out; and they commonly passed some hours in the morning together. The progress which Louisa's passion had made, was the greater, as it was not checked by those twinges of self-reproach she was daily feeling at Beechwood, nor by the salutary and strengthening counsels of her mother, nor yet by the sobering influence of religious exercises; it had now attained its utmost height. The interval appeared inexpressibly tedious, which passed between the times of meeting, during which hours flew like minutes, and were scarcely perceived, except by the recollection. Gildon gave himself up to the intoxicating influence of this most seductive of all pleasures, and, careless of the future and the past, he thought only of the present; or rather, engrossed by the delicious feelings of the moment, he did not think at all— he banished reflection.

As he and Jones were commonly together, when not in company with their mistresses, he soon became well acquainted with him, and found him sensible, well informed, of great integrity of character, but very ignorant of mankind. Gildon would endeavour to drive away those disagreeable anticipations of the future, which would occasionally obtrude themselves on his mind, by inquiring into the management and police of a large plantation—a subject into which he had obtained some insight during his residence in Frederick; and he now wished to see the difference between a slave estate on tide water, and one beyond the mountains.

Stanley was a large tract of four thousand acres of flat sandy land, three fourths of which were covered with a thick wood, in some places of pine, in others of pine and oak, intercepted here and there with swamps and glades; the other fourth, consisted either of land in cultivation, or old fields, exhausted by a severe course of tillage, and which now afforded a scanty pasturage to horses, cattle, and sheep; or had grown up in young pines, standing so thick as to be impassable on horseback. There were more than an hundred and fifty slaves on the estate. The tract had been larger, but two pieces had been taken off, of about eight hundred acres each: one for Mr. and Mrs. Jones, and the other, called the Glades, had been assigned to Frank Barton. Here he had an overseer, or manager, to whom the entire superintendence of his farm, and the sale of his crop, were confided; as Frank concerned himself very little about his estate, except in receiving its profits, and in attending to the horses which he raised. This man had been recommended to him by his father, who had known him as the son of the most judicious and faithful steward he ever had; and such was his success in raising crops, in disposing of them to the best advantage in Baltimore, and in honestly accounting for all that came to his hands, that he had so contrived as to administer to Frank's wants for the five years that had elapsed since he was put in possession of the estate.

Frank soon became tired of the regularity of Stanley, and on the third day after his arrival, he proposed to Gildon to ride over, and see if he could please himself in a horse. Mr. Collins, his manager, had the whole stud paraded; and Frank, with great animation, and a sort of technical eloquence, descanted on the merits of each. A large bay, of very fine form and carriage, first attracted Gildon's attention, which being perceived, Frank told him that gelding would suit him exactly; he had purchased him two or three years before, when a colt, and he had been for a long time his favourite riding horse, but having got poor, he was letting him run in the pasture this summer, to get in flesh, and supple, and springy, as formerly.

Gildon asked if he would part with him.

"To you I would, especially since I am now wedded to my phæton and dun ponies."

Gildon asked him his price.

He said he would take four hundred dollars, which was one hundred less than he could have got for him at the last Fredericksburg races.

As Gildon's funds were now very much reduced, and were not likely to be replenished while he continued to prosecute his present suit, he thought it prudent to decline the friendly offer; and the price, moreover, appeared to him rather high. Casting, then, his eyes around, he said, " what would you take for that fat, round, chestnut sorrel, that seems in better condition for present use?"

"Oh, he would not suit you; he wants size and fig re."

"That's the best horse on the land," said Collins.

Gildon still continuing to eye him, knowing that the large bay was beyond his reach, Frank, in his hasty way, as he always acted on some sudden impulse, said, " I must suit you better, as you won't suit yourself. You may have the bay for three hundred and fifty dollars."

Gildon still looked at th e sorrel.

"You shall then have him for three hundred; and so much for ill luck."

Gildon, attributing Frank's seeming unwillingness to let him have the horse he rated lowest, to the inconvenience of paying the difference in money, and knowing that it was equally inconvenient to himself to give money, in part, thought the last offer would accommodate both, and he accordingly acceded to it, congratulating himself on being so handsomely mounted, on such easy terms; and determining, however, that Frank should be no loser by his generosity, when he should hereafter be in a situation to make an adequate return for it.

He then inquired of Collins, about the age and qualities of his purchase, and learnt, that he was nine or ten years old, and well gaited ; that one of his eyes had been a little injured, but having been rowelled, that he had now recovered ; and that he was, upon the whole, a very valuable gelding; should, however, his eyes be again affected, he kindly recommended several remedies, which had been tried with great success.

"Oh, d——n it," says Frank, " if any thing should be the matter with his eyes, sell him, or swap him off. I would not plague myself with so much doctoring."

Gildon now began to doubt, whether he had made as great a bargain, as he had at first supposed ; and to suspect, that the proverb, which respects *a gift horse*, applies also to a *horse* that is won. The truth was, that Frank, from early familiarity with the practice, had very little scruple in getting more for a horse than he was worth, or even in concealing his defects ; and on the present occasion, he was willing to discharge his losses at cards by a horse, which, though once a very superior animal, had been broke down, and was likely soon to become totally blind. Some such peculiar morality must have prevailed with Collins, who was a very honest man, and who, out of pure good nature, intimated to Gildon the defects of his purchase. Indeed, it is not unfrequent to meet with men, who, however just and fair in all their other dealings, will cease to be so in the sale of a horse ; and while false representations, and even studied concealments of great defects, are generally reprobated as " cheating," there is not one in a thousand who hesitates to get more for his horse than he knows he is worth, if he can do so by not deviating from the truth.

Gildon and Jones used sometimes to ride over the extensive farm together, and sometimes, when the weather was cloudy, and not sultry, walk out to witness the labour of the slaves. A machine for threshing out wheat, which had just been erected by Col. Barton, the first in the county, was sometimes visited. He was amused at seeing the alacrity of the slaves, and hearing their rude songs in gathering fodder—that is, in stripping the long blades from the Indian corn, which are cured and put away for the horses in the winter.

" These expressions of joy," said Jones to him one day, " are peculiarly gratifying from the slave, because it pleases us to see them happy under that privation, which we have been taught to believe is greater than any other ; besides, the exercise of our sympathies is always more or less agreeable, and it is doubly so, when we sympathize with feelings of joy.

" But the corn songs of these humble creatures would please you still more ; for some of them have a small smack of poetry, and are natural at expressions of kind and amiable feelings—such as, praise of their master, gratitude for his kindness, thanks for his goodness, praise of one another, and, now and then, a little humorous satire. The air of these songs has not much variety or melody, and requires not more flexibility of voice than they all possess, as they all join in the chorus. Some one, who feels himself qualified for the office, strikes up, and singly gives a few rude stanzas, sometimes in rhyme, and sometimes in short expressive sentences, while the rest unite in chorus, and this he continues, until some other improvisatore relieves him. One of the favourite occasions, on which their talent for music and poetry is thus exercised, is when they are 'shocking' out the Indian corn—at which time, all the negroes of the plantation, and sometimes many from the neighbourhood, are assembled, and sit up nearly the whole night. This is a practice prevailing more or less throughout this state, and, I believe, the other slave states; but it prevails most in the lower country, where the negroes are in the greatest numbers, and the plantations the largest ; and yet, there are thousands among us, who never attended a cornshocking, or even heard a corn song—so entirely separated are the two classes of black and white, and so little curiosity does that excite, which is, and always has been, near us. I have heard of persons who were born and bred, or raised, as we say in Virginia, within sight of St. Paul's Church, in London, the proudest monument of architecture the kingdom can boast, and who yet were never tempted to enter its walls, and view its truly magnificent interior. No wonder, then, the rude ditties of our hewers of wood and drawers of water, should not provoke curiosity, or interest humanity."

CHAPTER V.

It happened, when Gildon had been about a week at Stanley, that there was to be a great barbacue, at a place not above six or seven miles distant, to which all the neighbouring gentry were invited. Gildon sent for his new purchase, being desirous of appearing mounted to the best advantage in the eyes of his mistress, and he found, that the malady which the knowing Mr. Collins had foreseen, had actually come to pass. The old defluxion at the eyes had returned, and rowelling, or some other operation, was necessary, before he could see well enough to be ridden. He was even content then to ride the horse with which Edward had furnished him.

They set off about eleven o'clock, and when within a mile of the place, they overtook, or were overtaken by, numbers on horseback, in coaches, chariots, phætons and gigs—many of whom had a most weatherbeaten and antediluvian air. Here was a youth, gayly mounted, dressed in silk stockings, with large bunches of riband at the knees of his buff casimere breeches ; there another, in a coat of peagreen, or some other colour, as lively and unusual

The gayety and variety of their habiliments, indicated the mirthful character of the company.

The ladies, too, were variously arrayed and decorated, nearly all with costly clothes, which were then, or had once been, fashionable; but many, in dresses that had been long since antiquated. Indeed, some of the leading modes for the last twenty years, might have been discovered there, in the gowns, or head-dresses, or shawls, or ornamental trimmings, of the ladies; and it is doubtful whether the most crowded promenade in Paris or London afforded as great a variety of fabric, or cut, or colour, as was at that day exhibited at the Cove Hills, in Choptank, on the Potomac.

The proportion of pale or sallow countenances was very great—some of them then labouring under tertian agues, and others, showing by their faces, surcharged with bile, that they were destined to some autumnal disease. A large crowd of servants were in attendance. Some were employed in preparing the dinner, which consisted of different articles, cooked over burning coals in the bottom of a long pit, dug about three feet deep, for the purpose of the barbacue—across the top of which, pigs, young shoats, mutton, lamb, and fowls, were fastened to wooden spits, all of which were ever and anon basted with vinegar and red pepper, by means of a piece of linen fastened to a long stick. The savoury fumes which arose from these reeking pits, regaled the nostrils of the epicures, and made them impatient for the tempting repast. A long, rude table, was prepared for the occasion, under a number of tall trees, that had been, perhaps, for half a century, used for the same purpose. The table cloths, knives and forks, bread and liquors, were contributed by the families concerned. The whole scene wore the appearance of bustle, and festivity, and joy.

In the adjoining house, which had once been a tavern, was a long room, where the young people were exercising their limbs in dancing reels, consisting of four, five, and even six couples, in which no regard was paid to suiting the figure to the tune, though, it must be admitted, they kept admirable time with their feet. Two fiddlers and one fifer, all black, rent the air with their enlivening sounds; and when they first struck up a favourite Scotch air, they set the whole room capering.

There were no useless ceremonials among the company, and very little reserve, but all was life, jollity, and exuberant mirth, unaccompanied with disorder or rudeness. The gentlemen, in their gayest apparel, vied in the profoundness of their respect to the ladies. Bow after bow prefaced every application to a lady to dance a reel, though many barely knew each other's names, and were not in the habit of meeting, except at some public place. Whenever a gentleman was remarkable for his awkwardness in dancing, or his uncouth and rustic appearance, the damsels would commonly make some slight excuse for not dancing, which they very readily forgot, whenever a more agreeable swain solicited the same favour.

The ladies seemed, as Gildon thought, to enjoy the sport yet more than their gallants. They could hold out longer in the violent exercise which the quick tunes of their dances occasion; and the moment after one was seated, she was ready to take the floor again, if invited : and so prompt were they to be led out, that Gildon, seeing a young lady he had been previously introduced to at Stanley, and going up to pay his respects to her, she held forth her hand to be led out in a reel. As he had never practised this dance, he was compelled to make an awkward apology, for declining the honour she had meant to confer, to the great mortification of both parties, and the infinite diversion of the bystanders.

The same unequal distribution of good and ill fortune was seen here, as in the rest of human life. Some danced continually, and some not at all. It was easy to see, that the ladies, who, from their beauty, fortune, skill in dancing, or adroit knack of getting themselves noticed, were oftenest taken out, and were objects of envy to those who were less distinguished, especially to those who were not utterly neglected; for most of the females who were habituated to this neglect, had either grown indifferent to it, or had learnt the art of concealing their mortification.

The party from Stanley took no greater share in

the amusement, than was necessary to avoid singularity ; and as Gildon did not dance at all, and Louisa, having consented to take a part in a reel with a genteel young man, (the same that was mentioned at Colchester,) and perceiving that it gave her lover pain, pretended a headach, and refused to dance again. Gildon was very much amused at the scene around him, and recovering his good humour, as well as gratified at the kind considerateness of Louisa, he diverted her and her friend very much with his lively and satirical remarks on the company—his whimsical comparisons—his ironical praises of the dress, and air, and movements of the motley figures, which were alternately springing, or swimming, or labouring, before them, as they severally happened to be ambitious of agility or grace.

By and by dinner was announced, when every rural swain was all eagerness to get possession of the hand of his favourite fair. The gentlemen stood behind the ladies, and assisted in carving and waiting on them. When these had dined, they were as courteously, though not quite so formally, reconducted to the ball room, where a few of the beaux had remained, that they might be more sure of some favourite lady for a partner, or of the possession of the floor, now that the number of competitors was reduced, while the greater part returned to take their seats at the dinner table. Among these, were the guests of Stanley, as Gildon, being a stranger, was particularly invited by one of the managers. A fresh supply of barbacued shoat, and mutton, and veal, was now served up ; and there was soon a happy mixture of speculative and practical criticism on their several merits. Gildon thought he had never seen such good judges of eating.

When the gentlemen returned to the dancing room, they found the floor covered with the dancers as before ; and the increase of animal spirits, which eating and drinking produce, even where there is no excess, gave a new spring to their merriment and festivity. The gentlemen jumped higher and oftener, attempted new and hazardous movements of the foot, and endeavoured to " snatch a grace beyond the reach of art." The ladies, too, caught the contagion. They turned around oftener, and danced with a brisker step and freer air, until some were visibly in the condition of a courser who has just finished his race.

A happier, merrier set, was never seen; and in the midst of this uproar of festive mirth, an elderly gentleman, who had taken the lead in conducting the festival, feeling himself grow young again, as he said, went to a gay young widow, whose spirits had risen with those of the company, and challenging her to a jig, by general consent of the bystanders, the other dancers gave way. The fiddlers then striking up one of the quickest and liveliest tunes they knew, this veteran lover of sport led out the little plump Mrs. Lacket on the floor, and they began their performance amidst the acclamations of the company. It was in vain that the old gentleman husbanded his strength and wind. In a few minutes his powers began to flag, while the little widow, becoming more supple and agile as she became more heated by her own motion, frisked round and round him, now setting, now rapidly shooting from one side of the room to the other, and now spinning like a top.

"Don't give up, Colonel!" "Keep it up, Colonel!" "Well done, Colonel!" were then shouted from all quarters of the room; but it all would not do—the old soldier had overrated his strength. He was fairly outdone, and must literally have fallen on the field of contest, if another veteran, (though a few years younger,) had not also sought similar distinction; and, jumping between the ill-matched dancers, "cut the Colonel out."

"Two to one is not fair," said some.

"I'll match the widow against them both," said others; and the little lady seemed so willing to try her powers, against this new reinforcement, that all opposition was withdrawn, and the spectators looked on with renewed interest, to see the issue of the contest. The widow seemed to have acquired new strength for the occasion. She made a pirouette much bolder and more rapid than she had before exhibited, as if to show the spectators the instruments of her wonderful agility and whisked, and spun, and sailed around the room, with such an au-tired spirit, that half a dozen voices cried, " Joetank for ever ;" and whether she had not made this new competitor also strike his colours, must ever remain uncertain, for the chief fiddler's string suddenly snapped, and thus, " by good luck," as Marmontel says, the lively widow's honour was saved.

She was highly complimented by the gentlemen, but it was easy to see, that more than one uncharitable remark was made by the ladies ; and it was doubtful, from her own air, whether she did not find, in the triumph of her success, somewhat to detract from her gratification.

About five o'clock, the company began to disperse ; and in the course of an hour, the place was entirely deserted, except by about a dozen young men, who staid behind to play at loo, and to finish the punch and wine which remained. There were several of these parties during the summer. Sometimes they were on the river banks ; and when the materials of the repast were drawn altogether from the river, these meetings are called " Fish Frys," and most commonly attended by the humbler classes in society.

Louisa had felt great compunction at first, in having disregarded her mother's injunctions in receiving the attentions of Gildon ; and she thought, that as she had, without any fault of her own, been thrown into his company thus unexpectedly, she ought to communicate the circumstance to her mother, and she at first resolved to do so by the next post; but, ere three days had elapsed, she felt unwilling to distress her parent, whose afflictions were already sufficiently heavy, with the apprehensions she would naturally entertain—apprehensions which she knew, indeed, to be without reason, and which, if they had been well founded, must, under existing circumstances, be unavailing. She expected that Gildon would soon leave Stanley; and to what good purpose, then, communicate the disagreeable intelligence? It was by such sophistry as this, that she excused herself for not doing her duty; and, indeed, it is by similar self-delusion that a majority of mankind, not hardened in sin and error, seek apologies for humouring their ruling propensities, and unlicensed inclinations.

After the first long walk she had with Gildon, when she had retired to her room, she reproached herself severely for her imprudence; and unfortunately, in communicating her regrets to her cousin, she found her, both from good nature and the love of romance, disposed to remove her scruples, rather than confirm them; and that young lady said so much, and was heard so favourably on this topic, that she began to think her mother's caution was unnecessary and ill founded.

She thought to herself, "suppose Mr. Gildon's father will not yield to the wishes of his only son, and should insist on sacrificing his happiness on the shrine of avarice, yet he himself is determined to persist in his suit; and in such a noble cause of disinterestedness, ought I to give him up? or can I do it? Give him up! It is impossible! I cou d much more easily render up my life. And if our future union is thus necessary and unavoidable, to what purpose, then, impose such severe restraints on myself, such punishment on him, whom my soul adores? Ought I not rather to make a kind return for so much devotion and love, and endeavour to soothe, so far as I can with propriety, the anxieties that must attend his present uncertain situation?"

When the evening came, and Julia Barton proosed their usual walk, she did not refuse to accompany her; and, to say the truth, it was that part of the twenty-four hours which she recollected with most interest, and looked forward to with most pleasure.

In these evening promenades, they sometimes extended their walk so far, that it was nearly dark before they reached the house; and Gildon and Louisa would be often some distance in the rear, while Jones and his mistress would have to wait some minutes at the great gate for them to come up. At these times Gildon had not forborne to repeat the trespass he had committed at the Elms; and while it was at first resisted as improper, and afterwards pleaded against, yet he finally prevailed, and it seemed at length to be a thing of course for him to snatch a hasty kiss, whenever they were shrouded from observation by the shades of twilight, or the turns of the road.

One evening, when the conversation had been more animated than usual, and there had been one of those little misunderstandings which sometimes take place between the most tender lovers, (which, indeed, but serves to fan the flame of love,) and it had been followed of course by an affectionate reconciliation, they passed a fork in the road—upon which Louisa, looking around with a more disengaged mind, began to fear they had missed their way. Her lover, however, assuring her they were right, they proceeded on. They had not walked far, before one of those thunder clouds, which often suddenly appear at this season of the year, had risen above the horizon, and threatened an immediate shower. They then turned on their steps, and concluded that their friends had, by some short cut, found their way to the house before the rain fell.

In a short time, they came to another fork in the road—the left leading towards the negro quarter, and the right towards the house. It happened that they took the left, and before they had proceeded an hundred yards, the rain began to fall. They quickened their pace, and the road grew darker from the overclouding of the sky, the increasing shades of twilight, and the greater closeness of the woods. Gildon naturally inferred he was moving further from the house, yet he hesitated whether he should not proceed, for he knew if he turned back, he must go some distance before he could reach any shelter; and he had a chance of meeting some person in the road they were in, in case they were mistaken; and they might, moreover, be right. Louisa was too much alarmed and distressed at the thought of missing her way, and of being alone with her lover at so late an hour, to be able to give any counsel, or to reason on the subject.

They accordingly walked on in the rain, which now fell very fast. Gildon insisted on pulling off his coat, to protect his fair charge; but she would not permit it, and on they trudged. After awhile, they came to a piece of open ground, where stood several old log cabins, that had once been negro houses, but had been long since deserted, for some more convenient situation. They went into the best of them, and, with some difficulty, seated on a log, in one corner, they found a shelter from the rain. Louisa was so much distressed at her situation, that her lover found great difficulty in calming her apprehensions. Seating himself by her, he reminded her, that she must be within a mile of Stanley; that the shower would soon be over; and that the path most used, no doubt, led to the house: that her friends would recollect, that as they were before, it was natural that Louisa and he should continue their walk; and quite as probable, that they should take the wrong fork as the right one, when they were strangers to both. These arguments would have been thrown away, if the shower had not evidently abated, and a negro man, with a basket on his head, carrying water-melons to the " great house," to traffic for bacon, had not passed by, and confirmed Gildon's conjectures.

Louisa's spirits were greatly revived by these circumstances, and Gildon was emboldened to renew the interesting subject of his passion. He said, he was more and more convinced of the impossibility of living without her; and if he found, on returning to New-York, that his father was obdurate, he should return immediately to Virginia, and put her professions of regard to the proof. He asked, if she would then refuse her hand, and drive him to despair? She confessed she would, in that issue, unite her fate to his; and, forgetting all the prudent advice of her mother, or rather, thinking that as in any event they were to be united, she no longer withheld the confession of her fixed and unalterable affection; which disclosure always breaks down a large portion of the restraint that education, and the forms of society, have created in the intercourse between the sexes. How could she, after this *epanchement de cœur*, refuse those little favours, which love delights in giving and receiving; and which are never so dangerous, as when they are most innocent. In a word, from the moment of this interview, Louisa considered herself as betrothed in the sight of Heaven, and gave him her whole heart, and unlimited confidence.

Jones and Julia Barton, who had taken the right

hand road, perceiving the approaching shower, had returned, and passed the forks of the road soon after the other couple had taken the wrong one. Not meeting with Gildon and Louisa, they took it for granted, on that account, that they also had turned back ; and it occasioned no little alarm when they found, on their return to the house, that Louisa was not there. Servants were immediately despatched on both roads with great coats and umbrellas, and one of them found the lovers just as they were about to leave the old cabin, and when it had nearly ceased raining.

Louisa, on reaching the house, hurried up stairs to change her wet clothes ; and, afterwards, complaining of being indisposed, she continued in her room. When left alone, the poor girl threw herself on the bed, overwhelmed with the most poignant grief and remorse. The errors of her late conduct—her imprudence in encouraging Gildon's attentions—her abuse of her mother's confidence—and, above all, the danger of forfeiting the good opinion of her lover, all rose in judgment against her, and put her on a bed of torture. Nor could she bring herself to disclose the whole extent of her imprudence to her friend ; it was bad enough to be known to herself and her lover—but insupportable, if it were known to another.

She passed a wretched and sleepless night, and the next day a severe head-ach furnished her with a well-founded excuse for not appearing at breakfast. It was followed by a slight fever, that continued two days; during which, Gildon felt the most painful solicitude, and sought solace for his anxiety by conversations with Miss Barton, in which Louisa was the perpetual theme. He sent her, by her cousin, the tenderest messages throughout the day, and indited the most impassioned and ardent epistles, that love, in the full blaze of its power, and in the spring-tide of success, could inspire.

On the evening of the second day, she ventured down stairs, just before candles were lighted; and, as Gildon was apprized of her coming, he soon entered the parlour, and approaching her in a manner equally respectful and tender, inquired into the state of her health. She felt so confounded as scarcely to be able to reply. The blood, for a moment, burnt in her cheek, which it then as suddenly left to flow back on her heart; while her limbs trembled, and her voice faltered, in a few short, broken sentences, she pronounced herself better.

Miss Barton having withdrawn for a moment, Gildon addressed her more familiarly, and, in the most earnest manner, besought forgiveness for the anxiety he had occasioned her. He entreated her not to punish him further for his transgressions, by such reserved beaviour; he affected, generously, to take the whole blame on himself; and so soothed her pride, that in a few minutes, when her cousin returned, she had sufficiently regained her composure to talk on indifferent subjects.

The next morning she kept her room, under the plea of indisposition; and, having come down stairs early in the afternoon, her cousin proposed their usual walk, but she peremptorily refused; nor could any arguments or entreaties of Gildon induce her to change her purpose. He then became displeased; and not sufficiently respecting the self-denial which she exerted, he upbraided her with want of affection, and maintained a silence and reserve the rest of the evening, which attracted the notice of the whole family. The displeasure of her lover was sufficient to induce her to make the utmost endeavours to restore his complacency, but not to depart from her resolve.

For three successive evenings she resisted, thoug' Gildon tried to enforce his own earnest solicitations, by the persuasions of her friend, until he announced to the family, that the time for his departure had arrived, and that, instead of proceeding to Williamsburg, as he had intended, he should forthwith return to New-York, in consequence of the last letters he had received. He also desired Miss Barton to tell Louisa, that he wished to have a short interview with her, for the purpose of making some important disclosure relative to his affairs; and to entreat her to afford him an opportunity of doing so on the following evening. At first she refused, alleging to her cousin, that such long walks subjected her to the remarks of the servants, and others; then she began to argue the matter; and, finally, she consented, as it was for the last time, to walk, as usual, for a short distance.

When they began their promenade, Gildon, according to custom, wished to fall behind, but Louisa insisted on walking before, and kept as near her young friends as she could, without giving them an opportunity of overhearing her conversation. Her lover then stated, that a more peremptory letter from his father than he had yet received, had just been forwarded to him from Frederick, according to directions left in the post office, which urged him to return immediately, and expressed a wish that he should enter into business without delay. He then exacted from her a promise of writing to him during his absence, and instructed her how to address her letters. He assured her, he should write to her at least once a week, to which there could be no objection; and he appointed some time in December following to be with her again, when his first wish on earth should be consummated, either with or without his father's consent.

She said but little, except that she was most unhappy. She was dissatisfied with herself; and she intimated her fears of some forfeiture of his good opinion: to all which he replied with the usual asseverations and protestations of increased confidence, affection, and gratitude. These sentiments, always so grateful to the ears of lovers, were doubly welcome at this time, and Louisa found them inexpressibly soothing to her distressed and mortified feelings. Her confidence in herself gradually returned, and she finished her walk with great self-approbation for the prudence and firmness she had displayed, and with delight at the sentiments expressed by her lover.

On the following evening, when a walk was again proposed, positively for the last time, Louisa at first hesitated; but, encouraged by the agreeable result of the one of the evening before, she complied once more with her lover's solicitations. They set out as on the preceding evening, except that Louisa, though she would not consent to walk behind, suffered Gildon to hurry her some distance in advance of her cousin; and, in the earnestness of their declarations of mutual attachment and eternal faith, they insensibly prolonged their walk to the fork of the road which had first misled them; when Gildon, whether by accident or design the writer of these pages has never ascertained, took the road which led to the old houses. As soon as Louisa saw where she was, she manifested the greatest impatience and uneasiness at finding they had again missed their way; but on her lover's reminding her that they must soon be separated by a distance of five hundred miles, and a painful absence of several weeks, she suffered him to impress on her lips those caresses, which, he said, could alone give him assurance of her real affection, and the remembrance of which would afford him such sweet consolation in his absence. They after awhile retraced their steps, but not until Jones and Julia Barton had been waiting for them nearly half an hour.

Louisa approached Miss Barton and her lover, with a silent, melancholy air, which was naturally attributed to the approaching departure of Gildon; and the amiable Julia sincerely sympathized with her in her distress; though, romantic as she was, she evidently thought there was as much to be admired as pitied in sufferings of this nature.

They sat but a short time after their return, and the young ladies retired at an early hour, at the earnest solicitations of Louisa. The next morning, Gildon, after expressing his lively sense of the kind and hospitable reception he had met with in a house, with whose inmates he was, three weeks before, a perfect stranger, shook hands with them all, except Louisa. She, dreading the effect of a farewell, the very idea of which was so terrible, excused herself by her cousin; and to make amends, sent her lover a note, breathing sentiments of exquisite tenderness, which had been plainly watered by her tears. He could have wished to have bid her adieu once more; but, finding it impossible, he mounted his new purchase, and, accompanied by Frank Barton's servant, set off for the stage road, which he reached in time to take a seat for Alexandria about ten o'clock in the morning. He thence proceeded, without much interruption, to the state of New-York, where we must leave him for a while, to attend to some other personages, to whom we have already introduced the reader.

Mrs. Grayson, after the departure of her beloved children, no longer called upon to make the efforts which their presence required, was not able effectually to repress the poignant feelings of grief which assailed her ; and it must be confessed, that it can seldom fall to the lot of any one, to have more or greater causes of affliction. Besides the regret which she felt for the loss of an affectionate husband, whose image, always tenderly cherished, came upon her recollection at times with so much force, as to make his death seem but as yesterday, she was about to be thrown from a state of ease and affluence into one of absolute penury, and thus the children, for whom alone she now cared to live, were soon to be deprived of those comforts and enjoyments which wealth can give, and that consideration which it procures from the world. But it was yet a greater source of anxiety and apprehension to her, that these children were both likely to be thwarted in their affections by the loss of their fortunes : for her daughter, indeed, she felt the most serious alarm.

With such an accumulation of present and of threatened evil, it is no wonder that she for a time yielded to its force, and that her piety was not able to support her. After a day of bitterness and tribulation, she recovered somewhat of her former composure, and began to make preparations for that change in her situation which was now become necessary, and to provide an asylum for her daughter before she returned to Frederick. She immediately wrote to Mr. Trueheart to come over, for the purpose of assisting her with his advice in the disposal of the property. She also wrote to Edward to proceed to make sale of the Easton estate ; and having executed these necessary pieces of business, she felt greatly relieved.

She then went, about twilight, to make a visit, as she often did, to the spot in which the remains of her husband were deposited. This had been surrounded with a neat railing, within which were two or three weeping willows ; and a small white urn had been procured from Philadelphia, around which had been carefully planted roses, and jasmines, and other fragrant flowers. Often, in the stillness of the evening, and the darker the more consonant was it to her feelings, would she take a lonely walk to this spot, and without any violent paroxysms of grief, ideally commune with his departed spirit, and secretly implore the aid and support of the great Author of all, to guide her in her difficulties ; for in her mind, the image of her husband was always associated with a feeling of religion and devotion, to which, indeed, pure and virtuous love in woman is very nearly allied.

She had often forborne to gratify herself in this sad luxury, for fear of attracting observation, or of being suspected by the unfeeling or narrow-minded of affectation, or of being ostentatious of her grief, and because she knew it distressed her children to see her give way to her feelings; but since they had left her, and she was not restrained by the last consideration, there never was a night, when she had no visitors, that she did not take this solitary walk. Sometimes, rapt in the contemplation of past scenes of bliss, or bewildered with the difficulties of the future, she would remain longer than was prudent at this season of the year, so near the fogs of the river.

Finding no inconvenience from the practice, she had been led insensibly to consider it as safe—until one evening, about the middle of September, when the night air began to be chilly, she happened to stay out longer than usual, and the next evening she was taken with a slight shivering, which was followed by a sharp ague, and the next day it assumed the appearance of a bilious fever.

She immediately sent for her family physician, a man of great prudence and experience, who, finding she was threatened with a disease of some continuance, rode over to Mr. Buckley's, and requested one of the family to call and stay with her. Fanny Buckley, who, from her intimacy with Louisa, was oftener at Beechwood than her sister, immediately rode over to attend her amiable friend; and, besides being a most assiduous nurse, endeavoured, by her cheerfulness and little attentions, to keep up the spirits of her patient.

Matilda Fawkner, as soon as she heard of Mrs. Grayson's illness, insisted with her mother on going to her ; and reached Mrs. Grayson's a short time after Miss Buckley. Both these young women were unwearied in their assiduities to this excellent woman, whose mildness of manners, and heavenly patience of temper, were never more conspicuous than on the sick bed. The ordinary remedies were tried without success, and in three or four days, it was circulated about the neighbourhood, that Mrs. Grayson was dangerously ill. The news flew rapidly over the county, and was every where heard with the liveliest concern. There was not a neighbour who had not, at some time or other, experienced her kindness in sickness, or in the way of charity; and who did not feel that her loss would be a general calamity. The servants, too, to whom she was so attentive a nurse, were seriously alarmed at her situation, and inquired a dozen times a day whether any change had taken place. Messages of inquiry came from all the neighbours, and even from persons with whom, on account of the distance, they had no intercourse— some bringing such little rarity or delicacy as was thought might be acceptable, and some recommending favourite remedies, or offering to set up with her ; and had the young ladies, who were staying with her, been so disposed, they need never have attended upon her two nights successively.

On the third day, when Matilda saw that her excellent friend was evidently growing worse, she proposed to her to let Louisa know of her situation; but the tender mother, always more anxious for her children's happiness than her own, positively forbid it—believing that she would probably soon mend, and it would be cruel in her to inflict unnecessary pain; still, on being strongly pressed by both her young visiters, she consented, if she was not better in two days, that Matilda might not only write, but that the carriage should be sent for her daughter.

The two days accordingly passed, and no change for the better having taken place, the carriage was directed to be prepared; and on the following morning, by daylight, Phill set off, with a letter from Matilda, so worded as to excite as little apprehension as possible, which reached Stanley shortly after Gildon had left it. Louisa and Julia Barton were walking by themselves, as Jones had departed the day that Gildon had left them, at the request of his mistress, that she might more effectually console her cousin, in the absence of her lover. They naturally turned their steps in that direction where they had most frequently walked, when they heard the sound of carriage wheels at a distance; and, not wishing to be seen by strangers, while thus unattended, they immediately hastened towards the house; but a lash or two of the whip quickened the pace of the horses, and in a little while the carriage overtook them, and was recognised by Louisa as the family chariot.

Her first emotion at the sight of old Phill, was that of joy; and, in a moment, recollecting where she saw him, she apprehended he was the bearer of some unwelcome message, and she trembled with alarm.

"How is mama, Uncle Phill?"

"She's not well, Miss Louisa."

"Oh, what is the matter? tell me. She's not sick, is she?"

"She has been sick two or three days, and Miss Matilda thought I had better come for you."

"Where is my letter, Uncle Phill?"

"Here it is," said the old man, taking it out of an old black pocket book, and handing it to her.

When she read that her dear mother was sick, probably in extreme danger, she felt almost beside herself. She determined on setting off the next morning; and, on going back to the house, she informed the family of her resolution; nor could they prevail on her to let the horses rest even half a day. Frank Barton was out of the way, but the overseer, a steady, decent man, was immediately put in requisition to escort her.

CHAPTER VI.

The next day, after an early breakfast, and an affectionate leave of her kind and amiable relatives, she left Stanley, with a heart rent with bitter and conflicting emotions. She recollected, that three weeks before, when she had approached that hospitable mansion, she thought herself supremely miserable; and yet, what was her situation then, compared to what it was at this time. Then her darling mother was in good health—she herself was in the act of complying with that mother's wishes, and was supported under her trials with self-approbation, nothing of which was the case at present.

She travelled on with a heavy heart, stopping as little as possible at private houses; and on the evening of the third day, as she came down the mountain of Ashby's Gap, at Berry's Ferry, and saw the dear mansion of her family, it awakened recollections and emotions which caused her to weep excessively. Good old Phill, discovering her distress, turned round, and said, "Miss Louisa, don't be uneasy. Mistress is not so very sick, and she will be distressed to see you take on so."

"I was only thinking of past times, uncle Phill.

I hope my mother is better; for, God knows, if I thought she were worse, it would make me distracted."

When the carriage came in sight of the house, Louisa thought it a favourable symptom, to perceive two young ladies walking towards them, one of whom she was sure was Matilda. They met at a short distance from the gate; in a moment, the ca riage door was thrown open, and Louisa and Matilda were in each other's arms—the question of " How is mama, Matilda?" having preceded every other.

" She is much better, I hope," said her friend.

As soon as, on further inquiry, Louisa's anxious fears for her mother's safety had subsided, her thoughts turned more on herself, and the reflections which then presented themselves, were of a still more painful character. With her desire to behold her beloved mother, there was mingled a good deal of undefined fear, and a feeling of shame and self reproach, that she could not meet her with all that ingenuousness that once made their intercourse that of two friends of unequal age, rather than of parent and child.

Belle ran out to meet her, exclaiming, " Oh, Miss Louisa, I am so glad to see you back! Mistress is better to-day, but she has been mighty ill. Lord! Miss Louisa, how pale you look! Mistress was afraid you would not have your health down the country. Granny will be so glad to see you!

Granny says she's had no good coffee since you went away. How did you leave Master Edward? Is he still in Williamsburg?" And thus the girl, with the freedom of a servant brought up in the family, chattered away from the gate to the chamber door, unconsciously, by every word, planting daggers in her heart.

Mrs. Grayson had been thought much better in the morning, both by her attendants and the physician, and she had prepared herself for the meeting. With a soul of the most feeling character, she had remarkable patience and equanimity. Her passions were delicate rather than strong. She was lying on her bed, with a white handkerchief round her brows, to relieve her from the slight head-ach which attended her disease; and this, with the effect of three days' fever, made her appear in her daughter's eyes still more altered than she really was. " My dear daughter!" " Oh, my mother, my mother!" were all they said when they embraced.

Mrs. Grayson endeavoured to allay the fears of her daughter, by giving as favourable answers as she could to her affectionate inquiries. In spite of all her exertions to appear cheerful, Louisa exhibited uncommon emotion. In her first embrace, as she laid her head on the bosom of her mother, she sobbed aloud. Matilda gently requested her to restrain her feelings, but it was some time before she sufficiently recovered her composure to converse with her mother freely, and to give full answers to her inquiries.

Fanny Buckley was delighted to see Louisa; but having made some remark on her altered appearance, Mrs. Grayson looked at her daughter more narrowly, and perceiving her much paler and more delicate than when she left Beechwood, she was apprehensive that the cause which had recommended her visit, had been still preying on her sensitive heart. She forbore, however, to say any thing that would lead the conversation to this delicate and painful subject.

In a little while, Dr. Selby arrived, and finding his patient's pulse quicker than the day before, and all the symptoms less favourable, he good-naturedly scolded his young acquaintances for their imprudence, and cautioned Mrs. Grayson against suffering herself to be agitated. This put a stop to all further conversation between Louisa and her mother, and thus spared her the pain of further disingenuousness—as she would have felt herself justified in concealing from her mother that she had seen Gildon, rather than distress her by communicating it in her present situation.

As soon as they had withdrawn from Mrs. Grayson's sick room, Fanny Buckley began to make close inquiries about Gildon—where he was when she had heard from him, and when she expected him;—all of which she was able to answer, without either deviating from the truth, or imparting the whole of it, but which it was mortifying in the extreme to be compelled to do; and she then found, that we are never exempted from the punishment which is sure to attend disingenuousness.

Often she was on the point of disclosing every thing to her young friend; but a sense of shame, and a distrust of Fanny Buckley's discretion, checked her. She was, however, resolved to be less reserved towards Matilda, on whose friendship and prudence she could equally rely. As soon, then, as Fanny Buckley went into Mrs. Grayson's room, to prepare and administer a dose of medicine, Louisa, who had been employed on some household matters, led Matilda into her room, and then gave her a disclosure of nearly all that had occurred. Matilda listened to her narrative with breathless anxiety, and experienced a variety of emotions and fears—none of which she ventured to express, except her regret for what she had heard, insisting, however, on a promise from Louisa, that she would not see her lover again without the consent of her mother, nor even then, unless he should be prepared to fulfil his engagements at once;—for she saw too plainly that her friend had not the strength of mind to pursue that course which her judgment might dictate.

Louisa wept tears in abundance, after her confession; and having given vent to her feelings, and readily consented to make the promise which her friend exacted, and of which she had seen the propriety before, she felt greatly relieved, and returned to her mother's room with a degree of composure which she had not felt for the last ten days. Such is the virtue in the balm of confiding friendship!

It was in vain, however, that she and her young companions made use of every art, and little soothing attention, in their power, for the benefit of the excellent Mrs. Grayson. The agitations of the morning, in spite of all her self-command, had heightened her fever, and it still continued to increase; she passed a bad night, and the day following the doctor thought her much worse. In the evening he returned again, and finding her no better, he proposed to call in a gentleman of eminence, from Winchester, who was accordingly sent for. This was a signal of alarm to Louisa, the servants, and the neighbours. There was not an hour in the day, in which some messenger did not arrive at Beechwood, for the purpose of learning how she was. Doctor Blodget arrived the following morning, when, Mrs. Grayson's fever continuing unabated, her strength had still further declined.

The two attending physicians had long been acknowledged rivals; and they had more foundations for their jealousy than commonly exist among the members of a profession, which is not remarkable for the harmony or liberality of its members towards each other. One had been educated in Edinburgh; the other in Philadelphia. One was a disciple of Cullen; the other an admirer of Brown. One was a man of cautious temper; the other bold, sanguine, and sometimes rash. The one was prejudiced against new remedies, especially if they originated here, or had been embraced and supported with zeal by Doctor Rush; the other an enthusiastic admirer of that gentleman, and favourably disposed to all new theories, new remedies, and new modes of practice.

As they sometimes came in contact, when Blodget first began to practise in Winchester, these foundations for collision had their natural effect. Selby, the graduate of Edinburgh, had used some expressions of contempt respecting Blodget, which came to his ears; and the two meeting in consultation soon afterwards, at the house of a wealthy man, then in the crisis of a fever, they differed, quarrelled, and, finally, came to blows. After this they held no sort of intercourse—but, as their quarrel was notorious, they were somewhat reserved in speaking of each other; and professional jealousy, finding less aliment to support it, and venting itself upon younger competitors, gradually subsided; and having been again called to a consultation, in the case of Colonel Grayson, whom they both greatly respected, they forgot their past differences, and in their hearty co-operation for the good of their patient, became, if not friendly, at least mutually civil and respectful. There was afterwards nothing to be observed in their occasional meetings, but a great deal of formality and politeness in their intercourse; and whatever one recommended, the other did not directly disapprove, but opposed in the form of a suggestion, a query, or a doubt.

On this occasion, however, it turned out, that their views were directly opposite as to the character of the disease, and, consequently, the character of the remedies; but, as time and experience had taught them to feel more respect for each other's talents, and to moderate their passions, or, at any rate, to conceal them better, they were led, to prevent a difference of opinion, to nothing more than an agreement to call in a third member of the faculty, Doctor Minorfee, with whom the reader has already been made acquainted.

He came, saw the patient, and hearing the arguments on both sides, did not hesitate to decide in favour of the depleting remedies, recommended by Doctor Blodget. He talked very learnedly and fluently on the increased action of the system, of the undue excitability, of direct and indirect debility, and would have resorted to the lancet, but both of the others united in deprecating this, in the exhausted state of the patient. Doctor Selby, somewhat chagrined at his decision, observed, that as the views entertained by a majority were different from his own, and he was bound to acquiesce, he must withdraw, though he would be always ready to aid with his advice when it was further asked.

Blodget began immediately to act rather boldly; and, finding no bad consequence to ensue, he persevered; and perceiving, the next day, a favourable change, though a slight one, he was encouraged further to proceed in the same course; and, in two days, he pronounced his patient out of danger.

This cure, as it was called, was a proud feather in his cap; not only because it had been performed against the opinion of his most eminent rival, but because it had restored to health the most respected lady of the county: and, although it is said to be very probable that nature (who, by reducing the flesh, and strength, and appetite of the patient, was effecting the same end as the doctor did by his medicines) would have wrought the same cure, yet as that could never be ascertained, "the worthy Mrs. Grayson," "the amiable Mrs. Grayson," "the dear Mrs. Grayson," had been saved by Doctor Blodget's skill.

The joy at her recovery, which was in proportion to their previous alarm and uneasiness, made the whole family forget their other misfortunes; and the pleasure which her recovery so obviously communicated, filled her own heart with gratitude, and gave a fresh stimulus to her benevolent feelings.

As soon as Mrs. Grayson was pronounced out of danger, Mrs. Fawkner came to make her a visit; and, having gone through the usual forms of congratulation, she insisted on carrying her daughter home, alleging, that nursing and sitting up had evidently affected her health.

Matilda's society had been Louisa's chief solace and support since her return to Beechwood; nor could that of her mother, now that she had, alas! ceased to repose entire confidence in her, supply its place. As to Fanny, she had so little of romance in her composition, was so inferior in understanding, and so apt to tell all she knew, that she could not bring herself to talk of Gildon to her, except in very general terms, much less to disclose to her the secret thoughts of her bosom.

In a few days Mrs. Grayson was able to ride out in the carriage; and, though extremely weak, the exercise rather strengthened than fatigued her. Returning from her morning's ride, greatly invigorated in strength, and refreshed in spirits, a gentleman and his servant were seen approaching the house, at a moderate gait, and in a little while Primus recognised them to be Mr. Trueheart and his valet. This worthy gentleman had intended to set off for Beechwood as soon as he received Mrs. Grayson's summons, but having, at the same time, heard the reports of her illness, he deferred a visit which must be useless, and might be unseasonable, and determined to regulate his movements by what he should learn from his friend, Doctor Blodget, of the progress of her disease. As soon as he understood she was decidedly convalescent, he set off; and, as it was about the time of holding the district court in Winchester, he concluded to call by Beechwood, and either arrange the business then, relative to Colonel Grayson's estate, or defer it until after the adjournment of the court.

The generosity and delicacy of this worthy man were never more conspicuous than on this occasion. He assiduously laboured to give the widow of his friend as favourable a view of things as possible, consistent with the truth; and in providing for her comfort, and that of her family, to make it seem rather as matters of course, than as the effect of his management or liberality—thus contriving to lighten the weight of obligation, while he increased its value. He endeavoured to show, that by disposing of the estate on a credit, and borrowing money at legal interest, on the faith of the bonds, (which he assured her would be very practicable,) enough might be saved, after paying the debts of the estate, to purchase a commodious house and farm for them;—that he himself had a claim against the principal creditor, which might be considered precarious, if hazarded on the uncertainties of the law; but which the same creditor was willing to settle in his debt against the estate;—that with this fund Mrs. Grayson might purchase such of the slaves as she was attached to, and repay him at her leisure, when her children were settled in life; and that this delay would be amply compensated to him, by making that secure which was contested, and might be eventually lost.

Nor did he forget to inform her, that the accounts he had received from Edward were of a very flattering character. The professors, one of whom he had seen the preceding week, gave him a most exalted character.

This exemplary man continued at Beechwood from Friday until Sunday, when, having attended Mrs. Grayson and Louisa to the chapel, to return thanks for her late recovery, he proceeded to Winchester, where the district court was to be held on the next day.

The Saturday's post brought, among others, a letter from Gildon to Louisa, dated in Philadelphia. He stated that he had travelled, without stopping, to that place, and a delay of two or three hours enabled him to say to his "beloved, angelic Louisa," how much he suffered in her absence; how flat, insignificant, and worthless, all that he met with appeared, when she was away; that her looks, and manner, and air, and words, were always fresh in his recollection; as were also those scenes where she had given him assurances of her affection. He begged her to write to him by every post— hoped he should be able to return sooner than he contemplated when they parted, as absence grew more and more insupportable—with much more to the same purpose, which, though very common-place, was read again and again with fresh delight by Louisa, after she had read them often enough to repeat every word from memory.

This precious proof of his faith and affection, after being shown to her mother, (as he had put nothing in it from which his visit to Stanley could be known,) was then deposited in her bosom, from whence she was often seen by Matilda to withdraw it, and after giving it a sly kiss, return it to its lovely sanctuary.

Mrs. Grayson was gratified at the warm sentiments of love this letter contained, though they would have been more to her taste if they had been expressed with more simplicity, and a less studied elegance. She was willing, however, to make allowances for the reigning fashion of florid and inflated writing, in which it was usual to avoid all natural modes of expression as tame and feeble.

Louisa readily complied with her lover's request of writing to him—for his will had now become a law to her; and she accordingly addressed a letter to him in New-York, thanking him for his letter, and avowing her affection in terms of great tenderness. But her epistle throughout exhibited an air of sadness and gloomy foreboding, which she could not conceal, and yet felt unwilling to confess.

This letter of Gildon's, nevertheless, had a very cheering effect on her spirits, and, as a natural consequence, was proportionally beneficial to Mrs. Grayson, and furthered her convalescence. She devoted so much of her time to making arrangements for the approaching sale, that she had not inquired into the particulars of her daughter's visit, as she would otherwise have done; and, consequently, Louisa was not much subjected to the pain that unwarranted concealment must ever give to an ingenuous mind, educated in such strict principles of integrity. She sought too, by her mother's earnest recommendation, the advantage of employment; she also wrote to Matilda almost daily notes; and set herself seriously about learning those household arts, which she had hitherto utterly neglected, but which the altered circumstances of her family made indispensable, while she continued under her mother's roof; and which the too probable refusal of Gildon's father to his marriage, would make equally necessary, if she should become his wife. These several occupations so filled up her time, that she found little leisure to indulge the painful, harrowing thoughts, that would sometimes obtrude themselves, and present to her imagination a horrible abyss, into which she was about to be precipitated. The society of Fanny Buckley, whose attachment to her seemed to increase with her unhappiness, and which that unsuspecting girl imputed as much to the change in the circumstances of her family, as to her anxiety about her lover, no longer afforded her any pleasure—for she could not converse with her on what alone created any interest in her mind.

Of all those who had flocked to Beechwood, to congratulate Mrs. Grayson on her recovery, there was no one who took more heartfelt delight in so doing, or was more cordially received, than their worthy neighbour, M'Culloch.

"My good madam," said he, approaching the easy chair in which Mrs. Grayson sat, and offering his hand, "I could put off seeing you no longer, though you, or rather these young ladies, must push me out of the room, the moment I am likely to fatigue you. But where's my Rose of Sharon?"

Louisa, hearing the voice of her old friend, came running in from the dining room; and he not only shook her by the hand, but gave her one or two kisses, that might have been heard in every room in the house. He then held her off at arm's length, to see if he could perceive in her face any indications of the ague and fever, with which the lower country was always associated in his mind; and this examination, by the train of ideas it excited, bringing the blood into her cheeks, he declared, with great satisfaction, that for once she had escaped it.

"I believe," said he, "your kinsman's place, madam, is one of the healthiest in the Northern Neck. And how many of the buckahoes have those blushes and dimples slaughtered? Some scores, I'll warrant."

Louisa, anxious to give the conversation another turn, inquired about Mrs. M'Culloch, and reproached him for not bringing her with him.

"The old lady considers me so boisterous, and and was so fearful of my fatiguing your good mama, that she wanted me to wait until to-morrow; but for once I ventured to disobey her, and I shall be sure to pay for it in a curtain lecture. Girls, if you want to know how to govern your husbands, take a lesson from the old lady."

"I don't know, indeed, a better model," said Mrs. Grayson; "but if she rules, it is by never seeking to rule."

He looked thoughtful for a moment, and, with more seriousness than was customary with him, said, "I believe you have it, madam; and it is the only way a husband, worth having, can be governed."

Bella now proclaimed that a gentleman was coming up the lane, and in a little while Primus came to the door, and said that Mr. Hatchett wished to see his mistress.

Mrs. Grayson seeming to hesitate, M'Culloch offered to go out and learn of him his business. He accordingly went into the parlour, and found the old usurer in the same rhubarb coloured coat and breeches, but a thicker waistcoat, to suit the slight change of the season. M'Culloch never disguised his contemptuous feelings.

"How fares it, old hard times? You are not aware, I presume, that the good lady of the house has just risen from the bed of sickness."

"I was apprized of it, Mr. M'Culloch, but my business is pressing, and can't be put off."

"Hoot, man! are you to learn that business must give way to sickness? Would you fatigue this worthy lady about that eternal compromise, which, after all, I predict you will never agree to."

"Every man, Mr. M'Culloch, understands his own business best, or thinks he does. It is to give her notice, that a claim on her late husband has been assigned to me, and to know of her if she has any offset or discount against it."

"Whose bond is it, and what is the amount?"

"It is to Sam Slocum, who was Col. Grayson's overseer, for one hundred and eighty dollars."

"What! has that rascal sold you his bond already? It has been but a few weeks since he settled his account; and this is the mighty and important matter, for which you would push that amiable and benevolent face of yours into the chamber of a sick lady. Suppose you were not to have given this notice to-day, could it not have been done as well to-morrow, or next day, or next week? Or if you had not given it at all, Joe could have made it good to you. Nay, even if you had lost it altogether, would you ever have felt it, or missed it, or even known it, except by your leger? And yet, you could find it in your heart to torment this worthy lady about such a trifle! For shame, man! if you have no bowels, at least keep up a show of decency."

"You have your way, Mr. M'Culloch, and I have mine. I don't interfere with you when you choose to waste your time or your substance, and I don't see what right you have to meddle with me for husbanding mine. I have borne your flouts long enough, and I have put up with them, because I love peace. But since, in spite of all I can do, you are ridiculing and insulting me whenever we meet, I hope you will pay me what you owe me before you make so free, unless you mean always to be more liberal of your hard words than of your money."

" And do you pretend to censure me, miscreant? You, who have not the soul of an oyster? Because I have used that money, which you, by rapacity, amass, and have not the spirit to spend? I am able, thank God, to pay you, but I shall be in no hurry to do so. I have other creditors, whose claims, upon every principle of honour and justice, are superior to yours ; and if you don't choose to wait my time, you may sue and be d——d." So saying, he left him, and returned to Mrs. Grayson.

M'Culloch was not without some fears, in the midst of his resentment against Hatchett, that he had lost all hold upon the money-lender's forbearance, and that his long deferred removal to the west would be precipitated somewhat sooner than he wished, by his bitter raillery of that morning.

CHAPTER VII.

On Matilda's return to the Elms, she found Frederick Steener there, though he had lately spent the chief part of his time on his own estate, and in making preparations for his marriage with Susan Tidball. He was also disposed to look a little more closely into the accounts of his guardian, in consequence of the advice which had been given him by old Tidball. This investigation was one of great labour to poor Frederick, and he had come down to ask explanations of his uncle.

He took the earliest occasion of informing his cousin Matilda, that when at Lexington he had seen a gentleman just from Williamsburg, who mentioned that Edward Grayson was thought a very promising young man, and a fine genius, though a little eccentric; and that two young ladies were pulling caps for him; one very pretty, but without fortune, the other not handsome, but very rich, and very accomplished; and that as his father's estate would be absorbed in paying its debts, it was generally supposed that he would marry Miss Allen.

Matilda had uncommon firmness of mind, as well as clearness of judgment, and she did not allow herself for a moment to believe there was any shadow of ground for the latter part of the report; yet no rumour of this kind ever yet reached the ears of a lover without causing some uneasiness.

She kept up a regular correspondence with Edward, and meaning to write the next day to confirm her former statement of his mother's recovery, she mentioned these reports as examples of the false rumours that malignant or inconsiderate people were constantly putting in circulation, and that it should be a warning to both not to credit any thing that was inconsistent with the good opinion they entertained of each other.

Frederick, who had never taken the possibility of the report being untrue into calculation, was ready enough now to admit it, and even was confident of its falsity, as soon as it was suggested. He, therefore, did not afterwards mention it to his aunt, who would not have failed to avail herself of it to renew her persecutions of her daughter, with better arguments than she had hitherto been furnished with. The truth was, that Edward boarded in the house of a Mrs. Robertson, of genteel connexions, and once in easy circumstances, but who, after the death of her husband, had settled herself in Williamsburg, for the purpose of having her children well educated at a moderate expense; and the better to enable her to effect her purpose, she accommodated with board three or four young men who were well recommended to her.

Edward's handsome person, the dignity of his manners, his serious and even pensive air, and his very polite deportment, all concurred to make him uncommonly interesting to the youngest of her daughters. At a ball given soon after his arrival, this young lady seemed to claim his particular attentions; for, as they were inmates in the same house, and she was without a partner, he danced with her.

This was sufficient to produce some bantering, and some little chit-chat, with the gossips of the place, until, by degrees, it made him her declared lover.

As soon as Edward discovered the fact, which was not the case until it was known by the whole household, he acted with all the delicacy and propriety he was capable of; not suddenly withdrawing his attentions, but endeavouring imperceptibly to give them a character of mere friendship, in a way that could not be mistaken. He even went further, and, on finding her alone one afternoon at her instrument, he intimated what, indeed, she had heard, but was willing to believe was not true, that his affections were engaged in Frederick.

It was also a fact, that Harriet Allen, who had come to pass the winter in Williamsburg, and who was the heiress of a large estate in Prince George, had again and again declared herself more pleased with Edward Grayson, than with any young man she had seen in the old city. The hairdresser, who attended Edward, (for at that time every student of William and Mary had his hairdresser,) had a wife at the house where Miss Allen was staying, and her maid communicated these civil and commendatory speeches to Chloe, the barber's wife, who transmitted them to her husband, who, in time, entertained his young customers with them, together with other intelligence of the same character, and was particularly forward in making them known to him to whom he thought they would be most acceptable.

Edward, who had felt nothing but regret at the report with Miss Robertson, was mortified and displeased at this new disposal of him, to which these flattering speeches of a wealthy heiress quickly gave rise. He could never tolerate the idea of being a fortune hunter; and one cause of his forbearing to press his suit with Matilda, had been, that he wished to avoid the imputation of being influenced by her fortune. He was therefore remarkably distant and reserved in the intercourse he necessarily had with this young lady, as they often met at the same social dinner, and at the evening parties of the city. But as he was known to be a reserved young man, and was really nothing of a coxcomb, the coldness with which he met her advances was attributed to sheer modesty, and had the effect of making the young lady indicate her preference yet more plainly—especially, as the flattery and attentions she had been in the habit of receiving, would not let her suspec that her favour could be a matter of indifference to any young man.

But the fortune and the forwardness of one, no more than the beauty and silent attachment of the other, ever made his fidelity to Matilda waver for a moment; nor did he know that any person ever seriously believed those reports, which, whenever they were mentioned, in the way of idle banter, he always promptly and flatly contradicted.

He felt, then, the pride of conscious rectitude, when he received Matilda's letter, though he could not but regret that such reports should have reached her ears—knowing how much a similar rumour respecting even Frederick Steener, had formerly distressed himself. He immediately wrote an answer to her letter, from which it may not be amiss to make the following extract:

"I thank you, dearest Matilda, for discrediting the idle reports which have reached your ears. I wrote you that I was boarding with a Mrs. Robertson, an amiable lady, in decayed circumstances, who had a daughter about sixteen; and as she is really a pretty, modest, amiable girl, and it devolved on me sometimes to escort her home from the little parties to which we were both invited, it was enough, in a place like this, where nothing of more moment occurs than the concerns of students and young ladies, to give rise to the report. But as soon as I heard it, and perceived that the young lady had also heard it, I lost no time in preventing the injury which such reports may prove to the character or prospects of a female; I sought an opportunity to let her know, without hurting her pride, that I entertained no such views; and I did what I hope you will deem pardonable—I partially made her my confidant, and imparted to her the secret of my attachment. She is really an amiable girl ; and so far from appearing to feel herself slighted, she seemed flattered by this mark of my confidence, and to feel a lively interest in my fortunes : So that I trust all danger of the mischief I most apprehended is now at an end, and the idle reports you have heard will soon die away. As to the great heiress, Miss Allen, I have never once either walked, danced, or been alone with that young lady, and cannot account for so silly and strange a rumour. It is true, I have several times been in her company, and it seemed to be assumed as a thing of course, that I should have no objection to an estate in Prince George, with two hundred negroes, now that I have lost my own ; and that, as she was pleased to bestow on me some trifling compliments, I should be found to join in the throng of worshippers at the shrine of Mammon. But if my heart, my dearest Matilda, had not been altogether thine, this young lady could never have interested it. She is not only not handsome, but has a confidence in her deportment towards our sex, and an air of haughty superciliousness towards her own, that are extremely unpleasing. This tale will be forgotten, of course, when it is seen that I pursue the same distant course as ever ; though I apprehend the young lady will soon put an end to all such reports herself, by marrying some one of three or four of our collegians, who are besieging her with their attentions. I feel very grateful to my friend Frederick for his seasonable agency, and have, in the letter which encloses this, written him that I will, one of these days, do his law business for nothing. I have applied myself so assiduously to my studies, that habit has made them agreeable ; and the thought of the prize which is to reward my labours, animates me to new exertion, and makes a study, otherwise tasteless enough, at once light and pleasant. In the spring, I hope to obtain a license, and then, if I do not succeed, it will be the fault of dame nature, who may not have furnished me with the qualifications, and not for want of my own diligence in study, punctual attention to business, and faithful discharge of my duty. I trust by the next post I shall hear that Frederick is married, but I know not whether I ought much to rejoice, as some other may be substituted in his place, when he is out of the way, to beset you, and torture me. I wonder I have never had a line from Gildon since we parted. He must have been in New-York for two or three weeks. I am uneasy at his silence. I know his relish for pleasure and society, and sometimes fear that the same facility of yielding to its seductions that has made him forget his promise of writing to me, may make him forget his professions to my sister. If he were capable of doing so, he would not deserve that she should bestow a thought on him; but I fear she could not be brought to see the matter in this light. It seems to me, my dear Matilda, as if there could be no lasting attachment that is not founded altogether on esteem. Let me know whether Louisa hears from him; and watch over the happiness of that too amiable, unsuspecting girl. You have my warmest thanks, my beloved Matilda, for your kind attentions to my dear mother. She speaks of your services in the strongest terms that her grateful heart can inspire; and says, that to your prudent counsels she owes her life. How much does my heart exult, to hear such praises bestowed on you, by one whose praise is always so just; and what visions of bliss does it call up, when I think that the virtue and excellence which are now the theme of every tongue, I may one day be able to call my own. The idea intoxicates me; I can no longer think, I can only feel, and bid you a fond and an abrupt adieu."

Matilda felt greatly relieved on receivng this letter; for, though touching the subject that was nearest to her heart, she found nothing in it of which she was not previously convinced; yet, still, there was a pleasure in having the assurances of her lover's fidelity under his own hand, especially when it was so seasoned with the liberal commendations of herself. There were, however, some passages in the letter with which she was not entirely pleased, and, according to her practice, she began her answer, when her impressions were fresh and lively. It was as follows:

"*Elms, November*, 1796.

"I was sure my esteemed and valued friend would confirm the opinion which my knowledge of his character had induced me to form, by telling me that the silly reports I mentioned were false. The young lady must now be convinced, that the hopes, if she ever entertained any, are unfounded, and nobody will long believe the idle tale; yet I cannot but think it unfortunate, that you should have established yourself in a boarding house where the attentions which mere civility would exact from you towards the young lady, would be some interruption to your studies, besides exposing you to such ridiculous reports; but I suppose you do not wish to hurt their feelings by quitting them just at this time. I am not sure you did right in making her your confidante. It is a delicate office between a gay cavalier, and so pretty, modest, and amiable a young lady; for if you are sure it is not dangerous to yourself, are you sure it may not be so to her? There is something very soothing, I admit, in her sympathy, but really I doubt whether both you and she would not be as well without it. As for that haughty Miss, who is content to receive the homage to her wealth which her charms cannot command, I think you are in no sort of danger; though I think she has given proof of her having the recommendation of a good taste, as well as a fine fortune. Your excellent mama is now quite recovered, thanks to the skill of Dr. Blodget, to whom, under heaven, the credit is due, though she would generously give a large share of it to me, who are entitled to no more than the horse which brought him. She not only looks better than before, but I think is in better spirits, especially since she saw worthy Mr. Trueheart, who, besides making a favourable report on the state of her affairs, told her some handsome things of you. You see of how much importance is your success. Louisa has received a very long letter from Mr. Gildon, which will be food for her meditations until she receives another. She is, however, very melancholy, in spite of his protestations and assurances, and I am half angry, half alarmed, to see her so wanting in firmness. If any thing should happen to prevent his return, I dread the consequences. Do you know I sometimes have my fears? Heaven forbid there should be any foundation for them. I always thought your friend wanted stability of character, and, to say the truth, I never had any great liking to habitual jokers. His conduct has been a little ambiguous of late, and his letters have a laboured elegance, that shows the heart has little to do in dictating them; but I check these fears when I recollect that he is your friend. Fanny Buckley mentioned the other day, in mama's presence, Mr. Trueheart's report of you, and I watched her countenance, but she said nothing, and I was not able to discover whether she was pleased or otherwise. Is not this a symptom that she is relenting. My father exulted, and said he always predicted you would be a credit to the county. So you see here is another reason why you should be diligent in your studies, and not suffer yourself to be drawn aside by ' pretty, modest, and amiable young ladies.' Oh, Edward! I often laugh, to keep myself from weeping; let us hope for the best; farewell, and remember your own

MATILDA."

When Edward read this letter, it appeared to him, for the first time, that he had been injudicious in selecting his lodgings, and that he ought certainly to change them; and the rather, as the susceptible girl with whom he lived, whose partiality for Edward was mainly founded on her admiration of his manly character and noble dignity of manners, was so far from being discouraged by the secret he had confided to her, that she felt herself flattered and honoured by the distinction. Without making any calculations about the future, she yielded herself up to the pleasure of being in his company, and of conversing with him for the little time that he could remain with the family. Hoping for nothing more, she sought, and scarcely wished for greater happiness, though to Edward the subject had been for some time a cause of serious uneasiness.

During, then, a short interval, in which the Professor of law was attending the meeting of the general court in November, he went to Easton; and on his return he determined to lodge in the college, and to eat at a boarding house hard by, alleging, that he wished (as was the case) to have a readier access to the college library. Mrs. Robertson, though not remarkable for her penetration, knew of her daughter's partiality for Edward, and took it for granted, that it met with encouragement, or was one of those growing intimacies, which, at that place, one or two winters are very apt to mature into marriage. Feeling great personal respect for Edward, on account of his good breeding, his family, and his misfortunes, she already began to regard him as a son-in-law, and was greatly surprised at this intimation.

" I am afraid something has happened, Mr. Grayson."

" Nothing, madam, I assure you; on the contrary, I feel myself greatly obliged by the kind reception I have ever met with in your house."

At this moment her daughter entering the room, Mrs. Robertson said, " Nancy, did you know Mr. Grayson was going to leave us?"

Nancy, taken thus by surprise, turned pale with alarm, and could with difficulty articulate, " No, madam, I did not know it."

" He's going to board in college."

This afforded the poor girl great relief, as she had at first supposed he meant to quit Williamsburg. Recovering herself, she forced a smile, and said,

"I'm sorry we cannot accommodate Mr. Grayson to his taste."

He then repeated the reasons he had given before, on hearing which she felt greatly consoled. The good lady expressed a wish to see him often, and invited him to come and drink tea with them, whenever he was not more agreeably engaged. He endeavoured to excuse himself, alleging that his present course of study would allow him little leisure, but that there was no house in Williamsburg he should take more pleasure in visiting. Both the mother and daughter appeared to be greatly gratified at this remark, and they all parted very good friends.

He procured of the college steward a bed, with other necessary chamber furniture; and by the assistance of old Lemon, one of the slaves then belonging to the college, and whose oyster suppers are fresh in the recollection of numbers now living, he was soon rendered comfortable. He boarded at a house in the neighbourhood, where, indeed, he missed the nice muffins of Mrs. Robertson in the morning—her soup and stews at dinner, and crisp biscuits in the evening; but, on the other hand, his studies experienced no interruption. He could come and go when he pleased, and he knew it would gratify Matilda, who, it was clear, had thought he had been a little too warm in his praises of Miss Robertson.

Among the young men who boarded at the same

house, was Richard Mawly, who had formed a great intimacy with Gildon. They were both wits—both epicures—both had rather lax notions on some points of morality. They were, in short, both men of pleasure; but Mawly's face was as harsh and disagreeable as Gildon's was handsome; and he had, moreover, great perverseness and obstinacy of temper. He had taken an early dislike to Edward, whom he called a moral prig; and as every man instinctively finds out his friends and enemies, Edward soon perceived his ill will, and returned it with undisguised scorn.

In this state of feeling, nothing was wanting but an occasion, to bring these youths to an open rupture. Gildon had written to Mawly two or three times since he had reached New-York, and as the latter was apprized of Gildon's attachment to Louisa Grayson, and of his father's opposition, he never lost an opportunity of communicating to his companions every thing which made it probable that the match would be broken off; nor did he fail to hint at the disagreeable qualities of Edward, as he called them, and dwelt at length on the approaching downfall of the family.

In Gildon's last letter, there were some expressions, which seemed to warrant the inference, that he was coquetting, if nothing more, with Miss De Peyster; and on the strength of this, Mawly took occasion to mention at the dinner table his belief that Gildon would, after all, be married to his old sweetheart. Edward saw the malice of the remark, and was at first disposed to resent what he considered an aspersion of an absent friend; but as Gildon was not actually engaged to his sister, he did not feel himself warranted in going that length, especially as the silence of Gildon had created some painful suspicions of his good faith. His first impulse was to cast a look of disdain towards Mawly, and the next to look away. The poisoned shaft, however, hit the point it was aimed at. Edward, after making allowances for the malignity of Mawly, thought he would hardly have ventured to go so far without some real ground; and in his next letter to Matilda, he mentioned the report, and his feelings on the occasion, but cautioned her about repeating it at Beechwood.

Let us now return to the gentle, but imprudent, Louisa. Every Saturday she looked with anxiety for a letter from her lover; and though she was sometimes disappointed, yet the following week brought an apology for the omission, so studded with professions of love, and with extatic praises of his mistress, that her forgiveness was readily obtained. These omissions had been of more frequent recurrence of late, but still, the following post had continued to bring the explanation. From the time that Primus was set off to Battletown till his return, she thought of nothing but the letter she expected. She was generally stationed at the window a half hour before his arrival; and sometimes, when she was not noticed, or noticed only by her mother, she would walk up the lane leading to the house, to meet him. She had done so one evening about this time, and having asked Primus for the letters and papers, and eagerly run over them, she found several for her mother, but not one for herself.

" Are these all, Primus?" said she, in a faint voice.

" Yes, Miss Louisa, there's all."

" Look in your pockets," said she.

" There was five, Miss Louisa," replied Primus.

She found the number right.

" Perhaps he hasn't sent mine?"

" Lord! Miss Louisa, Mr. Taylor always sends your letters; and the young man who keeps the office, says ' here's one for your young mistress,' and sometimes, ' here's one from New-York;' but when I asked him if there was one for you, he looked again, and said 'No.' I reckon the gentleman doesn't write, because he's coming himself."

Louisa felt mortified, amid her disappointment, that she had discovered so much anxiety as to expose her feelings to this servant, who, it was clear, as well as the postmaster, seemed to be well acquainted with the relation in which she stood to Gildon. She walked on, much depressed, and delivered the letters to her mother.

They were all on business, but one of them was from Trueheart. Mrs. Grayson, after reading this letter, handed it to her daughter, saying, "Though this worthy man is sufficiently occupied with his own and other people's business to distract a weaker head, yet he gives more full and satisfactory answers to my inquiries than some who have nothing else to do. It was but last week that I wrote him the long letter to which this is a reply. A friend in need is a friend indeed. How should we get along without this capable and kind adviser?"

Louisa, engrossed by her disappointment, heeded not what her mother said; and mechanically taking the letter, and holding it in her hand, her eyes ran over the lines, without comprehending any thing of their meaning.

"On what credit does he think the poor negroes should be sold?" said Mrs. Grayson.

"Madam!—Yes."

"They will sell so much lower for cash. What length of credit does he recommend?"

"I don't see it, madam," said Louisa, recalled to herself; and after reading nearly half the letter, for the first time she found that he mentioned a credit of one or two years.

"Is any thing the matter, Louisa? you seem very abstracted. Have you received any intelligence?"

"No, madam."

"Are you sure?" said her mother.

"There came for me no letter, mama; at least Primus brought me none."

"You expected one, I presume."

" I thought it was probable I should receive one."

Her mother now perceived the cause of her anxiety, and, without seeming to notice the circumstance at the time, she endeavoured to inculcate the necessity of fortitude and patience under misfortune; and, above all, she determined to engage her daughter's mind busily in domestic occupations, until she should regain that portion of tranquillity she had recently possessed.

When another week had slipped around, Primus was again sent off as before, and Louisa's anxiety was now so increased, that she trembled when she asked him for the letter. The arch boy said, " there's a letter for you now, Miss Louisa." She looked over the parcel in his hand, and immediately recognising the well-known hand, she seized it, and hastily pressed it to her lips before she broke the seal. But it was not that healing balm her devoted heart craved, and so fondly expected. After a long detail of the various interruptions which had prevented him from writing in time for the post on the last week, and the week before, and the most vehement declarations of the strength of his passion, he said, " I have been endeavouring to make arrangements to be with you by Christmas, as I expected, for, believe me, my most adorable Louisa, nothing but necessity could control the impatience of my heart to be once more with you; but circumstances, which it would be tedious to unfold, will not enable me to set out till some time in the spring, by which time I shall return to Frederick, on the wings of love; and hope, then, to be able to call you mine wholly and for ever. I shall know little peace of mind till then, and nothing but this sweet hope could support me under the cruel privation. I have now not a shadow of expectation that any thing can soften the obduracy of my father; but while he does all in his power to make me miserable, I do not see that I am obliged to unite with him to the same end. I shall, therefore, feel myself justified in seeking my happiness in the only way in which it can be attained, which is in the possession of the fairest and sweetest of nature's works. Assist me, adored Louisa, to beguile this tedious interval of its weariness,"—with a good deal more of the same stamp.

Though her joy at getting a letter was greatly damped by learning that her lover had postponed his return, yet she was so soothed by his tender assurances, and had so much confidence in his affection, that she believed his protracted absence to be necessary, and lamented it only as an unavoidable misfortune.

The secret anxiety which had been preying on the mind of this lovely girl, had now visibly affected her appearance. Her colour had nearly left her cheek, her eyes were hollow, and the whole of her air and manner was languid and drooping, so as to be noticed by all the servants, even by

Granny Moll; who, attributing the change partly to regret for the absence of her lover, and partly to the prospect of leaving the family seat of her ancestors, endeavoured to cheer her with such arguments of consolation as occurred to her. She would banter her about pining so much before marriage; and asked her how she would do when she had a husband, if he went to the wars, as her father had done, or to foreign countries, or even away to Kentuck or New-York, and be gone five or six months. She endeavoured, too, to find some consolation for the loss of the estate; but this was a sore subject to the old woman herself, as well as to all the servants, and she made but a lame hand as a comforter; she, however, told Louisa, she had no doubt, that her young mistress and that pretty young man would ride in their coach, as his father, they said, was very rich; and thus she touched on a string of all others least likely to give a cheering or soothing sound. "As for mistress," said she, " poor soul, since master's death, a little would do for her; and master Edward was born to be a great man, and would make his fortune by the law, as old lawyer Scrip, and Mr. Trueheart," and many others, whom she enumerated.

The old woman's cabin had, indeed, always been a favourite place of resort to Louisa; and she had found it more grateful than ever, since Granny Moll invariably introduced the subject that her knowledge of her sex taught her was the most acceptable topic on which she could speak.

"And do you really think so highly of him, Granny?" would she sometimes ask, well knowing what the answer would be, but never tired of hearing it.

After receiving the letter, which she showed to her mother, who was unwilling to disclose the apprehensions it suggested, Louisa was desirous of paying her promised visit to Matilda, and of showing her the letter.

CHAPTER VIII.

The next day old Phill was directed to get the carriage to go to the Elms; a visit which he would gladly have declined, as the servants were now aware, that they, with the rest of the property, were soon to be sold, and they felt the mortifying reverse the more severely, when they were compelled to witness the new-born wealth of their ostentatious neighbours, where pride of purse was felt as much, and shown as plainly, by the servants, as by their haughty and ambitious mistress. As, however, he was to make a drive, perhaps for the last time, he determined to put his best foot foremost; and little Ben and himself were employed the evening before in cleaning the harness, scrubbing the carriage, and giving to every thing the most glossy and polished appearance. He felt keenly for the honour of the family, now about to be shorn of its beams; for he had all his life been accustomed to pride himself on its consequence, and make a boast of its wealth too, when his master was as superior to his neighbours in fortune as in dignity and standing.

So tediously minute was he in his preparations, that it was past eleven before they set off. It was, however, a good day; not a cloud intercepted the soft and grateful warmth of the autumnal sun. The rich foliage which had lately painted the mountain forest with all the brighter hues, had now disappeared, and the few leaves which were yet to be seen were dried and straggling, except those that were to be seen on a few scattered pines. The trees along the river, lately impervious to the sun, were stript of their leaves, which now formed a soft bed for the horses' feet, and occasioned a rustling sound as the carriage drove over them.

The whole of the road, which she had not travelled before since her return, reminded her of her lover, and of the rapturous delight with which she had listened to his " flattering tale." Not a turn of the way, a remarkable tree, a bend in the river, or view of the distant mountains, but brought to her recollection some of those fond scenes, which, after they are past, differ so widely from the common concerns of life, and are so bedecked with the brightest hues of the imagination, as to have at once the strangeness of a dream, and yet greater freshness in the memory than belongs to our waking perceptions.

Her thoughts then wandered still further back, and she remembered a yet earlier period of time, when, in the careless gayety of childhood, she rambled along this road with her brother, to meet Matilda, or to accompany her part of the way home, sometimes on foot and sometimes on horseback—

when her mind was free from care or disguise, her heart filled with benevolence and affection, and she was innocent and happy. Her present wretchedness, then, appeared the greater by the force of contrast. And such, she thought, are the wretched consequences of imprudent love, of disingenuous concealment, and disobedience to the best of parents!

Matilda had been expecting her friend, and had walked up the avenue to meet her, and to enjoy the fine day. Louisa alighted from the carriage when they met, and the two friends walked together arm in arm towards the house.

Mrs. Fawkner's fears of an alliance with the Graysons, had been much moderated by Edward's absence; and finding that her daughter's firmness was not to be shaken, and that her plan with Frederick Steener was in a fair way of being frustrated, she had not objected to an intercourse with the families; and began to think, that if Edward should realize the predictions of his friends, though he might not be a fit match for Matilda, as he wanted what she deemed most essential, yet he might be tolerated, rather than an only daughter should be consigned to an unprotected celibacy. She, therefore, received Louisa with more cordiality than she had shown for some time before; and, indeed, her wan and pallid countenance was calculated to soften a yet more unfeeling heart than Mrs. Fawkner's. She imputed Louisa's evident dejection of spirits to the impending sale of the estate, and endeavoured, with more of compassion than of delicacy, to say something consoling—as, that we were all liable to changes, that Fortune's wheel might soon take another turn, and that she heard Barbawl say, that if some of the claims belonging to the estate were properly managed, they would produce something handsome to the family after all,—though (she added immediately afterwards) it might be that Barbawl only wanted to get himself into business.

Louisa's depression was too deep to be reached by the consolations or admonitions of her who used them. They were received in silence. Major Fawkner was really pleased to see her; and he had several times, of late, ventured to hint to his partner, that Matilda's unfortunate attachment seemed incurable; that it had already seemed to have an effect on her health and spirits; and that if Edward should succeed at the bar, as seemed not unreasonable, he would be able to take care of the estate, if not improve it. He even went further, and supposed the no very improbable case, (considering the character of their daughter,) of her dying unmarried and childless, and of their estate going to Frederick Steener and the Tidballs.

This idea the good lady could not for a moment tolerate. She denied that Matilda was ever in better health; and said that she had seen girls bent on throwing themselves away, but being prevented from doing so by their more prudent parents, take on a good deal at first, and in a few years bless their stars, and the considerate caution of their friends, for the advantages of a more suitable match. If, indeed, she added, Edward should become a great lawyer, there would not be so much objection to him, but she never " reckoned her chickens before they were hatched." As to Frederick, if he threw himself away upon such " trash" (one of her favourite terms of contempt) as the Tidballs, he not only should never inherit a penny of her money, even if she had to give it to the poor, but should never set foot in her doors again.

After sitting about half an hour with the old people, Louisa asked Matilda to take a walk with her in the garden. The spot where Gildon had first made his declaration of love, was viewed by her with the liveliest emotion. She then showed her friend his last letter, and asked her candid opinion on the reasons he gave for delaying his return.

Matilda read over the letter again and again, and it was now too plain to her, that from some motive of ambition, or from the influence of his father, or, perhaps, the mere love of change, he was paving the way to break off the connexion altogether : but she had not the heart to communicate her opinion. She, however, told Louisa, that as her lover's return had been thus unexpectedly prevented, it might, from the same, or a similar cause, be still further delayed, and advised her to prepare herself for the worst. " Follow my example, my dear Louisa," said she ; " I believe I am as devoted in affection as it is in the power of you, or any other woman, to be ; and yet I am always acting, and preparing my mind, as if your brother and I were never again to meet. I never can consent to be his, but on terms which will subject neither of us to repentance, or the reproaches of the other ; and if the difficulties that now present themselves to our union can be removed, our bliss will, of course, be so much the greater. We shall enjoy our haven of rest the more, for the tempests we have encountered in reaching it."

" Oh, Matilda, what you say is perfectly reasonable and proper," cried Louisa, " but it is beyond my feeble powers. I can admire your fortitude, but cannot imitate it. There is the same difference between us, as between this convolvulus that withers at the first approach of frost, and yonder perpetual rose that defies its utmost rigour. I am a poor weak mortal, unable to struggle with those sorrows which I fear fate has in store for me. Oh, my dear Matilda, tell me that they do not await me, rather than vainly attempt to teach me how to bear them. Can he be inconstant? Is this the language of the heart? Does he write as one who is pouring out his whole soul? I sometimes think he does not express himself as he used to do; and then again I think my fears have misled me. Tell me, Matilda, you whose perceptions, always clear, are not blinded by the same passions which agitate me, tell me what you think? I see you hesitate. You think him false—Oh, God! look down upon a miserable sinner—pity and forgive her errors, and receive her into thy merciful bosom, ere this cruel suspicion be confirmed. But, no, it cannot be; you are prejudiced Matilda; I think you never appreciated Gildon justly; you judged of him by my brother, without considering the different dispositions of men; you intimated once he was selfish; I could give you the strongest proofs of his generosity, and charity, and beneficence; but which is the part which makes you distrust him?"

"My dear Louisa," said Matilda, striving to appear calm, "moderate your feelings, and call in the aid of the good sense you possess. Do not magnify evils unnecessarily; do not add to the distress of your excellent mother, who has already had her full share of trouble, and who affords you a bright example of heavenly patience, under trials with which yours cannot be compared. I have no particular reason to distrust Gildon's fidelity more than yourself; and if a doubt has arisen, it is merely a sudden suspicion, and you may be right, and I wrong; all I wish to inculcate is, that it is our duty, in difficult situations, to prepare for the worst, and if your lover should"—

"Oh, do not name it," said Louisa, interrupting her; "the thought is insupportable; the misfortune would be greater than you are aware of." Here she paused, hesitating whether she should proceed or not; and Matilda, waiting an explanation of her mysterious expressions—" But," she added, " I could not survive it."

" My dear Louisa, it pains me to see you possessed of so little fortitude; I sincerely hope you may have no greater occasion for it than you have had. But one can hardly expect to pass through life without great trials ; and upon our own account, as well as for the sake of those whose happiness is dear to us, we should learn the severe duty of resignation. Misfortune is, indeed, the only effectual instructress ; but I believe we may so prepare our minds, as to lessen the severity of her discipline."

" What, then, would you have me do?" said Louisa, in a tone of complaint.

" I would have you," replied the other, " contemplate the worst that can happen, and determine on a course of conduct which you will steadfastly pursue. I would have you prepare, in any contingency which can befall you, to do your duty to your best of parents, and to yourself. I would have you to remember, that if your lover is capable of deserting you, it must be either that he never loved you, or that he sacrifices his love at the shrine of avarice and ambition; in either of which cases, he deserves not your regard."

" Oh, Matilda, you talk like one who had learnt love only out of books. Can you erase from the heart the image which is engraven on it? Can you at your will and pleasure, banish from your mind all the recollections of the past, all the fond hopes of the future, which have occupied your thoughts by day and by night, for weeks and months? Can you possibly loathe and despise what you lately loved and admired? Can you pluck from the heart that which gave it life and motion? You can do it only by plucking away life itself. To tell me not to love Gildon, is to tell me not to live; and to tell me that he does not love me, is yet more cruel."

"Far be it from me," said Matilda, " to suggest such a thing. I never doubted that he did love you passionately; and if he did, so much do I agree with you on the force of the passion, that I must believe he loves you still. But I was merely arguing, that his love might be overpowered by other temptations, or by the influence of his friends; and granting these suppositions to be extremely improbable, as I admit them to be, I was merely considering how you ought to act if they were to prove well founded, without meaning to express an opinion on their probability. But since you think yourself incapable of supporting such a trial, in which, however, you do yourself injustice, and moreover do not suppose it possible, I see not why you should be so much distressed at the letter. It is comparatively of little importance whether Gildon comes in December or April."

Louisa looked distressed and embarrassed. "Yes, but I dreaded what might intervene. I did not know"—and with a violence of emotion she could not control, and which alarmed Matilda, she burst into a flood of tears, and said, " oh, Matilda, I am ruined in my own estimation, let what will happen; I am a lost being—I am unworthy of your friendship."

Matilda listened with amazement, and feared, at first, her friend's intellects were disordered; but after sobbing and weeping plentifully, she, with much hesitation and embarrassment, intimated the apprehended consequences. Her culpable weakness, and her contrition and sufferings, seemed so acute, that Matilda, after the first shock was over, used her best endeavour to calm her troubled spirits, and to offer the best consolations that sympathizing friendship could suggest.

While this lovely young creature, like a tender flower nipt by a too early frost, was pining under the heart sickness of disappointed hope, her mother was meekly bowing to the will of heaven, and endeavouring to support herself against some of its heaviest dispensations. The evening before the sale, Mr. Trueheart, arrived at Beechwood, in company with a man of genteel appearance, apparently about thirty. He was met by old Phill, with a sorrowful face, as he passed near the stable, where the ancient domestic had been brushing up the carriage to make it show to the best advantage, for the credit both of the house and its coachman.

" My daughter Patty," said he, " wants to know of you, sir, if she's to be sold—as, if she is, the gentleman who owns her husband will buy her."

"I cannot tell which of the servants will be kept yet, old man. Your mistress will make out a list of those she most wants, and, if possible, they shall be purchased for her; but the creditors must have their money first. I know she means to keep you and your wife; and the carriage and horses will be purchased too, if they do not sell too high."

Before the barrister had fairly entered the house, Phill ceased his well-intended labours on the carriage and harness.

"What a fool I have been," said he to himself, "to show off every thing to the best advantage, just to make my poor mistress give more for them—and all to pay money for which my master never got the value of a chew of tobacco. No, they ought to give her up the carriage, and horses, and driver, if nothing else; and if they don't, I'll try that she shan't pay much for them."

He then threw the harness into a dirty corner of the stable, where the greasy blacking that had just been put upon it, caught up the dust and litter, and made it look worse than at first. The carriage was drawn to the river, and, in returning, made to pass through the muddiest places he could find. The horses were slightly fed over night, and kept without water, to give them as gaunt an appearance as possible, and the currycomb was used as a modern beau's confusion brush, to produce as much disorder and roughness as possible.

Trueheart found an air of sadness and melancholy in the face of every slave he met. Even the brisk and lively Primus partook of the gloom which he saw reflected in the countenances of all. The worthy advocate dreaded to meet Mrs. Grayson, whose attachment to her servants, and keen sensibility, were as remarkable as her patience. She had been taking her favourite evening walk to the grave-yard; and about ten minutes afterwards, just as candles were lighted, arrived Mr. Trueheart and his companion. She met him with the same sweet serenity as ever—indeed, he thought there was even more cheerfulness in her manner than he had seen since her husband's death.

He then introduced Mr. Stokes, from Georgia. Mrs. Grayson rather wondered at the appearance of a stranger at such a time; but had no doubt that her friend could give some good reason for it. He, however, soon put an end to her conjectures, by informing her that Mr. Stokes, hearing of the approaching sale, and wishing to purchase slaves under a good character, had made him an offer, and they had actually been in treaty for the purchase of the greater part of them. Mrs. Grayson felt very much relieved by this information; for the pain of separating from the servants, to whom she had been accustomed from her infancy, would be greatly softened, if she could be sure they would be sold to a good master, and all, or nearly all, to the same person. Mr. Stokes was slightly known by character to Mr. Trueheart, and in the introductory letter he had brought, stating his responsibility for any pecuniary engagement he might make, his qualities as a master were also well spoken of.

In the course of the evening, he told Mrs. Grayson, with a communicative frankness not uncommon in his state, that his father had moved from King William county, in Virginia, to the state of Georgia, a little before the breaking out of the revolution, with a few negroes, and a numerous family;—that he had taken up a large quantity of land, which had been found particularly adapted to cotton, now becoming a common article of culture in Georgia; that he himself had been very successful as a cotton planter ; and from small beginnings, by means of industry and good management, which his father had learnt on the poor sands of King William, and had practised in a kinder soil and climate, he had made a considerable sum, which he wished to vest in negroes, and thus extend his cotton plantations. He stated, that his father had been once manager for Counsellor B——, whose only daughter Colonel Grayson had married; and asked, if she was the lady.

Mrs. Grayson replied she was. She remembered Mr. Stokes very well—that he often brought her peaches, and that she used to go to his house to eat sweet potatoes, with his daughter Polly, of whom she then inquired. He told her that his sister had married very well. She had grown very fat, and was now a widow with nine children. He then detailed many particulars, that he had heard from his father when a child, of the grand style of living of Counsellor B——, all of which had made a lively impression on his youthful mind ; and from the respect he seemed to feel towards one of his descendants, it seemed not to have been then entirely effaced.

Mrs. Grayson excused herself for withdrawing at an early hour, that she might have breakfast over the next day, in time to make arrangements for the sale, and to receive the attending crowd ; and retired to the small building that has been mentioned before, fitted up for her accommodation during the few days it would be necessary for her to continue at Beechwood.

It was soon whispered by the house servants, who had overheard a part of the conversation, to those in the kitchen, who reported it to those at the quarter, that there was a gentleman at the " great house," who meant to buy them all, and carry them to Georgia—some said to make cotton, but Granny Moll said to make indigo ; and to those who had most dreaded a separation from one another, the news afforded matter of congratulation ; but to others, to be sent out of Virginia, where they experienced the abundance that prevails on a grain farm, to a country, where provisions, not being raised on the plantation, were less liberally supplied, appeared more like a punishment than an accommodation, and among these was the old grandam, who has been so often mentioned.

In common with the other servants, she had arrayed herself in some of her best attire. A clean white cap, bound with a half worn black riband, covered her grisly locks; and a wrapper of white homespun, nicely starched and ironed, connected with her wrinkled features and wan complexion, gave her a funereal appearance. She hobbled up to the house, and going to her mistress's chamber, there stood leaning on a stick, and shaking and panting with fatigue from the unusual exertion. Bella was told to hand her a cricket to sit down upon, when she said, "I thought I would come up to see my mistress in her troubles, though the old woman can't lend a hand to any thing now. My Rachel tells me that you are a going to sell the people to a rich man from Georgia, to make indigo. But let me beg and pray my dear mistress, not to sell my Peggy and her children there. They live so hard, as they tell me, in making indigo. I remember my husband went with his young master to the Charleston races, and he told us that the black people worked up to their necks in water—that they have little or no bacon, and now and then a salt herring, and that the overseers are mighty strict. Do pray, my mistress, let that man keep his money, and sell them, as they must be sold, (for I'm sure you'd keep them if you could,) to your own country people. Let them make corn—let them make wheat—let them make tobacco—though, for the matter of that, they havn't much rest on a tobacco plantation—but don't send them away, where we never shall hear of them. Don't send my Peggy."

Mrs. Grayson had much difficulty in persuading the old woman that her fears were groundless. That in the part of Georgia in which Mr. Stokes lived, they made no indigo, and provisions of all kinds were as plentiful and cheap as in Virginia. That peaches, watermelons, and sweet potatoes, all favourites with the negroes, were better, and more abundant than in Virginia. The old woman was greatly comforted by this representation of her mistress, in whose accuracy she had implicit confidence. She, however, still repeated, " but, mistress, let Peggy stay; sell her to somebody that lives in old Virginia."

" Well," said Mrs. Grayson, " it shall be as Peggy pleases."

The fact was, that the old woman had several other children, but as Peggy was the youngest, and had continued longer with her before she took to herself a husband, her heart yearned more strongly to her than the rest, contenting herself that they would be well provided for if they were purchased by the gentleman from Georgia. Mrs. Grayson then asked the old woman if she would choose to remain where she was, or would go to live with her near the Opeccan—as if she would rather continue on the spot to which she had been accustomed, Mr. Trueheart would stipulate for it in her behalf with the purchaser, as well as for her maintenance.

" Oh ! no, my mistress," said the old woman, " I must go with you. To be sure I love this cabin ; I have a fine little garden ; I have drank water out of the Poplar spring there these thirty years, but I must live and die with my old master's child"—wiping her eyes. " They tell me it's a wild sort of a place upon the 'Peccan ; but what should I do for my coffee ? and who is to nurse the old woman when she's sick ? and who's to bring her wood ? and how should I do without my Louisa ? God bless my child ! She looks mighty thin. When did you hear from her ?"

" She was tolerably well yesterday, granny. I expect her home to-morrow."

" Yes, I must keep with you, my mistress, while I live, and the old woman won't trouble you long."

Her mistress's susceptible heart was greatly affected at this instance of attachment, though the old woman did not disguise that her own personal comforts had some weight in inducing her choice. Mrs. Grayson then bade Bella go out, and tell all the women to come to her. The order was promptly obeyed, and the sorrowful looks they exhibited, contrasted strongly with the neatness, and even gayety, with which some of them were attired. She informed them of Mr. Trueheart's plan of disposing of them to Mr. Stokes, for the sake of keeping them together—communicated what she had heard of his character as a good master, and advised them to make no objection to the sale, assuring them that although it would be an advantageous one for the estate, it should not be made if it were against their wishes. She then consulted them one by one; the greater part, on the faith of her recommendation, were willing to live with Mr. Stokes. One said she would rather have remained in the country in which she was raised, and continue at the sort of work she was accustomed to; yet, as it might be of advantage to her, who had been a kind mistress, and had saved her life with her last child, she would rather be sold than not. Three or four, however, persisted in saying, that they would rather remain in Virginia, either because they had some expectation of being purchased by particular persons who owned their husbands or sweethearts, or because of the undefined fears which they had of a country they had never seen, and which their mistress's representations were not able to remove.

Having written down the names of those who preferred staying behind, and taking the chance of a good master in Virginia, rather than the certainty of a good one in Georgia, she opened a wardrobe, from which she took a large collection of her old clothes, most of them not past wearing, but no longer suiting the sombre dress she had prescribed to herself the rest of her life, and distributed them among the crowd,—rather regarding the size of their families, than their several merits, in this last act of her bounty. They received the presents with a curtesy, and a " thank you, madam," or " God bless my dear mistress," or " we shall never get such another," or with a simple curtesy, and a silent tear, as gratitude or affection, or that flattery which servitude naturally engenders, happened to prevail. One or two might have been observed, in which there was rather more of discontent, that their presents were inferior to those of some of the others, than of gratitude for what they had received. There was, however, not enough of these unamiable characters to affect the beauty of the moral picture of genuine benevolence, active under the severest pressure of misfortune on the one part, and gratitude and affection taking the place of servile obedience on the other. Caps, handkerchiefs, remnants of muslin, cambric and silk, ribands, dresses, stockings, curtains, and counterpanes, were borne off in triumph ; and the women, in their wrappers and short petticoats, without shoes or stockings, (except those who belonged to the house,) for a while forgot that they were soon to change their homes, their habits, their associates, and many of them to be exiled even from their country.

Before this distribution was entirely over, a few persons had arrived, and in a little while, the crowd gathered thicker and faster, until the lower rooms of the house, and the yard, were quite filled. The lane, formed by two high fences leading from the road to the house, was lined with horses from one end to the other. Among the company, were a few females, drawn there partly by curiosity, and partly by a wish to purchase some article of furniture, that had been admired and talked of by their plain neighbours, or, mayhap, because it had been the property of persons so much beloved and respected.

About twelve, the auction began with selling the kitchen utensils, and the coarse tools and implements of husbandry; from thence they proceeded to the household furniture, and when Mr. Trueheart happened to bid, a whisper immediately went round, " that is for the widow;" upon which there was a general unwillingness in the company to bid further, though some of the most rigorous creditors, and a very few besides, with some grumbling to conceal their own want of generosity, showed that they were to be restrained by no considerations of that kind. Their efforts, however, only had the effect of making Mrs. Grayson give a little more for the articles she wished. Old Hatchett was there, and although he was cautious of bidding for what he did not want, yet he was ready enough to encourage the biddings of others; and he earnestly complained of the injustice of a man's creditors going unpaid, that his family might purchase articles at half price; articles, too, that did not suit their present circumstances,—remarking, " that people should lay aside their pride when they had lost their property ; but that with some people poverty was no cure for prodigality and waste."

Amidst a good deal of respect and delicacy manifested towards the widow of the deceased Colonel Grayson, there were some harsh comments on his inconsiderate facility in being every man's surety, as well as on his ostentatious style of living, and a few coarse jests on the different articles of furniture, many of which excited the wonder and curiosity of the vulgar throng around. They passed from room to room, staring and inquiring into the uses, and cost, and value, of such articles as were new to them, and with irrepressible curiosity, thrust themselves into the bedrooms, where they diligently scanned the minutest particular.

The auctioneer was a man of cleverness and despatch, and the most valuable articles had been disposed of before three. The little manœuvres of the bidders were amusing to those disposed to laugh at the foibles of their fellow creatures, but somewhat mortifying to the sticklers for the dignity of our nature. Pure selfishness never appears so naked and undisguised, as in a great crowd, actuated by some common feeling or motive, for it is not then restrained by the fear of shame, (far more potent than conscience ;) but one, in giving indulgence to his feelings, is kept in countenance by another. There you might have seen them, pushing forward and elbowing each other, without the usual deference to age or sex, as the stream followed the auctioneer from room to room. Their little artifices in undervaluing the quality of the article, with the bystanders, that they might make better bargains—their hostile feelings at the rival bids—their envy at a lucky purchase—the absence of every thing that indicated a benevolent or even a social nature—all seemed to favour the hypothesis of Hobbes, that war is the natural state of man.

"An excellent Wilton carpet, ladies," cried Mr. Winkornod, the auctioneer, "as good as new."

"It is burnt in several places," said one little woman, with sharp peering eyes, and looking through a pair of spectacles at a small scorch from a cinder.

"This would suit your large room, Mrs. Williams," said the auctioneer.

"Oh, sir, I can't buy Wilton carpets, now wheat has fallen."

"Her husband has just sold his crop for two dollars per bushel, however," whispered a bystander.

"The Brussels carpets are more fashionable now," said Peggy Buckley.

"This was a very pretty carpet before it was so faded," Mrs. Vaneer said.

Yet, when it was set up, this carpet, though burnt and threadbare, and fitted to no room but the one it was in, was bid for very eagerly by all the ladies, and it was finally knocked off by the auctioneer to Mrs. Still, who had been sitting in the corner, and had not said a word.

"A very fine stuffed easy chair, ladies," said the man of the hammer.

"It is rather too narrow," said Mrs. Micklebairn, a short thick woman, who had been sitting in it.

"Is it stuffed with hair or moss?" said another.

"Hair, I presume," said the auctioneer.

"Will you warrant it?" said the other.

"No, madam, but I will inquire."

"It is not worth while, but it feels like moss."

After a long contest, in which Mrs. Micklebairn took a conspicuous part, it was purchased for Mrs. Grayson.

"Every handsome thing is bought in," said one of the ladies, colouring.

"Mr. Winkornod, set up this bed and furniture."

"Shall I set up the bed and mattress together?"

"Separate," said one.

"Together," said another.

"I won't bid," said the lady who last spoke, "unless they are set up together."

"I must accommodate the widows," said the polite auctioneer, and the widow accordingly made the purchase.

CHAPTER IX.

About three o'clock, notice was given, that the residue of the furniture, stock, &c. would be sold on the following day, and they proceeded to make sale of the slaves.

A pine table, about four or five feet square, was brought out of the kitchen, and placed on the lawn before the south door, on which these people were made to ascend, one by one, unless there was a family, in which case they all stood on the ground. One not accustomed to this spectacle, is extremely shocked to see beings, of the same species with himself, set up for sale to the highest bidder, like horses or cattle ; and even to those who have been accustomed to it, it is disagreeable, from their sympathy with the humbled and anxious slave. The weight of his fetters, the negro, who has been born and bred on a well regulated estate, hardly feels. His simple wants are abundantly supplied, and whatever of coercion there is on his will, it is so moderate and reasonable in itself, and, above all, he has been so habituated to it, that it appears to be all right, or rather, he does not feel it to be wrong. He is, in fact, a member of a sort of patriarchal family.

But when hoisted up to public sale, where every man has a right to purchase him, and he may be the property of one whom he never saw before, or of the worst man in the community, then the delusion vanishes, and he feels the bitterness of his lot, and his utter insignificance as a member of civilized society.

The countenances of the dullest and most phlegmatic of them, showed some emotion when thus exposed—mostly of anxiety about the persons who should purchase them, and sometimes mortification at answering the inquiries made by the bidders, about their health, their age, ability, and willingness to work. Some of the women, who had chosen in the morning to run the risk of being sold to some person in Virginia, when the risk they were about to run was thus brought fully before them, would willingly have recalled their words; and one wept loudly while the auctioneer was, in the way of his trade, crying out, " three hundred dollars—will nobody give more for this likely wench?" Her extreme distress induced an inquiry on the part of Mr. Trueheart, and, after much sobbing, she admitted that she had just married, or as good as married, a young man, the servant of Mr. M'Culloch. As soon as the old man heard of it, he declared the hussey and his man Jacob must not be separated, though Jacob was an idle chap enough; and he forthwith made a bid, though he knew that the bond he should give, would probably get into Hatchett's hands, and that he would be sued on it immediately. But Trueheart, thinking that his friend would be better off, under his present circumstances, by disposing of a part of his slaves, than by purchasing more, suggested another plan of accommodating all parties. This was, to sell both Jacob and Molly to Mr. Stokes, and thus the girl could go with the rest of her family, and the lovers be gratified; and M'Culloch be relieved from an old debt, as well as an unprofitable servant, instead of adding to his difficulties—to which arrangement he finally consented, provided Jacob would agree to it.

On one occasion, a likely mulatto girl, about eighteen years of age, whose husband was owned in the neighbourhood, was about to be sold; and as slaves of this description often command very high prices, when they happen to suit the tastes of some of the libertines of the French or Spanish settlements, or even as house servants or ladies' maids, they are eagerly sought after by the negro traders. Those who were present, readily sought to avail themselves of this object of speculation; and soon going beyond the limit, which the prudent farmer, who owned her husband, had prescribed to himself, he had stopt, and they continued to bid against one another.

The girl looked extremely alarmed, when she saw she was bid for by men whom she did not know: and one of them, who was very well dressed, and a likely man, having asked her if she would be willing to go with him, she suddenly, and rather petulantly, said, " No !" The auctioneer, who had directions to dwell awhile, whenever a slave was about to be sold to a master they did not like, immediately sent for Mr. Trueheart ; and he, finding how matters stood, authorized a bystander to make the purchase for him. The trader, piqued at what he called the girl's impudence, which he felt the mean desire of punishing, in order to gratify his humour, and to make some little display of his cash, had bid for the girl forty or fifty dollars more than she was worth ; but having time to cool, (as the sale now proceeded slowly,) and fearing to make himself a laughing stock with his companions, by the price he should be made to pay, he ceased bidding, and the girl was put down to Mr. Trueheart.

"There's a piece of extravagance for you," said Hatchett, to one standing near him ; " here's a woman whose husband died insolvent, or nearly so, and his widow can afford to buy a field girl for four hundred and twenty dollars. I hope they'll not talk of compounding after that."

"The old lawyer has taken a fancy to that mulatto girl ; I wonder if he's married," said one of the negro buyers.

"You'd better mind how you talk, young man," said the farmer, in ill humour, both with the negro buyer and with himself, " about respectable people in a strange place. That may be the practice where you came from ; but the girl would have had a husband of her own colour, if something of that sort had not been running in your own head."

The sturdy appearance and angry looks of the farmer, and the laugh raised at the expense of the trader, made him check his anger. In a few minutes, Trueheart, who was engaged in separating those negroes which were to be sold at auction, from those who were to be retained by Mrs. Grayson, or purchased privately by Mr. Stokes, returned, in a short time, and taking the farmer by the arm,

"Hark ye, neighbour Wilkinson," said he, " I will either sell you this boy, or buy his wife. The price is high, to be sure; but I will wait with you a twelvemonth for the money "

The farmer, who had reproached himself for flinching from such a contemptible fellow as he now thought his competitor to be, and who knew that the girl would not be dear, at the ordinary difference between cash and credit, consented to the offer; and the pretty mulatto, who was delighted that she was to remain in the county, was still further pleased to find that she would hereafter be with Anthony always, instead of seeing him only once a week, as had been the indulgence allowed him hitherto.

The next that mounted the table, was a tall, athletic man, between forty and fifty, by the name of Absalom. He had a look of firmness, and of what some might consider sullenness, and others, dejection. The auctioneer looked at his list, and asking his name, read aloud, " Absalom, and his wife Judy. Where is your wife ?"

"She's going to Georgia," said he.

"That must be a mistake," said the other.

Mr. Trueheart was sent for ; and Absalom was asked how it happened that he chose to be sold, when his wife had preferred going to Georgia. He made no answer at first ; but, on the question being repeated, he said that Judy and he had parted. Upon Trueheart's suggesting that they might be reconciled again, he said it was impossible,—on which he was sold, and purchased by Mr. Trueheart. It seemed, on further investigation, that he had detected his wife, with whom he had lived for about fifteen years, in an infidelity with little Tom, and had repudiated her, though it had cost him a great struggle; and after some interference on the part of their friends, and great contrition on the part of his spouse, and promises of future amendment, they were reconciled, and he was sold to Mr. Stokes.

Although there was no separation of husbands from wives, or mothers from young children, yet, in some instances, those who were going to Georgia, were very near relations to many of those who remained behind—the first, choosing to separate from their friends, rather than encounter uncertain risks.

As Mr. Stokes had an agent there ready to take charge of them, and had already provided the means of transportation, they were required to prepare for starting immediately ; while many of those who were purchased by the neighbours, were told to go to their new homes that evening, and that their little articles of furniture and stock could be sent for afterwards. In such cases they took an affectionate leave of their friends and fellow servants, with whom they had been born and bred, and from whom they were about to be separated for ever. The solemn shake of their hard hands, and " Good bye, Dick," " God bless you, Sal," "Farewell, Aunt Nelly," " Cousin Charles, God bless you," were very affecting. Their simple hearts are very susceptible of warm attachment; and many of them on this occasion, especially when they went to take leave of their mistress, as they still called Mrs. Grayson, could not refrain from tears, accompanied with some such benediction as this : " Heaven bless my kind mistress wherever she goes, and send her good luck !" and " Remember me to Miss Louisa."

Many of those who were going to Georgia, made presents to those who stayed behind, especially of such articles as they had not been able to sell. They were all dressed in the coarse white cloth called napt cottons, at once cheap, warm and strong, and thick stout shoes, which had been made on the estate by some two or three of the number.

Bella came frisking among them, with an air of conscious superiority, crying out, " mistress says you must all go to the store-room for some sugar, and bring your bottles for molasses."

"God bless my mistress—we never shall get such another!" ejaculated two or three.

"And, Effy, mistress sends you this flannel for Mary Ellen, and says you must be sure to give it the drops every night and morning."

Eight slaves were selected for Mrs. Grayson, four house servants, and four for the field, besides Granny Moll. There were several superannuated, whom Mr. Trueheart concluded to attach to the estate, when it should be sold the next day, as they would be an inconsiderable incumbrance on its value; and it would be far better for them to remain where they had been accustomed to live, than to go off, even for the purpose of being better used.

After the sale of the negroes was over, the carriage and horses were brought up, and Mr. Trueheart, attending for the purpose of bidding for them, would not have recognised them to be the same that he had seen "smartened up," as old Phill termed it, the evening before—so successful had been his pious fraud in metamorphosing their appearance for the worse. He smiled at the device of the old man, which he purposely endeavoured to counteract by expressing his surprise openly at the change. The old servant said afterwards, "Mr. Trueheart be a great lawyer and a sensible man, but he no great hand at a bargain. After I had fixed my carriage and horses, so as they look like Joe Holliday's hack, he throw all the fat in the fire, by saying 'Phill, what have you been doing to the carriage and horses, they look so rusty ?' 'But,' says I, ' ah, massa Trueheart, we are all getting old, carriage, and horses, and driver.' 'But, Phill,' says he, 'you have not got much older since last night.' I wink and wink, but he do nothing but laugh. He's a mighty green man sometimes ; but I told them all the carriage and the horses were a mighty good carriage and horses, except that, like the old man, they were the worse for wear, and they took me at my word ; and Mr. Trueheart have them at his own bid, and when I smartened them up, you would not have known them."

The following day, the stock, horses, provisions, and old articles, were disposed of, and then the estate itself was sold. As the land was good, there were two or three bidders, besides old Hatchett, who, disappointed in getting it for half price, let it slip through his fingers, under the persuasion that there were by-bidders employed to make him run up the price, to his infinite mortification when he discovered his mistake.

The succeeding day was one of still greater bustle than the others. The purchasers attending to receive and take away the articles they had bought—calling incessantly on the auctioneer and his clerk—moving tables and chairs, bedsteads, presses and bureaus—here a parcel of glass, there a case of knives and forks, with a mattock and spade—a kitchen jack, with a set of window curtains, a carpet and a wheat fan. The most heterogeneous mixture was seen in the different lots—some standing in one corner of a room—others moved into the yard, and other again already placed in a cart or wagon to take them away.

Mrs. Grayson, seated in the out-building, was quietly signing receipts, or receiving bonds, or executing such papers as Mr. Trueheart advised, and had already made herself comfortable in her temporary residence, on the same scale as she expected to be in her intended establishment on the Opeccan. The zeal, assiduity, judicious management, and delicate generosity of her worthy friend, had filled her heart with the liveliest gratitude; and she prevailed on him to accept, as a small memento of her grateful friendship, a pair of diamond ear-rings for Mrs. Trueheart, which had belonged to her mother, and a London copy of the Encyclopædia Britannica for himself.

Having adjusted every thing with equal despatch and correctness, this worthy man quitted the house of Mrs. Grayson, leaving both black and white cause to bless him for his well-directed and disinterested benevolence. It was believed, that but for his judicious management, the estate, instead of leaving a handsome surplus, would have fallen far short of paying off Hatchett's claim; and every one rejoiced at the result, as much from their regard to Col. Grayson's widow and family, as their dislike to the hard-hearted usurer.

On the morning after the sale, Louisa returned

from the Elms; and, as much as she was engrossed by her own misfortunes, she could not be insensible to the effects of the change in the circumstances of her family. When she entered the house, the bare floors, and the nakedness of the rooms, had such a forlorn and desolate appearance, that her heart sunk within her. She passed by her mother's chamber, and though the bedstead was yet standing, it was stripped of its bedding and furniture, and drawn out of its place. What articles remained, were scattered in disorder over the middle of the floor, defiled with the marks of the feet, or with the stain which the chewers of tobacco had left on it. Brooms, and fire irons, and old trunks, all indiscriminately heaped together. The best articles had been first removed, and there remained old bedsteads, old trunks, boxes, and casks, and other lumber, or such as had been purchased by persons at a distance. She hurried along to where she was told her mother was, and found her sitting with the same serene and resigned countenance, as if she was in her easy chair at the window, in her own room, reading a sermon, or penning one of her pious effusions to some distant friend.

"Are we not snugly fixed here, my dear?" said she, after an affectionate embrace, and inquiries concerning her daughter's health. "Mr. Trueheart tells me our house on the Opeccan is pretty much like this, except it is of stone; and I think, as it is so small, Rachel and Bella will be able to keep it neater than they did this, without the necessity of scolding."

Louisa was rejoiced to find her mother so satisfied with the change, and she reproached herself more than ever for having concealed any thing from so much goodness. Mrs. Grayson saw, with great concern, amid all the cheerfulness which Louisa assumed, that her health was not improved by her visit. She was thinner and paler. She was persuaded that the anxieties of love preyed on her daughter's too sensitive heart, and a state of painful uncertainty was impairing her health, and undermining even life itself. They laboured to conceal what they suffered, and in amiably endeavouring to lighten the sorrows of the other, each alleviated her own.

The next post brought another letter from Gildon to Louisa, which converted her doubts and fears into the most cruel certainty. It was in these words:

"*New-York, Dec.* 15, 1796.

"My beloved Louisa's heart, tender and affectionate as it is, will not make known to her what I have suffered since I last wrote. I informed her of my plan of engaging in business in the city of New-York, and this plan had my father's ready approbation and support; he procured me a partner—agreed to become one himself, and to advance two thirds of the capital. All this went just as I wished; but, as if he suspected my too ready acquiescence, he inserted a clause in the articles of agreement, that neither of the partners should leave the state, without the permission of the other two, under the penalty o. forfeiting his whole interest, and that the chief management and control of the business was to be in Mr. Van Dyck, a young man whom he has brought up, and in whom he has the greatest confidence. My first impulse, on reading this provision, was to spurn the proffered advantage ; but, would you believe it? the means, even of getting from this to Virginia, were wanting ; he has so limited my pecuniary supplies, and has been so successful in closing the other avenues by which they have heretofore been obtained. What to do, under such circumstances, I knew not. I then thought, that after our term of partnership expired, I might, from the profits, which my father would have no right to control, be able to gratify the first wish of my heart, and make my Louisa mine by the rights of law, as, I trust, she already is in affection. But, on further reflection, I felt it would be an act of gross injustice to the most lovely and most amiable of her sex, and a most ungrateful return for her kindness towards me, to keep her so long in a state of suspense, and subject to the anxieties that ever attend it, as well as to the remarks and sneers of the illiberal. She, whose beauty, and manners, and accomplishments, have resounded throughout the Valley of Shenandoah, and at whose feet the worthiest and most accomplished youth of the land would be proud to throw themselves, if permitted—I could not, my most lovely, my never-to-be-forgotten, Louisa, be thus unreasonable. Love, such as mine, seeks the real interests of its object, still more than its own gratification. I feel myself called upon, by every principle of justice, generosity and honour, to release you from your engagement, rather than expose you to the perils and disadvantages of a three years' separation. My own heart, I know, could never change. I fear thy too pleasing image is destined ever to reign there triumphant, and to unfit me for any other business or pursuit. But is it not among the things possible, too, that in this long interval, besieged as you would certainly be by wealth and talents, and the entreaties of friends, these cruel intermeddlers with the happiness of lovers, you might forget your Gildon ? If so, ought I not to enable you to do it without blame, as it is not in my power to place you in that situation from which I should take you, and which you are so eminently qualified to adorn ? I shall anxiously await your answer. Be assured, that it has cost me pangs not to be described, to take this course ; but in my cruel situation, I had no other alternative. It was a choice of evils, and in making the selection, I have regarded your interest, not my own inclinations ; for, believe me, when I swear to you, that the happiest moments of my life have been in your sweet and innocent society, and that the world has nothing for me, that can compare with that bliss, if circumstances would permit me to enjoy it. Farewell, my amiable, my ever-loved Louisa. I shall always be your devoted, though unfortunate,

"GILDON."

CHAPTER X.

The unhappy Louisa had not half read this evidence of her lover's perfidy, before her eyes became dizzy, and her brain confused. She endeavoured to get up and retire, but in the effort at concealment, she swooned away, holding the letter in her hand. Her affectionate mother ran to her assistance, and taking possession of the fatal paper, and putting it in her pocket, she endeavoured to give such aid as her situation required In a few minutes, she came to herself, but it was only to utter the most piteous and heart-rending cries of distress.

" Where is it ?" said she, looking around her.

Mrs. Grayson told her, if she meant the letter, it was safe in her pocket, and had not been seen by any one.

" Read it, then, my dear mother, read it, and judge what I must feel. Oh ! could he be so cruel ? Stay, it may not be his hand-writing—it may be a forgery."

" It has the New-York post-mark," said Mrs. Grayson.

" Let me see. It may be some contrivance of that odious Miss De Peyster."

She took the letter, and saw too plainly that it was Gildon's hand. She now finished reading it, and the high wrought compliments it contained, looked so much like insults, that they brought a momentary indignation to her aid ; but this feeble support soon deserted her, and resentment gave way to pure unmingled grief, and the blackest despair.

Mrs. Grayson ran over the letter hastily, and saw enough to satisfy her, that it was the pitiful shift of a mean, mercenary lover, who was abandoning the object of his affection, because she was poor ; and began to call to her aid the precepts of religion, the vanity of all worldly hopes and expectations, and that " there's nothing true but heaven." With the calm dignity that was natural to her, and had been strengthened by misfortune, she said, " My child, this man has proved himself unworthy of you ; and self-respect requires you to despise the wretch, who could thus sport with your feelings."

Louisa seemed all the while following the course of her own thoughts ; but, catching at the last words,

" Yes, sport with my feelings," she repeated. "Oh ! Gildon, could you read the heart you are thus lacerating, you could not have written that letter. And has it come to this ? Have, then, all my fond dreams of happiness vanished for ever ? Is this the result of your professions and vows of never-ending love ? Oh ! mama, pity me, pity me."

" Comfort yourself, my child, and trust yourself to our heavenly Father."

"I deserve not the favour of Heaven—I deserve not your pity—I merit *his* scorn. Oh! mother, mother, let me hide myself from the face of the world—I am unworthy of you—I have deceived you—I saw him at Stanley. He followed me there without my knowledge."

"Oh! my child, how could you conceal the fact from me? Have I deserved this want of confidence?"

"I have been a culpable wretch. I see it—I know it. Oh! forgive me."

"My child," said her mother, unable to reproach her when she was so self-accusing and so afflicted, "I do forgive you, and I regret it more upon your account."

"My dear mother," said Louisa, interrupting her, "you will not, you cannot forgive me. I have not told you all. I saw him privately—I saw him too often—I——Oh! I'm the veriest wretch that lives."

Her mother guessed too plainly at what her daughter intimated; and she thought now that the cup of her afflictions was full. One painful thought followed another in rapid succession. The forlorn and unprotected condition of her child—her blasted affections—the stain on the hitherto unblemished honour of her house, so tortured her, that it required all her natural fortitude, and all her habitual resignation to the will of Heaven, to support her.

"And have we nursed a viper in our bosoms, to

sting us to death ?" said she, in a tone that was rare with her. " And have you so far forgot what was due to yourself—to your family—your father's honour—" here she could not refrain from weeping.

" He is not altogether to blame," said the generous girl. "I have been as much in fault as he; but he never could have loved me. I see it now too plainly; and death will soon come to relieve me from a hateful existence."

" Is that the way you insult an offended Providence, Louisa? Instead of seeking to atone for your errors, by penitence and amendment, to wish to rush unasked into the presence of your Creator! Are you prepared for the change ?"

" Forgive me, my dear, my angelic mother. I know not what I say. Despair deprives me of my reason; but I cannot, I'm sure I cannot, survive it."

The wild and frantic looks of Louisa now awakened all the tenderness of the mother, and for a time suspended her indignation towards Gildon, and the deep mortification she felt for the degradation of her family. She used some soothing expressions; but these seemed to throw the wretched girl into more violent paroxysms of grief, her mother's gentleness and tenderness but enhancing the pain of self-reproach.

" Do not pity me, my dear mother—I deserve nothing but scorn and reproaches. Do not pity me, or you'll drive me to madness."

After this burst of passionate grief had subsided,

her pale and haggard face showed the exhausted state of her system, and that she had need of repose. Mrs. Grayson sent for Isabel, her favourite maid, and requested her to attend to her daughter, whom she then advised to seek some rest, and withdrew to her room to meditate on this unlooked-for calamity, and to brace her mind up to endure and to bow to the will of Him, who striketh where he listeth, and who often chasteneth by affliction those whom he loveth.

She began now to fear a new danger, and that Edward's fiery temper would, on receiving the intelligence, resort to some violent steps; and, incensed as she felt, in spite of all her Christian forbearance, against the author of her calamity, she determined that her son ought not to be made immediately acquainted with Gildon's desertion.

After Louisa was put to bed, she was found to have a burning fever. Her tears, with some intermissions, continued to flow; and she uttered short ejaculations at intervals, which showed the steady current of her thoughts—" Cruel man!" "Impossible! he must have loved me!" " What shall I do?" " What! oh, my mother, my mother!"

Mrs. Grayson sat awhile, till she appeared to be more composed; and exhorting her to address herself to the Throne of Mercy, she approached her bed, and kissing her as usual, wished her a good night. Poor Louisa, overcome by her mother's unabated affection, could make no reply, her sobs stifling the few words of love and gratitude she would have uttered.

The next morning, Louisa was so ill, that Mrs. Grayson proposed to send for a physician ; but she objected, and asked for Matilda. A pressing note was accordingly written for her to come over to see Louisa, who was in bed. Mrs. Fawkner inquired as minutely as she could of the messenger into the nature of the fever, and insisted on her daughter's fortifying herself with a small bag of camphor around her neck, lest it should be infectious, as some cases this autumn had been regarded. Matilda lost no time in setting out, and reached Beechwood before twelve o'clock. The meeting was a very affecting one. Matilda did not hint at her former predictions, and Louisa admitted her own blindness and folly. Sometimes she railed at the perfidy and cruelty of her lover ; but if any remark of the same character was uttered by her friend, she always threw in something by way of extenuation, that showed it was painful to her to hear him censured by another, and that the love which he had planted in her heart was too deep rooted to be torn away at once. Louisa insisted on having the letter brought to her ; and after reading it, and pondering on it awhile, she asked Matilda, if " he did not appear to feel a good deal at the step he was taking." But Matilda's looks implying distrust,

" Fool that I am," said she, " I have taken no

pains to secure his love. I have done all I could to change it to contempt."

Matilda dwelt on every topic which affectionate friendship could suggest, to alleviate her sorrows; and so far as her wounded spirit could receive comfort, it was soothed by the efforts of her sympathizing companion, with whom she felt nothing of the bitterness of self-reproach, which her mother's presence occasioned.

One morning, soon after the receipt of the fatal letter, Louisa seemed in better spirits than usual, and looked very much refreshed by her night's sleep. She had experienced, during her slumbers, one of those visions which cheat us for a time of our misery, more completely, perhaps, than any of the realities of life; and on this occasion it was not followed by the pain of finding it was but a dream, for it had cheered her desolate heart with a ray of hope. She dreamt that she was walking in Matilda's garden, about the middle of winter, when every plant was killed by the frost, or drooping and leafless, and that she had here complained to Matilda, that she feared her lover would never return. On which her friend had advised her to write. That she had accordingly written him a letter, in which she poured out her whole heart, and many passages of which were still fresh in her recollection. That, overleaping time and distance in her dream, she thought the letter had reached him; on which, he had immediately returned, and that they were about to be married in the summer house; on which, the whole scene was immediately changed: every shrub in the little garden was in full bloom, and every flower shedding delightful fragrance. In the suddenness of the transition from wretchedness to bliss, her feelings were so strong that she awoke.

This creation of her fancy, on the subject which occupied all her waking thoughts, so haunted her imagination the next morning, that she communicated it to Matilda, and insisted on writing to Gildon. The good sense of Matilda in vain attempted to dissuade her from a step, which would but delude her with false hopes, and was inconsistent with the respect due to herself. She was inflexible in her purpose; and Matilda consented to furnish her with materials for writing, provided she would consent to her disclosing it to Mrs. Grayson. She agreed that her mother might be informed of it, after the letter was sent off, but on no account before, lest she should be opposed to a scheme, from which her own fond hopes augured so favourably. Accordingly, while her mother, worn down by the watching of the preceding night, was sleeping the next morning, she sat up in the bed, and in the following letter poured forth the feelings of her heart to her faithless lover:

"*Beechwood, Dec.* 1796.

"In spite of appearances, I am sure, oh! Gildon, you were not aware of the effect your cruel letter was to have, at the time that you wrote it. I cannot yet believe that your heart is changed. I, who know what it is to love, and how impossible it is to eradicate the passion, when it is truly felt, but with death, cannot believe that you are already indifferent to your Louisa. I can truly say, from the period of our last interview, I have not seen one happy moment before last night, in a dream, when about to join our fates at the altar, I was raised from the lowest abyss of misery to the summit of human bliss; and it is the hope, inspired by this blest vision, which induces me now to address you. They say dreams sometimes come from heaven, and are the harbingers of truth. God grant that such may be the character of mine! It is in your power, Gildon, to realize the blessed vision; and can it be possible that you will not do it? I have a full persuasion that I was not indifferent to you. You told me so—you swore it—your looks, your actions, all proclaimed it as plainly as your words; and it was not extraordinary, that you should have been gratified at as warm, as tender, as true a devotion, as was ever felt by woman's heart. You could not have feigned the passion you professed—it was impossible—I could not have been deceived. Love, such as mine, is too jealous and sharp-sighted for that. Nothing but sincere attachment on your part, could have inspired love such as mine. If, then, you were sincere, what has happened to lessen your regard? Am I not the same? Have I altered in person, mind or heart? It is true, the fever which the fear of your desertion has occasioned, has reduced me to the brink of the grave; but your presence, your smiles, the assurances of your affection, would act on me like rain on a withered flower. Oh! Gildon, the very hope which my dream has inspired, has already renovated my strength, calmed my troubled spirit, and brought colour to my faded cheek. Is my heart altered? Yes, it is changed; for that which was once a cold and regulated sentiment, is now a passion that consumes me. Not a moment passes in which your image is not present,—sometimes appearing to my entranced imagination with those sweet smiles and fascinating looks, that won my virgin affections; but often of late, oh God! what a difference! with a stern, unrelenting visage, and averted looks! And what have I done, Gildon, that you should turn away from me? Is it to have loved you as woman never loved before? Is it to have forgotten the dictates of prudence, the advice of friends, the commands of the best and most affectionate of parents, to please you, that you thus turn from me? Is it that I have done more—have disregarded all the precepts of education, of morality and religion, that you have forgotten me? Oh! Heavenly Father! and can there be a heart that would first use its unlimited power to lead a defenceless victim astray, and then urge that very error as a cause of desertion? And can, then, that being be my Gildon—once the pride as well as the joy of my heart? It cannot be. The Gildon whom I knew in these shades, conversed with in that porch, and walked with on yonder beach, was as remarkable for his generosity as his tenderness. If the act is ignoble, it cannot be his. Ah! what were my remonstrances! what where my expostulations! What did I not say to you on my knees, when you, hurried on by the impulses of passion, sought to abuse the power you possessed over me? And what were your arguments? what your promises? what your protestations? Have these arguments lost their force. Are these protestations forgotten—these promises annulled? It cannot be. After that fatal evening, your love seemed to have acquired a new tenderness, and more lively ardour. What, then, is it which can have made such a change? But whatever it is, let me recal you to the path of truth, and honour, and justice—of pity and humanity. Oh! Gildon, if your breast can be steeled against my sufferings, have mercy on——must I tell you?—but why not? We are ——————. My mother does not know it, nor have I the courage to tell her. You and Matilda are the only beings on earth to whom I could mention it; all others shall know it only by my death. Speak then a word of comfort, to restore me to peace and happiness—make me what I was when here you found me, innocent and gay. Do all this, as you may in one word, by telling me, and showing me, that you still love your own devoted Louisa. Oh! Gildon, could you see me, propped up with pillows, wan and emaciated, and supported only by the hope which my own heated fancy has created; could you see the wreck and desolation which you have caused in a once happy family—a family lately the object of your esteem and regard; could you see my broken-hearted mother, watching half the night over the feeble frame of her still more wretched daughter,—it is not in your heart, it is not in the breast of the veriest monster in the human form, to turn a deaf ear to my supplications. No, it is impossible. You will not stab to the heart, her, whose only crime has been her too great love of you, and ——————————. You cannot have so forgotten the love that you lately felt; and if you have lost the ardour of a lover, you cannot have laid aside the feelings of a man. Forgive me, Gildon, if I have said any thing harsh or displeasing. I would suffer any cruelty that can be inflicted, rather than willingly give you a moment's pain; for, with all that you have made me suffer, you are, beyond all expression or conception, dear, oh! too dear, to your own

"L———."

When Louisa first began to write, she derived so much strength from the excitement of her feelings, that she was not sensible of fatigue, and the same cause supported her to the end. But the moment she had finished, her strength, put to so severe a trial, deserted her all at once, and she fell back senseless on her pillow. Matilda, who was reading at the fire, heard a noise in the bed, and, looking round, saw the face of her friend exhibiting the paleness of death, with her eyes closed. She first ran to Louisa, and then called for assistance. Bella, who was at hand, came running in, and seeing the situation of her mistress, screamed out that she was dead. This alarmed the rest of the servants, and the bustle awaked Mrs. Grayson, who had been sleeping about an hour. She hastened in, and finding her daughter in a fainting fit, and at the same time seeing the writing implements on the bed, which Matilda had not had time, nor even the thought of removing, she asked if Louisa had been writing. On being answered in the affirmative, she said to Matilda, in a tone of reproof she had never used towards her before, "I wonder, my child, you could be so imprudent as to suffer it."

"I see, madam, how wrong it was," said Matilda; "but I have not time to explain what led to it."

Mrs. Grayson took the letter, and saw it was to the man whose name she had of late held in utter abhorrence. She was too anxious about the situation of her child then to read it, but she folded it up and put it into her pocket. When Louisa came to herself, she looked around with an inquisitive, anxious eye; but Matilda, who understood her, told her to compose herself, and not to talk in her present weak state.

Mrs. Grayson, after a while, retired to her room, read over the letter, and found her dreadful apprehensions but too truly confirmed; but her daughter gave such a touching picture of her sufferings, and seemed so overwhelmed with remorse and shame, and the pangs of blasted affection, that she felt more of maternal pity for her woes, than of blame for her errors.

"Wretched child!" said she, "how light are all my misfortunes, grievous as they certainly are, when compared with thine! I thought, too, that I had reached the last point of human wo, and yet this is the moment of the most unmixed bitterness I ever yet experienced. While we act up to our duty —while we conform to the great law of Him who made us, we never can be completely wretched; we always have some sources of consolation. But whither, oh! whither, can this unhappy girl now turn for comfort? Such is the hopelessness of her situation, she cannot even impart her feelings and sentiments to me—to me, from whom she never had a secret before! Father of Mercies! help thine unworthy servant in this hour of affliction; and if it is not according to thy divine will to afford relief to her sufferings, at least enable her to bear them."

Thus fortified by the aid of religious meditation and prayer, she returned to her daughter's room, and taking her hand, mildly said, "My dear Louisa, I know every thing. I pity you still more than I blame you."

"Oh! mother," said Louisa, sobbing, "can you then forgive me?"

"Compose yourself," said her mother ; " pray to the Giver of all good for forgiveness, and ask him for aid in this hour of trial. There alone is to be found a balm for the wounded spirit. Kneel, my daughter, and pray, or let a mother's prayers be offered up, and do you join your humble supplications to the Throne of Mercy."

She then, inspired by the high-wrought state of her feelings, poured forth a prayer of the most touching eloquence, by which her daughter, though melted, was soothed. Louisa called her mother to her bed-side, and asked permission to kiss her, saying to her, if ever there was an angel upon earth, she was one, and that she was too forgiving, too good.

" My child," said Mrs. Grayson, as the tears, in spite of her habitual composure and self-command, coursed one another down her pallid cheeks, " I feel for you the warmest affection, and I know you reciprocate it."

" I ever have, indeed, my mother ; and oh ! that my heart had never known any other."

Matilda had been a silent spectator of this affecting scene, but her tears flowed in unison with those of the mother and daughter. Mrs. Grayson told Louisa, that her advice was, that the letter she had written should not be sent, or, at all events, not by the post, as it would aggravate their sufferings if it should miscarry, or fall into strange hands. Such a contingency had never occurred to Louisa, and she agreed to wait for a more certain mode of conveyance ; and that in this, as in every thing else, she would be governed by that advice, which she had been so severely punished for disregarding.

Mrs. Grayson, seeing her daughter was more composed, retired to her room ; and, no longer feeling the necessity for the exertion she had used there to conceal her emotions, she lamented the fate of her lost and disgraced child in a burst of unrestrained grief. Nor could she think of any plan, by which the stain upon the hitherto unsullied honour of their house could be kept from the knowledge of the world, or that any thing like happiness or respectability could again attend her in life. She dreaded also the consequences with Edward, whose proud and lofty spirit would never suffer the author of such a disgrace to escape with impunity.

After Louisa's bosom had been disburthened of the painful secret which oppressed it, her mind became greatly relieved ; and she found a consolation in the religious exercises of her mother, that she had before been a stranger to, while there was any thing concealed. Nor was she without some hope, that the aberration of her lover was a temporary one, and that he would yet return to that faith, in which she could not be persuaded he was not once sincere. She resolved, should it be otherwise, to give herself up wholly to religious duties, and the society of her mother, abandoning the world and its vain pleasures, to which she was persuaded her heart would then be for ever dead.

In this consolatory frame of mind, her health gradually returned, so far as to enable her to set out for the Opeccan—though the glow which brightened her emaciated and delicate cheek, gave fearful indications that the seat of her disease was permanently fixed.

Matilda returned to the Elms the day before they were to set out for the Opeccan, promising to visit them as soon as they were settled in their new habitation, and to spend with them the greater part of the winter. Her mother's opposition to Edward having subsided into a silent discontent, seeing that all her schemes had been frustrated, and no offer, that she deemed more eligible, had been made.

The following day, Mr. Trueheart, who had been sent for, as he had requested, came down about ten o'clock, and they set out from that seat, where Mrs. Grayson had passed the happiest and the bitterest hours of her life. It was a cold, but clear and cloudless December day, when the brightness of the blue sky contrasted strongly with the desolate aspect of the country around, and when all the trees were leafless, except a few scattering pines, whose lugubrious foliage was still more in unison with the cheerless season than the bare trunks and branches of the other tenants of the forest. It was a melancholy day to a woman of her amiable and tender feelings. The house, the grounds, the trees, the distant mountain, and the glassy surface of the river, beautiful as they were in themselves, were rendered interesting chiefly by the melancholy recollections with which they were associated. In this spot, she had witnessed years of as uninterrupted connubial bliss as it can fall to the lot of mortals to know. Here, she had reared the most lovely and promising children; here, she had been severed by death from that husband she had idolized, and had bid a lasting adieu to the vulgar pleasures of life; here, the remains of that husband were deposited. All these circumstances made the spot inexpressibly dear to her heart; for the very melancholy they inspired, constituted its mysterious charms. But the sufferings she had of late experienced here, were of so painful a character, that they served to weaken the force of local attraction; and she was glad, on Louisa's account, to remove from a spot, where every thing she saw must revive feelings of shame, regret and remorse.

A part of their small household had been sent on the preceding day, to make suitable preparations for receiving them; and a part set out a little before them that morning in a wagon, driven, as it happened, by the identical wagoner with whom Gildon had had the fracas, and who would have exulted in the verification of his prophecy, that " he would come to no good," could he have known all that was known to his employers.

Louisa was carefully wrapped up in woollen and

fur; yet the shock was evidently too great for her tender lungs, as her frequent coughing indicated. They reached "The Retreat" about two o'clock, having travelled a distance of fourteen miles from Beechwood. They found the house to consist of two small rooms below, with a passage between them, and two rooms in the garret. It stood on a piece of flat ground, to the south of a range of hills, which were covered with wood, and defended the mansion from the north and northwest winds. The Opeccan ran obliquely before the house, and made to the right a small piece of rich bottom, while to the left, a ridge of land covered with pines, was the beginning of an extensive forest, which was the asylum of numerous deer, foxes, and other wild animals, for the sport of the huntsman, and the annoyance of the poultry yard. The land was hilly to the south, on the other side of the Opeccan, and covered with woods and fields intermixed—it being a body of hilly fertile land, which was pretty thickly settled; and the houses and settlements, built mostly of the blue limestone, but occasionally of wood, gave cheerfulness to the scene. The furniture was already disposed in its proper place—the house put in neat order, and the floors well rubbed, where it was not carpetted. One room served them for eating and sitting. The other room below was the chamber of the mother and daughter; and a little closet, built out beside the massy stone chimney, was used as a dressing room. Such convenient out-houses, as were not there before, had been put up by the provident care of Mr. Trueheart, in the simple style that suited the rest of the establishment. A comfortable dinner had been provided, and Mrs. Grayson felt more as if she was visiting a neighbour, than that she had made a change of residence. The place was more improved than she had expected, and she found there every thing that was essential to comfort. She was particularly pleased with a spring house to the left of the dwelling house, which was placed a little below a rock, from which gushed out a bold and perennial spring of the purest water, which, passing over the floor and one side of the spring house, immediately assumed the character of a respectable stream, and was. about half a mile below, sufficient to turn a small mill, whose ever revolving wheel gave animation and picturesque beauty to the quiet scene.

"Here," thought Mrs. Grayson, "shut out from the more busy and ostentatious portion of the world I can prepare my mind for that state to which we all are fast tending. Here, I shall have ample time to pour out my adorations to my Heavenly Father and invoke his mercy and forgiveness for me and mine. Yonder settlements will furnish me with sufficient opportunities, as far as my humble means extend, of being useful to my fellow creatures. Oh! God! even in this day of tribulation and grief, I yet have cause to return thee thanks for thy goodness and mercy."

Mr. Trueheart described to her the limits of the farm, as well as the course of husbandry he had been pursuing; and then added, " But I had like to have forgotten to tell you, that I had written to Edward to-day, and urged him to return to Williamsburg without delay, or perhaps he had better come up to Frederick at once, and continue his studies in my office. There are two very promising young men now with me, who will afford him both society and exercise in argument, and I want him to get a license in the course of the next year. I have a project of giving him a good start, by the collection of the debts due to a house in Alexandria, that is winding up its extensive concerns, and which suits a young man just entering into practice better than it does me."

"I too have written," said Mrs. Grayson, " as has another person, whose letter may have more effect than both of ours."

" Ay, I think the wind begins to set fair in that quarter. The old lady inquired the other day how many students I had—whether I expected any more —the prospects for a young lawyer at present; by which I saw as plainly as if she had told me, and something plainer too, that her views and temper are changed. A bright evening yet awaits you, my dear madam, after all your stormy trials."

" My trust is in heaven, Mr. Trueheart. If my children could be happy and respected, 'tis all I now seek," said she; but the recollection of her unhappy daughter checked her speech, and she was not able to stifle a deep, long-drawn sigh. The worthy man saw the rising emotion, and hastened his departure, amidst the grateful benedictions of those he had befriended.

CHAPTER XI.

A little before those scenes of wo which we have detailed had occurred at Beechwood, Edward had gone to Easton to superintend the sale of that estate. The distress among the slaves at parting from one another, and of being separated from scenes endeared to them by early pleasures, and by habit, were pretty much as have been described in Frederick, except that the gentleman who had purchased the Easton estate, bought also the greater part of the slaves. And Mr. Cutchins, the manager, as he was not able to purchase the little corner he wanted, it being thought by good judges to be the most valuable part of the tract, and before the present year, had produced excellent crops, had, as one of the creditors of the estate, bid very freely for the slaves and stock, and some of the best of the furniture. Nor did the field negroes show as much regret on being sold, as those of Beechwood, inasmuch as they, for a long time, had less intercourse with the family, and were under the management of a steward, who had treated them with less kindness and indulgence than the others had received from Mrs. Grayson.

Having executed the no very agreeable office of selling the land of his forefathers, the scenes of his infant sports and joys, for the purpose of paying the debt of another, he returned, as soon as it was over, to Williamsburg; and sending off old Lemon to the post office, he soon returned with a letter from Matilda.

In this letter, she had stated, as she felt herself bound to do, her fears of Gildon's constancy, which the postponement of his return had occasioned; and though she did not venture to acquaint Edward with the extent of his sister's imprudence, she informed him of her lover's visit, and their frequent interviews at Stanley. The unaccountable silence of Gildon, had given Edward increasing uneasiness; and when he learnt that he had postponed his visit to Virginia till the spring, he was persuaded that it could have proceeded only from a change in his feelings towards Louisa. He intended, therefore, to write to her, to rouse her pride, and to remonstrate with her against longer feeling an attachment for one so undeserving of her. He intended also to write to Gildon, demanding an explicit declaration of his views. In the picture which Matilda gave him of his sister's anxiety, he felt nothing but pity for her, and indignation at the unworthy cause; and, for a time, forgot his own sorrows and difficulties. He went to bed, greatly fatigued with his ride; and the uneasiness which the intelligence he had received, had excited, kept him awake the best part of the night.

The next morning, he did not rise till after he was summoned to breakfast. He went to the ordinary, and soon perceiving that he was viewed with eyes of curiosity by several of the students, he was induced to ask one, who was more in his confidence than the rest, what was the cause of it. On which, he learnt that Mawly had declared at table, that he had just received a letter from Gildon, in which he had said the match with Miss Grayson was entirely broken off, and that he had spoken of her in terms of levity, which had incensed some of the students, though Mawly had undertaken to defend him. Edward immediately said, "I will know the truth of this, and either Mawly or Gildon shall answer the consequences."

Mawly, who, though of a vindictive character, and well enough disposed to make mischief, was not over willing to support it by his courage, had no hesitation in showing Gildon's letter, in which he spoke of his late engagement with Louisa—of the necessity he found himself under to break it off, and of his address in doing so, with great levity and want of feeling. He even extolled the beauty and personal attractions of Louisa, as if he was speaking of a cast-off mistress, rather than of a delicate female, who had honoured him with her affection.

"It is enough, sir," said Edward, proudly. "I

see that your friend has been capable of writing what may bear you out in your statements, though I give you no credit for propagating it. I wish you a good morning."

His course was now taken. He paid off his bills that evening—took the stage the next morning for Richmond, where he stopped only long enough to get as much money from his agent as would defray his expenses, and proceeded on, without loss of time, as far as Philadelphia. When he arrived in that city, he wished to pass a day or two with some students of medicine from Virginia, for the purpose of procuring intelligence of the movements of Gildon, and of recruiting somewhat from the fatigues of his journey. The session of congress, too, had just commenced, and he was desirous of being present at a debate.

He learnt, (through his Virginia friends) of some students from New-York, that Gildon had renewed his addresses to Miss De Peyster, and was expected to marry her, by some; though others thought he was merely playing the agreeable with her, as, it was said, he had been doing with a young lady of family in Virginia. On hearing this intelligence, Grayson's indignation boiled within him. He resolved that he would make an example of such a wretch, who had profited by the hospitality that had been extended to him, to blast the happiness of his entertainers. He began to review his whole conduct, and while some parts of it seemed to favour a system of duplicity and perfidy, he was obliged to admit, that its general character seemed to indicate i could have proceeded only from unfeigned attachment to his sister, and real friendship for her family. He was lost in perplexity to reconcile these seeming incongruities; but the fact is, he did not make sufficient allowances for the variable character of Gildon, who, very different at different times, was, according to the prevailing humour, either the impassioned lover, willing to sacrifice "all for love;" or the cold-hearted, calculating man of the world—making the higher duties of honour and justice bend to the dictates of an ignoble ambition.

Though in a frame of mind, which ill prepared him for viewing what was most worth seeing in Philadelphia, yet he suffered himself to be conducted about the city by his young friends; and concealing his thoughts and purposes from all but one friend, Charles Campbell, of Jefferson county, he was able to bear a part in the frolic and youthful jollity which prevails among the southern students at that medical institution, when a countryman comes among them.

He visited the alms house, jail, hospital, and state house. None of these afforded him so much pleasure as the jail, or penitentiary house, then making the noble experiment (first suggested by speculative philanthropy) of endeavouring to reform the criminal, instead of taking away his life, and of graduating punishments to crimes. The neatness and regularity with which every thing was managed; the mildness with which counsel was given, and punishment was enforced, seemed more in the character of parents superintending their children, than officers of justice executing the sentence of the law. He was struck with the silence of the prisoners, even at their meals, for he saw them at dinner ; and with their grave and serious deportment, indicating, in general, sorrow and dejection, rather than sullenness or despair. He asked the keeper, a sensible, obliging man, animated with the zeal of the society of Friends, of which he was a member, how they proceeded, when they met with persons who would neither work nor submit to these regulations. He said, they were condemned to close confinement in small dark cells, where the privation of light, and their unpalatable diet, (they being then restricted to bread and water,) and of all communion with their fellow prisoners, being shut out from every cheering sound, particularly of that of the human voice, soon humbled them, and made them submit to the commands of their superintendents. Grayson asked him if he did not sometimes meet with refractory tempers, who would not yield even to this severe discipline. He said never, except, in one instance, they had a negro who would not work ; and when of course condemned to solitary confinement, he soon fell asleep, and waking when they brought him his allowance of bread and water, would take them, and go to sleep again ; and he seemed to prefer thus dozing away an inert existence, to a state of comparative enjoyment, incumbered with the necessity of labour.

Grayson then asked if there was any striking difference in the number of prisoners furnished by the different nations. The superintendent said there was more than a just proportion of Irish, and an unusually small proportion of Scotch, which he imputed to the benignant influence of their public schools. As to the portion furnished by the different states, he said there was no uniformity. Grayson went away, filled with admiration for this triumph of philosophy and benevolence over vindictive feelings, and resolved that he would exert himself, if circumstances should ever put it in his power, to introduce the same wise and benevolent system into his own state.

In Congress Hall, he was highly gratified to behold the leading statesmen of his country; though in that early period of the session, the business was but of little moment. He applied to the representative from his district, by whom he was well known, to give him an introduction to the illustrious Washington, the president of the United States, whose approaching retirement from publie affairs had softened the virulence of his opponents, and was viewed with alarm and anxiety by the rest of the nation. He then had regular levees, or mornings for receiving company, at which the heads of departments and foreign ministers attended, together with such citizens as were known, or were introduced by some officer of the government. He lived, at that time, in the upper part of Market-street. When Edward and his friend entered, they found a great many already assembled in a large oval room, in which the company were standing around; while the President, in a suit of black velvet, with his hair powdered white, and tied behind with a silk bag, was in the middle of the circle, conversing easily and readily with those about him. He found something to say to every one, and habit had enabled him to be always provided with easy pertinent questions, without labour or premeditation. As soon as Edward was presented, "You are a son of the late Col. Grayson, I presume—I see it by the likeness. I hope Mrs. Grayson enjoys her health," said he, with more of feeling than his manner commonly indicated. Then turning to the member, Mr. S——, he observed, "The late Col. Grayson commanded a company at the battle of Princeton, and was very near poor Mercer when he fell." This was all that fell to Edward's share, as he had to give place to two or three elderly gentlemen who were then present.

It was not the fashion to stay long, as there was a constant succession of persons going and coming, during the whole time Edward was there, so that the room was constantly full, and yet seemed never, for five minutes together, to consist of the same individuals. He thought he could never be tired of looking at this, the most distinguished man of his age and nation. He watched every turn and movement he made, caught every word that fell from his lips, and thought he had never seen so much grace and dignity united. He was so delighted, and so engrossed, that he was surprised, when his friend, jogging him by the elbow, told him it was time to withdraw. After he retired, he went to the boarding house where his friend Campbell lived, and there some of the students insisted on carrying him to the museum and the library, and to the large marble house, then building in Eighth-street, and deemed, by its magnitude and costliness, more an architectural curiosity than any other edifice in the city.

He passed a social evening with six or eight Virginians, who went to sup at the Indian Queen, in South Second-street; but while he exhibited the outward signs of youthful gayety, his thoughts were running on the melancholy reverses of his family.

He went to bed about eleven, and a little before day, was roused by a waiter holding a candle, with " Sir, the stage is ready," and the moment afterwards, heard the blast of the horn that sounds so ungrateful unto the drowsy traveller on a winter's morning. But Edward had been an alert fox-hunter, and though the air was something sharper than he had been accustomed to in Williamsburg, he was up and dressed in a few minutes, and in a few more had paid off his bill, and was seated in the stage beside a fat land speculator, who, having supplied the

Philadelphians with rich western lands, was now going to accommodate those who were in New-York.

When day at length dawned, he found there were five persons in the stage besides the driver—a young lady, and a middle aged man beside him, who proved to be a great mechanical genius from Connecticut, who had come on to get a patent for a brick making machine ; he was also a zealous democrat, and very gallant to the lady, whose escort he offered to be. The others were a speculator in land from Richmond, and a student of Princeton College, from Maryland, who had been nodding all the morning, but who made ample amends for his past silence as soon as his eyes were fairly opened.

Edward maintained a cautious reserve, but the Marylander flew from subject to subject, until he unconsciously struck upon a string which awakened all our traveller's attention, though he was probably the only person in the stage who paid any regard to it. When the speculator wondered that he had come so far to attend college, and why he had not stopped in Virginia, the youth began to rail out very freely against William and Mary. He said the professors were men of no talents, their books were obsolete, their apparatus not fitted to illustrate modern discoveries, and that the town was filled with old maids, or young girls, sent there to catch rich students ; that twelve out of sixteen in one boarding house were either married, or about to be so, at the last session; that a gentleman from New-York had sent his son there to divert him from an imprudent connexion, and that he had formed one a great deal worse; but that his father had lately succeeded in getting him back, and was going to marry him to his first love, whose father, not long since a bankrupt, had, by a lucky turn of fortune, got rich.

While this youth was thus giving vent to whatever came uppermost, Edward was on thorns; he was unwilling to enter into an altercation with one for whom he felt no respect, as he did not wish to discover himself; and yet was afraid that the freedom with which the young man spoke of all persons and things, and the heedless facility with which he blended truth and falsehood, would compel him to give a check to his censorious levity. But as none of the company made any comments on this episode, its loquacious author soon passed on to some other subject.

They dined at Trenton, and stayed at Princeton that night. The next morning they found some change in the passengers. The lady had complained of fatigue, and said she should remain in Princeton till the next stage; the student, of course, remained at his college. There was, however, an accession of two more students, going to pass some days in New-York. They entertained the company with college anecdotes—talked politics with the speculator—abused the British treaty—complimented Mr.

Jefferson—execrated the Electors in Virginia, by whom he had lost his election—and the next evening they reached Paulus Hook, opposite to New-York, just after candle-light. The twinkling of the numerous lights in the city, made a very gay and striking appearance, and gave, perhaps, a livelier impression of the active population which inhabits it, than a view by day, because it is more picturesque. Grayson reached the Tontine Coffee-House, in Wall-street, about nine o'clock. With some difficulty he made one of the waiters attend to his wants; and having taken a cup of tea, he retired early to rest to refresh himself after a fatiguing and uncomfortable journey of nine days.

The speculator finding, from some expressions which Edward had dropped, that he was from Virginia, was at first disposed to show him attention, and to aid him with the advice which it was evident he wanted; but as he had several times reinforced the Marylander, when too hard pressed by his adversary, in reprobation of the British treaty, he conceived such a prejudice against him, such was the force of political intolerance at that time, that he was very cold in his civilities, and was put down at a boarding house in Wall-street, as soon as they arrived, and Edward never saw him afterwards.

He had learnt in Philadelphia that his false friend was then in the city of New-York, and he determined to try what temperate measures would do, before he proceeded to harsh ones. His first object was, to ascertain where Gildon could be found. His father resided in Albany, and Edward did not know at what hotel or boarding house the son might be then staying. At length, remembering to have heard Gildon speak of a Mr. James Cox, at whose house he was intimate, he called for a directory, and found there were four persons of that name. He thought he would inquire at the house of the one most likely to be Gildon's friend, and seeing one of them had no designated occupation, Edward set him down for a gentleman, and accordingly went to his house, far up Greenwich-street, then containing but a few scattering houses. To save time, and prevent the mistakes which the irregularity of the city is so apt to cause in a stranger, so little conversant with crowded streets as himself, he called for a hackney coach, and having directed the coachman where to drive, he was immediately whirled along from the Tontine, by many windings and turnings, to the place required. Edward had expected to see an elegant mansion, and had supposed the gentleman had wished to avoid the dust and bustle of the more crowded part of the city. He was conducted, however, to a small wooden house, with a piazza from one end to the other; and behind it was a garden, containing two or three small summer houses, in a very dismantled condition. The whole had the air of a house of entertainment of some sort, though there was no sign before the door. Two or three men of ordinary appearance, were in the front room, before a coal fire, playing backgammon. Addressing himself to a dirty-looking servant girl, who came out, he asked if Mr. Cox was at home? "No, he's been gone these two days."

"When will he return?"

"That's more than I can say; he said he might be back last night."

"Does a gentleman by the name of Gildon visit here?"

"Ay, that's what he does, and other gentlemen too."

"Well, give this card to Mr. Cox when he returns," said Edward, leaving his name and address, and drove off.—He bade the coachman, by way of finding himself employment, drive out further in the same direction, and bring him back by a different route, that he might see something more of the city, whose singularly happy position, between two such noble pieces of water, he admired exceedingly. The coachman, with alacrity, obeyed his commands, and whisked him at a pretty brisk rate towards the Bowery, then across to the East river, and thence, by several meanders, into Pearl-street, to his hotel. Edward asked his charge, and he said, whatever the gentleman chose—but he supposed three dollars in all would not be too much. Edward, who had never contested a bill in his life, felt unwilling to do so in a strange place, especially now that he knew himself poor; he paid it in silence, but thought if his expenses should prove of a piece with this, he would soon be pennyless, in a place in which he knew but one individual, from whom nothing could have induced him to accept a favour.

He went into the large room of the coffee-house, and saw a throng of persons, talking news and politics, reading newspapers, looking over lists of arrivals or importations—engrossing pursuits to those engaged in them, but foreign and unimportant to Edward. He felt utterly friendless and forlorn, and could scarcely have thought it possible that he could have been any where in the United States, and seen so many persons in earnest conversation on subjects in which he could take so little interest. He walked about some time, and, recollecting he was in a coffee-house, with great simplicity called for a cup of coffee. The bar-keeper, respecting Edward's appearance, and seeing that he was a gentleman, immediately directed one of the waiters to bring the gentleman a cup of coffee.

"Where will you have it, sir?"

"In my room, No. 36, if you please."

The obsequious waiter stared, looked at Edward with an inquisitive glance, and disappeared. He then seated himself in a chair in a corner, where he sat observing the faces of those who came to the bar, and by and by saw a thick, well-set man, with a great quantity of hair, plaited and fastened behind with a large comb, booted and spurred, and having a heavy whip in his hand, go to the bar, and looking at a card, ask if Mr. Grayson of Virginia was within—Edward immediately stepped forward, and being told the stranger's name was Cox, asked him into his room. When there, he began to apologize to Mr. Cox for the trouble he had given him.

"Oh, don't say a word of that, my dear fellow; it's all the same to me—here as there; but we should have been more snug at my quarters, in Greenwich—what say you? Let's adjourn."

Edward looked at him, and suspecting some mistake, began to explain. The other, who had been rumaging an inside pocket while he was speaking, now drew out a pack of cards, and without noticing Edward's attempt at explanation, said, "You see, Mr. Grayson, I come provided—but, pray, what's your game?" Edward's blood mounted into his cheek, and with a look of anger and contempt, replied, "Why, sir, what do you take me to be?"

The other stared in his turn. "What do I take you for? why a thorough-bred Virginian—Is this your card?"

"Yes."

"Well, and what could I think you left it for, but to have a little sport? and I thought if you wanted to meet me on your own ground, I'd show you I wasn't afraid—but then you see I fight with my own weapons," taking up the cards—"or turn and turn about, that's fair."

"Sir, I wanted to inquire for a Mr. Gildon, of this state—I knew him to be well acquainted with a person of your name, and supposing you were the person, I called at your house to make the inquiry."

"I know nothing about your Gelding," said the other, with that sort of forced laugh with which a man backs a bad pun—" he's not been found by me— and if you don't like to try your hand—or these books don't suit you, there's no harm done. But I can tell you, Mister, you broke up a merry set that was just seated, when they brought me this bit of pasteboard; and I'd advise you hereafter to be sure of your card before you play it."

"I'm sorry, on more accounts than one," said Grayson, " that I have fallen into this mistake ; but I want no advice from you, and will take none—and either you or I must leave the room immediately."

"Sir, I'm a gentleman," said the gamester, "and will take an insult from no man, damme; but I scorn to stay in any gentleman's room, when I'm not welcome;" and putting the cards in his pocket, walked out with a swagger, muttering something about "Virginia dons—the better for a little currying."

Edward was greatly mortified and disappointed; though at another time he might have been diverted at the incident.

After some little delay, he was served with the coffee he had ordered, which he found, on inquiry, they were not in the habit of furnishing, except at breakfast or supper. While he was drinking it, a waiter came in and said, " a gentleman wishes to speak with you, sir."

"Ask him in." On looking towards the door,

his eyes were greeted with the sight of a young merchant from Frederick, with whom he indeed had often dealt, and greatly esteemed, but had no particular intimacy. He never had before experienced so much pleasure from meeting a friend. Mr. Young, though not equally delighted, was, in truth, very much pleased to see him. He told Edward, that he had come on to New-York in September, to purchase goods, but had been seized with the yellow fever, from which he had a narrow escape. That he had been completing his purchases since his recovery, and on looking over the list of persons in the house, in the book kept for that purpose, at the bar, and seeing Mr. Grayson's name, he thought he would satisfy himself whether he was the person, and was delighted that he had found him out.

The merchant then paused, and expected that Edward would be equally communicative.—The latter was indeed so pleased at meeting with one whom he knew, from his own county, that he, regarding Mr. Young as a particular friend, briefly related to him the object of his errand, softening the disagreeable parts of the affair as much as he could, consistently with the truth, and acquainted him with his present difficulty of finding Gildon in such a crowded place. Young smiled, and said that difficulty might be easily overcome by one acquainted with the city; and having obtained the very slender clue that Edward was able to give, he took a memorandum, and said he had no doubt he would, in the course of the next day, ascertain whether Gildon was now in the city.

They continued together, in Edward's room, talking about Virginia and Frederick, with a patriotic interest which is known only to persons abroad, until past midnight; and when Young got up to retire, Edward would have tried to detain him yet longer, if he had not recollected that his companion was a man of business, and could not take from the next day what he borrowed of the preceding night. The following day, Young, who knew what inquiries to make, and of whom to make them, soon ascertained that the Mr. Cox whom Gildon probably visited, was a wine-merchant in Pearl-street, but who had lately built a house in Broadway, as he and Mr. Gildon were associated in some foreign adventures. He had, accordingly, visited that Mr. Cox, and learnt from him that Gildon was then in the city, but expected to leave it in two or three days, and that he lodged at Mrs. ———'s, near the Battery.

Grayson, as soon as he received this intelligence from his friend, set out for Gildon's lodgings, and found he was out. He learned, on inquiry, that he would probably be in at dinner at 3 o'clock. He called at that hour, and finding Gildon was within, in order to avoid the embarrassment of a meeting in the presence of others, he gave the servant a slip of paper, on which was written with a pencil, that E. G. wished to have an interview with J. G. at any place the latter would appoint. The servant was gone longer than seemed necessary, and returned with an answer on the same paper, that J. Gildon would give the requested meeting at 5 o'clock, at the old Coffee House, and that Mr. Grayson might inquire for him at the bar. Edward returned to his lodgings, and the conflicting passions with which he was agitated prevented him from eating.

The hour at length arrived, and curbing his rising indignation, Edward went to the place appointed, and inquiring at the bar for Mr. Gildon, the bar-keeper said he was not in the house, but that he had sent a letter to be delivered to a gentleman who was expected to call for him, and presuming him to be the person, it was delivered to him. It ran in these words:

"My dear friend—for, in spite of appearances, such I feel myself to be, and so I would still be considered by you—I have not attended you according to appointment, because I thought it more prudent, until we understood each other, that our intercourse should be only in this way. I am aware that you may, judging from appearances, be disposed to believe that I have been a systematic deceiver; but believe me, Edward, the attachment I professed, I sincerely felt, and nothing but the most cruel necessity could have induced me to adopt the course I have pursued. I resisted the wishes of my father as long as there was a chance of resistance being of any avail, and finding him inexorable, and on the point of abandoning me, I thought that a true regard for your —— should induce me to make a sacrifice of my own inclinations, and that it was better to incur the blame of bad faith, than to deserve her reproaches as well as my own, for entailing on her the certain miseries of poverty, and the too probable chance of a bitter repentance. You are, no doubt, apprized that I have now put it out of my power to change the course, which justice and real regard dictated, no less than prudence; and I trust your good sense will see, that while any altercation between us cannot undo what is done, it may give to the affair a publicity which all parties ought to avoid. Nothing shall be said on my part that is calculated in the smallest degree to lessen the standing of ——— in the eyes of the world; and if she sustains any other injury than what may arise from a disappointment, which I trust is but temporary, it will assuredly not be owing to me. Believe me, Edward, I deserve your pity rather than blame. I have never ceased to cherish sentiments of exalted respect for every member of the amiable family of Beechwood, and I hope the time may yet come when I may show with what profound sentiments of gratitude and respect their hospitality and kindness is remembered by their, and your, most obliged and devoted servant, JAMES GILDON."

The fiery temper of Edward could no longer contain itself, on reading this piece of insolent mockery, as it appeared to him; though, in truth, the greater part of Gildon's letter was written in perfect sincerity. He stamped, bit his lips, and made ejaculations which were heard by some of the by-standers, whose inquisitive looks suggested to him the necessity of retiring. He went to his room, and with hurried steps paced it backward and forward for more than an hour, before he acquired self-possession sufficient to determine on the course he should pursue. He knew not to what Gildon alluded, when he said he had put it out of his power to change his course; but his resentment and contempt were so great, that at that time he would not have consented that his sister should be allied to so utter a wretch.

Ere the fever of his wrath had subsided, Young knocked at his door, and his voice being recognized, he was admitted, and the letter shown to him, after which Edward consulted with him on the course he should pursue.

CHAPTER XII.

While the friends are engaged in this deliberation, let us take a brief review of what had befallen the inconstant Gildon after he left Stanley. He took the stage at Stafford court house, and proceeded on to his father's in New-York. When he left Louisa, he was as much attached to her as he was capable of being, though he had lost some portion of the high respect he had previously entertained for her; such is the suicidal tendency of illicit love in its unceasing efforts to effect that which works its own destruction. But her beauty, her guileless, artless manners, and her devoted affection, produced their legitimate effect of filling his heart with the most ardent attachment; and ere he had reached New-York, he had several times very nearly resolved to return, and, yielding himself to the intoxicating draughts of love, to forego every thing else which he had hitherto deemed desirable.

He, however, continued to travel on, and when he reached the city of New-York, he there found his father. At first he was received very coolly, as the old gentleman soon perceived that he had come on, not because he was cured of his ill-fated attachment, but because he hoped to obtain his sanction to gratify it; and there was, in consequence, but little intercourse between them. Mr. De Peyster was settled in New-York, and success continued to attend him in all his undertakings. His daughter, who was a showy, dashing girl, was now thought a capital match for any one, and it afforded old Gildon a perpetual source of chagrin, that his son had thrown away so valuable a prize. Gildon learnt of her eclat as a belle and a fortune, at first with indifference. His heart was so filled with the image of the little rural beauty he had left behind him, that he had even lost his former desire of making himself agreeable; nor did he ever put himself in Miss Emily's way. Had he done so, the young lady would probably have repelled his advances with haughtiness, in revenge for former slights; but she, who received homage from all quarters, was piqued at Gildon's indifference, and sought an opportunity of meeting him, and of adding him to the train of her lovers.

Having once conceived the plan, there was no want of schemes for putting it in execution. She first endeavoured to meet Gildon at public places; but in that she failed, as he had not yet begun to frequent them. She tried to catch his eye at church, having gone to the one he usually attended, for that purpose. She tried also to meet him in the street, or on the promenade of the Battery, which is so fine as to tempt the citizens of every description at all seasons, when the weather is fine; but all these schemes proved abortive. He was observed, however, to have become more lively than on his first arrival, and she ascertained that he had been making inquiries of late about her.

Thus foiled in all her previous attempts, she adopted a more decisive course. Gildon was very intimate with a young man by the name of Cox, son of his father's friend, who was gay, lively and dissipated, and they passed much of their time together. This young man had a sister, who was a homely girl, and had much of the humility that conscious plainness of person often inspires. Miss De Peyster had frequently met Miss Cox, especially since her father had launched once more into the fashionable world, but had never taken any more notice of her than of any other of the common place beings who were continually passing and repassing before her. She, however, availed herself of the first occasion, at a small cotillion party, near Miss Cox's residence, to cultivate her acquaintance; and as this young lady felt very grateful for the attentions received from an established belle, and was ambitious of getting a certain standing in the fashionable world, there being a very nicely graduated scale of rank in a large city, Miss Emily soon succeeded to the utmost extent of her wishes in obtaining the good graces of the other. She was from that time constantly dwelling on the praises of Emily De Peyster, on her " elegance, and grace, and wit; and then, too, with so much flattery and attention, to be so free from airs." These praises she took occasion to utter in the presence of Gildon, for whom she felt a great deal of good will, though she had never aspired to make a conquest of him. At first, these commendations were not heeded by Gildon, as they were little more than what had been dinned in his ears from several quarters; but one morning, the young lady said to him, "Cousin James," as she always called him, "is Miss Grayson as handsome as Emily De Peyster?"

"Yes, a great deal handsomer. You might as well ask if a poppy is as handsome as a rose."

"Well, now, I much question it, and I have some reason for doing so; for there was a young gentleman here from South Carolina this summer, who said that Emily had as good features, and was so superior in manners and grace, that she was, beyond comparison, the finest woman."

"Pshaw!" said he, "some flattering coxcomb! Don't I know them both?"

"Yes, but you have no idea how Emily has improved."

"In complexion, I suppose."

"No, I'm sure she don't use rouge, for the other day she was here, the morning we thought there was snow enough to sleigh, and some person coming up stairs, I observed, ' Ay, there's cousin James coming, now the snow is all gone;' and she turned as pale as ashes. I'm convinced she feels her old attachment, and that she'll never get over it. She's always talking of you, and sometimes I think it is on your account, that she seems of late to have taken such a fancy to me. But I don't care, she's a sweet girl, and I'm delighted with her."

"She's the veriest coquette in the city of New-York, and that's a bold word, as they say in Virginia."

"There, too, I'm convinced you do her injustice. Has she not turned off every young man who has addressed her? and I impute that also to her attachment to you. Before your arrival, it was generally thought she was to have married young Rutledge, from South Carolina, but she has finally discarded him."

These remarks sunk deeper into Gildon's mind than he seemed to admit, or indeed was aware of at the time; and he soon began to think it possible that she, who was a coquette to others, might be sincerely attached to him, or that she had in fact altered for the better in disposition, as all admitted she had done in person and manners. He was gradually led by Schuyler Cox into parties of gayety, until the pain of separation from the lovely Louisa grew fainter and fainter, and he was getting to be a mere man of pleasure, when this conversation with Miss Cox took place. His father (unwilling to attempt too violent a reform) was impatient to get him established in business; and after looking about for some time with his usual wariness and caution, concluded he could not do better than by forming the partnership that has been mentioned.

While he was calling in the money he had lent out, and introducing the new house to his distant correspondents, James, his son, had little else to do than to lounge about, and partake of the frivolous or sensual pleasures that were within his reach, and to which he was further invited by the precept and example of young Cox. In this dangerous state of idleness, when the soft scenes on the Shenandoah, or the more impassioned and culpable ones on the Potomac, were fast fading from his recollection, or remembered only as pleasing dreams, he was asked by Eleanor Cox to attend her to the theatre, to see Mrs. Merry, who had recently arrived from England. As her brother was ill with an influenza, he could not refuse; and indeed the little anecdotes which his cousin told of Emily, had now began to interest him, and he really wished to see her, but was ashamed to propose it. When he waited on Miss Cox in the evening, on opening the door of the parlour, he found there a lady alone, and who, to his not unpleasing surprise, proved to be Miss De Peyster herself. She was really agitated, and affected to be more so. He was somewhat confused, but emboldened by her apparent embarrassment, and the favourable footing he believed he yet retained in her heart, he accosted her with respect, but with much of his wonted easy assurance.

"He was happy," he said, "that he, at last, had an opportunity of congratulating her on her return to the city, where she had so many friends, and which agreed so well with her health."

She made a short and guarded reply, reserving herself, like a skilful boxer, who never aims a blow till he sees where to strike ; and added, " I did not know that Eleanor expected company this evening I came to take her with me to see the Honey Moon."

" She has consented to put herself under my protection," said Gildon ; " and if you would honour me with your company, we will have the satisfaction of being envied by half the audience, even if we should not be gratified with the performance."

Looking in his face, very significantly, " I believe you have lost your relish for plays," she remarked, " by your residence in Virginia, though, perhaps, this one may be to your taste."

" I find my old tastes returning very fast," said he, " since I have breathed my native air. You know I used to be devoted to the drama, and first love, they say, will return."

He was not aware of the obvious application that might be made of these words when he used them. The moment afterwards, perceiving their full import, he felt a slight confusion and hesitation, but the current of ideas once put in motion, could not be stopped.

" I have no faith in that," said Miss De Peyster.

"I don't believe it, either, of your sex," said he.

"If true at all," said she, "it is true only of them. But here comes Eleanor; why, what have you been about, you naughty girl; you take as long to put on a tippet as I do to dress. Here's Mr. Gildon, who insists that he is as fond of plays as ever, though, I believe, I have not seen him at two since he returned from that earthly paradise."

"You mistake me a little, Miss De Peyster. I say, I think I shall be as fond as I ever was."

"I'll believe that when I see it."

This partiality for the drama, by one of those tacit agreements, that diplomatists in love and gallantry so well understand, was thus made the type of his former attachment, and enabled them to carry on a conversation, in which they could express their sentiments more freely, and were quite as well understood as if they talked openly and directly. It had the advantage of being taken literally by Miss Cox and her Mama, the daughter of a rich ship chandler, of Dutch extraction.

The play was acted here for the first time, and was very well received, as it deserved to be. But there were few of the audience who were as much gratified as Mrs. Cox's party. She and her daughter had the satisfaction of thinking that two of the most fashionable young persons in the city were in their box. Emily De Peyster exulted at the success of her snare, and Gildon found himself pleased and flattered that he had so easily reinstated himself in her good graces. He found her greatly improved in appearance; she was dressed to the greatest advantage, and the more as there was an air of simplicity, and of graceful negligence, which concealed the labour that had been actually bestowed in her decoration.

The young lady, too, had become more an adept in disguising the thousand little artifices by which coquettes allure, interest, and please. During her residence in the country, she had narrowly watched, and successfully imitated, those reserved and retiring manners which she found to constitute much of the charm of rural beauties, and which she naturally supposed had been so instrumental in gaining the affection of Gildon. Amidst all her gayety of heart, which she could not entirely rein in, she was occasionally serious and even pensive; and as her manner was not uniform, Gildon, deceived by his vanity and self-love, thought that her *penseroso* mood was natural, and the *allegro* assumed. He asked permission to wait on her the next day, to which request, with a look of well-feigned surprise, she assented. Their sitting in the same box, and their frequent conversations, evidently animated and mutually agreeable, were not unnoticed by their acquaintances, and gave rise to many humorous sallies and grave remarks, most of which, as is usual on such occasions, would have given no great pleasure to the objects of them. Between the acts, however, their box was thronged with the young men of the city, who pressed round the then reigning belle, as uniting more than any other the strong recommendations of beauty, fortune, and wit, or who, like other light substances, most felt the electric attraction of fashion. The little divinity they had created, smiled propitiously on them all, and though she said little that was witty, or intended to be so, but was more reserved than usual; yet, as she was known to be variable in her humour and character, according to the caprice of the moment, she gave no offence. They contented themselves with observing, that she was playing the *penseroso* this evening.

The next morning Gildon called on Miss De Peyster, and they passed an hour or two very agreeably, in which their former *penchants* were still spoken of under the disguise of a taste for the drama. But the morning after he called again, when even this slight veil was laid aside, and in the course of a week they both found themselves desperately enamoured, and vowed eternal love and constancy. The young lady had not intended to go thus far; she wished, indeed, to add Gildon to her train—she even had as much partiality for him as a professed coquette is likely to have; but she was unwilling to surrender her liberty so soon or so easily; she had not meant to forego the habitual triumphs of conquest, which she found so sweet, until her captive territories should be wrested from her by younger competitors, or, at any rate, until she found herself less competent to wield the sceptre. But she was caught in her own snares. The meshes which she had so artfully woven for the prey she had set her heart on catching, had entangled her own feet; or, to quit the metaphor, she began to feel the passion she had at first merely feigned; and Gildon, who had been led on step by step by his own vanity, his facility of temper, and natural inconstancy, became really attached to her; and since every consideration of prudence recommended her as an excellent match, he was earnest and ardent in soliciting her hand. Her prospects of fortune were considerable; his mercenary father would be overjoyed at the union, and he himself would have the glory of conquering where so many had failed.

Yet all this was not without many misgivings, and compunctious visitings of his conscience, when he thought of the sweet, the gentle, the lovely Louisa, whose beauty, as well as artlessness, he could not disguise from himself, were of far greater worth than the more glaring attractions of his countrywoman; and when he received a letter from Louisa, its simple and pathetic complaints, and expressions of affection and contrition, brought back his original feelings almost in their original force; but these good impressions were but short lived. The fascinations of Miss De Peyster were constantly operative, and his intercourse with Cox and his gay companions, aided by the force of ridicule, (so powerful with weak minds, to cure him of his romantic fancy, as they called his attachment to Louisa. To put an end to this conflict of feelings and motives, he pressed for an early day, and the lady consented to marry him early in December, that is to say, about a week after Edward arrived; and it was after the preliminaries were settled, that he wrote the cruel letter to Louisa that has already been laid before the reader, in which, to do him justice, there was more sincerity than he gained credit for.

He had received a timely intimation from his friend Mawly, that Edward had left Williamsburg for New-York, to call him to account, as was supposed, and he was advised to put himself on his guard. He, therefore, kept a steady look out, and learnt, the day before he received Edward's visit, that he was in New-York. He would, indeed, have kept himself out of the reach of Edward's resentment, from shame rather than fear, if he had not been restrained by the same feeling of shame and dread of ridicule. He resolved, however, to elude his adversary for the present, and to soften him, if possible, by fair words, in the critical situation in which he stood.

After taking a review of Gildon's conduct, Young agreed it was that of an ungrateful and perfidious villain, who, indeed, merited the severest chastisement, but whom, he was clearly of opinion, deserved no serious notice from Edward. But his friend declared that his course was fixed and unchangeable, and that he would punish such unprincipled baseness, or perish in the attempt; on which Young, finding him immovable, generously offered to act as his friend on the occasion, if he wanted one. The offer was gratefully accepted, and he wrote that night a note to Gildon, demanding satisfaction for the injury done to his family. Young called at Gildon's lodgings the next morning about breakfast time, and asked if he was at home; the servant said he was not: he was asked when he would be; the servant did not know, he supposed at dinner. As Young turned from the door, suspecting some evasion, he walked slowly under the parlour window, and recognized Gildon's voice (for he had known him in Frederick) at the breakfast table, with several other young men. He then entered a bookseller's shop in the same street, and determined, under the pretence of looking over the new publications, to remain there till after breakfast. In about an hour, a hack drove to the house, and he saw a man hastily enter it, whom he knew to be Gildon. He saw the carriage drive off towards Mr. De Peyster's. He immediately conjectured that the servant had been ordered to deny him, and pushing along as fast as he could towards Mr. De Peyster's, which was nearly a mile distant, he saw, when he came into the street, the same coach, as he believed, returning. He went to the house of Mr. De Peyster, and told one of the servants, who appeared at the door, that he had a letter for Mr. Gildon, who had just gone in, which he wished to deliver in person. The servant said he would call Mr. Gildon down. He soon made his appearance, and seemed at once surprised, confused and vexed, when he found that he had not been able to evade his pursuer. He then came forward, and said, bowing formally to Young, " If you have any business with me, sir, it must be transacted at my lodgings. I am a stranger here, as well as yourself."

" That certainly would have been the most proper place," said the other, " if you had not ordered yourself to be denied to me this morning when you were at breakfast. As you would not receive this note there, you must take it here."

Gildon, suspecting treachery in the servant, and thinking it vain to deny what was so undeniable, took the letter, and on reading it, bit his lips, and turned pale.

" Sir," said he, " do you know the contents of this letter ?"

" I do, sir."

" And do you know the risk you run, of being accountable for such a violation of the law ?"

" I have brought a letter from one gentleman, addressed, as I supposed, to another," said Young, " and I did not expect to be thus questioned. Mr. Grayson will expect your answer in the usual way ;" and, with a slight bow, was about to depart.

" Stay, sir," said Gildon ; " I have no wish to give unnecessary publicity to this disagreeable business.

by using the intervention of a third person. I will send an answer by you, if you will do me the favour of being the bearer of it."

"Certainly, sir." He then asked Young to take a seat in the adjoining parlour, while he went up stairs to make his apology to the family. He returned in a few minutes, and taking Young into the next public house, he went into a private room; and after an absence of more than an hour, returned with a letter to Edward.

"Sir," said he to Young, "I have not accepted the invitation of Mr. Grayson, which must have been dictated on a sudden impulse; for had he reflected on the whole history of this unpleasant business, as well as the consequences of the course he is pursuing, he would see that it is calculated only to aggravate the evil of which he complains, and which, from the bottom of my heart, I sincerely deplore."

He then entered into a laboured vindication of his conduct, by such arguments as he had before dwelt on with Edward, and urged Young to use his exertions to appease a resentment, which was altogether unavailing, and might lead to the most injurious consequences. The other excused himself from taking any part in the business, except so far as he was invited or authorized by his friend, and withdrew.

Edward received his letter, which was a reiteration of what he had said to Young, with the most violent resentment—"After inflicting," said he, "injury on injury upon a family, known to him only by their hospitality, he refuses to give one of that family the satisfaction he demands. He first insults us, and then bids us defiance.—The villain shall not escape me."

Young again endeavoured to persuade him that Gildon's conduct was so thoroughly base and contemptible, as to be utterly beneath his notice. He urged every argument of which he was master, but all in vain. Edward swore he would horsewhip him in public, let the consequence be what it might. He accordingly provided himself with that instrument of disgrace, and taking with him a pair of pocket pistols, well loaded and primed, he sallied forth towards Gildon's lodgings, before which he walked backward and forward, several times, in company with Young, who, finding he could neither assuage his wrath, nor divert him from his meditated course of violence, accompanied him from motives of friendship, and to prevent mischief as far as he could.

Edward was in such a state of excitement, that he paid little regard to what was passing around him; but Young, more cool and self-possessed, perceiving that they were eyed rather suspiciously by a mean looking man, whom he took to be a constable or bailiff, urged him to change the course of his walk for a short time at least. He then went to the boarding house, and inquiring of a mulatto servant, who made his appearance at the door, whether Mr.

Gildon was at home, he was again answered in the negative.

The fellow, after Young was gone, began to think it strange that two persons should be so desirous of seeing a man, who had been constantly going in and out, especially as he had observed Edward standing off in a watchful attitude, and with a lowering look, and conceiving that mischief might be intended, concluded it best to disclose what had passed. Accordingly, when Gildon came home, as he did at a late hour, in a hack, Thomson, as the mulatto called himself, followed him to his room, and gave him a recital of what had occurred, for which Gildon thanked him, and gave him a gratuity. He sent for Cox early the next morning, and acquainting him with the occurrence, consulted him on the course he should pursue. Cox, who, amid all his dissipation, was not without spirit and family pride, advised him to accept Edward's challenge; or, if it was now too late for that, to throw himself in the way of a personal rencounter.

"These chaps have been so accustomed to lord it over their slaves, that they think they are to do as they please every where. But I'd soon teach them the difference, if I was in your case."

But Gildon, though not deficient in personal courage, was unwilling to take either of these steps. He hated to confront Edward's honest indignation; and still more, to give publicity to an affair, which he was conscious would be regarded as a violation of the dictates of honour, friendship, and hospitality, and would cover him with disgrace. He, therefore, determined to avoid a meeting, if possible; but if one should ensue, to be prepared for it.

Cox was accordingly despatched to procure him a dirk; and he was already provided with an excellent pair of pocket pistols. Thus armed, he also thought it advisable to remain at home the rest of the day. But in the evening, knowing that he would be expected at Mr. De Peyster's, as usual; and fearing the disgrace and ridicule that would be attached to his longer staying at home, he ordered a hackney coach, and rode off without interruption.

Edward, who had changed his lodgings to the Hotel, for the purpose of profiting by the first opportunity of meeting his enemy, had kept within sight of the bar, looking every moment at the door in the expectation of seeing his agent come in to give the intimation agreed on, nor did he abandon all hope of receiving it until late at night. The next morning, after waiting some time, he grew impatient, when Young went to Gildon's boarding house, and knocked at the door; after some time, another servant came out, who said Mr. Gildon was not within, and immediately withdrew. While he stood fretting at being thus sported with by one servant or the other, a gentleman walked out; and Young, addressing him politely, asked if Mr. Gildon was within, observing that there seemed to be some mystery on the occasion with the servants, as he could not obtain the necessary information from them. The gentleman expressed his surprise at what he heard, and told him that Mr. Gildon had just gone into his room, and that he would make free to take him up, if his business was pressing. Edward, who had approached the door during this conference, forgetting every thing but the dictates of vengeance at the time, advanced and said, " You will confer a great favour on me, sir, by showing me to Mr. Gildon's room." But as he and the stranger were turning to go up stairs, Young, whispering a few words to Edward, reminded him of the danger and impropriety of such a step ; and having succeeded in stopping him, he said aloud, " Mr. Gildon is probably engaged at this time, by the servant's denying he was at home ; we can call again by and by, when he may be more at leisure ;" and thanking the gentleman, they wished him a good morning.

Convinced now that no reliance was to be placed on the information obtained from the servants, Edward determined to keep watch and ward for himself, in spite of his friend's renewed remonstrances, at a small distance from the house, until the object of his resentment should make his appearance. After walking to and fro more than an hour in the cold, for it was a sharp frosty morning, and seeing nothing of Gildon, Edward's anger began to subside into contempt. On further reflection, too, on the course he was pursuing, he entertained more serious doubts of its propriety. If, in a personal conflict, brought on by his attack, he thought, he should chance to take Gildon's life, the laws would undoubtedly pronounce him guilty of murder, nor would his conscience absolve him altogether from its guilt; he could have no certainty of inflicting the disgrace he meditated, except by the assistance of arms; and if the death of his adversary should ensue, after thus lying in wait for him, it would have the air of an assassination, at which his proud and honourable mind revolted. The interest which his mother and Matilda had in his safety, would have strongly enforced these arguments, but, by a determined effort, he would not allow his mind to dwell upon that subject.

While he was occupied with these reflections, Young, who had gone to see first about some business of his own, and then to the post office, returned, and brought him a letter from Matilda, which was in these words:

"Dear Edward—Since we heard of your departure from Williamsburg for New-York, circumstances have developed themselves, to prove that Mr. G—— is as unworthy of the journey you have taken, as he is of the regard of your sister; and I have no doubt I shall in time make her sensible of this; but real affection is not easily eradicated from a woman's heart. I write this, then, my dear Edward, my most valued friend, to conjure you to bestow no farther thought or consideration on one every way so unworthy of you. Silent contempt, believe me, is the only course consistent with what you owe to yourself and your family. Oh! Edward! remember the high and important duties, I beseech you, which you are now called upon to perform. A widowed mother, an orphan sister, have no other protector but you ; and I trust I too have some claims on your prudence, and some influence on your conduct. If I have, let it be shown in your instant compliance with my earnest injunction, to return immediately to Virginia, and prosecute those studies, which are so essential to your own success in life, the welfare of your family, and the happiness of your own faithful MATILDA."

After he had read the letter, he showed it to Young, whom he now regarded as a confidential friend, and observed, " I really begin to think the cowardly villain is beneath my notice."

Young thought this a favourable time to reinforce his former arguments; and Edward finally consented to change his course, and content himself with publishing Gildon to the world as a poltron and a villain, which was immediately done by placards stuck up in the Tontine Coffee House, and two or three other public places.

Although these were quickly removed by Gildon's friends, or some peaceable citizens, who disliked what had a tendency to disturb the public tranquillity, yet they were sufficient to give publicity to the affair, and to furnish ample materials for the gossip of the city. When Gildon found that he was held up to public scorn, and that the notoriety he so much dreaded was given to what all the world would call his dishonourable conduct, in the first instance, and the greater part of it, his cowardice afterwards, he repented that he had not accepted Edward's challenge at once ; and under the disgrace which the story, now circulating with a thousand exaggerations and distortions, heaped upon him, he almost felt, in his turn, the resentment of an injured man. His success with a reigning belle, made him an object of envy, moreover, with a number of young men, who exulted in his present difficulties, and readily propagated every injurious rumour concerning him. Young, who was extensively acquainted with the mercantile part of the city, had told of his engagement to Louisa, of her beauty and sweetness, of the character and standing of her family, of its hospitality to Gildon, and of his coming to New-York, under the pretext of soliciting his father's consent to his marriage.

Several of the citizens, either because they were incensed against Gildon by this tale of baseness and perfidy, or from the generous motive of giving countenance to an injured and a friendless stranger, sought Edward's acquaintance ; and his handsome person, cultivated talents, and very dignified manners, never failed to make those respect him for his own sake, who had at first shown him civility from some extrinsic motive.

Amidst the buzz of rumours which were in circulation, one was, that the young Virginian meant to horsewhip Gildon whenever they met ; and another was, that Miss De Peyster was so greatly mortified at the want of gallantry in her lover, that she had broke off the match. These reports, as is usually the case, were partly true and partly false. Edward, as we have seen, once had the intention of making a personal attack, but afterwards declined it ; and Miss De Peyster had not discarded her lover ; but her pride had been so mortified at the disgrace he had incurred, that she had postponed their marriage until he could clear up the imputations against his character, which, she said, were not more inconsistent with his honour, than with the account he had given her of his conduct towards Miss Grayson.

If at any place of fashionable resort, Gildon happened not to be present, it was immediately whispered by his enemies, that he was afraid to show himself ; and not a few mischief-loving idlers and street loungers, busied themselves in reporting the alleged taunts, or threats, or abuse of the parties, for the purpose of bringing about a meeting between them.

Cox, who was more in the way of hearing these rumours, insisted with his kinsman, that it was indispensable for him to prove to the world, that he had not refused to meet Grayson from pusillanimity, but from the generous motive of forbearing to inflict further injury on a family, whose feelings he had already been the unwilling instrument of wounding.

Goaded thus by the dread of public shame and ridicule, the fear of losing his mistress, and by resentment at the immediate cause of his vexations, he resolved, after three or four days, that he would no longer shun the places of public resort, but go well armed, and prepare himself for the worst.

In the mean time, the civil authority, hearing some of the reports in circulation, was disposed to interfere, to prevent the threatened mischief; and the peace officers were instructed to arrest the young men, and bring them before a magistrate, if there should be the least symptom of disorder at a political meeting which was that day to take place at a Hotel in Broadway, where, it was rumoured, they would both probably be. Gildon had gone there, in company with Cox, and seeing nothing of Edward or his friend, they, and the small party which supported them, exulted at this refutation of the slander that had been circulating against Gildon; and to make their triumph more complete, they determined to walk down Wall-street towards the Tontine Coffee-House, and mingle in the crowd which assembled there every day at that hour; among whom they would be certain to find one, and probably both.

Edward having now staid in New-York as long after he had published Gildon, as the most fastidious honour could require, began to think of returning to Virginia. He had passed the early part of the morning in writing to his mother and Matilda, after which he took his customary walk with his friend Young; and when, on their return, they had got within twenty yards of the coffee-house, Gildon and Cox, walking arm in arm, were just leaving the crowd, and were chuckling and exulting at their fancied success. Edward, who was the first to perceive them, boiling with indignation at the sight of the author of so much misery to his family, so apparently happy and triumphant in his villany, forgot his previous determination; and running up to him, said, "Villain, take the punishment of a coward, since you would not risk that which may be inflicted on a man of spirit," and gave him several strokes with his cane. Cox, disengaging himself, cried "close with him, close with him, Gildon." The latter, recovering from his first surprise, did so; and being somewhat stronger in the arms, was about to wrest the cane from Grayson's hand; but he, letting go the cane, took out one of his pistols, at the sight of which Gildon drew his dirk, and as a last effort of self-preservation, stabbed the unfortunate Edward to the heart, whose pistol going off at the same time, wounded his antagonist slightly in the arm. Edward reeled, and was falling, just as Young, who, as well as Cox, in the first surprise, knew not what part to act in this deadly conflict, received him in his arms. He barely was able to say, "Heaven forgive me—I'm a dead man—my poor—mother," and expired.

The report of the pistol brought great numbers to the spot. There were indeed several present before they had drawn their weapons; but the fear of receiving injury, and that suspension of the faculties which such scenes occasion with the generality of men, prevented any one from interfering, until interference was useless. The crowd, in a populous city, is constantly receiving new accessions, until the number of those whose curiosity is satisfied, is equal to those with whom it is yet keen. A constant buzz of inquiry ran through the crowd; while many told what they had seen, or heard from eye-witnesses, and made out stories that bore little resemblance to the truth. Some saw the murderer in a green coat and yellow top boots give the first blow, and then draw his dirk and stab the deceased three times. Others saw the deceased cock his pistol, and snap it twice before it went off, or the other drew his dirk. So various and so contradictory were the accounts of the bystanders, that it would have been impossible for a stranger to have ascertained the particulars of the affray on the very spot where it took place.

Gildon was immediately taken into custody, and carried before a magistrate, followed by a large crowd of the rabble; while the body of the ill-fated Edward, attended by a more numerous and respectable multitude, was carried to the coffee-house. His handsome features, unchanged in death except as to paleness, and his genteel dress, profusely stained with his blood, greatly increased the favourable prepossessions of the bystanders; and the narratives given of the rencounter were, nearly all, more or less coloured by the lively pity which his youth, beauty, and untimely end, contributed to excite.

Every proper respect was paid to his remains by Young, assisted by some of the most respectable persons of the city. They were deposited in the south-west corner of Trinity church yard, and the young men of the city placed a marble slab over them, as a tribute of hospitality to virtue and misfortune; and in raising the fund for the purpose, it was observed, that among the most liberal subscribers were the discarded lovers of Miss De Peyster; so mixed are the motives of all our actions, whether good or bad. This memorial, so honourable at once to its authors and its object, may be yet seen in a mouldering state, almost hid by the rank grass which surrounds it.

The painful task of communicating this mournful occurrence to Grayson's friends, devolved on Young. He sat down and made several attempts to write, first to Mrs. Grayson, and then to Major Fawkner; but he finally declined it, concluding, that as he should set out immediately for Frederick, it would be better to be the bearer of the melancholy tidings himself.

CHAPTER XIII.

This tale of the ruin of a once prosperous and respected family, draws to a close. Young, having paid off the bills for the funeral expenses with mercantile punctuality and exactness, set out in the stage for the south, and proceeded without delay to Alexandria, where he found no difficulty in sending up his baggage by a wagon to Frederick, and of hiring a horse for himself. His object was to go directly to the house of Mr. Trueheart, knowing his intimacy with the Grayson family, for the purpose of communicating the melancholy tidings.

Not finding him at home, he proceeded to Mrs. Grayson's new residence, and met the worthy man on his return from the visit which has been mentioned. The barrister was pleased to see him, and congratulated him on the recovery of his health, and return to Frederick, but was struck with the seriousness of his countenance, and the solemnity of his manner.

"Yes, sir," said he, "I return in good health myself, but am the bearer of melancholy tidings to some of my Frederick friends."

"Why, what's the matter," said the old man, eagerly; "has any thing happened to Edward Grayson?"

"He lost his life in a scuffle with Gildon."

"Oh, the viper! were you present?"

"I was, sir; I caught him as he fell, and I waited to attend his funeral."

"Why did you not take the villain's life, before he could have perpetrated such an act? Alas, alas, this unexpected stroke of fate must overwhelm his poor mother, who has supported herself under unexampled calamity, with the patience of an angel. The ways of heaven are dark and unfathomable. Here is a family possessing every virtue and grace, fitted to enjoy happiness and comfort beyond any other I ever knew, that are overwhelmed with every species of affliction. Death, sickness, poverty, treachery of friends—but it is not for us to arraign what we cannot understand. The whole world, and all it contains, is an inexplicable mystery. But what shall we do, my dear sir? how disclose this terrible piece of intelligence to the good lady?"

"That is what I wanted to consult you about," said Young—"I have been to your house, and hearing you were here, without staying but one night at home, I rode over, in the hope of reaching Mrs. Grayson's before you had left it."

"Stay, we must consider," said Trueheart—"I have just left them in a state of comparative quiet and comfort. Louisa has been dangerously ill from distress of mind, at that monster's conduct towards her, and she has now so far recovered, as to walk about and ride out. She is even cheerful, either from the precepts and heavenly example of her pious mother, or because she nourishes some secret hope of her lover. To disclose the news abruptly, in her present weak state, might be the death of her; it must be broke to her by degrees. Mrs. Grayson is a woman of wonderful fortitude, strengthened by a firm and implicit conviction that all she suffers is by the immediate ordinance of God, and for some good, though often unknown end. Give her time, and she will bear it. But, poor lady, to what purpose prolong a life deprived of its last comfort.—I am persuaded her heart has been for some time dead to all pleasure, except what she derived through her children, or from her charities or religious exercises.—Well, poor Edward! cut off in the flower of youth and hope—knowing nothing but sorrow, and anxiety, and crosses, since he came to man's estate, but with better prospects opening before him.—He is like a mariner, who, after weathering the most furious storms, has been wrecked just as he was going into harbour. Did he get any letter from me?"

"He did, with several others besides, and they determined him to change his intended course—but for a casual meeting, when his indignation got the better of him, he had been safe now in Frederick."

Young then gave a circumstantial detail of what the reader has already learnt, to which Trueheart listened with painful interest; and ever and anon a tear stole down his wrinkled cheek.

" Well, Mr. Young, there is no help for it now; it behooves us, as we cannot restore the dead, to do what we can for the living. We must prepare them for the shock. But what is the best mode?—let me see. It will not do for you to go, or for me to return. They would suspect the truth. I will write, and while I shall state nothing but the truth, I will take care not to state the whole truth. Nothing has so afflicted me since the death of her father, one of my best and earliest friends."

He accordingly, with Young, proceeded on to the first house on the road, and stepping in, sat down and addressed a letter to Mrs. Grayson, in which he stated that Morgan Young, whom she knew, had just returned from New-York, and had left Edward there—that her son would not be able to leave that city immediately—that he (Trueheart) would endeavour to learn the cause of his detention, and let her know it either by letter or in person.

He requested the master of the house to allow his son, an active lad of about sixteen, to carry the letter to his farm on the Opeccan, where the widow of Col. Grayson was now residing. The man made some difficulty at first, but upon Trueheart's saying to the lad he would give him a dollar, he removed all obstacles, by saying he would ride the " stud ;" and accordingly he was desired to give that letter into the hands of one of the white family, or a house servant, and without staying until it was read, or to answer questions, to return immediately.

The boy took the letter, and in less than two hours was at the little gate of the enclosure round the house. The quick pace at which the large and clumsy horse, on which he was mounted, proceeded, lumbering over the hard frozen ground and stony road, was heard for some distance before he reached the house, and the eyes of Mrs. Grayson and of the servants were directed that way. When, instead of proceeding on, he turned down the road which led to the house, that lady had a fear of some ill tidings, and as it has appeared to her since, a strange presentiment that the boy was the messenger of bad news. In a trice the lad was at the fence, dismounted, opened the gate, and was at the door; and, holding the letter in his hand, said, "this is for Mrs. Grayson."

"I am the person," said she, much agitated.

He delivered it into her hand, and with as much haste as he had come, he returned, mounted his horse, and was out of hearing before the good lady had read the letter, or at least, had the thought of inquiring of the messenger where he received it, who was present, and who Mr. Trueheart had seen in the short time since she had parted from him. Finding that no satisfaction could be obtained from this source, she began to form conjectures on the cause of Edward's detention, and naturally apprehended that he was engaged in a controversy with Gildon. She sometimes thought that Mr. Trueheart must have formed some unpleasant apprehensions himself, by his sending off an express to give her information, that was better calculated to make her uneasy, than to give her satisfaction—but his known character for candour and fair dealing, soon repelled this impression.

She was, upon the whole, more uneasy than the intelligence strictly warranted; and if there be any mysterious and inexplicable connexion between our feelings and distant events, as the experience of every close observer has often almost persuaded him, then had Mrs. Grayson somewhat of this preternatural warning of the calamity that had befallen her. In spite of all the efforts of her reason, her fears overpowered her, and she wept in bitterness, she hardly knew why. She was not able to conceal the letter from Louisa, but she concealed her unfavourable auguries from her. Louisa, on the other hand, always disposed to hope, where she could perceive the least ground for it, drew an auspicious inference from her brother's detention, as if a favourable result should be hopeless, or a rupture with Gildon should take place, his stay would not be so protracted as Mr. Trueheart's letter would lead them to expect. That night was, therefore, spent by Mrs. Grayson in the prayers and tears of an alarmed and devoted mother—and by her daughter in the sanguine hopes of love.

The next day was passed without any occurrence worthy of notice, except that Mrs. Grayson's fears were somewhat abated, and Louisa's hopes somewhat confirmed. The day after, the arrival of letters from the nearest post-office was anxiously expected. They, accordingly, received one from Mr. Trueheart, saying, that he had it in his power to give them some further particulars of Edward's movements in New-York. That he had been so violently incensed at Gildon's manifest evasion, and want of faith towards his sister, that he had sent him a challenge; but Gildon having refused to accept it, that Edward had threatened him with personal chastisement. Trueheart then added, that he had good reason to believe, that the letter which he told her he had written to Edward, advising moderation, and an immediate return to his studies, had arrived before he had carried his threats into execution; but on the other hand, if he had meant to take his advice, he might have returned with Mr. Young, as his letter must have reached New-York some days before Young left the city.

This letter, which strengthened Mrs. Grayson's fears, extinguished the last remaining hopes of her daughter. She relapsed into her former state of grief and despair; and all that her mother could say and do, seemed to have no sort of effect for the first night, in allaying the acuteness of her sufferings. She herself endeavoured to prepare for the worst.

"It is the will of God," said she, " that I am

no longer to know the comfort which children can give. Perhaps I have had my share of happiness in this life, and then I was not sufficiently sensible of it, or thankful for it. The Lord giveth, the Lord taketh away, and I must submit."

Mr. Trueheart further mentioned, that he had fallen in with Mr. Young, who knew the particulars of the quarrel, and he would bring him over to see Mrs. Grayson the next day.

They, accordingly, arrived the next morning about 11 o'clock, with heavy hearts, on one of the most ungrateful of all missions. They both entered with that serious air which suited their feelings and the occasion; and Mrs. Grayson was so agitated when they entered, that she could scarcely ask them to sit down.

"How long is it since you left New-York, Sir."

"A fortnight to-morrow, madam."

"I understand you saw—my son there," her voice faltering.

"I did, madam."

"You left him behind, I understand."

"Yes, madam," said the kind hearted young man, his lively pity for the mother not permitting him to undeceive her; but his feelings rejecting all artifice, an involuntary tear came into his eyes. This could not escape the vigilance of a mother, who then unravelled their well-intended plot at once.

"Oh, my God!" she exclaimed with vehemence, "my son is dead—tell me, gentlemen—let me know the worst—oh! I see it—I see it—he's shot—he's stabbed—he's murdered—he's fallen in a duel."

Her clasped hands raised to Heaven, her upturned eyes streaming with tears, and her pale, wobegone visage convulsed with agony, would have melted stouter hearts than those who then saw her. Unable longer to act their parts, they also burst into tears, and sobbed like children. In this communion of feeling, it was long before they could give the wretched, heart-broken mother, any particulars of the tragic event; nor, stunned and overpowered as she was, by the fact of her son's death, did she seem desirous of learning any thing further. In the first burst of her grief, all her precepts of religion, all her habitual resignation and fortitude, gave way; and nature resumed her power uncontrolled. She had hitherto been commonly silent in her grief, but she now went about the room like one bereft of reason, as was in fact the case for the moment.

"Oh, my Edward," she exclaimed, "the joy and pride of my life; born to honour his country, and his species; oh, how my heart exulted in my noble-minded son. Forgive me, gracious Heaven, I thought too much of the creature, too little of the Creator. I am humbled for my pride—humbled to the dust. Why, oh God! am I suffered to live?—oh, my Edward, my son, my noble son—my glory—the day-star of my existence is extinguished for ever;" and thus she went on in ejaculations of praise, or of bitter complaint, and almost of expostulation. Sometimes a torrent of tears would drown her voice, and sometimes their sources appeared to be dried up; now she would stop, and seemed lost in reverie; then, suddenly starting, she would pour forth the feelings of a mother in strains of the most melting and impassioned eloquence.

As soon as Mr. Trueheart had sufficiently recovered himself, he asked her, in a gentle tone of voice, to endeavour to compose herself, and since she knew the worst, to hear the recital of the particulars from an eye witness. She sat down, but before Young had proceeded far in his narrative, her feelings were so much excited, that she again rose from her seat to indulge in the same extravagance of grief as before.

Louisa, who felt extreme repugnance to see strangers, had left the room, when she saw the gentlemen enter, but returned as soon as she heard her mother's exclamations; and inferring the truth from the few words she heard, she threw herself into her mother's arms, and they had a warm embrace; but in a little while Mrs. Grayson extricated herself, and without further noticing her daughter, walked about the room, wringing her hands, and ejaculating as before.

Several unsuccessful efforts were made before the poor woman could hear out the whole melancholy tale. When it was ended, Trueheart, who knew she must be exhausted by such violent agitation of mind, recommended her to seek some repose. She shook her head, and broke out into a fresh burst of grief. The kind-hearted man then left the room where the mother and daughter were mingling their bitter tears, and having requested the woman Isabel to attend on her mistress, and to prevail on her to take some rest, he and his companion took their leave; he, for the friendly purpose of sending Mrs. Trueheart, as had been previously arranged, and of requesting Mr. M'Culloch to carry his wife, who was known to be a great favourite with Mrs. Grayson.

As soon as the dreadful news reached the servants, they, one and all, rent the air with shouts of grief. They were all strongly attached to Edward, on account of his kindness and generosity; for, though he would often, hasty and impetuous as he was, give them angry words, and, until he had learned to curb these sallies of passion, occasionally a blow, he more than made them amends by his liberality, by his ready disposition to indulge them in all their wishes, and by the frank and familiar manner in which he often conversed with them. The tribute of affection which they rendered, on hearing the afflicting intelligence, came warm from the heart, though their manner of showing their grief is ostentatious, and has so much of a theatrical air, as often to give suspicions of its sincerity. Wretched as were this helpless mother and daughter, there was another heart in Frederick which was about to feel the loss of this generous youth yet more severely.

When Matilda Fawkner returned to her paternal seat, the day before the Grayson family quitted Beechwood for the last time, her heart was filled with anxious apprehension for the safety of her lover, and sympathy for the distresses of his wretched sister and mother. In her generous efforts to afford consolation to her friends, she had alleviated her own sufferings; but when the necessity for those efforts had ceased, she viewed with dismay the perils that one of Edward's fiery temper must incur, in vindicating the injured honour of his family. She had already written to beseech him to return, and it appeared to her that she could urge new arguments, and press them with still greater force. She resolved, therefore, that she would write to him a long letter on the following day, which was the post day for the north.

She had been greeted by her father when he met her, with his usual warmth and tenderness; and there was more of kindness in her mother's manner, than had been common for some time; both because of the change in her sentiments that has been adverted to, and because the distress of mind, and the fatigue of watching and nursing her friends, having greatly affected Matilda's appearance, had roused her maternal fears for the safety of an only child.

"Indeed, Matilda," says she, " you never go to

Mrs. Grayson's, but you return as haggard as a witch, and as pale as death;" but lest her daughter should suppose she was actuated by her former feelings, she added, " not that I have any objection to your spending as much of your time as you can spare, as there is no family in the county I would so soon see you intimate with as that; but you must not stay so long, for you will wear out your constitution in nursing them."

" Oh, mother, they need all the attention and sympathy their friends can bestow; and I ought not to grudge the trouble it may cost me, if my society could afford them any gratification, as I trust it can. They set out to-morrow for their new residence on the Opeccan, and I have promised to visit them as soon as I hear they are settled. I trust that Louisa no longer needs my nursing, but I fear that she and her mother will long require consolation."

She then detailed to her, as they withdrew to her chamber, as much of their affairs as she thought her friends would not object to her disclosing, on which Mrs. Fawkner remarked, " there is a letter from Frederick Steener, who apologizes for not delivering it, as he had been requested. I made free to open it, and found a letter from New-York, which I hope may enable you to give some welcome news to Mrs. Grayson."

Matilda eagerly caught the letter from her mother, who thus, indirectly, for the first time, had given her sanction to her daughter's correspondence with Edward, though she had long known of it.

This letter, the reader will perceive, had been written by Edward immediately after he had sent the challenge to Gildon, to excuse his conduct to her in case he should fall; and after the challenge was refused, and he had abandoned all thought of personal satisfaction, he had neglected to destroy the letter, but suffered it to remain on the mantle-piece in his room. Young, seeing it there after Edward's death, and knowing nothing of its contents, put it in the post office the same day.

Matilda hastily opened it, and, pale and breathless, read to the following purport:

New-York, November, 1796.

How shall I justify myself to my beloved Matilda for the course I am about to pursue? Ere this reaches her, she will be apprized of the motives which brought me here, and which will regulate my conduct. The present is one of those occasions in which reason points one way, and feeling impels another. Oh, if all the world were like you, Matilda, the case might have been different; so far as the sentiment of vengeance is concerned, or my individual indignation, the eloquent arguments I have heard you urge on this subject would be successful; but, unfortunately, they are lost upon the world in general; and the opinion of the world, however we may affect to despise it, who is it that dare disregard? Who can venture to brave its decrees of ignominy?

or, if he has this superior firmness, where is the man who would not be ruined by his rashness? The very persons who would advise him to such a course, would be among the first to despise him. No, Matilda, trust me, I had no alternative—I had come here for a certain purpose; when I arrived, I found the legitimate causes of resentment—the injuries to those whom it is my duty to protect, far greater than I had supposed them to be. I had taken my course, that course which those who set themselves up for judges in such cases pronounced to be right, and I had gone too far to recede—I was obliged to go on, or to return to you, and to my family, dishonoured and disgraced. That could never be; I must offer you a name and a reputation on which rumour had never breathed reproach, nor suspicion left a stain. I have demanded satisfaction for the injury to my family's honour, in the only way in which it can be obtained, and I put my own life to hazard on the attempt. That honour would not have been worth preserving if I had hesitated. Should I survive, all will be well, and I shall trust to making my peace with you in person. But if Heaven adjudge otherwise, to its wise decree I submit. This letter will inform you of the fact, and I trust plead my apology. Oh, then, sweetest, noblest, loveliest of women, do not, in the censure which you may pass on my conduct, lose any of your regard to my memory; for it will be my sweetest consolation in death, as it has been the joy and pride of my life, that I possessed your regard. This subject is a dangerous one; I dare not give utterance to all that I feel, or I should be ill-qualified for the course I have prescribed to myself. In one word, then, forgive, pity, and remember, your devoted EDWARD.

Matilda's colour had been seen to come and go as her eye ran over the paper, and when she came to the conclusion, which made its reception depend upon his fate, she let it drop, and, clasping her hands, and turning her eyes in beseeching agony to heaven,

"Oh, God," she exclaimed, "suffer not a wretch to live, who is no longer fit to discharge the duties of life," and hurried out of the room.

Mrs. Fawkner, who, though not of very acute sensibility, had suffered very much by her daughter's apparent distress, being desirous of informing herself of the cause of her violent emotion, took up the letter, and inferring from it that Edward had fallen in a duel with Gildon, forgot her former animosity, and sincerely regretted his loss; but was chiefly excited by maternal fear for the effect the intelligence would have on Matilda. She followed her daughter into her chamber, and finding all was still, she doubted whether she was within. She opened the door softly, and found her in one corner of the room, by the side of the bed, on her knees, with her face and eyes turned towards heaven, expressing at once despairing grief, and ardent devotion. She was so struck with the force of feeling delineated in her countenance, that she was held some moments in suspense, but maternal sympathy overcoming every other feeling, she went up and cried, " Oh, Matilda, don't take on so—do not, my dear Matilda—it is sinful to grieve so."

And as if it would soothe her daughter's sorrows, she added, " Oh, he was a fine young man, every body thought well of him—and your father and I have both been talking of him and you of late, and of his prospects. But do not grieve so—Matilda! —Matilda!—my child, why don't you speak to me? Are you displeased with your mother? It was all intended for your good." Matilda turned her eyes on her mother, and shook her head, as much as to say, nothing was farther from her thoughts.

She continued, however, her supplicating attitude, and seemed yet engaged in the act of prayer. Her mother endeavoured by the kindest and most persuasive manner of which she was capable, to draw her attention.

" Oh, Matilda, you will break your poor father's heart—and mine too."

At the mention of her father's name, the poor girl, who had concluded her act of devotion, started from her trance, while her eyes shed a few scalding tears, and exclaimed, " My poor father, where is he?"

" In the parlour," said Mrs. Fawkner, who had been alarmed at the fixed stare, and tearless eyes of her daughter. " Shall I bring him to you?"

"If you please, madam," said Matilda, with apparent composure.

Mrs. Fawkner soon returned with her husband, and the kind-hearted man, who almost idolized his daughter, seeing in her face, though she did not weep, the agony that was rending her heart, went up to her, and unable to speak another word, but "Oh my daughter!" sobbed on her neck, as if his heart would break—Mrs Fawkner all the while endeavouring to check him in thus giving way to his feelings, and increasing the distress of Matilda. She again shook her head, and said with some calmness, "Mother, nothing can add to what I feel."

The Major then seated himself by his daughter, and took her hand without speaking—and often casting his eyes on her face, on which he saw utter despair, and a fixed look that he thought indicated a wandering of the mind, his grief returned in all its violence. But neither the entreaties of Mrs. Fawkner to her daughter, nor her expostulations to her husband, nor his lively grief, seemed to have any effect upon Matilda, or to direct her thoughts from the strong current in which they ran.

After an hour had been passed in this way, which seemed like three or four to the anxious parents, Matilda rose from the seat she had occupied ever since her father entered, and going to her toilette, she took up a cambric handkerchief, tied it tight round her brows, and began to walk up and down the room. Her mother inquired if she had the head-ach, offered her volatile salts, and said she would bring her a mustard plaster; all of which she rejected as before, without speaking. But Mrs. Fawkner insisting she should take something for the sake of her parents, if not for her own, she consented, and immediately preparations were made to bathe her feet, and give her a composing draught.

Major Fawkner now asked his wife how Matilda got the news, on which she showed him Edward's letter. He was greatly relieved when he saw the hand-writing.

"Why, Molly," said he, "this cannot be the letter, this is from Edward Grayson himself."

"Read it," says she; "it was not to be sent unless he should fall."

He then read it, and remarked there might yet be some mistake. It might have been sent without his intending it, or he might be wounded, and have recovered. "I heard yesterday that Young, the merchant, had returned, and had gone to Mrs. Grayson's with Trueheart; no doubt he can give an account of the whole affair."

At that moment the servant said, that Mr. M'Culloch was in the parlour. When he entered, the Major saw in the face of his old friend the melancholy errand on which he had come.

"I suppose, Major, you have heard the news," said M'Culloch.

"Of Edward Grayson?" said the other; "is it true that he was killed in a duel."

"No, not exactly that," said M'Culloch, "but he's no longer for this world of wo;" and he then related the particulars as he had learned them from Young. "And does your daughter know it?"

"She does."

"And how does she bear the news."

"Bad enough, my dear friend; I fear she will never get over it."

"Matilda is a girl of a strong mind, and good understanding, Major. Leave her to herself awhile; it is natural and right she should grieve at first; for, to be sure, he was a noble youth, and I know not where you could find such another in all the valley. But her good sense will bring her right, Major; may be she would not dislike to see an old friend; though it may grieve her too, to see one that she knows was so partial to the poor fellow that's gone," wiping his eyes.

Major Fawkner then briefly stated what had passed; that she was in bed, and they were endeavouring to compose her to rest; on which the old man took his leave.

Matilda rose betimes the next day, and in answer to the inquiries from her parents, she said she was better, but her looks showed that she had had no sleep, or none of that rest which refreshes and invigorates. Her parents both went to her chamber before breakfast, but barely went to see her and speak to her, without remaining in the room. They were pleased to find her dressed; but she had the same wan, haggard look of despair, as the day before. Major Fawkner, taking her hand, said, my dear, your old friend Mr. M'Culloch called last evening to see you.

"Oh!" said she, lifting up her hand, "the last spark of hope is then gone—there is now no doubt;" still looking at her father, as if, however, some spark of hope yet lingered in her breast; but his streaming eyes answered her inquiries, and she again threw herself on her knees, and in a few words uttered audibly, "oh, God! pity my weakness, and aid me, while I henceforth devote myself to thy service."

The parents both wept freely; but Mrs. Fawkner occasionally exhorted her daughter to allay her grief, by all the topics that are so commonly and so vainly used on such occasions. By and by her little dog, which had been purposely kept out of her sight by the considerate servants, on whose neck was a collar, which Edward had given her, and had put on the last time he was at the Elms, having, while they were engaged at their breakfast, found means of escape, came patting up stairs, and made a noise at the door, by which he usually gained admittance. Major Fawkner went to the door, and opening it, little Fido ran up to his mistress, wagging his tail, and looking wistfully in her face, as if waiting for the caresses to which he was accustomed. Her eyes being turned towards the floor, and lighting upon the dog and his collar, the sight awakened a train of tender recollections, and for the first time she wept aloud. When her tears had once began to flow, they ran in a stream, and crimsoned her cheek, that was before of a death-like hue. Her parents, though rather pleased to see her grief venting itself in a natura. way, mingled their tears with hers in silent sympathy.

She did little on that, and the two following days, but weep, and walk about her room; and in spite of all that could be said, she scarcely took nourishment enough to sustain life. The first subject on which she conversed, was to inquire about Mrs. Grayson and Louisa, and the next was to know the particulars of her lover's fate. She seemed to feel great relief, when she found that he had not fallen in a duel, and that her letter had had, in a great measure, its intended effect. In the course of a week she left her room to go to the dining-room, which she afterwards continued to visit when there was no person present but her own family. She expressed a wish to see Mrs. Grayson, from whom she heard every day, but her mother appeared so unwilling that they should add to each other's grief by an interview, that Matilda desisted. After a fortnight spent in gloomy and silent meditation, she began to read some favourite religious anthems, but it was observed that she seldom read long in any one, but would pass from one to another with a feeling of disappointment. The sermons of Bourdaloue were said, however, to be her favourites. A Roman Catholic priest of Baltimore, returning from from the springs, where he had been passing some weeks during the summer, was sent for by her, and they had a long interview. He was invited to repeat his visit, as Matilda was observed to be less abstracted, and more disposed to converse, than she had been before. The next day another long conference took place, with the same perceptible effect, and on the fourth day, she declared to her father and her mother the intention of joining the Catholic persuasion. Her father said nothing, except that she had better deliberate well, but if she was conscientious, as he made no doubt she was, it mattered little he thought to what sect she belonged. Her mother undertook to argue against it, but finding that Matilda, without wishing to enter into a controversy, was steadfast in her purpose, she desisted, especially as she gave signs of being more cheerful since her conferences with the priest.

Her parents remembered that she had heard this gentleman, who was both learned and eloquent, in Alexandria, and that she was greatly pleased with him; that afterwards she had met with him at Bath, and had heard him again with equal delight. While his discourses had only produced the transient admiration, that pulpit eloquence never fails to cause in the sensitive souls of the fair sex, without her entertaining the least thought of abandoning the church in which she was educated; yet the remembrance of the effect he had produced, the sermons of Bourdaloue, and the accordance of some of their doctrines, and ordinances, with the present state of her feelings, induced her to solicit this conference for the purpose of seeing if he could clear up the difficulties she entertained on the subject of transubstantiation, the worship of saints, and other catholic tenets, that are repugnant to the common understandings of men; and he was so successful in explaining away the difficulties, or in supplying her with faith for what he could not reconcile to reason, that her scruples were entirely removed, and she became a sincere and confirmed Catholic.

Another motive probably had some influence on her in making this choice. In a short time afterwards she declared it was her fixed purpose to enter the convent at George Town. To this her parents made the most decided opposition. But neither the vehement remonstrances of her mother, nor even the tender entreaties of her father, could divert her from her purpose. Old Mr. M'Culloch and Mr. Trueheart, one of whom she loved, and the other she respected, more than any persons out of her family, joined to dissuade her with as little effect.

She took the veil about six months afterwards, purposely putting it off, to prepare her mind for so important a step, and, to show that she was not influenced by a sudden impulse, but that it was a well-weighed and deliberate purpose; for, alas, we can never be indifferent to the opinion of the world on our conduct, however conscience. may approve of what we do. Many years afterwards, strangers who visited that institution, which is a sort of curiosity in this country, and was almost the only one in the United States, before the acquisition of Louisiana, were struck with the appearance of a tall young lady, with large dark eyes and hair, long eye-lashes, a fair skin, who shone among the rest like Diana among her nymphs, and who engrossed by the fervour of devotion, never seemed to heed what was passing around, or to steal a look of curiosity, or of wishful regret, on the worldly beings who visited them, but who was unwearied in her watchings of the sick in her chamber, her liberality to the poor, and in the taste and simplicity of her dress, and her success in cultivating rare and beautiful flowers. Her father allowed her a liberal annuity during his life, and continued it by his will, and if I mistake not, the lady still remains in that convent, unless, as I have heard, she has been prevailed upon to go to the convent in Louisiana, for the purpose of superintending that institution, in which it was said there had been some relaxation of vigilance, and some mismanagment of their funds.

The subsequent history of the excellent Mrs. Grayson, and her unfortunate daughter, may be soon told. Louisa was taken sick in the night after the news of her brother's death reached her, and she continued ill some weeks, and it was long before she was considered to be out of danger, during all which time her mother staid in her room, and never left her day or night. The necessity this amiable woman was under of nursing her daughter, to keep life in her, was, perhaps, fortunate for her, as it diverted her mind from brooding over her afflictions until time had applied its softening hand to her sorrows, and aided her natural patience, and mild resignation, in bowing with submission to the will of Heaven.

Of all her neighbours, the first to visit her, and offer their services, were young Freeman and his wife, the new married pair of whom we have spoken. They spent more time, too, at the Retreat, than any others, and seldom a day passed without receiving some mark of their kindness.

After a while Louisa recovered from her illness, and, such was her attachment to Matilda, that it was thought she would have followed her example and become a catholic, if Mrs. Grayson, whose religious faith was too firmly fixed to be shaken, and whose influence over her daughter was unbounded, had not exerted herself to prevent it. But she was little less of a devotee than her young friend. She joined her mother in her religious exercises regularly; but religion, which gave firmness and patience, and even cheerfulness, to her mother, had produced a settled pensiveness on her daughter. She seldom went into company—never into gay circles; and as her mother had never thought it consonant with real religion to rely upon faith in exclusion of works, or safe to omit the practice, as well as the profession of virtue, she engaged her as an assistant in every kind and charitable act which her neighbours required. She died about two years afterwards, without having ever regained her health or spirits, of a lingering disease, and her mother yet resides, an aged woman, on the Opeccan, the Lady Bountiful of the neighbourhood, a monument of the efficacy of religion in enabling us to bear up against the ills of this life, as well as in preparing us for a better.

After this sad catastrophe of Edward's fate, Miss De Peyster, who saw her lover with very different eyes since he was disgraced in the eyes of the public, and only wanted a decent excuse for rejecting him, found that excuse in his being a murderer of a friend and benefactor, whose sister he had deserted after having seduced; and by a little of the same finesse by which she had drawn on Gildon to a second courtship, she had succeeded in getting one of her lovers to renew his addresses, and had married him.

Gildon was tried, and acquitted without difficulty by court and jury, but condemned to lasting infamy by the public; and, torn with remorse for shedding the blood of one of the noblest characters he had ever met with, he sought relief from the reproaches of the respectable, by courting the favour of the worthless. Plunging into the excesses of pleasure and dissipation, he lived and died a confirmed sot, and his father, who survived him, is yet undetermined how he shall dispose of his large wealth, and views with so much suspicion every attempt made to conciliate his favour, that it is not yet known who will inherit it.

Of the other characters who have appeared in this narrative, we have been at some pains to learn their subsequent history, and, after diligent inquiry, have understood that M'Culloch, after selling off his land piece after piece, was finally compelled to remove to Kentucky, where, though he had a valuable tract of land, he soon found the inconvenience of debts, courts, and sheriffs, as he had done in Virginia; and seemed to prove, that he who, with a piece of good land, cannot keep out of debt in one place, will not be apt to do so in another. He, however, retained his health, his spirits, his taste for hunting, and for bantering his meek wife as a termagant, as long as she lived, which was but two years after she changed her residence.

Miss Margaret Buckley is yet single, and annually visits Alexandria, and imports the new fashions in dress, manners, furniture, &c. together with the oracular dicta of her aunt Browne. Fanny, after Louisa moved out of the neighbourhood, became the victim of ill health and melancholy, set herself diligently about bringing on her former lover, but finding his taste had changed, as she had other game in view, she tried her skill on a young deputy sheriff, raw in the world of fashion and etiquette, but dexterous enough in turning a penny, and whose father's land joined Mr. Buckley's, she succeeded, and a large family has crowned their loves, and they now live in the mansion house of their father, who, as well as Mrs. Buckley, has been long since dead.

Frederick Steener married Miss Tidball, and they live in a handsome style. His wife succeeded so well in paying court to Mr. and Mrs. Fawkner, that, after providing a liberal annuity for Matilda, as has been mentioned, he settled the rest of his estate on Frederick's second son, who bore the name of James Fawkner, and of whom the old lady became extremely fond in her dotage. The old Major never recovered his spirits after Matilda left him, and died several years before his wife.

Mr. Trueheart lived to a green old age, and died as he had lived, universally loved and respected.

Some further particulars have been learned of other characters, but it is thought that the acquaintance the reader has formed with them during their short appearance on the stage, is too slight to make their history interesting. And thus, gentle reader, you may see, in this true, but melancholy history, something of the life and manners which prevailed about twenty-five or thirty years ago, in Virginia, and especially in that part of it which is called the Valley of Shenandoah.

THE END.